# SONG OF TRAILS

A HANSEL AND GRETEL RETELLING

THE SINGER TALES
BOOK 5

DEBORAH GRACE WHITE

LUMINANT PUBLICATIONS

# SONG OF TRAILS: A HANSEL AND GRETEL RETELLING

By Deborah Grace White

**Song of Trails:**
**A Hansel and Gretel Retelling**
The Singer Tales Book Five

Copyright © 2023 by Deborah Grace White

First edition (v1.0) published in 2023
by Luminant Publications



ISBN: 978-1-922636-70-6

Luminant Publications
PO Box 305
Greenacres, South Australia 5086

http://www.deborahgracewhite.com

Cover Design by Karri Klawiter
Map illustration by Rebecca E. Paavo

*For anyone walking a trail they never expected.*
*May you find peace amidst the twists and turns.*

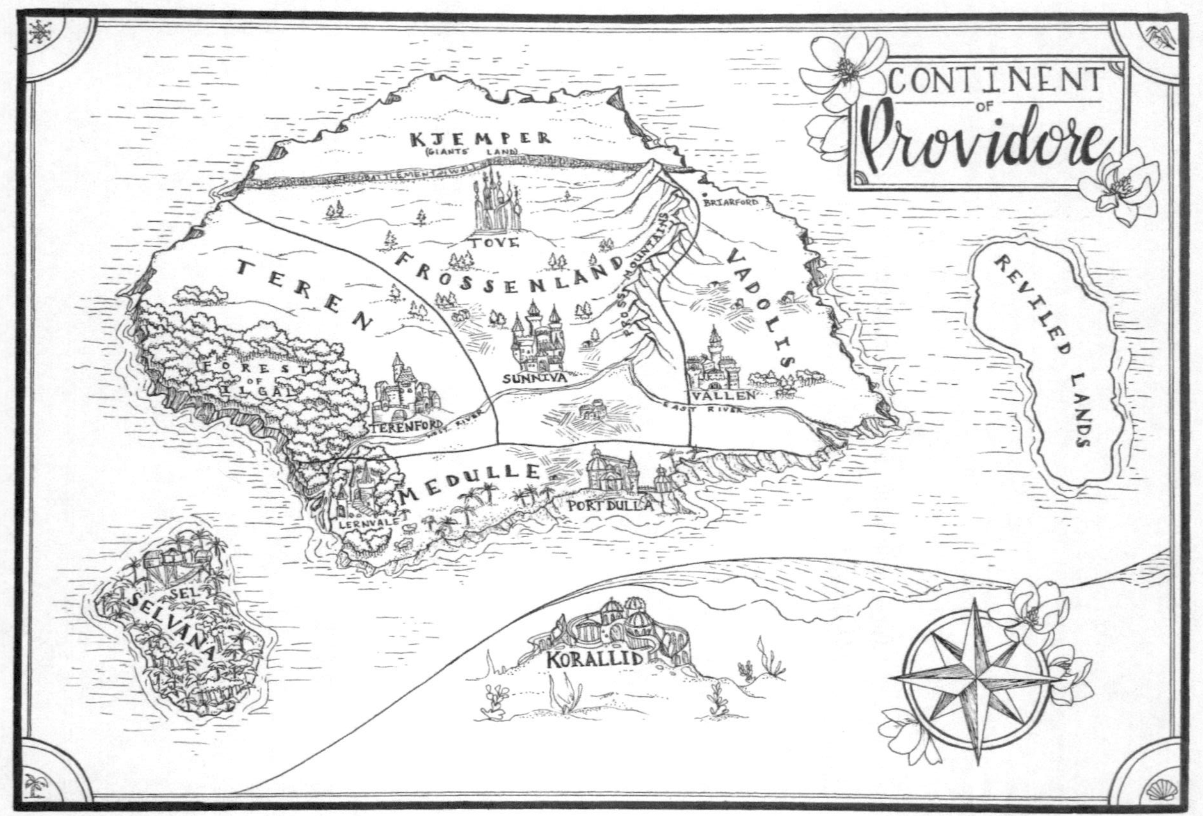

CONTINENT OF Providore
KJEMPER
(GIANTS' LAND)
BATTLEMENT WALL
TOVE
FROSSENLAND
BRIARFORD
VADOLIS
FROSS MOUNTAINS
TEREN
FOREST OF ILGAL
SUNNIVA
VALLEN
EAST RIVER
TERENFORD
WEST RIVER
MEDULLE
PORTDULLA
LERNVALE
REVILED LANDS
SEL SELVANA
KORALLID

# PROLOGUE

# Gisela

"All right, my darlings, that's enough stories. Time for sleeping."

Gisela smiled at the soothing tone of her mother's voice, snuggling down into her covers. Predictably, her four-year-old brother Haiden wasn't so easily appeased. He began to protest, asking for one more tale. Just as he'd done after the last tale. And the one before that.

Gisela pulled the covers to her chin, guarding against the cold. It was winter, and although it didn't snow in the Forest of Ilgal, it was cold enough that she could see a whisper of her breath on the air. Her brother was still protesting, and she gave him a lofty look. At seven, she was far too old for such a display. But Haiden was too distracted arguing with their mother to see her sisterly disdain.

"No, you must sleep now, both of you," said their mother again. "I have no more stories left in me tonight."

Gisela pushed up on one elbow, the cold air rushing in as she let the blankets fall.

"Does it make you sad, Mama? Telling stories about the homeland?"

Her mother shushed her, although her voice was gentle. "Don't speak of it, Gisela. No one must know where the stories come from."

Gisela nodded soberly. She was well aware of the need for caution because her mother had drilled it into them from earliest memory. They were never to let anyone know of her ancestry in the island to the east of the continent of Providore. No one on the mainland spoke about the two kingdoms of the Reviled Lands. Providore cut off contact with them long ago after a bloody coup was carried out against the monarchs of both the island's kingdoms. Her mother didn't go into detail about what had happened—after all, it had all occurred long before living memory. But Gisela still grasped why the monarchs of Providore wouldn't wish to continue contact with the Reviled Lands. Presumably the successors of those treasonous rulers shared the same views about monarchies.

None of that troubled Gisela, however. She was Terenan, like her father, born and bred in Providore's westernmost kingdom, far from the Reviled Lands from which her mother's ancestors had fled. But she still loved to hear the tales her mother would tell of distant lands, so different from her own.

"And yes." Her mother's soft voice drew both children's attention. The pause had been so long, Gisela had forgotten about her question. "It does make me sad. But when something is precious, it's better to be sad remembering it than happy forgetting it."

"But I don't understand," said Haiden petulantly, still disgruntled about losing the argument. "How can it be precious to you when you never went there? You were born here, and it all happened forever ago!"

"Hush, Haiden," said Gisela quickly, not liking the look on her mother's face. She'd learned long ago that this topic was touchy.

"Enough questions," said their mother, not looking at Haiden as she spoke. "I want you both to go right to sleep."

A large form appeared in the doorway of their room, and Gisela noted that her father wore his heavy coat.

"Are you going somewhere?" she asked, looking between her parents. "Aren't you staying here, with us?"

"We won't be gone long," her father said reassuringly. "The elves are holding a winter festival nearby with a market stall, and we're just visiting it briefly. We'll bar the door—you'll be safe until we return."

Gisela bit her lip, not pleased to be left alone with only her brother.

"You'll be asleep, you won't even know we're gone," her mother said briskly. "Now come on, you two."

She started to speak the words of a familiar lullaby, her voice more rhythmic and soothing than any other Gisela had heard. The words almost danced off Mama's tongue. Gisela supposed everyone felt that way about their mother. But as her eyes drifted closed, she was sure no one could be as soothing as Mama.

"Gisela!"

A clumsy hand shook Gisela awake, and she blinked in confusion. All was dark, except for the narrow band of moonlight slanting into the bedroom from one high window.

"Haiden?" she asked groggily. "What is it? Why are you awake?"

"I don't think it's fair Mama and Papa get to go to the market and we don't," pouted Haiden.

Gisela groaned and rolled over. "We're kids, Haiden. Nothing's fair. Now go back to sleep. You made me let the cold in."

"No." Haiden marched around the bed to Gisela's other side, his little face set in determination. "I'm going too."

"No you're not," said Gisela, exasperated. "You can't get

outside, and you wouldn't be able to find your way even if you could."

"Yes I can, and yes I would," Haiden contradicted. "I can hear the sounds of the festival from here. It won't be hard to get there."

Gisela stilled, straining to listen. Her brother was right. Faint sounds of merriment drifted to them, suggesting the festival must be very close. It surprised her, because they lived in a deep part of the forest. It was rare that they encountered groups of any kind. Usually only the most intrepid individuals ventured this deep. Gisela's bleary eyes passed around the room, and she realized why the sound was carrying.

"Haiden!" she accused. "You opened the window! No wonder it's so cold in here."

"I wanted to see the festival," said Haiden, his unapologetic gaze following hers to the two chairs stacked on top of each other just under the window. "But I couldn't see anything. I reckon I can climb out, though. You too."

"I don't want to climb out," Gisela protested. "I want to stay in my bed where it's warm and safe."

"I've thought of that," said Haiden proudly. He held up their two coats, both looking a little threadbare.

"And the safety?" Gisela asked dryly.

"You'll be with me," said Haiden, puffing out his skinny little chest. "I'll protect you."

Gisela rolled her eyes. "I'm the older one. *I* do the protecting."

Haiden scoffed his disapproval of this sentiment. "Come on, Gisela. Don't you want to see it? It's a real elf festival!"

Gisela sat up slowly, wavering. It did sound intriguing. Their parents had told them to stay put, though...

"Well, I'm going, anyway," said Haiden, shrugging into his

coat and marching toward the stacked chairs with purpose. "I'll tell you all about it."

Gisela threw the covers fully off, slipping into her shoes and grabbing her coat as she ran after him to hold the chairs steady. He was going to fall and break his head if he wasn't careful. After all, she couldn't let him go alone. He was only four.

The excuse sounded flimsy in her mind, but Gisela banished thoughts of rules and punishments. She had a sniff of adventure, and she wasn't about to let Haiden see an elf festival if she didn't get to as well. It only occurred to her after they'd shimmied through the window and fallen—rather painfully—to the grassy ground below that they had no way to get back through.

Ah well. They'd have to face that problem when they got there.

Haiden had gone first, and he was already running through the undergrowth, moving with the sure-footedness of someone who'd lived all of his four years in the depths of the forest. Gisela followed after him, trying to move silently like her father had taught her. But she wasn't really worried about predators when the festival was so close.

Soon they could see light through the trees, and they crept forward, entranced. It wasn't the warm yellow light of fire or lanterns, like Gisela had expected. It was a silvery white light, as if the moon had tripled in brightness and flooded the clearing.

Clearing. Gisela frowned, confused. She knew this patch of woods well, and there wasn't usually a clearing there.

"Where did this space come from?" she asked Haiden, feeling vaguely uneasy.

"I dunno, maybe they chopped trees down," he said, his eyes riveted on a nearby shelter where an elf was showing off some kind of magical ware.

Gisela gave a scornful snort. "Chop down this many trees

since this afternoon? So close to us, without us hearing? I don't think so."

Haiden didn't answer, obviously not interested in the practical details. Gisela fell silent as well, her eyes wide as she took in the silvery-white orbs that floated, suspended, around the place. They were the source of the light, and were undoubtedly magical. She should have expected that from elves, whose whole business was mining magic from the power-saturated ground and turning it into talismans like these. It was a breathtaking effect, anyway, and much more appropriate for a winter festival than roaring yellow fires would be.

"Let's get closer," said Haiden eagerly.

Gisela's protest fell on deaf ears, the four-year-old already sneaking from behind one tree to the next. By the time Gisela caught up, he'd decided to abandon caution and jog out into the circle of enchanted moonlight.

No one took any notice of their presence, and it was no wonder. The place was full of humans and elves alike, eating food from the various vendors, marveling over the wares and feats of the merchant elves, and watching delightedly as a group of elves played music on wooden flutes.

"It's like Mama's lullabies," said Haiden, staring at the performers.

Gisela nodded absently, her eyes drawn to the far end of the clearing. Everyone over there had gone still, as if responding to something that had yet to reach the rest of the merrymakers.

"Who's that?" she asked, as a group of elves made its way across the clearing, the crowd going silent in their wake.

Haiden obviously didn't know, and gave no answer. But judging from the respect on the faces of the elves in the clearing, and the fascinated glances of the humans, Gisela guessed it was someone important. She edged forward for a better look, jostling against others in the crowd.

An elderly elf led the group of newcomers, his alabaster skin marked by deep grooves, but his eyes—the same piercing green as all of his kind—still sharp. Two stripes of an earthy green had been painted onto his face, traveling down his cheekbones. And around one upper arm he wore a wooden circlet, intricately carved.

Could she be looking at the Imperator, the hereditary leader of elves? Gisela held her breath, suddenly feeling keenly aware of the fact that they weren't supposed to be there.

"We should go," she murmured to Haiden.

"What? No way!" protested her brother. "We just got here."

He shifted forward, his eyes also on the approaching group that had so effectively paused the whole festival. As they drew close, Gisela noticed that there were younger elves walking just behind the leader, almost childlike in their appearance, although from what she knew of elves, they were probably much older than she was. Behind them were other adult elves —even at full height, they were perhaps half as tall as her father.

When the group reached the precise middle of the clearing, they stopped, and the elderly one in the front raised his high, cool voice.

"Winter, we embrace you. May the blessing of life lay dormant but not forgotten, and may your rest produce life and growth in time."

A cheer went up from the gathered crowd, and people started moving again.

"Is that it?" Gisela asked, a little disappointed.

"I hope so," said Haiden. "Who wants to listen to a bunch of speeches?" He was eyeing a nearby cart which appeared to be selling some kind of sugary dessert that looked like edible snowflakes. "Let's get one of those!"

"We have no money," Gisela reminded him.

"Maybe they'll give us some for free," Haiden said optimistically. "Because we're kids."

Gisela snorted. "It doesn't work that way," she informed him. "No one gets given things for free, not even kids."

Haiden's face fell into a pout, but he didn't argue. The musicians had started up again, and Gisela noticed her brother's foot starting to tap. She didn't blame him. It was a captivating sound. She started tapping along too, by drumming her fingers on her leg. Next thing she knew, Haiden was doing it with his voice, his eyes shining with an enthusiasm she'd never seen as he wove his voice wordlessly around the music.

"What are you doing?" Gisela demanded, awed and bewildered. She'd never heard her brother make sounds like that before.

"I don't know," said Haiden, breaking off the strange verbal dance he'd been doing. "But it feels good. It feels amazing!"

Putting a little more power into it, he started up again. But this time, Gisela realized that others were starting to notice. The people closest to them were turning to look, some looking enchanted, others just surprised. But worst of all, the elves in the middle had noticed.

At least, one of the younger ones had. She was watching Haiden with bright, curious eyes, and Gisela was terrified to see her brother come to the notice of someone so exalted. The main rule they lived by was to keep their heads down. Whatever new ability Haiden was discovering, this wasn't the time or place for it.

She tried to shush her brother, but he ignored her, his body swaying to the music as his voice somehow added to it. With her heart in her throat, Gisela saw that the young elf from the important group had detached from the others and was walking toward them. Desperately, she stepped in front of her brother, trying to speak confidently to hide her nerves.

"My brother means no harm," she told the elf when she'd drawn close and come to a stop. "Please don't be angry with him, or punish him."

The elf girl looked surprised. "Angry? Why would I be angry? Singing isn't a crime."

"Singing?" Gisela gasped the word, and even Haiden fell silent at last.

"But I'm not...I don't...I'm not a singer," he stammered.

"Of course you are," the elf laughed. "How else were you just singing?"

Both siblings stared at her, open-mouthed.

"Why do you look so horrified?" the young elf asked, perplexed. She glanced between the two of them, able to look them in the eye as wouldn't have been possible if they were adults. "Being a singer isn't a bad thing. The reverse, in fact."

"But...but..." Gisela's mind was whirling, trying to make sense of the impossible turn their adventure had taken. "But singers are the ones who ruined everything. They're the enemy."

"The enemy?" The elf's gaze was shrewder now, her manner so much more like an adult than a child. Somewhere in the back of her mind, Gisela wondered how old she actually was. "Whose enemy?"

"Ma—" Haiden started to answer, but Gisela shoved him to cut him off, hastening to speak over him.

"Never mind. I guess I was wrong."

The elf narrowed her eyes, not as if she was mad, but as if she was thinking hard. Then her expression changed, her delicate features looking dreamlike. The tips of her pointed ears quivered ever so slightly, and her voice sounded more melodic than it had a moment ago.

"You are an enemy indeed, young singer. You will bring down a rising kingdom."

Gisela froze, bewildered by the strange message. The words

sounded ominous, but the elf's demeanor didn't match them at all. She was still dreamy, but there was a smile on her face, and kindness in her eyes. Gisela didn't know what to make of it at all.

"Asivah! What are you doing?"

The shout caused all three of them to turn, and another gasp escaped Gisela. The speaker was one of the adult elves who'd entered with the important group, but it wasn't him who caught her eye. It was the two much more familiar figures standing a few feet away, looking like they'd been hurrying over when they were stopped in their tracks by the elf girl's words.

Their parents.

"Now we're in for it," muttered Haiden, apparently not as alarmed by the elf's cryptic words as Gisela had been. The four-year-old was clearly more worried about getting in trouble for sneaking out.

"Gisela, Haiden, what are you doing?" The deep voice of their father signaled his approach, and Gisela winced as she looked up at him.

"I'm sorry, Father," she said. "We just wanted to see the festival."

Behind him, Gisela could see the young elf being marched back to her own group, but most of her focus was on her father as he knelt down in front of his children.

"I thought you were both safe in your beds!" His voice was somber. "Can you imagine how it feels to find you out here instead? Don't you two realize how dangerous it is to be wandering the forest alone?"

"We didn't have to wander far, Father," said Haiden in a wheedling tone. "We could hear the festival from our room."

Their father let out his breath in a huff. "Elves and their blasted gates."

"Gates?" Gisela asked. "There were no gates."

"No, I don't mean physical gates." Her father shook his head. "Never mind. It's time to go home."

Gisela was more than ready to go home. The adventure had already been more frightening than she'd bargained for. She leaned sideways to look around her father's kneeling form. She was sure she'd seen their mother with him. Where was she? Why wasn't she also berating them for sneaking out?

Bewildered, Gisela realized that her mother was standing right where she'd last seen her, staring at her son in horrified shock. Even when their father stood and called to her, she made no move to join her family.

"Come on," Gisela's father repeated.

"He's...did you hear?" Their mother's voice was a strangled whisper, the sound unfamiliar and alarming.

"Yes, I heard," said their father in a clipped tone. "We can discuss it later."

"But she said...she said he'll bring down the kingdom."

"Pay no mind to the idle words of a stranger." The uneasy note in her father's voice sent fear trickling down Gisela's spine. Why was her mother acting so strange?

"She wasn't just a stranger." At last their mother drew close, but she wouldn't look either child in the eye. "She's elf royalty. There's power in their blood. They can tell the future, or at least...tell things others can't see."

"I know the stories," said Gisela's father. "And this isn't the place to talk about it. Come on."

He took Gisela by the hand, but when he reached for Haiden, the boy held out his hand instead to his mother. For a charged moment, she just stared at it, her expression unrecognizable to Gisela. Then she took her son's hand, and Gisela let out a breath of relief that she felt mirrored by her father. Striding with purpose, he led the family out of the clearing, back toward their home.

As they made their way into the trees, Gisela glanced back. To her confusion, she saw that her mother was taking a different route, Haiden's hand still clutched in hers. Instead of walking straight between the tree trunks, they'd veered sharply to the right once they left the clearing.

"Papa," said Gisela, uneasy for a reason she couldn't tell. "Papa, I want to walk with Haiden. I want to hold his hand."

"All right," her father said, releasing her hand. "As long as you go straight to—what?"

He must have just realized that his wife and son weren't right behind him, but Gisela didn't stay to hear his questions. As soon as her father had let her go, she'd dived toward her brother, seizing his free hand just as their mother led him between two thick trunks.

"Gisela?" Haiden turned to her in confusion, and Gisela could understand his uncertainty.

Suddenly, their surroundings were completely different. The trees grew even more thickly together on this side of the clearing, and instead of the oaks she was used to, the dominant tree seemed to be some kind of walnut. But it made no sense. They hadn't gone far from the new clearing, which meant they weren't far from home. And yet she was sure she'd never seen this area before.

More concerning than the change in the trees was the absence of their mother. She'd been holding Haiden's hand a moment ago, and now she was just gone. Gisela turned back, listening to the faint sounds still emanating from the clearing.

"Where did Mama go?"

"I don't know." Haiden drew close to her. "It's dark, Gisela. I'm scared."

Gisela bit back her own fear, instead taking his hand and squeezing it reassuringly. "They can't be far away. Home is this way, come on. They're probably just past the next tree."

She struck off in what she thought was the right direction, but their parents didn't appear. An owl hooted dolefully from nearby, and both children jumped. Gisela's fear grew, and it was hard not to show it to her brother. She'd never been out in the woods at night before, let alone without their parents.

When they'd been walking for a couple of minutes without encountering anyone or anything familiar, she stopped.

"I don't think we should keep going, Haiden," she said. "We'll just get more lost. We should try to go back to where we last saw Mama and Papa and wait. They'll come for us."

"All right." Haiden sounded tearful, and he didn't try to argue.

Gisela led them back the way they'd come, counting trees as her father had taught her to do. She was glad she'd kept her head and hadn't neglected to do it on the way out from where they'd lost their mother. She didn't want to admit it to Haiden, but that was why she'd stopped when she had. She didn't know how to count any higher.

"One, two, three, four, beech," she whispered, tapping the trees as she passed, trying to remember if the rhythm worked in reverse. "Six, seven, eight, nine, walnut."

When they stopped, she was fairly confident they were at the right place. But there was no sign of their parents. The sounds of the festival still issued faintly, though, so she knew they weren't too far from where they should be. She debated suggesting they return to the clearing, but her father had told them that if they ever got separated in the forest, they should stop in the place they last saw him and wait.

He would come for them. He had to.

Squeezing Haiden's hand more tightly, Gisela leaned against a tree, telling herself to be patient. Minutes passed, but for how it felt, it could have been hours. The cold seeped through their worn coats, and Gisela's feet were starting to go numb.

Haiden was getting restless, and Gisela was wondering whether they should move after all, when they finally heard a familiar whistle.

"Papa!" Gisela cried, surging forward with her brother's hand still clasped in hers. "Papa, we're here!"

"Gisela, Haiden!" He came into view between two trees, his expression changing instantly from anxiety to relief in the moonlight. "Are you all right?"

"Yes, we're all right," said Gisela.

"I'm not," Haiden said, sniffling. Now the uncertainty was over, his tears seemed to have permission to fall. "I'm cold."

"Of course you are," their father said, wrapping Haiden in a bear hug. "Let's get you home." He lifted the four-year-old in his arms, extricating one hand enough to hold Gisela's.

"We did like you told us, Father," Gisela said proudly. "We tried to follow you, but we couldn't find you. And I remembered to count the trees like you said, saying the type of every fifth one to make sure we were on the right track, and we found our way back to where we'd last seen you and waited."

"You did very well." The approval in her father's voice wasn't as warm as usual. Something was still troubling him, and Gisela suddenly realized the glaring absence.

"Where's Mama?" she asked, her fear returning. "Is she lost, too?"

There was a moment of silence before their father answered. "No. She's back at home. We'll go there now." He stepped out of the trees and into the silvery light of the clearing. But instead of rejoining the festivities, he skirted the edge and made his way back to the point of the clearing where they'd entered the first time, plunging straight back into the trees.

Gisela followed readily, but her forehead wrinkled in confusion. "Where were we, Papa? It should have been close to home, but it...wasn't."

Her father nodded. "You weren't close to home at all. The festival isn't really at our doorstep. It's in a different part of the forest altogether."

"Then how did we get there so quickly?" Haiden asked sleepily from his perch against his father's shoulder. "We didn't walk for very long."

"Ilgal is a complex place," their father answered. "The magic of the forest is strong, and things are possible here that wouldn't be on the plains. The elves have learned how to create gates in the forest. The clearing where their festivals are held is surrounded by them, but they're only open when a festival is happening. We entered through one near our home, but..." He hesitated. "But your mother took you through the wrong one when we left. You ended up...I don't even know where. When I realized you weren't with us, I came back to the clearing and went through each gate until I found you."

"I knew you'd come for us." Gisela leaned against his leg. It made walking awkward, but he didn't chastise her. She felt much more secure now that their surroundings were so familiar. Even in the darkness, she could find her way home from here without her father's help. "Why didn't Mama come with you, though?"

Her father didn't answer, and Gisela looked up to see that their little cottage had just come into view. She let out a sigh that was half relief, half weariness. Their father carried Haiden through the door—he seemed to have fallen asleep on the journey.

Gisela's mother appeared, giving her a swift hug with arms that trembled, but saying nothing. She looked stricken as she watched her husband lay Haiden on his narrow bed. She must have been anxious for them as well.

When it was Gisela's turn to be tucked in, her mother had already disappeared to the other room. Gisela's father kissed her forehead, but although she was ready to sink straight into sleep, he hovered.

"You did well, Gisela," he murmured, repeating his praise from the forest. "Not just when you were lost, but before. You somehow knew to go to your brother even when I didn't realize what...well, you're a good sister."

"Thank you, Papa," said Gisela, proud.

"Gisela..." He hesitated over his next words, and the fog of descending sleep cleared a little from Gisela's mind. What had him so troubled? "Gisela, you need to help look after your little brother, all right?"

"Why?" Gisela asked, not sure she liked the direction the conversation was going.

"Because you're his big sister," said her father, sounding like he was struggling to explain. "You must promise me that you'll always protect him—and yourself—from anyone and anything that might try to harm you both. You have to be careful of everyone, all right?"

"Not everyone," said Gisela. "You and Mama I can trust."

Her father swallowed, taking a moment over his answer. "Even with people you think you can trust, you must always be careful."

"What are you saying, Papa?" Gisela asked, reaching for his arm in the darkness. "Are you saying you might hurt us?"

"I would never hurt you," he said emphatically. "Never on purpose. Gisela, I want to keep you both safe. That's why I'm telling you this."

Gisela frowned over his answer, confused as to *what* exactly he was telling her.

"I'll be careful," she said, sensing that she was supposed to say something. "For Haiden too."

Her father nodded, laying one large hand over her little one where it still squeezed his arm.

"You're a good girl, Gisela," he said. He placed a kiss on her forehead, then moved quietly from the room.

Sleep tugged at Gisela, but she resisted it. She was too unsettled by what her father had said, too bewildered as to his meaning. Why did she have to protect her little brother now? Was it because he was a singer? Could it really be true that he was?

Her reverie was broken by her parents' voices issuing softly from the next room. Her father was trying to be quiet, but he didn't seem able to lower his emotion enough to properly do it.

"What were you thinking?"

The harsh tone brought a crease to Gisela's forehead. She'd rarely heard her parents fight, and she didn't like it at all.

"I wasn't thinking." Her mother sounded hollow, distraught. "I'm sorry. I...I lost my head, and I—"

"I can't talk to you right now." Her father cut his wife off brutally. "I can't even look at you."

Gisela heard his heavy tread on the floorboards, but her mother had one more thing to say.

"I don't blame you, and I won't try to excuse it. But he can't sing, understand? We must teach him never to sing."

Her father didn't even respond, and after a few short minutes of them moving about the house, silence fell.

Sleep was now far from Gisela. Her body was exhausted, and her mind was completely overwhelmed. But she couldn't take refuge in sleep. Not when the pieces of the night's events were starting to come together in her mind in a way that she didn't understand at all. In a way that surely couldn't fit.

Could it...could it be possible her mother had abandoned them—or at least Haiden—in the wrong part of the forest on purpose? But why would she do that? Gisela pulled the blanket over her head, shivering as she remembered the darkness and cold of that strange part of the forest. Her mother loved her and Haiden. She would never want them to be lost and alone in the forest at night. She'd always taught them to be careful.

Careful. The word brought her father's warning immediately back into her mind.

*Even with people you think you can trust, you must always be careful.*

Gisela swallowed nervously. She couldn't bear to think it. But she'd also promised her father she would be careful, and would look after Haiden. She glanced at her brother, snoring peacefully in the bed next to hers. How she wished they'd never left their beds that night!

An hour ticked by, and still Gisela couldn't sleep. All she could think about was how dark and scary the forest had been when they'd been lost. And how she'd had to turn back because she'd run out of numbers in her head. That trick was useful, but it wasn't enough. She needed something that didn't depend on her own memory.

Silently, she slipped out of bed and pulled her coat back on. The night was far advanced now, and the fire was low in the hearth. There was silence from the room where her parents slept, not even a mouse disturbing the stillness of the little wood cabin.

Gisela eased the bolt off the front door and pushed it open a crack. A quick glance showed no movement outside. For a moment she hovered, her instincts set against returning to the forest at night. But she wouldn't have to go far. Gathering all her courage, she forced herself out into the cold. At the corner of the house there was a small decorative garden, with white pebbles tastefully scattered around it. They gleamed in the moonlight like silver coins. Stooping, Gisela pocketed a generous handful of them.

Then she turned and fled back to the house as if a wolf was chasing her. Once the door was closed and barred behind her, she let out a breath of relief. Then she crept back to her room, the pebbles a comforting weight in her coat pocket. She left them there when she removed the garment, pulling out just one to take into bed and hold, as a reminder. These wouldn't run out so quickly, or be too hard to think of if she was scared.

No, she told herself firmly, as she sank into her bed and at last let sleep claim her, one white pebble clutched in her fist. If anything awful like this ever happened again, she would be ready. She wouldn't be caught out another time.

# ELEVEN YEARS LATER...

# CHAPTER ONE

# Gisela

"Come on, Haiden." Gisela frowned at her brother, who was idly watching a robin flutter to land in its nest on a branch above him. "Talk it out backwards. We're not even halfway to where we left the gear."

Haiden brought his attention back to her with a sigh. "Uh... five more trees makes seventy, and the fifth one should be a....beech."

"Elm," said Gisela flatly. "Haiden, you're not taking this seriously!"

"I don't need to take it seriously," her brother told her with a long-suffering expression that was almost comical on a fifteen-year-old. "My object control magic is solid now, Gisela. It's not like when we first started using the pebbles. I can sense every single one of them, and could find them with my eyes closed." He raised his hand, palm upward. "I could make any of them move from here, have them fly right into my hand if I wanted. I wouldn't even need to sing—the magic's already in them."

"I know what object control magic is," said Gisela, unimpressed. "I don't need the lesson. And don't make them fly into your hand—that would defeat the whole point of marking our trail with them."

"Precisely," Haiden agreed, lowering his hand. "The whole point of them is to *mark our trail*. So we can find our way home even if we lose track of where we are in the forest."

"But you shouldn't rely on only them," argued Gisela. "We need to be able to navigate the forest in a variety of ways, to cover all possible scenarios. It's treacherous out here."

"Is it?" Haiden asked sarcastically. "Oh, I didn't realize. Thanks for letting me know."

He waved his arm around in a theatrically floppy manner, drawing attention to the scar he carried from an encounter with a lone wolf. Gisela winced. They'd been lucky to get out of that one with their lives.

Haiden took in the look on her face, and his own expression softened, although his irritation still showed in his tone.

"Gisela, I've lived in Ilgal all my life. And we've been on our own out here for five years. I'm well aware of the dangers, and I know my way around. Don't you think it's time to stop the constant lessons?"

"No," said Gisela shortly. "We never stop needing to train, not if we want to survive."

Haiden gestured around the quiet, dappled clearing, the edge of which they'd been skirting. "This is a pretty safe part of the forest, Gisela."

"Which means we're at risk of letting our guard down," she countered. "You might be overconfident, Haiden, but I don't have magic to help me. If we stumble through an elf gate, or stray too far, I can't use the pebbles to find my way out."

"Of course you have magic," said Haiden, indignant. "You have my magic. Do you think I'd ever leave you to stumble your way home alone?"

Gisela frowned. "It's not your job to look after me, Haiden."

"By that logic, it's not yours to look after me," he retorted.

Gisela pressed her lips into a thin line, the ghost of her father's words dancing in her mind.

*You must promise me that you'll always protect him.*

"It's different," she informed him. "I'm older, and I'm not being hunted for what I am."

"Hunted?" Haiden raised his eyebrows in disbelief. "That's a bit of an exaggeration."

"You remember what Mother used to say," Gisela insisted. "There are those in the forest who'll try to harvest your power, to—"

"Yes." Haiden's voice was hard as he cut her off. "I remember what Mother used to say. All of it."

Gisela let out a long, quiet breath, regretting her words. She shouldn't have brought up their mother. It wasn't a pleasant topic for either of them, but especially for Haiden.

"Even Papa said it, Haiden, just in a different way. He said there will always be people who want to exploit you for your magic."

Haiden said nothing, his expression still mutinous. Gisela sensed that there was nothing to be gained from pushing the point. It was time to change the subject.

"Just count the trees, Haiden," she said.

Haiden groaned, shifting the wooden pole he carried further up his shoulder. A pair of rabbits dangled from it, the results of their morning's hunt. They would eat well that night, and it was about time. Winter was well advanced, and the last few weeks had been lean.

Haiden had just resumed counting when he suddenly paused, stiffening.

"What is it?" Gisela asked, always alert to any shift in his mood. "Do you sense something?"

He nodded. "Magic," he murmured. "Up there."

Gisela followed his pointing finger with her gaze. She could neither see nor feel anything, but then, she never could. She wasn't born with the singing ability, and she couldn't sense the magic of Ilgal. At least, not in the way singers could. The last thought was rueful, and she found herself rubbing her chest.

"What kind of magic?" she asked.

"I think…" Haiden frowned. "I think a gate is opening."

An elf gate? The pair exchanged a look, then picked their way quickly and silently into the undergrowth further in from the clearing. Without the need to discuss it, they chose separate trees, scaling them quickly and concealing themselves in the foliage. Haiden had chosen one too close to the clearing for Gisela's liking, but she couldn't fault his skill. She couldn't see so much as a glimpse of him or his pole of rabbits once he was settled.

His senses proved correct. Soon Gisela heard the high voices of elves filtering through the trees, although they were far from any elf settlements, and she was sure no one had been nearby minutes before. By the sound of it, they were moving across the clearing, but she couldn't actually see them. She was also too far away to hear their conversation properly, although she strained her ears with interest. It was rare to encounter impromptu elf gates like this. It was complex and nuanced magic, with many risks inherent, and the ruling elf kept strict boundaries on its use. Mostly they created them to allow everyone to congregate for events such as festivals, or important meetings. The group of elves in the clearing didn't sound large. What purpose would justify the creation of a gate for their use?

"…too close to the Imperator's backyard, if you ask me."

The voice of an elf, slightly louder than the others, drifted up to Gisela's hiding place. She frowned. She'd always heard elves speak of their leader with great respect. But this elf's tone had been off somehow. Her vision blurred as she remembered the one—disastrously memorable—occasion on which she'd seen the elf leader herself. She'd been only seven the night of the fateful winter festival, but she could picture his wrinkled skin and piercing green gaze with ease. Every detail of that night was burned in her mind.

The elves' quiet voices were moving further away, and Gisela was just starting to relax when a flash of movement sent alarm through her. She watched in horror as Haiden dropped silently from his tree, dropping the rabbits on the grassy ground as he sprinted after the elves.

What was he doing?! Gisela didn't dare call after him, for fear of alerting the elves to his proximity. But inside she was seething, anger and fear vying for position. She'd taught him better than this. They were supposed to always be careful. How could he be risking himself—risking both of them—like this?

She scooped up the pole with the rabbits, her stomach grumbling at the thought of leaving their catch behind. She was a fast runner, though, and she wasn't far behind Haiden when she saw him sprint across the clearing, disappearing quite suddenly on the other side.

Gisela checked for a moment, a gasp escaping her. Then she doubled her pace, hoping desperately that she wasn't too late. Because Haiden hadn't just disappeared between tree trunks— he'd literally disappeared. Which meant that he'd run through an elf gate.

The longer the distance to be covered by a gate, the more sophisticated the magic required. Not to mention the conspicuousness of that great a volume of magic. These elves must have made two gates to break up the required magic into more manageable components, and used the clearing as the halfway point. Haiden could be literally anywhere within Ilgal right now.

As she dove after him, her surroundings changed. Her

breath of relief that she'd made it formed a visible cloud in front of her. This part of the forest was colder. She barely caught sight of Haiden's dark hair where he crouched in the undergrowth ahead, and she hurried after him.

"What are you doing?" she hissed, grabbing at his coat once she drew near.

He made a shushing motion, gesturing with his head. Gisela dropped down to his level, wincing as the rabbit pole made the leaves rustle.

"What am I looking at?" she breathed, peering through the foliage to where the elves seemed to be waiting, motionless.

"I don't know." Haiden's voice was equally quiet. "But they're up to something."

"What do you mean they're up to something?" Gisela demanded, irked. "What wild speculation did you base this life-threatening chase on?"

Haiden rolled his eyes at her dramatic language. "I think they were using magic-covering talismans. I could only sense the gates when they first opened, then the elves did something, and suddenly I couldn't feel magic anymore."

"So?" Gisela hissed.

"*So*, they're probably up to something illegal," said Haiden. "The use of magic-covering talismans is strictly regulated, remember?"

Yes, Gisela remembered. They'd learned as much a few years before when they'd attempted to acquire one in a market, thinking it might help them cover their tracks—or more specifically, Haiden's tracks. It turned out that while the elves usually kept their distance from everyone but their own kind, they had strict rules regarding the use made of the talismans they sold to humans.

"Even if they are doing something illegal, why does that mean we have to follow them?" she protested.

Haiden ignored the question, his eyes narrowed as he tried to see what the elves were up to. "The only reason a group of elves would need to hide the magic of a gate would be if it wasn't authorized," he mused. "If they're under the protection of the tribe, they would have nothing to fear from any non-elves able to sense magic. And the Imperator is the only one who could take issue with how much or what type of magic they use. They must be hiding it from the rest of the elves."

Gisela frowned. She couldn't fault Haiden's logic, but even so, he was only speculating. And even if he was right, she still couldn't see what it had to do with them. The affairs of the elves were no concern of theirs, after all.

"Haiden, what's going on?" she demanded, feeling like she was missing something. Haiden was more curious than her by nature, but he wasn't usually obsessed with discovering the activities of any strangers they encountered. "Why did you follow them?"

"To find out what they're up to," Haiden said. "And..." He flashed her a self-conscious look, immediately confirming her suspicion. "They mentioned Asivah."

Gisela stilled at the name. The elf girl—a princess of her kind, as they'd later learned—was another tense topic. No wonder Haiden had been tempted into pursuing the elves. Before now they'd never managed to hear or see more of the elf girl whose dire prophecy had effectively ripped their lives to shreds. Logic told Gisela she should hate Asivah, but she couldn't find the emotion in her when she pictured the open, friendly face of the elf. Her words had been terrible on the surface, but they hadn't *felt* that way. Gisela didn't know how else to describe it.

"What did they say about her?" she asked, captivated in spite of herself. "She's not with them, is she?"

"I don't think so," Haiden muttered. "I didn't catch exactly what they said, but the tone wasn't very complimentary."

The elves had been speaking quietly among themselves, but they suddenly stopped. The siblings froze, afraid they'd been spotted, but no one came toward them. Instead, they all looked up in the opposite direction, and Gisela realized someone new was approaching.

It took her a moment to identify that the newcomer was also an elf, given there was no gleam of unnaturally pale skin through the gloom of the forest. But when he came fully into view, his diminutive size and adult features confirmed him to be a member of the elven species. It was just that his face was painted in the greens and browns that suggested he spent much of his time alone in the forest, trying to escape notice. He might be a hunter for the main elf community. He might also be a lone elf, choosing not to belong to any formal settlement but to eke out a solitary existence in the forest. Like them.

One of the elves strode forward from the group to meet the new arrival. The two of them dipped their heads to one another, neither taking his eyes off the other's face. Clearly their relationship wasn't one of any great trust.

"Do you have the message?" the camouflaged elf asked.

"I do." The other elf pulled a missive from his clothes. It was rolled up and sealed, and the newcomer quickly stashed it out of sight.

"No gold to be transported?" he asked curtly.

The first elf shook his head. "That's not your concern. They'll get what they've been promised—a shipment will be arranged separately. The message explains it all. You know your role?"

The lone elf nodded. "I should clear the forest by nightfall. I'll rendezvous with the next group tomorrow, or the day after at latest. Do I expect a return message?"

"It's not certain," piped up another elf from the group. "The other party will notify you. But we should arrange to meet again in case there is a return message."

The camouflaged elf nodded, and the one who'd given him the message spoke.

"Do you agree to return to this same place, a week from now, telling no one of any of this, and bringing no companions?"

"I so agree on the provision that you agree to speak of my role in all of this to no living soul," the elf replied.

"Agreed," murmured each elf present, followed by, "witnessed," as they all confirmed each other's oaths.

Intrigued, Gisela glanced at Haiden, watching the wonder on his face as he sensed whatever magic was passing around the group, binding them to their promises. It was rare that they got the opportunity to witness an elf bargain. By the time she looked back at the elves, the lone one was already disappearing through the trees. The one who'd approached him rejoined his group, and they began to retrace their steps toward where the gate had been.

"We have to hurry," Gisela whispered frantically. "They'll close the gate behind them this time for sure. If we don't make it through first, we'll be stranded here."

For some strange reason, Haiden hesitated.

"Haiden!" Gisela hissed. The last of the elves had disappeared from view. "Let's move!"

"But they're coming back here in a week, and if we go now, we'll never be able to find this place again," Haiden protested. "We won't have any way to discover what they're up to." His eyes lit up with an idea. "A pebble! If we leave a pebble, I'll be able to find it."

"I'm all out," Gisela told him. "I used them all when we were hunting."

Haiden groaned. "I don't have time to try to cast new object control magic." He closed his eyes, taking stock of himself. "Or enough energy, to be honest."

He held his palm out in a gesture Gisela recognized, and she shook her head, seizing his hand and tugging him toward the gate.

"The stones must be hours away now, Haiden. There's no time to wait while you bring them to you. We have to go!"

She dragged him behind her as she ran toward the gate, the rabbit pole still gripped awkwardly in her other hand. As Haiden had said, the elves would be back here. She didn't care for them to find the decaying remains of the siblings' hunt as evidence that they'd been observed.

"Is the gate still open?" Gisela asked, her eyes searching the forest for any abrupt change. Up ahead, she thought she caught a glimpse of dappled light shimmering incongruously in a patch of deep foliage, and she made for that. Could it be the clearing where they'd first encountered the elves, showing faintly through the gate?

"It's there, but it's fading," Haiden said.

The words had barely left his mouth when their surroundings changed abruptly, and they found themselves not in the clearing Gisela was expecting but in a particularly dark patch of ash trees.

Instinctively, they parted, ducking behind different trees as they scoped out the area.

"The gate is closed," Haiden murmured, glancing behind them. "We just made it."

"There," Gisela breathed, pointing ahead to where one solitary elf could be seen wending her way between the tree trunks.

Haiden frowned, his singer senses clearly picking up something Gisela couldn't feel. "There's another gate. Come on."

The two of them took off, moving as silently as speed allowed. But they were too late. They'd seen only one elf, and she was gone in moments. By the time they reached the spot where she'd been, all was still and quiet. A glance at Haiden's grimace told Gisela all she needed to know. The gate was closed, and they were stranded.

Emotion rose up in her, and she tried to beat it down. Getting angry wouldn't help the situation, and neither would panicking.

"Where are we?" she asked instead. "This isn't the clearing they passed through on the way."

"No," Haiden agreed. He peered through the trees in all directions before answering. "It's dense here, isn't it? I can't see any sign of a clearing nearby."

"They must have created new gates on the way back," Gisela said. "And used a different midpoint."

"To further avoid detection," Haiden pointed out. "Which means I was surely right that they're hiding something from the rest of the elves."

"Which *means*," Gisela corrected, "we're stranded somewhere completely random."

## CHAPTER TWO

# Otto

Dappled sunlight fell onto the path ahead, the shadows dancing in the light breeze that was rustling the leaves. It was beautiful, Otto acknowledged to himself. He'd always loved teasing Rosa, his stepsister, about her love of the forest, insisting that he preferred the luxuries of castle life. In fact, volunteering for this mission was in part his attempt to rectify his former disconnect from her second life in the Forest of Ilgal. Perhaps if he'd been part of her visits to her grandparents in the forest, things would have unfolded differently.

But the longer he spent under the trees, the less his guilt motivated him. He was starting to feel the magic of the place himself. And not just in the bad way, he thought, rubbing one hand over his chest.

"It's strong, isn't it?" The voice of his friend Monty came from beside him, where the young nobleman rode his horse close alongside Otto's on the narrow forest trail. "The magic, I mean. It's getting stronger."

Otto nodded, noting that Monty's voice was at its usual cheerful best.

"It's going to get worse, too, the deeper in we go," he informed his friend. "All our inquiries now suggest that the tale we were told previously about the problem being worst in the region near Terenford was blatant falsehood. I'm sure the aim was to target that region with the evacuation plan first, then eventually expand it out to the rest of Ilgal." He shot his friend a look. "It's not too late to turn back."

"Yes it is," said Norris, the head guard, from in front of them. Otto hadn't even realized that the older man could hear their conversation. "I don't have the manpower to send guards back with anyone just because they have cold feet, courtier or not."

"I don't have cold feet," said Monty, affronted. "I never said anything about wanting to go back. I'm going to stick it out, the same as the rest of you."

He turned to Otto, shaking his head when he saw his friend grinning at his expense.

"Thank you for that, Otto," he muttered, low enough for Norris not to hear this time. But with his usual good nature, he quickly let the matter go. "It makes sense that the magic would be thicker in the middle of the forest rather than at the edge." He glanced nervously at the gloom between the trees just off the path. "Does that mean the wolf issue wasn't isolated to the region near the capital, either?"

Otto shook his head, trying not to start grinning again at his friend's obvious alarm. "If you mean the giant, magically-enhanced wolf problem, that really was only near the capital. Obviously there are normal wolves out here, but not as many as you'd think. And none that would attack a group our size. Their style is more to pick off the vulnerable lone prey."

"Much like your approach to the young ladies of the court, from what I hear, Lord Montague." The new voice came from a middle-aged woman riding just behind the pair.

Monty grinned, shooting a glance over his shoulder. "You malign me, Lady Louisa, and I'm affronted."

Her only response was to snap the feather fan in her hand into a thin line with a loud wooden clack.

"I still can hardly believe you brought that thing all the way into the forest," Monty commented, eyeing the feathers. "Surely it's a bit too fancy to be carted on a trip like this."

"A lady should never be without her fan," said Lady Louisa prosaically.

The words were accompanied by a look that would quell a less confident soul than Monty. But Monty had always been a bit shameless. Otto smiled, seeing no real malice in the older woman's glare. Lady Louisa had accompanied the group in representation of the king's Council of Nobles, but she wasn't at all like most of the members of Otto's father's court. The easygoing but no-nonsense countess had quickly become a favorite of both his and Monty's.

"He's really not that bad, Lady Louisa," Otto felt compelled to say in Monty's defense. "Just a bit too dashing for his own good. I don't think he can really be accused of breaking too many hearts."

"Tell that to my niece," Lady Louisa said shortly. "Apparently she's in a decline after you slighted her. Although I daresay you don't even remember one conquest among so many."

Monty gave a snort that caused his horse to sidle. "I remember her perfectly. And I find it hard to believe any slight from me broke her heart. I can tell you with absolute confidence that her interest in me was entirely a means to the end of catching Otto's eye for a chance at the crown."

"Ah, you're probably right," said Lady Louisa in a practical spirit. "I've never had much patience with the girl. But my lord has a soft spot for all his sister's family, so here we are."

"Speaking of which, where exactly is *here*?" Monty asked,

exchanging a smile with Otto. The noblewoman's habit of referring to her husband always as "my lord" was one of her most endearing features. A couple of days into the trip, Monty had received a rap from her fan for inquiring innocently whether she'd forgotten her husband's name.

Strictly speaking, it was the count who held a hereditary position on the Council, but his health frequently prevented him from filling it. Somehow, through a process Otto had never quite managed to nail down, the countess had taken over on these occasions. Which seemed to be all the time now. She'd even managed to secure a place on this expedition under that guise. Since she'd been the only member of the Council of Nobles willing to consider trekking deep into the Forest of Ilgal, perhaps that particular appointment wasn't so mysterious.

"Here is nowhere in particular, Lord Montague," said the head guard, Norris, in response to Monty's question. He was now riding two rows in front, at the head of their sizable group. "If the chief of that last village is to be believed, we're still about a day's ride from the closest elf settlement."

"And I wouldn't wager much on his word," said Otto dryly. He shook his head. "This trip is excellent for deflating my ego. We've only been gone from the capital for two weeks, and any illusions I had as to the power of my position as crown prince have already been thoroughly punctured. That's the fifth village where even the chief has been disinclined to give me either information or encouragement."

"It probably will be good for you," said Lady Louisa frankly. "It's an excellent thing for a leader to have a modest ego. It's also an excellent thing for you to get an authentic picture of how life is for those of your future subjects who live in Ilgal. The forest makes up a significant portion of Teren's population, after all. But I must say, the lack of cooperation is not especially helpful for our purpose."

"No," agreed Otto, deflating. "That last village was especially disappointing. It was twice as big as the last few. In a town that size, you'd think there would be at least one singer. But none at all."

He glanced back at the group behind them. All told, they numbered three dozen, mainly guards. It was a lot for such narrow trails.

"Do you think they were telling the truth about the singers, Valerie?" He directed the question at the only woman in the group, other than Lady Louisa.

"I do," said Valerie slowly, as if not quite confident of her answer. She saw Otto looking at her inquiringly, and sighed. "I don't think they were lying about there being no singers there. But there did seem something odd about their reluctance to talk even about the ones who'd left."

"I noted the same thing," Otto agreed. "They didn't even want to identify the families or friends of singers. It was like they wanted us to think singers had never been there at all."

"When that clearly wasn't the case," Monty agreed, nodding. "The village well was definitely enhanced by magic at some point in the past, and didn't they say the boundary wall kept out predators but not humans? Surely that's a product of magic."

"Undoubtedly," Valerie agreed. "I could sense the power on it. It's strange that they would lie."

"Perhaps they were afraid you'd be angry with them if they admitted they'd let all the singers leave," Lady Louisa suggested, tapping her ever-present fan against her leg. "Given that you were open about your goal of recruiting singers."

"Perhaps," Otto said, unconvinced.

"At any rate, I don't think they were lying about there being no singers there now," Valerie repeated. "It's consistent with what I've heard. Singers have been leaving Ilgal in droves over the last decade or so. A number of my classmates at the academy came from Ilgal originally, either them or their parents. From what they say, it's pretty normal that as soon as singing ability is detected, a family will start exploring the option of moving to the city."

"Why?" Monty asked, frowning. "So they can study at the academy?"

"That's part of it," Valerie acknowledged. "But not the only reason."

She paused to think, twisting a strand of fiery red hair around her finger and trying to coax it back into the loose mess of curls on top of her head, from which it had escaped. Otto noticed one of the closer guards watching the process surreptitiously, and held in a sigh.

Valerie was much younger than the countess, around Otto and Monty's age. She was also very pretty and, to Otto's eye, had caused a fair bit of distraction among the younger members of the guards. It was unfortunate, but it was in no way her fault, and Otto remained grateful to her for her presence. They'd had great difficulty finding a singer to volunteer for the expedition until the Academy of Song suggested Valerie. As the academy head had predicted—somewhat dryly—she'd had no hesitation in throwing herself into the adventure. She wasn't as experienced a singer as he'd hoped for—she was only one year out of the academy—but by that stage Otto had been very ready to take what he could get.

"To be honest, I think the volume of magic here is as big a motivator as the academy," Valerie went on. "There's just...too much of it."

"What do you mean?" Monty demanded. "That makes no sense. Singers don't have their own magic—they have to draw it from the earth. Surely the more magic coming out of the ground, the better."

"Thank you, Lord Montague, for teaching me the basic principles of magic," said Valerie sweetly. "As a mere singer, a graduate of the Academy of Song, I naturally know nothing of the matter. I'm sure that your father's patronage of the academy makes you, on the other hand, an expert."

Monty grinned. Otto had yet to see his friend abashed by the young singer's very public dislike of him.

"Well, I don't know if I'd say expert," Monty said comfortably. "But if you'd let me, I could probably teach you a thing or two."

Valerie narrowed her eyes at this brazen flirtation, but thankfully Lady Louisa cut in before the spat could escalate.

"Children, children," said the countess idly. "Lord Montague, try not to be any dafter than you absolutely must. And Valerie, from what I understand, the earl is incredibly generous in his sponsorship of the academy, so it won't kill you to speak of him with some respect."

"Oh, I have no problem with the earl," said Valerie, without the hint of an apology. "Except perhaps as regards his parenting skills, I suppose."

Otto couldn't help chuckling. It was entertaining to see Monty brought down a peg. His friend was always confident to a fault. Not that Monty seemed especially chastened, judging by his grin.

"Yes, he's an excellent sort, my father, but you're right that his parenting could use some work. Maybe when we get back to Terenford, you could have a word to him, Valerie, and back me up. I've been telling him for years that he should give me more license."

Valerie snorted. "I don't think that's your issue, somehow. And it's not *when* we get back to Terenford, it's *if*. I was reliably informed that this expedition comes with great risk, and I for one am hoping you fall from a tree or something."

"Now you're insulting me and my men," said Norris mildly.

"We fully intend to see every member of our expedition returned safely to their homes."

"I meant no offense, Norris," said Valerie with deceptive respectfulness. "You're an excellent guard. But couldn't you make just one exception?"

Otto could have sworn he saw the grizzled guard's lips twitch, but it was hard to be sure. Norris was pleasant enough in manner, but he rarely showed much emotion.

"Can we return to the original question?" Otto interjected. "Why would more magic make singers want to leave the forest rather than stay?"

"Oh yes," said Valerie, shifting in her saddle. "Sorry, Your Highness."

Otto waved a hand. "I've told you all, no need for the title in a group this small. We'll all be traveling together for a long time, and in far from exalted conditions."

Valerie dipped her head in acknowledgment of the words, but didn't use his name. She'd get there.

"As for the magic, such a high volume as this can be problematic." She rubbed one hand slowly across the space between her collarbones. "Well, we can all feel it, can't we? There's a lot of it. And even though you'd think that would make it a paradise for singers, it actually makes it harder to harness the magic. Especially for inexperienced singers. The quantity is just too much to control when you're learning. It pours right through us and straight back into the environment unused, rather than being a manageable flow that we can harness and direct. A trick I heard the Ilgal singers talk about is trying to get off the ground, to limit the direct flow of the magic. So right now, sitting on my horse, I can feel an excellent supply of magic ready for me to use. When I'm actually standing on the ground though, it's overwhelming. I'm not saying it can't be used. Just that for those learning their craft, it's not the ideal environment."

"Which is why all the young singers like to leave the forest to study at the academy," Otto mused.

Valerie nodded. "I think our best bet is to find older, more established singers. Ones who learned to harness the power of Ilgal successfully enough to want to stay."

Otto nodded, but inside he was discouraged. He'd felt so hopeful when he set out from Terenford, proud his father had trusted him with the responsibility of this expedition, and sure that he could succeed. The plan that Teren had copied from Selvana seemed simple enough: gather a significant number of singers and—with their assistance—develop a strategy to harness the maximum amount of power. The theory was that if enough of the magic lingering in the forest could be used, the amount pouring from the ground would become manageable. It was essentially a clearing of the air. It would take a long time and many separate attempts to perform the process throughout the whole forest. But it was at least a way forward.

Of course, the magic would just build up again over time if they didn't find enough singers willing to stay in the area and use the magic as it flowed out of the ground. But in his naivety, Otto had thought that the singers of Ilgal would be happy to oblige, and some of the singers from outside of Ilgal might be so captivated by the place when they joined the expedition that they'd choose to stay.

That had all been optimistic to the point of lunacy.

First of all, they'd been able to find almost no singers outside Ilgal willing to take part. A number had agreed to assist once there was a plan, in exchange for a fee, which would fall to the crown to pay. King Ryker, Otto's father, was willing to pay. But few of those singers would commit to the length of time and the number of exercises that would be necessary to clear the forest. It was likely most would help only once or twice. And Valerie was the only one who'd been willing to actually come into the forest for the first exploratory trip.

Determined not to be stumped, Otto had turned his attention to the forest itself, sure that the singers within Ilgal would be more invested in the wellbeing of the area and therefore more willing to assist.

The only problem was, there were no singers within Ilgal. Or at least, none he'd yet managed to find. And it was necessary to search in person, slowly and tortuously, because the forest settlements were so sprawling and far apart that there was no reliable census of their inhabitants. It was discouraging, but the quest was far from over. In the two weeks since they'd left Terenford and ridden west into the forest, they'd covered only a fraction of Ilgal. There was still time to find singers, or so Otto kept assuring himself.

"Halt."

Norris's voice brought the group to a stop, and he called some of his guards forward to hack at the branches that made the next section of trail impassable. Otto barely stopped himself from rolling his eyes when he saw a couple of them looking to see if Valerie was observing their manly efforts with their axes.

She wasn't.

"It's a shame singers can't magically recognize other singers on sight," Otto mused, directing the comment to Valerie. "Because I've wondered if any of the chiefs might be lying about having singers in their villages."

"They might be," Valerie acknowledged. "But I don't see what difference it would make, Your Highness. If the singers don't even want to be identified, then they surely won't agree to help." She gave him a sharp look. "And I was under the impression that His Majesty doesn't intend to force anyone to participate."

"He doesn't," Otto assured her. "But honestly, I'm starting to wonder if he might have to consider a decree if we can't find singers willing to help."

"I can tell you now that the leaders at the academy would have plenty to say about the dangers of that as a precedent," Valerie said wryly.

"Yes, I'm sure they would." Otto sighed. "Obviously my father and I would both prefer it didn't come to that."

"I don't know why everyone is so unwilling," said Valerie brightly. "I think it's very exciting!"

"I imagine they're afraid of being crushed by the magic of the forest," said Lady Louisa, refraining from rubbing her own chest like the rest of them periodically did.

"Hm, they shouldn't be," Valerie told her. "The magic passes straight through singers, thanks to our ability to channel it. It might be uncomfortable to feel it converging, but it's not a danger. I think they're all just big cowards."

Monty laughed, causing her to shoot him a dark look.

"What?" He raised his hands in a defensive gesture. "I'm agreeing with you."

"Don't do that," Valerie informed him. "It makes me uneasy when we're in agreement about anything."

"I can't help agreeing with you when you're right," said Monty reasonably. "And it's not just the singers. The nobles are just as bad. They should know better. If King Ryker is sending his son and heir, he obviously doesn't anticipate any dire risk." Monty gestured at the guards who weren't currently hacking foliage, all of whom had formed a loose ring around the rest of the travelers, and remained on high alert. "We're not exactly being sent into the depths of the forest unprotected."

"It's a good point," Lady Louisa agreed, snapping her fan open then shut. "But you don't need to convince us. We're the ones who were willing to come, after all."

"All right, path's clear."

At the word from one of the guards, the group nudged their horses back into motion. They hadn't gone far, however, when Otto pulled his horse, Bullion, back to a walk. Always responsive to his rider, the stallion slowed.

"What is it, Your Highness?" Norris asked, instantly taking note of the prince's change in demeanor. "Is all well?"

Otto nodded slowly. "Where does that path go, do you think?" he asked, pointing at a branching trail up ahead. "I thought the village chief said it was a straight path all the way to the elf settlement, with no turn offs larger than deer tracks. But that's definitely a trail."

"It is," the guard agreed, with a frown. "We'd best stay the course, I think, Your Highness."

But Otto had already pulled to a stop. He found himself drawn to that path, fascinated for some reason. Was it his imagination that it shimmered a little compared to the path they were on?

He looked back ahead, and let out a cry. "Where did the other path go?"

"What?" Norris swung his head around, looking uneasy as he saw what Otto had seen.

The path ahead, the one they'd been following, was simply gone. Instead of being a branching side route, the trail that had caught Otto's eye was now the only path, turning in a sharp bend.

"What is this?" Monty asked, frowning.

"I've heard of things like this." Valerie pulled her horse up alongside Otto's, looking excited. "I've heard that when you get deep enough into the woods, where the magic is strong, the paths can shift of their own accord."

"Of their own accord?" Lady Louisa sounded skeptical. "They're not sentient."

"Magic almost feels alive sometimes," Valerie said with a shrug. "Not sentient exactly, but not entirely passive, either."

"That makes no sense," Monty informed her.

"To one of your intellect, Lord Montague, I would imagine not."

"What do you feel from this path, Valerie?" Otto hastened to jump in before they could escalate to a quarrel. "Does it feel sinister, like there's an enchantment on it?"

Valerie frowned in thought. "I feel magic, definitely, but it doesn't really feel like an enchantment. Those are specific and concentrated. It feels more like the natural magic that's all around in this forest. It's just...especially potent here."

Otto glanced back at the place the path had previously been, which was now a thickly wooded grove.

"Well, I guess we're going this way," he said.

## CHAPTER THREE

# Otto

"I don't like it, Your Highness." Norris's forehead was furrowed as he examined the path that had appeared out of nowhere. "We don't know where it leads."

"We didn't know with any confidence where the last one led, either," Otto pointed out. "Surely it's safer to follow a path—any path—than to wander through the trees."

"Not if the path can't be trusted to stay put so we can find our way back," Monty muttered. But he made no real objection to Otto's plan.

Even Norris said no more. He was well within his role to express his concerns, but leadership of the expedition was in Otto's hands, as everyone was aware. Soon the group was moving cautiously down the new trail.

To Otto's amazement, only about an hour after they started on the path, Valerie drew up alongside him with a look of great excitement.

"I feel magic, Your Highness," she said. "More than just the natural magic of the forest, I mean. It's like many talismans gathered in one place. I think we must be near."

"Do you mean near the elf settlement?" Otto asked. "But I thought it was still a day away!"

"Maybe it was," said Valerie cryptically. "By the old path."

Otto blinked at her, but there was no time to explore her vague comments. A row of ash trees came into sight ahead, spaced too evenly and growing too perfectly to be entirely natural.

"I think it's a boundary," Valerie commented, her eyes on the trees as well. "Around the settlement."

She proved to be right. When they neared it, Otto could see that the row was actually a ring, curving out of sight in both directions. The slightly shimmering trail came to a stop when it reached the ring, and the group pulled up their mounts.

"Greetings," Otto called to the air. "I am Crown Prince Otto, son of King Ryker who rules this kingdom, and I have come to speak with the leader of this settlement, if he or she will welcome me."

"Just the right balance of grandiose and approachable," Monty muttered approvingly.

Valerie sent the young nobleman a withering look, but Otto smiled. He was glad his friend had decided to come with him. It certainly lightened the long, boring days of riding.

A small figure stepped out from between the ash trees, his expression showing none of the deference Otto might hope for.

"Your Highness," he said, in his high, clear voice. He bent into a bow that could only be described as reluctant. "Your visit is unexpected."

"Had it been possible, I would have sent word ahead of my party," said Otto coolly. "But it was not an option. Will your leader meet with me?"

"She will," the elf confirmed. "Do you and your party come in peace?"

"Of course," said Otto, a little taken aback.

"Then you may all enter," the elf said, with the tone of one making a concession.

Otto exchanged a dry look with Monty, but made no comment as he dismounted. Following his lead, the rest of the party did the same, leading their horses through the ring of ash trees. Two guards moved to flank Otto closely, the rest forming a circle around the group.

The inside of the ring wasn't anything like the simple human villages Otto had so far visited. They tended to consist of a central square of some kind, with simple wooden dwellings scattered around it, no trees between them. But the elf settlement wasn't clear of trees. It had another ring of trunks inside the ashes, pines this time. And in the center of those, a third ring of small beech trees. And, from what Otto could see, as many of the dwellings scattered among them were found in the trees themselves as on the ground.

The group was led to a large building at the center of the middle ring. The house had been cut into the dead stump of what must have been a truly enormous tree during its life.

The elf signaled for them all to wait and ducked inside the building. A moment later, an elderly elf emerged, her hair white and her skin wrinkled. She looked Otto over thoughtfully with her emerald eyes, ignoring the rest of the group.

"You are Prince Otto?" she asked.

"I am," said Otto, inclining his head slightly. He didn't want to seem overbearing, but it was hard to behave in a casual, approachable manner when he towered over the elf.

Perhaps she sensed the same thing, because she gestured toward a collection of small stumps which appeared to have been lopped from elsewhere and planted in a circle on the grass near the leader's dwelling.

Otto sat as directed, his long legs splayed awkwardly on the low seat. His guards remained standing around him, but Monty,

Valerie, and Lady Louisa all joined him on the stumps. A few other elves joined as well, although there was a distinct lack of pomp and ceremony around the elderly leader.

"What brings you to our settlement, Your Highness?" the elf asked.

"Speaking literally, it was an unexpected path that brought us here," Otto said. "We thought ourselves still a day's ride away when the path shifted, bringing us right to your home."

The elf frowned, not seeming pleased with this information.

"And for what purpose were you coming to find us?" she asked.

"To explain that, I must first explain my reason for being in Ilgal," said Otto.

"If you refer to the king's plan to gather singers and make concentrated attempts to vent the magic of the land from the forest, we are aware of it," said the elf, her voice carrying no particular emotion.

Otto leaned back on his stump, regarding her in surprise. Word of their errand had gone ahead of them, even to this isolated settlement far from human habitation?

"I'd give a great deal to know how you learned of it," he said unthinkingly.

The elves all straightened on their stumps, several pairs of emerald eyes gleaming identically at him.

"Would you indeed?" the elf leader asked. "What precisely would you give, Your Highness?"

Realizing his error, Otto held in a laugh. "Nothing," he said. "I wouldn't actually give anything. I spoke figuratively."

"Not a wise thing to do among elves," said the leader, as the rest of the group slumped a little in disappointment. Otto shuddered to think what the bargain-loving creatures would do with the whiff of a promise from the prince of the kingdom. He knew that bargains with elves were magically binding, and as the heir to his father's throne, a bargain made by him would have extra power.

"Do you tell me that fact as a gift freely given?" he asked cautiously, called back to the elf etiquette in which he'd been meticulously trained before departing Terenford.

"I do," said the elf leader, with the hint of a sigh.

"Then I thank you for it," said Otto. "But it is information I already held. Please disregard my earlier words." He examined the elf. "If you know of my errand, perhaps you know why I'm here in your settlement."

"I do not," the leader said promptly. "I understood that you intended to visit human villages in your search for singers. I can assure you there are no singers here. Elves do not cohabit with humans."

"I'm aware of it," Otto said. "However, since you've given me information as a gift freely given, I will do the same with this information. Namely, that I have yet to identify any singers in the human villages through which we have passed."

"Is that so?" Again there was no particular emotion in the elf's voice, and Otto couldn't read her reaction. "Do you expect me to help you find singers?"

"I expect nothing from you," Otto said comfortably, not about to fall into any traps. "But I came to explore your willingness to share information with me."

"My willingness or otherwise will depend on the nature of the information you seek," the elf informed him. "And the exchange offered."

"Does my father's crown not provide me with any credit on which to expect information?" Otto asked lightly.

He was met with silence and hard stares, and deemed it wisest not to push the point.

"You know already that I wish to find singers," he said. "You're correct that my intention was originally to visit the human villages. But having met with no success so far, I formed the plan of seeking out some elves."

He glanced around the settlement, or what little of it he could see from inside the ring of beeches.

"I have no doubt that you are well aware of the sprawling and uncharted nature of Ilgal. I know that the elves have their own ways to both tame and traverse the forest. I suspect that your kind have a much better idea than the humans of the true inhabitants of the forest, both their numbers and their attributes." He kept his voice level. "You may even have some idea of why there appears to be an unnatural lack of singers in this forest."

The elf leader remained expressionless, but a couple of her fellows shifted slightly at these words. Otto kept his eyes on the leader, but took mental note of the reaction. It seemed more was going on in Ilgal than he understood.

"That is the information you seek?" the elf leader asked.

"It is," Otto confirmed.

For a long moment, she regarded him in silence. Then her masked expression relaxed into what was almost a smile, the corners of her green eyes crinkling. "I am sorely tempted to form a bargain with you, Your Highness. It is difficult for one of my age and experience to resist exploiting your youth and inexperience, particularly given the power you so clumsily wield."

A few of Otto's guards drew closer, clearly not liking her disparagement of Otto's abilities. For his part, Otto just waited to see if there was more to the elf's thoughts.

"But I could not do so in good faith," she went on, with only the tiniest hint of reluctance. "Because I do not carry the authority to treat with you on these matters. If you wish for these answers, you must apply to the Imperator."

Otto raised his eyebrows, surprised by the mention of the chief leader of the elves of Ilgal. He knew that there was one ruling leader, who filled a hereditary position similar to the kingship he would inherit one day. He also knew that it was not a role that came with specific territory, but rather the loyalty of a specific group of elves. Most elf leaders across Providore commanded small tribal groups. As far as he was aware, Ilgal was the only place where those small groups all deferred to one overarching leader, whom they called the Imperator. Even so, Otto had understood the individual groups to mainly enjoy autonomy. It seemed the authority of the Imperator was greater than he'd realized.

"Will you tell me where I can find this Imperator?" he asked the leader before him.

"In exchange for what?" she replied promptly.

"Are you interested in gold?" Otto asked.

"Not especially."

He considered her. "What do you suggest?"

"How about a promise to recognize Ilgal as under the sole authority of the elves once you ascend your father's throne?"

"How about no?" Otto said flatly.

The elderly elf chuckled, her eyes crinkling. "You can't blame me for trying. I think a simple information exchange would be best. I have two questions regarding your group, and for their answers, I will tell you where to find the Imperator."

"I want to know what the questions are before I decide whether to agree," said Otto, aware that the elf wouldn't hesitate to exploit him as much as he let her.

She sighed, but appeared to accept the request as reasonable. To Otto's surprise, her eyes passed to Valerie, seated next to Lady Louisa.

"The questions relate to her. First: is she a singer? Second: does she have a brother?"

Otto blinked. "Why would you want to know that?"

"Do you wish to change the terms of the bargain so that my

answer to that question provides satisfaction for the answers I've requested?"

Otto tapped his foot impatiently on the grassy ground, wondering why he bothered trying to have a normal conversation with the impossible creatures.

"No," he said. "I prefer the original terms." He looked at Valerie. "But it's up to you. If you'd prefer not to provide the information—"

"No, I don't mind," she said, looking as bewildered as he felt. She looked like she was about to give the answers, not realizing she'd be providing information for free and taking them back to square one, so Otto hastened to speak.

"Very well," he told the elf leader. "We will give you the answer to those two questions in exchange for the information as to where the Imperator can most frequently be found."

The elf to the leader's left looked a little disappointed at his phrasing, and Otto wondered if they'd intended to tell him something obscure and useless, like where the Imperator could be found at full moon in summer. He would have to be more on his guard if he was going to spend much time treating with the bargain-loving species.

"Very well," the elf leader said. "Agreed."

"Witnessed," murmured several nearby elves, and Otto glanced uncertainly at Monty.

"Er...witnessed?" the young nobleman offered. Otto turned back around, catching in his peripheral vision that Valerie was rolling her eyes.

"I will go first," the elf leader said. "The central settlement of our kind, where the Imperator lives, is located right in the heart of the forest, about a week's ride from here. If you continue to travel northwest, you will find it. I will even give you a warning as a gift freely given. Human roads will not take you there." She met his eyes. "Nor will the forest's paths."

"Thank you." Otto inclined his head. "And for the information you sought, yes, Valerie is a singer. As for a brother..." He looked to Valerie questioningly.

She shook her head. "I have no family," she said.

"You have no family now?" the elf clarified. "Or you never had a family?"

"Obviously I once had parents," she said in a matter-of-fact tone. "But I never had a brother."

Otto caught Monty looking at Valerie in surprise, and he felt the same way. He'd had no idea that the confident singer was an orphan without family. A flash of sympathy went through him, but he put it aside. He had more pressing matters to consider.

"I trust you consider our exchange satisfied," he said to the elf leader, not phrasing it as a question.

The elf smiled. "Trust is something you should not employ with my kind, Your Highness," she told him. "Or in Ilgal in general. But yes, our exchange is satisfied."

"We will take our leave of you, then," said Otto, standing. The elf stood as well, but said nothing to discourage their departure. Had it been a human settlement, Otto would have asked for shelter for the night, but he shuddered to think what kind of exchange the elves would attempt to extort for that magnitude of favor.

The party made their way out of the settlement the way they'd come, watched by many pairs of green eyes, but stopped by no one.

"Well," said Lady Louisa, when they stood outside the ring of ash trees. "That was an interesting experience."

"Why did they ask about Valerie?" Monty demanded, not looking cheerful for once. "What interest do they have in her?"

"I don't see what business it is of yours," Valerie pointed out.

"Does that mean you know, then?" Monty asked.

She hesitated, then shook her head. "I have no idea," she admitted. "It was bizarre."

"Do you really intend to seek out the Imperator, Your Highness?" Lady Louisa asked Otto. "A week's ride into the heart of the forest is surely not the trip that your father initially intended."

"It's not," Otto acknowledged. "But plans change, and my father understands that. He gave me autonomy in how to direct the trip once I'm here."

"I'm not sure he intended you to stray so far off the path, Your Highness," said Norris uneasily. "Metaphorically speaking."

"I know it's a big ask of you and your men, Norris," said Otto. He looked around the group. "Of all of you. Things will be less predictable and no doubt more dangerous if we leave human paths altogether. But I do wish to speak to the Imperator. I strongly suspect he'll have a way of identifying the singers in a domain which he clearly considers his. But it's also becoming increasingly evident that something is going on in Ilgal of which my father and I have no idea. And in addition to it being a barrier to my original mission, that's not a desirable state of affairs."

"Of course, Your Highness," said Norris staunchly. "I didn't mean to complain. We are capable of protecting you in whatever situation your duty requires you to enter, and willing to follow where you lead."

"As am I," said Monty amicably. "I'm along for the whole ride, Otto."

"I don't object," shrugged Valerie. "I was already curious, and now doubly so if I'm going to have elves asking questions about me in particular."

"I'm up to the task," said Lady Louisa regally. "I'm not about to abandon the venture halfway through."

"Thank you," Otto told them all. "Truly. I'm grateful to all of you for helping me on this expedition. I know you're putting up with long days in the saddle and far from comfortable conditions." He looked up at the patches of sky that showed between the branches. "The afternoon is advancing. It would be ideal to find a human village to sleep in rather than camping in the open."

Norris pulled a by-now familiar map from his saddlebags and smoothed it out across the flank of his patient horse.

Otto bent over it, trying to decipher it with the head guard. It was a map of Ilgal, with a rough X scratched in numerous locations on the parchment, each one marking the position of known human dwellings. It was years out of date, but better than nothing.

"There's the last village we visited," Norris said, pointing to an X. "And we rode only half a day north, so I suppose we're about here? That makes us a long way from any known human villages."

"I'm not sure we are there," Valerie commented, leaning over the guard's shoulder. "I have a feeling that shimmering path we took changed our course in some way."

Otto glanced at her. Apparently he wasn't the only one who'd seen the shimmer.

"Let's assume, for a moment, that we're actually at the point where the village chief said we'd find the elf settlement," Valerie said. "That would put us three times as far north, right? Maybe here?" She tapped one slim finger on the page. "So there would be a human village only a short distance to the west, right?"

The guard nodded. "Only two hours' ride, probably."

"Let's try it," said Otto decisively. "If we're wrong about our location, it only means we'll have to find a place to camp, which leaves us no worse off than we were."

The group rode mostly in silence for the next two hours, on

a trail that was partly overgrown but still visible. Otto's excitement on seeing buildings appear through the trees quickly died when the riders emerged into a small village square and realized it was completely overgrown. Whoever had lived there had abandoned it long ago.

"Probably moved to Terenford with the singers," muttered Monty beside him, clearly considering the defectors to have shown great sense.

It was disappointing not to have a human welcome, but the abandoned buildings were better shelter than they'd find in the forest. A few of the guards went out to hunt, and the rest of the group set about making the former village home for the night.

The guards managed to catch a deer, which cheered everyone up immensely. They'd be able to enjoy a full meal once they added the provisions they'd brought with them.

Valerie began making a fire, her voice raised in a song that did much more than the flint Monty was attempting to use. When the gathered sticks and logs went up in a blaze, she shot a smug look at the young lord. Monty just gave an admiring whistle as he examined her handiwork, and although she showed every sign of irritation with his reaction, Otto was sure he saw the hint of a smile on her face as she turned away.

He was sitting on the porch of a dilapidated building, watching the pair feed the blaze, when he saw a skulking figure at the edge of the village square. Otto had barely bolted upright in his makeshift seat when the man strode confidently into the clearing, swirling a short blade in his hand, and grasping something in the other.

"Lovely voice you've got, my dear," the man said in a grating tone. "Not many singers to be found round these parts."

Valerie stared at him open-mouthed, and Monty sprang to her side with a speed Otto had rarely seen from the easy-going lord.

"I beg your pardon?" Monty said coldly. "I suggest you move along, friend."

"I don't think I will, *friend*," the man said, his mouth stretched in a smile that showed off a few broken teeth. "Unless the pretty young lady would like to come with me."

"I don't think so." Valerie and Monty spoke in unison, her voice indignant, Monty's frigid.

Otto stood, leaping over the broken steps of the porch just as the man raised the hand without the blade. At that moment, the guards who'd been preparing the kill nearby reappeared, most hastening to flank the prince while a couple went to stand alongside Monty and Valerie.

The stranger started, his eyes widening in alarm at the sight of all the armed men. Clearly he'd thought Valerie and Monty were a pair of lone travelers.

"Grab him," Otto urged the guards, but the man had already turned and plunged back into the trees. The guards gave chase, but it wasn't long before they returned, empty-handed and apologetic.

"It's not your fault," said Otto. "This is his territory. He'd know how to evade us with his eyes closed, probably." He frowned. "I think staying here is safer than relocating at this advanced hour. But I want double shift all night, Norris."

The head guard nodded in grim agreement. "I'll make it triple, Your Highness."

"How dare he?" Monty raged, so affronted anyone would be excused for thinking the man had targeted him instead of Valerie. "How dare he think he could just carry Val off like that?"

"Don't call me Val," said Valerie shortly. "And no one was carrying me off. I'm a fully qualified singer, remember. I know how to look after myself. I don't think I was in danger."

"Don't think?" Lady Louisa picked up on the note of uncertainty, and turned her piercing gaze on the younger woman.

"Well...he had a talisman," Valerie admitted. "In his hand. I couldn't tell its purpose, but I could feel the magic."

Monty looked horrified at this information, and Otto laid a hand on his friend's arm.

"You saw his reaction when the guards appeared, and two thirds of our number are still setting up camp in the other buildings or tending to the horses. Whatever the talisman does, it wasn't something that could overcome a group our size."

Valerie nodded, looking relieved, but Monty still seemed anxious.

In spite of Monty's fears, the night passed without incident. Nevertheless, they were all quick to break camp when dawn came. Otto had slept uneasily, and was eager to be on the road again. To his relief, the path that had led them there was still intact, and they followed it back toward the elf settlement.

They didn't go all the way there, however, turning north as soon as a branch appeared on the left of their path. Norris checked his map, and seemed fairly satisfied that they were heading in a northwesterly direction from the elf settlement, as the elf leader had indicated. Of course, so much of it was guesswork under the endless canopy of the forest.

The elf had told them it would take a week's ride to reach the Imperator's settlement, but she'd also said that the roads wouldn't go all the way there. Otto was therefore encouraged that the northwestern trail showed no immediate sign of petering out.

Every now and then the path would branch, and they would pause to allow Valerie to discern which one led more northwest. On one of these occasions, Otto watched with interest as she piled her hair on top of her head. It seemed to allow her to think better. Then she began to sing, her voice soft and low, the words of the melody too quiet for him to hear. The pitch started low but traveled briefly up to be high and piercing before returning to its starting point.

Otto glanced sideways and saw that Monty was watching, rapt, as the young singer spun gracefully on the spot, the movement slow and controlled. Otto hid a smile. From the look on his friend's face, anyone might think he'd never witnessed singing before, when in fact his father's patronage of the Academy of Song meant he'd basically haunted the place all his life.

"Due north is that way," Valerie declared with confidence, pointing to a spot partway between the two branching trails. "So we should take this one if we want to go northwest."

The group waited for her to mount her horse again before nudging their steeds toward the lefthand fork of the path.

"That's a handy bit of magic," Otto commented to Valerie, finding himself right behind her on the narrow trail.

"It is, isn't it?" she agreed brightly, casting a look over her shoulder. "I learned it especially when I found out I'd be coming on this expedition. It doesn't take much magic. Once I've let the song free, I just turn on the spot, and northward sort of...tugs at me."

"Doesn't seem very precise," grunted Norris disapprovingly from in front. "We have ways of telling direction, Your Highness."

Otto grinned at the older man's back, but Monty beat him to a reply.

"Of course it's precise." He sounded indignant. "Magic is much more nuanced than old forester's tricks. Your methods would get you an estimate at best."

Far from appreciating this defense, Valerie cast the young lord an irritated glance. Otto could only shake his head. Monty was famed for his charm with the ladies, but he was clearly struggling to find the right strategy to reach this particular one. Valerie urged her horse forward a little, initiating conversation with Lady Louisa, who was between her and Norris.

"Otto." Monty's quiet voice made Otto glance back. Conversation was difficult on such narrow trails. "Do you think that man might follow us? He seemed to really have his sights set on Valerie, didn't he? And with so many of us, our trail won't be hard to find."

Otto looked at his friend, surprised by Monty's serious expression. "I really don't think so," he told the other young man earnestly. "There are so many of us. He'd be mad to try to attack us. I doubt he'd consider one random girl worth it."

Monty didn't look at all convinced by this, but he said no more, and when nightfall came and went with still no sign of the stranger, he seemed to relax.

For four days, they made good progress, diverting to human villages twice, but otherwise camping in clearings, always with double guard shift. No disasters befell them—once or twice Otto thought he spotted wolves through the trees in the twilight hour, but the creatures didn't make any attempt on a group their size. Lady Louisa also had a near encounter with a lethal-looking snake, but thankfully Norris was near at hand and quick in dealing with the creature. All in all, the mood of the group was growing more comfortable in the forest surroundings.

Although their pace was good, Otto suspected they weren't quite halfway to their destination yet, given that they had to make camp early each day in order to allow time for hunting, foraging, and food preparation—an extensive task for a group their size. He wasn't sure the elf leader had factored that into her estimate.

On the fifth day, something happened to break the monotony. They were riding along at a good pace when a shout from the front caused them all to stop. Otto pushed Bullion forward to join Norris.

"What is it?"

"The path has ended, Your Highness," Norris said.

Otto followed his gaze and realized the guard was right. The path beneath their horses' hooves, which had showed a faint shimmer for some time, simply faded to a stop in front of Norris.

"What do we do now?" Monty asked uncertainly, pushing through the foliage to join Otto.

"Maybe we're getting close after all," Otto said optimistically. "The elf leader did say the road wouldn't take us all the way there."

"Or maybe we're lost," muttered Monty.

"We're not lost," said Otto firmly. "And we keep going. Valerie." He looked back at the group. "Can you please find northwest for us?"

Nodding, she slipped down from her saddle, leaving Lady Louisa to hold her horse's reins for her. A feat she achieved by tucking her feather fan under one arm. Otto restrained a smile as he watched her carefully positioning it so it wouldn't fall. He wouldn't have guessed the stalwart countess would be so attached to her accessory—she'd brought no other finery—but he supposed they all had their foibles. And she certainly used it to good effect in fulfilling her role as mother hen of the group.

"I don't like it, Your Highness," Norris said uneasily. "Leaving the path doesn't seem a good idea to me. If we lose our way entirely, we may find it impossible to retrace our steps."

"I know the risks," said Otto. "But we've come this far. I'm convinced it would be safer to continue to the elf settlement—which must be only a couple of days away—than to turn back after all this progress."

He waved to one of the guards at the back, who had a small

cage attached to his saddlebags. The man rode forward, and Otto smiled at him.

"I'll send an update to Father with our best guess as to our current whereabouts, and a summary of our plan."

Norris frowned as the guard pulled a pigeon from the cage, and Otto flapped a hand reassuringly.

"I'll use code, Norris. If the bird is intercepted, the thief will be none the wiser as to our location."

Valerie had completed her direction-finding song, and having told Norris which way was northwest, she approached Otto, watching with interest as he scratched out a message on a small scrap of parchment.

"Did you say you're writing in code? That's exciting. I suppose it's something your father's intelligence agents came up with?"

"Something like that," said Otto noncommittally.

Monty snorted, and Valerie raised an eyebrow at him.

"Go on, tell the truth, Otto," the young lord said with a smirk.

Otto grunted, his focus still on his message. "I don't know what you mean."

"You're hopeless." Monty shook his head before turning to Valerie. "It's a code Otto and his stepsister, Princess Rosa, came up with as teenagers. They mainly used it to make secret plans to avoid their tutors."

Valerie looked uncertain whether to believe him, turning suspicious eyes to Otto. "Really?"

He nodded, affixing the message to the bird's leg. "Find your way home, little friend," he said, releasing the pigeon. It fluttered up and out of sight among the branches. Otto turned to Valerie. "In father's defense, he wasn't using some child's doodling. It was an excellent code. He only made a few changes before adopting it."

Valerie laughed, and Otto saw Lady Louisa shaking her head smilingly as well.

"Come on," he said. "Which way are we going?"

Norris, still mounted, directed his horse into the undergrowth according to Valerie's instructions. The head guard didn't look happy, but he was clearly ready to follow Otto's leadership to whatever end.

It was both gratifying and sobering, and Otto could only hope that his decision to take them off the path didn't end up betraying their trust in him.

# CHAPTER FOUR

# Gisela

"Haiden." Gisela glared at her brother, who was avoiding her eye. "If the elves used a different midpoint the second time, we're stranded in the middle of nowhere, aren't we?"

There was a moment of pained silence as Haiden grimaced. "Yes."

Gisela drew a deep breath. They could be anywhere in Ilgal. "Use the object control magic, Haiden," she said. "Can you use the stones? They should guide us back to where we left our gear, and we can find our way home from there."

"Of course." Haiden brightened, closing his eyes in concentration. A moment later, his expression fell.

"Can't you sense them?" Gisela asked, anxious.

"No, I can," said Haiden. "But they're nowhere near us. Their presence is the faintest flicker in my mind. They're probably several days' hike away."

Gisela let out a groan. "In what direction?"

Haiden pointed, and she followed the direction of his hand.

"Which way is that?" she muttered.

She was speaking to herself more than to her brother.

Haiden didn't know any magical way to tell direction. Given their lifestyle, he'd been able to learn only a fraction of the potential of his songcraft.

She looked at the trees around them, trying to ascertain which side of each plant grew more densely. Theoretically, that should tell them which side got the most sun, and from there it was a simple calculation to establish the direction.

Haiden shook his head, grasping her intention. "They're all growing too close together in this part of the forest. We won't be able to tell north from the trees. None of them get enough direct sunlight for that."

Gisela sighed, giving it up. He was right. "We'll have to find some more open ground," she said.

Haiden nodded, not needing her to explain herself. "Let's hurry, while the light is still good."

The two of them moved forward without another word, spreading out to their usual distance in foraging trips—just out of each other's sight, but still within comfortable hailing distance. They were so practiced at their methods they didn't need to think about what pace to move to ensure they didn't lose one another, or how frequently to quietly employ their imitation birdcall to make sure they were still moving together. It was all second nature.

The forest was unusually dense, the gloom seeming more like evening than late morning. Gisela's nerves were on edge as she listened for the sound of animals, and checked for dangers among the underbrush. Thankfully, all was quiet, only the normal songs of birds and rustles of small creatures surrounding her. After less than ten minutes, she brightened at the sight of the light growing stronger ahead. She paused to whistle to Haiden, but he emerged into her view a moment later, moving to intercept her. He'd obviously seen it as well.

"There's a small clearing ahead," he told her unnecessarily.

They both hurried toward it, pleased to find the grassy area big enough to allow a strong circle of sunlight to show.

Gisela wasted no time in finding a long, straight stick and planting it in the middle of the clearing. Haiden didn't need to be asked—by the time she'd positioned it, he'd retrieved a tiny stone from the forest floor and placed it at the end of the thin shadow cast by the stick. Then the two of them sat down, their backs to trunks at the edge of the clearing. Haiden rummaged in his rucksack, pulling out some roasted chestnuts and tossing one to Gisela. She received it gratefully, her stomach growling after the morning's unplanned exertions.

"What do you think those elves were up to?" Haiden asked while they waited.

"I don't know, and frankly I don't care," Gisela said shortly.

He gave her a wheedling look. "Come on, Sis, aren't you a little bit curious?"

"I can't afford curiosity, and neither can you," Gisela told him seriously. "What if they'd seen us spying on them, Haiden? What if we found something out that compromised us?"

Haiden snorted. "So dramatic. The more information we have, the better, I say."

Gisela said nothing, unable to agree. She was too conscious of her own guilt in that regard. Because even though she'd been willing to give her whole life to support the opposite argument, there was a small, ashamed part of her that wished they'd never even gained the knowledge of Haiden's songcraft. If they'd never found out, they would probably all still be together, and probably still be very happy.

But that was a foolish thought. One way or another, it would have come out eventually. And, more importantly, Haiden's singing was a gift, not something to be hidden or ashamed of. He deserved better than to have to stifle it all his life.

"Did you see the message they passed to that other elf?"

Haiden went on, his mind still on the suspicious meeting they'd witnessed. "I think it had the Imperator's seal on it."

"What?" Gisela said. "That doesn't seem likely. Why do you think that?"

"It was just like the seal we saw on that edict that was posted around the market warning everyone about fraudulent vendors. Remember? The seal was wax, but it glowed, and magic sort of pulsed gently from it."

Gisela snorted. "I'm pretty sure you're describing any elf seal. They probably all sign their correspondence like that."

Haiden didn't look convinced. "Did you hear them talking about a shipment of gold? I wonder if whatever that message was might have something to do with fraudulent vendors or faulty talismans." He drew in a sharp breath. "Or not faulty, but forbidden. Maybe they're mining magic they're not supposed to touch, or using it to create something contraband, like magic-draining talismans, or paralysis talismans."

Gisela gave him a look. "Why did that merchant's stories about magic-draining talismans stick with you so much? You know *he* was a fraud, right? None of his wares did what he said they would."

Haiden snorted. "Of course he was a fraud. He was a human selling talismans in the forest—the heart of the elf talisman trade. His wares weren't talismans at all, let alone powerful ones. I couldn't sense a hint of magic on them."

"Sometimes it's handy having a singer around," Gisela said, shouldering him.

Her brother pulled her braid by way of reply.

"It's just fascinating magic, is all," he said. "And in the end, it doesn't matter if the talismans are real. It's not like we'd have any gold to buy them."

"Plus we'd have no use for a talisman to *remove* magic," Gisela pointed out, kneeling to peer at the stick in the clearing. "We need every bit of magic you can harness just to get by."

Haiden said nothing, and she sat back down. It hadn't been long enough yet.

A couple of minutes passed in silence before Haiden spoke again.

"I think we should try to find out what those elves are up to. It could be important."

"Haiden, no." All Gisela's instincts rose up in alarm, and she turned to fully face her brother.

"Think about it, Gisela," Haiden said. "The messenger said he was leaving the forest. Who would he be communicating with? The elf leadership is all in here."

"The elf leadership of the Ilgal elves," Gisela corrected. "There are plenty of other elf tribes across the continent. Surely there's communication between the Ilgal elves and those ones."

"You think that was an official messenger of the Imperator?" Haiden asked sarcastically.

Gisela sighed. He was right.

"The question is, in which direction was he leaving the forest? Not west, since the forest goes all the way to the ocean. Probably not east, as that would take him right to Terenford, and I doubt he was an official messenger to the capital of our fair human kingdom. South, do you think? North is mainly just wasteland, right?"

"I don't have an opinion, and I don't want one," said Gisela firmly. "We shouldn't get involved. We have nothing to gain, and everything to lose."

"What do we have to lose?" Haiden contradicted mulishly. "Our lives are miserable. I can't see what we're really risking."

"Miserable, are they?" Gisela narrowed her eyes, trying to cover the hurt caused by her brother's words. She knew the life she was giving him was far less than he should have, but she was doing her best. "You might feel like our lives aren't much to lose, but I disagree. I value mine, and have no intention of throwing it away."

"No one's talking about dying," Haiden said impatiently. "You always think everything is so much more dangerous than it is."

"Do I?" Gisela asked. "Then you always think you're much more invincible than you are."

Haiden tossed a twig at her petulantly, and she dropped the tone.

"Haiden, I'm not preaching caution for nothing. The danger is real. What about today? You ran off and dove straight into a random elf gate, without stopping to find out whether I wanted to take the risk."

"You didn't have to follow me," Haiden said quickly.

Gisela shook her head, her tone gentle but unyielding. "That wouldn't have been any better. You probably thought you'd come back for me, but it turns out the gate didn't take us back to that clearing, did it? If I *hadn't* followed, I would have been stuck alone in that clearing, far from home, with no way for the pebbles to guide me. And that was after you'd just assured me that I can rely on you and your magic because you'd never leave me to wander home alone. The truth is, you didn't even think about what would happen to me if you left me behind."

Haiden bit his lip, and for a long moment there was silence. "You're right," he said at last, only a hint of resentment in the admission. "I didn't even think about it. And I'm sorry."

Gisela let out a sigh. "I know. And I'm not angry. I just...want to keep our lives as simple as possible."

Haiden frowned, and she took his silence to mean that he wasn't convinced. But mercifully, he let the matter drop. "I saw you rubbing your chest earlier," he commented. "The pressure is getting worse, isn't it? And it's particularly bad in this area. I really felt it when we were running before."

Gisela nodded. "I know the rumors about Selvana back it up, but I'm still always surprised to remember that you feel it too. Since you're a singer and all, it seems like you should be immune."

Haiden looked troubled at her mention of the island kingdom to the southwest, which had been cut off from Providore for generations, and only recently made contact again. The reason it had been cut off in the first place was that the magic in its jungle had grown so wild, the ground had become lethal to humans.

"If we're to believe the gossip from the traveling merchants, even the Selvanan queen feels the pressure on the ground," he said. "Being a singer doesn't prevent her from being assaulted by the magic. It just means her body can channel it rather than being consumed by it."

"Just like your body," Gisela pointed out, relaxing slightly. When they'd heard the latest tales about Selvana, it had been a great relief to her to discover that no matter how wild the magic grew in Ilgal, it wouldn't kill Haiden outright.

"But not yours," Haiden said quietly. His eyes were heavy as they met hers. "If we're going the way of Selvana, the pressure is only going to get worse, Gisela. You can't stay here forever."

"Can't stay, can't leave…I'm singularly useless, aren't I?" Gisela said lightly.

"I didn't mean that," said Haiden, sounding upset.

"I know you didn't," Gisela assured him. She pushed herself to her feet, eager to change the direction of the conversation. There was nothing to be gained from discussing their most devastating restriction. "It's been long enough. Let's check the shadow."

Haiden followed her, watching as she assessed the shadow,

which had shifted a decent chunk since they'd planted the stick. Stooping, she placed a second small stone at the new tip of the shadow, and Haiden pulled the stick out, laying it so that it formed a straight line that ran across the two stones.

"So if that way is east," Gisela muttered, following with her eyes the direction indicated by the end of the stick closest to the new stone, "and that way is west…" Her eyes flicked back to the other end of the stick before she squinted at Haiden. "Which way are the stones again?"

He raised his arm, biting his lip in concentration as he sensed the location of the white pebbles from their childhood home that were now doused in his own magic. Both siblings turned their heads that way, making their silent calculations.

"The stones are several days south?" Gisela asked, aghast.

Haiden nodded. "South and a little bit east, I'd say."

"So home is further south again, which puts us days northwest of our usual area," Gisela said, her lips numb. "Haiden, we're in—"

"The very heart of Ilgal," Haiden finished for her. "No wonder it's so thick here, and the pressure of the magic is so strong."

Unease washed over Gisela, and she hastened to remove the stick and stones and toss them back among the trees. It would be as well not to leave signs of their presence.

"Come on," she said, moving back to the tree line and lifting the pole with the rabbits. "If we have that much ground to cover, we'd better get moving. Who knows how long it will take us to find a good place to camp?"

"Let me take that," said Haiden, his guilt from her earlier chastising showing in his tone as he took the pole and hoisted it over his shoulder. "At least we have dinner for tonight."

"True," said Gisela slowly. She was reluctant to risk the attention a fire could bring, but then again they would be too vulnerable without it. It all depended on what kind of shelter they found.

They'd barely started moving, however, when a steady thudding reached their ears.

She and Haiden exchanged a quick glance. "Is that... hooves?" he asked.

Gisela understood his bewilderment. It was rare to hear horses in the forest, except on the established roads. And they'd always taken care to avoid those. All of their various makeshift homes had been located far from any human settlement or thoroughfare.

"We don't know this part of the forest," she said. "It's possible that there's a road here somewhere."

Haiden glanced at the suffocating thickness of the foliage around them. "Not likely."

There could be no doubt it was hooves, however. Soon voices joined in, ones that were distinctly human. It had been a while since Gisela had spoken to any human other than her brother, and the sound made her breath catch in her throat from more than just fear.

"This is impossible, Otto. Why did we have to leave the blasted road?"

"Because, Monty," responded a second voice without heat, "the roads don't lead where I want to go."

Gisela and Haiden exchanged another glance, before diving sideways in opposite directions, Gisela into a thick patch of undergrowth, and Haiden behind a large tree.

Not large enough, however. Peering through the foliage, Gisela realized with horror that her brother had forgotten to account for the pole with the rabbits. He was concealed, but their catch dangled conspicuously in the air, inviting attention in a way that would be comical if the situation wasn't so dire.

She had no time to warn him, however. The next moment a

blade flashed through the air uncomfortably close to her hiding place, clearing the greenery to reveal a group of riders, a tall dark-haired man with pale skin and a pleasant expression at their center. An older man was the one hacking away at the foliage.

"Otto..." The bewildered voice issued from a second young man, this one with tawny hair. Gisela could only watch in horror as the dark-haired man followed the other's gaze to where Haiden's rabbits dangled improbably. "It looks like someone has helpfully caught our dinner for us."

There was a shout from the man clearing the greenery, and the next moment he was off his horse and diving forward.

Haiden, well-trained to be cautious of revealing his singing ability, didn't attempt to defend himself. Expression defiant, he was pulled from his hiding place.

Gisela didn't hesitate. She charged out of her patch of brush, hands curled into fists as she glared at the man who held Haiden in his grip.

"Let him go!"

# CHAPTER FIVE

# Gisela

Gisela's chest heaved with anger as she stared down the grizzled man. He seemed to be looking to the young, mounted man for guidance, so Gisela looked at him as well.

He was younger even than she'd first realized, and his expression was anything but threatening. His dark hair looked a little unkempt, and he bore all the signs of extensive travel through the forest. However, that did nothing to disguise the expensive nature of his clothes, or the quality of the horse he was riding.

"I beg your pardon," the young man said pleasantly. "Norris, let the boy go, of course. They were doing us no harm."

"Looked to me like they were setting some kind of trap," the older man grunted, but he released Haiden nevertheless. Evidently the young dark-haired man was in charge.

"I wasn't setting a trap," Haiden said indignantly. "If a pair of rabbits would be enough to lure you into a trap, you have no hope of surviving out here. It wouldn't provide so much as a snack for a group your size."

"Very true." The words came from the tawny-haired young

man mounted beside the one in charge, amusement dancing in his eyes.

Gisela studied both him and the dark-haired man for a moment, before letting her eyes travel back over the rest of the group. She'd been too distracted by Haiden's plight to take proper stock of the strangers, but she realized now that her brother was right. The group was a large one. Possibly the largest she'd ever seen outside of gatherings like festivals. Usually people moved through the forest in smaller parties, for greater ease of travel.

What she saw as she studied the group filled her with unease. The man who'd seized Haiden wore some kind of uniform, and she saw now that several others were in view who wore the same uniform. In addition to that, a middle-aged woman and a red-haired young woman were mounted on horses just behind the pair of young men. And it didn't appear to be the whole group, either. Men in uniform kept appearing through the trees behind the others. Who knew how many were being blocked from her sight by the foliage?

She could have kicked herself. She and Haiden had been unforgivably careless not to avoid such a large group. They should have identified the sounds of their approach much earlier than they had, and hidden themselves better.

"Who are you?" Haiden asked, bolder than Gisela. "And what are you doing out here?"

"Maybe we should ask you the same," said the grizzled man who'd seized Haiden.

"Peace, Norris, we're the strangers here," said the young man who radiated authority.

"Good point, Otto." The tawny-haired one bounced a little in his saddle. "Maybe they can help us find our way."

"We're not lost," growled the one called Norris.

"Well, we don't know where we are with any precision," the tawny-haired one said fairly.

"Monty is right," Otto said, his eyes both kind and curious as they passed between Gisela and Haiden. "We could benefit from directions."

"We can't help you," said Gisela quickly, reluctant to get more involved with the strangers than they already were. "We're not from these parts ourselves."

"Oh." The tawny-haired one—Monty—looked surprised. "Are *you* lost then?"

"Of course we're not," said Haiden indignantly. "We're just... a long way from our destination."

"That doesn't sound very convincing." The red-haired girl nudged her horse forward, wending her way around a tree trunk. "And why do I sense magic from the two of you? Do you have a talisman on you?"

The men in uniform immediately stiffened, the man called Norris shifting to stand in front of Otto's horse.

"If we do, what's it to you?" Gisela asked, her eyes narrowed. "We have nothing on us that wasn't acquired in full compliance with the Imperator's regulations."

It was true. The talisman she carried wasn't strong. If it had been, they would never have been able to afford it, with only rabbit pelts to trade. Its magic provided limited assistance in locating edible plants. They mostly had to rely on their father's training to find foliage which would sustain them, but the talisman should prevent them from eating anything fatally dangerous. She'd hoped to be able to purchase one that would help them find live game, but that had been far outside their means.

The one called Otto looked thoughtful at Gisela's answer, and Haiden hurried to fill the breach and back his sister up.

"That's right. If the rumors of the Imperator's ban on elves selling talismans to humans are true, they're recent. They definitely weren't in place when we bought ours."

"Ban?" Otto said, startled. "The Imperator has forbidden elves from selling talismans to humans? We've heard nothing of that."

"Only to humans within the forest, apparently." Haiden shrugged. "Or that's the rumor. It's been a while since we've been to an elven market." His eyes traveled to the young woman with the group, his expression brightening as a thought occurred to him. "Wait, if you can sense talismans, does that mean you're a singer?"

His eager expression caused alarm to spike inside Gisela. Surely he wasn't about to reveal his own abilities?

"You'd be wise not to bandy that information about so freely," she told the red-haired woman, her words hard. She didn't look at Haiden, but he would know the warning was for him. "Not everyone is as trustworthy as you folk no doubt are."

The flint in her voice wasn't missed by her audience. Monty gave a low whistle, his whispered aside to Otto clearly audible even from Gisela's distance.

"I don't think she likes us much, Otto."

"Hush, Monty." There was a definite note of reproof in Otto's words, and his tone was faintly apologetic as he addressed Gisela. "Thank you for the reminder to be cautious. You mentioned the Imperator before. Are we in the right area to reach the central elf settlement and find him?"

Gisela stared at him. "I don't know," she said. "I've never been there, and I have no desire to go."

"Is that where you're headed?" Haiden asked, again sounding eager. He glanced at his sister. "It's a good point, Gisela. We figured out that we must be close to the heart of Ilgal, and that's where the Imperator supposedly moved."

"Moved?" Otto asked quickly, while Gisela was internally wincing over Haiden's carelessness in revealing her name.

"That's right." The unexpected human company seemed to have gone to Haiden's head, because he was prattling as brightly as if he was still an innocent child. "The main elf settlement used to be further south. But some years back, they moved it. There was some tension with the human crown, I think, pestering them to do something about the thickening magic. Plus there were apparently giant wolves, that the elves claimed humans had created with magic." He shrugged. "I don't really know what's true and what's not, but those were the rumors."

Otto looked taken aback by this information, and he exchanged a glance with his companion before responding.

"How many years ago was this?"

Haiden looked to Gisela, uncertain.

She shrugged stiffly, uncomfortable with how much information they were sharing. "Not very long. Five, maybe."

"Well." Otto shook his head. "I didn't even know that, which demonstrates my point about how dangerously uninformed we are regarding the state of Ilgal, and the politics of the elves."

Gisela raised an eyebrow. Who were these strangers, and why would it be dangerous for them to be uninformed about Ilgal?

"You're not from the forest?" she asked cautiously.

Monty shook his head. "Heavens, no. We only left Terenford, what...less than three weeks ago?"

Gisela looked them over, taking in all the little signs of being out of their depth. That tallied.

"Well, the giant, magical wolves we knew about," the red-haired girl pointed out cheerfully.

"Yes." Otto sounded rueful. "In far too much detail. They're gone now, though, so the elves needn't be concerned about them."

"Really?" Gisela perked up, for the first time feeling like there might be some benefit to this chance meeting. "Are you absolutely certain?"

"Positive," said Otto.

"Well." Gisela let out a breath. "That's one less thing to worry about, then."

She exchanged a pleased look with Haiden. Maybe they would be able to expand the area of the forest they considered safe to roam. Since the stories of giant wolves near the capital started circulating, she'd made a point of staying well within the western half of the forest. The thought reminded her how far they were out of their familiar territory, and she hoisted her small pack up her back.

"Thank you for the information," she said politely.

No matter how suspicious these city-dwellers were, hacking their way through a part of the forest they had no business being in, politeness was a wiser policy than hostility. She bent her upper body in a half-bow, uttering the traditional parting of Ilgal.

"May the canopy shelter you and the trails remain straight under your feet on your journey." She turned to her brother. "Come on."

He deflated, clearly not as eager to leave the strangers as she was. But he didn't argue, tilting the pole with the rabbits back across his shoulder and picking his way toward her.

"Hold on." It was Otto who spoke, and to Gisela's surprise, he dismounted, handing his reins to his friend. With a couple of short strides, he reached them. "Where are you going? You said you're not from this area."

"That's right," said Gisela firmly. As it stood, they had no idea where she and her brother lived, and she intended to keep it that way. "Our destination is far, and we cannot afford to waste time."

"Of course not," muttered Haiden sarcastically. "We have such pressing schedules."

Gisela kicked him in the ankle, although she kept her eyes on the young man now standing right in front of her.

"Forgive me, I know I'm a stranger in these parts, and I don't mean to be impertinent, but...is it safe for the two of you to travel so far alone?"

"Not really, but that's never stopped us before," Haiden said cheerfully. "We're much less likely to fall afoul of a poisonous snake, tumble into a swamp, or get eaten by a galboar or a wolf than city-dwellers like you, at least."

"Galboar?" Monty, still on his horse, sounded distinctly uneasy. "What's that?"

"It's a species of boar native to Ilgal," Haiden explained helpfully. "They're vicious, especially in their mating season."

"Which is summer?" Monty asked hopefully.

Haiden guffawed, and Gisela couldn't help grinning in response to the look he threw her.

"Optimism might serve you well in the city, but it's a poor friend out here," she informed Monty. "Galboars usually mate in the late fall...sometimes into early winter."

"But that's now," said Monty in dismay. He glanced around him, as if expecting a boar to leap from the undergrowth. "I wonder if we've passed any without realizing it."

"Unlikely," said Gisela dispassionately. "They travel in large herds, so they're hard to miss. But the benefit of that is that they're not everywhere, like lone animals can be. Their herds usually have defined territories, so if you stay out of them, you'll be fine."

"Is this in a defined territory?" Monty asked.

She shrugged. "No idea. Like I said, we're not from this area."

"How did you end up here, then?" asked the red-haired girl.

Gisela cast a wry look at Haiden, who winced a little. "By an unfortunate accident. Now we really must be off."

"Maybe we can travel together," said Otto, before she'd taken so much as a step. "It would be safer than traveling alone, surely."

"Thank you, but we'll be fine," said Gisela.

"Gisela, we should at least think about it," Haiden said quickly. "Look how many of them there are. We'd be safe from just about any animal in a group this large."

"And an easy target for other humans," Gisela murmured, too low for the group to hear. "Haiden, they're total strangers. We can't trust their intentions." A glance up showed that Otto was watching her, and she wondered uneasily if she'd underestimated his hearing. Raising her voice, she added, "You're clearly going north. We're going south."

"We'll be going south again once we've discharged our errand," Otto offered. "We could see you safely back wherever you're going if you can afford the delay."

"We can't," Gisela said flatly.

"We can," Haiden contradicted. "Gisela, you're being ridiculous. What pressing engagements do we have? Besides, it might not be a delay at all. If we make it to the central elf settlement, it might be possible to use a gate to get home. Or at least part of the way there. That would be safer than trekking so far through unfamiliar territory."

"A gate?" Otto repeated, looking confused.

Haiden gave him a disbelieving look. "You really don't know anything about Ilgal, do you?"

The young man's expression was rueful. "Not as much as I thought, or so I'm learning daily."

"But why would you offer for us to accompany you?" Gisela demanded suspiciously. "You claim you're concerned about our safety, but how does it benefit you?"

"Isn't it obvious?" Otto asked with the hint of a laugh. "We need guides, and local advice. You may not be from this area, but you clearly know Ilgal." He gestured back at the group. "And we just as clearly don't. We didn't even know about the galboars. We've done well to make it this far, but we were following roads most of that time. We've only just left the road, and we're already floundering. Besides which, I have a feeling that travel is going to get more complicated as we near the central elf settlement."

Gisela eyed him thoughtfully. So he'd gleaned that about the elves, had he? He wasn't quite as clueless about Ilgal as he appeared.

"Gisela." The murmured plea came from Haiden this time. "Aren't you a *little* bit curious about the Imperator, and...all of the elves? Don't you want to find out more?"

Gisela bit her lip, not immune to the entreaty in his eyes. So that was why he was so quick to support the idea. It was no wonder. If the prophecy had been about her, she'd probably want to know more, too. But the idea of seeking out Asivah, or any of the royal elves, terrified her. Since that night, she'd done all she could to *avoid* Haiden coming to the notice of anyone important. Approaching the Imperator's own settlement was the opposite strategy.

"I don't know, Haiden..." she said reluctantly.

"We'll never get a better opportunity," he told her.

Still Gisela didn't reply, her mouth set in a line as Haiden watched her in hopeful silence. He must have seen that she wasn't convinced because all at once his demeanor changed. He turned away from her back to Otto, and smiled.

"My sister is uncertain, and that's understandable. But even if she prefers to keep traveling south, I'd be delighted to take you up on your offer."

"Haiden," said Gisela, exasperated.

He just shrugged at her. Clearly he didn't intend to follow her lead this time. In the past, she would have pulled rank, but she could see in his eyes that it wouldn't work now. He wasn't a child anymore, and if she wanted to protect him, she'd have to stick with him, even if it meant taking a path she didn't wish to choose.

"Fine," she said, not very graciously. "We'll go with you for now at least. I won't promise to see you all the way to the elf settlement."

"Excellent."

Otto seemed genuinely pleased, but Gisela didn't trust his reaction, not when she knew nothing of him. Was it possible he'd figured out that Haiden was a singer, and was eager to get the teenager—and his magic—in his power? She'd have to remind her brother not to let anyone know his secret.

Otto was looking around at the group with a critical eye. "They'll need horses. Perhaps they can ride double with someone? Which horses can best bear the extra weight?"

"Absolutely not," said Gisela, horrified at the idea of being perched up on one of the beasts alongside a stranger, totally in his or her control.

Otto glanced at her, hesitating. "Or perhaps two of our people can ride double, and you and your brother can share a horse."

"Of course," said Monty eagerly. "I can ride double with Valerie, and they can share my horse."

"Absolutely not." The red-haired girl—Valerie, apparently—used just the same words and just the same tone that Gisela had done.

"Is it hard?" Haiden asked, causing Otto to pause.

"Have either of you ridden before?"

The siblings shook their heads.

"Well, then," he looked apologetic, "I'm afraid you'll both

have to ride double with an experienced rider. It's not something you can just pick up all at once."

Haiden shrugged, apparently unconcerned by this turn of events. But Gisela was far from pleased. She wavered for a moment, wondering if she'd really made the right call to give in to her brother's tactics. But what right did she have to deny him answers to the questions that had defined his life, through no choice of his own?

"Haiden, can I speak to you alone for a moment?" she asked tightly.

Haiden looked mutinous, but Otto hastened to interject. "Of course you would want the chance to discuss your plans. Take as long as you need."

Gisela inclined her head to him then seized her brother's arm and tugged him through the trees.

"Haiden," she said, once confident they were out of earshot. "I don't like this."

"I can tell," he said, unimpressed. "But if you tell me I'm not allowed to—"

"I wasn't going to tell you that," Gisela interrupted.

He paused. "You weren't?"

"No, I wasn't." She sighed. "In spite of what you think, I am aware that you're not a child anymore, Haiden."

"Wow." Haiden's expression was somewhere between amusement and astonishment. "That's news to me."

Gisela ignored his cheeky comment. "But I'm still concerned that you don't fully grasp the danger you're putting yourself in."

"I know they're strangers," said Haiden seriously. "And I'll be on my guard."

"It's not just that they're strangers," Gisela told him. "They're suspicious. That head one, Otto, is clearly someone important, and we have no idea of his errand here in Ilgal. We might be getting mixed up in something we don't want to be involved in.

Besides which, there's a singer with them. What if she can figure out what you are? And all of this is without even touching on the dangers of approaching the Imperator's settlement."

"Yes, about the singer," Haiden said eagerly, apparently uninterested in the rest of Gisela's warnings. "She doesn't seem to be oppressed or exploited, does she? Maybe it's not so risky to let my skills be known. These people seem to treat singers well."

"Haiden!" Gisela gripped his shoulder, alarmed. "You've just acknowledged yourself that they're total strangers. We know nothing of their intentions, or the dynamics of their group. How do you know she's not being exploited? Or that she isn't betraying her own kind for gold?"

"*Her own kind*?" Haiden rolled his eyes at her dramatic language. "I'm not a different species, Gisela."

"Yes, you are," she said heartlessly. "The irritating and impossible species of teenagers."

Haiden shoved her with his shoulder. "Last I checked, you were still eighteen. As in, a teenager."

"I'm an adult," she said loftily. "It's different."

"Sisters are a more impossible species than teenagers," Haiden declared. "If you're done lecturing me, can we go now? I'm excited to ride a horse for the first time, even if you aren't."

"Not until I know you understand what's at stake," said Gisela stubbornly. "I want you to promise me that you won't tell any of them what you are. Or about the elf princess's prophecy," she added quickly.

"That part I'm not likely to tell anyone." Haiden's voice was dry. "Do you really think you have to warn me not to tell other humans that a royal elf foretold that I'd bring down our kingdom? If they're from the capital, they're probably blindly loyal to the king, and would immediately throw me in a dungeon at best."

Gisela squeezed his shoulder, torn between sorrow at the

heaviness of his voice and relief that he wasn't as careless of the dangers as he'd made it seem.

"No one is throwing you in a dungeon while I'm still breathing," she told him firmly. "But I agree we'd be wise to be careful what we say. Does that mean I have your promise?"

Haiden nodded, still looking disheartened.

"You won't tell them you're a singer, either?" Gisela pressed.

"Yes, all right." Haiden didn't sound too pleased about it, but Gisela didn't push the point. More words from her wouldn't help anything.

The two of them wended their way back through the trees, moving around in an arc and coming at the group from a different side. They emerged next to Monty, the tawny-haired young man whose horse was still alongside Otto's. He jumped when Gisela cleared her throat, his eyes flying to her in alarm.

"I didn't see you there," he said. "You move so silently."

"Well, we did grow up in the forest," said Haiden, with a hint of scorn that sounded much more like youthful pride than he would have intended. "Learning to walk through it is more or less the first skill we master."

"So what did you decide?" Otto asked cheerfully, casting an eye over the two of them. "Will you join us?"

Gisela nodded tersely, and the young man smiled in what appeared to be genuine pleasure.

"Excellent."

"Hold on." The older man, Norris, moved forward. "I have a few questions I'd like answered first."

Gisela tensed up, but Haiden didn't seem troubled. "All right."

"Is it just the two of you?"

"Every day, and it gets very dull, to be frank." Haiden's voice was much too cheerful, and Gisela wanted to roll her eyes. He was childishly elated at having won his point regarding joining the group.

"Thank you for that, Haiden," Gisela said.

"You're brother and sister?" Norris pressed.

Monty laughed. "Do you need to ask, Norris? It's fairly obvious."

"Appearances can be deceiving," the grizzled man said shrewdly.

Gisela's respect for him grew. Besides, he had a point. She took more after their mother in looks, while Haiden's features were more like their father's, down to the darker shade of his skin.

"We are brother and sister," she acknowledged. "And it's just the two of us. We're not part of any group. I swear it." She didn't like making themselves vulnerable by revealing the information, but she recognized that if their new companions suspected them of being scouts for a larger party, they would be much more suspicious of the pair. And that wouldn't make them safer, since the truth was they *were* alone and would be completely in the larger group's power.

"And what's your purpose here?" Norris persisted.

"Here as in the forest?" Haiden asked in an affronted tone, raising one dark eyebrow. "We live here."

"You said you're not from this area," Norris said, narrowing his eyes at the teenager.

"We're not." Gisela jumped in, the instinct to deflect negative attention from Haiden so deeply ingrained she wasn't even aware of its prompting. They'd decided to throw their lot in with this group, and she had to acknowledge that their new companions therefore had some right to know such basic details about them. "Our purpose was simply to hunt for food, until a misadventure took us far off our intended path."

"And brought you across our path, so perhaps it wasn't such

a misfortunate after all," Otto said pleasantly. His voice was mild, but Norris desisted at once, and Gisela recognized in the young man the voice of authority. Otto turned to Haiden. "Haiden, isn't it? Monty has offered for you to ride with him, if you're willing."

Haiden eyed the tawny-haired one, not looking eager about the idea, and Monty grinned.

"Don't worry. I'm useless at traversing the forest, but I'm actually a very good rider. We'll manage just fine."

Gisela saw Haiden soften at the other man's lighthearted acknowledgment of his own ineptitude.

"And...Gisela, right?" Otto smiled when Gisela confirmed it. "Would you be willing to ride with me?" He must have seen the way she looked around the rest of the group, and his smile took on an apologetic edge. "I'm afraid the guards need to be unencumbered to respond to any crisis that might arise, and Monty and my horses are the best trained and most likely to submit without complaint to a second rider."

"It's true," said the young woman who'd identified herself as a singer. "I wish I could offer to take you, but my mare is very particular."

"What a well-suited pair you make," Monty said to Valerie, in a pleasant tone that didn't fool Gisela for a moment.

"Only a man aware of his own insufficiency would think it a fault in a woman to be particular," said Valerie, the sweetness in her voice as artificial as Monty's tone had been.

"I didn't say it was a fault," said Monty with feigned astonishment. "Quite the reverse."

"Enough, Valerie, Lord Montague." The older woman spoke up for the first time since the group had appeared, sounding long-suffering. "Our new members will think you have no more control than children."

Gisela and Haiden exchanged startled glances at this reference to a title. The tawny-haired young joker was a lord of some kind? He wasn't anything like Gisela would expect a lord to be. And what was someone titled doing out in the middle of Ilgal, anyway?

She was so distracted by the revelation—and in all honesty, intimidated by Monty's rank, that she went along unresisting as a guard helped her mount Otto's horse. Before she knew it, she was settled in front of the near-stranger, her bow attached to the saddle out of her reach, and Otto's arms reaching around her to hold the reins. Haiden, on the other hand, was perched behind Monty, holding on around the other man's waist with wide eyes and a distinct lack of dignity. Gisela understood his feelings. The horse's backs seemed much higher from on top of them than they had from the ground. At a word from Norris, the group started to move forward.

"Bullion is strong." Otto took one hand from the reins to give the horse's shoulder a fond slap. "But it's still a lot to ask him to carry us both. Normally I wouldn't attempt it unless the situation was dire, but I figure it will probably be all right at the snail's pace we'll have to travel through these trees."

"Yes," said Gisela, struggling to marshal her thoughts. She didn't really know what he was talking about when it came to horses, but forest travel she understood. "It will be slow going for such a large, mounted group. I imagine there will be times we'll have to walk."

"Probably," Otto agreed, his arms warm and far too close where they rested against Gisela's. "I'll defer to your knowledge on that matter."

Gisela cleared her throat, wishing her head could be cleared as easily. "To tell the truth, I won't be able to advise you much. Mounted travelers usually keep to the road, and we usually avoid them."

She caught the sharp glance Haiden threw at her, and

wanted to bite her own tongue. What was she doing? She'd lectured Haiden about it, but she was the one letting slip unnecessary information. She sent her brother an apologetic grimace, hoping Otto wouldn't pick up on her words.

She had no such luck.

"Why do you avoid the roads?" he asked curiously, ducking along with Gisela as they traveled under a low-hanging branch.

"Too much traffic," she said curtly. "On foot, it's faster to travel through the trees."

The words were unconvincing, their obvious flaws painfully clear in Gisela's ears. Otto was polite enough not to challenge her claim. Contrarily, Gisela found herself resenting his friendly politeness a little. Gruff, threatening strangers she knew how to respond to. Kind ones with open smiles and deferential manners were more alarming. It made the young man seem trustworthy, which was the most dangerous pitfall of all.

Of course, the sudden physical proximity wasn't helping her to sort out her reactions to the stranger. He couldn't be much older than her, and she was honest enough to acknowledge that he had an attractive frame and pleasant features. His arms were strong around her, the muscles taut but by no means beefy. Everything about him declared a life of privilege, but he didn't give an impression of indolence at all, challenging her perceptions regarding the wealthy.

Because wealthy he undoubtedly was. Gisela found herself studying the velvet sleeve of his blue tunic, marveling at the quality of the fabric. She'd even noticed gold embroidery on the chest of the garment, although she couldn't see it now, and she wasn't about to twist around to look. In fact, it was taking quite a bit of concentration to stay upright enough not to lean back against his chest. Gisela was alarmed by how appealing the prospect was. It made no sense, because her logic told her to be wary of this man—of everyone in the group. And being physically in his power to this extent should be terrifying. But she didn't feel afraid. There was simply nothing threatening about this Otto.

And if her instincts were telling her to trust a complete stranger, she clearly couldn't trust her instincts.

It was no doubt the proximity to an attractive young man that was muddling her thoughts, and the realization was humiliating. She and Haiden had been so isolated for so many years, it was no wonder she was easily rattled. She didn't think she'd ever been this close to a man, with the exception of her father. And even that had been a long time ago. She hadn't even seen him for five years, and she had most certainly changed in that time. For a moment she was lost in memories of time with him, the way he'd put his arms around her when teaching her to shoot a bow and arrow, or guided her hands as they fished in forest streams.

Those were happy memories, of times when she'd felt safe and at peace. When she'd known that someone wiser and stronger was in control of her world, and would take care of everything.

It was a distant time, and Gisela pushed it from her mind. It would do her no good to dwell on the past. She would do better to keep her wits about her in the present. Coming back to reality, she took stock once again of her position.

Being this close to Otto felt nothing like those childhood memories of her father.

Nevertheless, much as she hated to admit it, there was something comforting and secure about sitting in front of Otto while he guided the horse, and his arms kept her in place. A glance at Haiden showed that he wasn't faring as well, his face screwed in concentration as he bumped up and down with the horse's motion.

Catching his eye, Gisela permitted herself a smirk. Haiden

rolled his eyes back at her, his attention quickly reclaimed as he had to duck to avoid a branch. This was surely not much faster than walking, and much less practical. The thought had just occurred to her when Norris called a halt from the front.

"I'm not sure it's going to be practical to travel for days longer like this. It's looking much denser ahead, Your Highness."

"Your Highness?" The words slipped out before Gisela could check them, her whole frame stiffening in horror. Her gaze slid once again to Haiden, seeing the same shock reflected in his eyes.

"Oh. Yes." Otto didn't seem to share her discomfort. "I suppose I never introduced myself properly, did I? I'm Crown Prince Otto, and I'm in Ilgal on behalf of my father, King Ryker."

# CHAPTER SIX

# Gisela

**W**ave after wave of blank horror washed over Gisela. She supposed some response was required, but she couldn't think of one. Her only thought was to prevent the prince learning anything of Haiden's situation, and a defensive instinct told her the safest way to avoid giving information was to remain silent.

"What do you suggest, Norris?" The prince must have sensed her tension, but he didn't comment on it, speaking to the guard as if nothing had occurred.

The guard. Of course he had guards. He was the crown prince. The future king. Of the kingdom Haiden was prophesied to bring down.

And they were now in his power.

It was all a nightmare, one too horrible to imagine.

But she and Haiden knew the forest like these city-dwellers never could, Gisela reminded herself. They would have no difficulty slipping away and would leave no trace of their passage, or at least none that could be found by this group.

"I think we might do better on foot," said Norris thoughtfully. "Perhaps we should send a few scouts ahead to better survey what's coming. It must be close on time to stop for the midday meal anyway."

"Yes, that sounds like a good plan," said Otto approvingly. "But we should ask our new forest experts. What do you think, Gisela?"

"Yes," she said mechanically, trying to keep her panic at bay. "Good plan."

Before she realized what was happening, Otto was sliding from the horse. He landed neatly on the forest floor, holding up his arms in an offer of assistance.

Instead of taking it, Gisela glanced quickly at her brother, her mind slowly churning into motion.

"Haiden and I can scout ahead, can't we, Haiden?" She sent him a meaningful look which he met with a blank stare. Clearly he was also having difficulty processing the revelation.

"No, you don't need to do that," said Otto, his arms still extended. "Norris will send some of his guards, won't you, Norris?"

"Of course, Your Highness," said the older man. With a gesture, he summoned three of his men.

"No, really, we'd be happy to do it," Gisela tried desperately.

"I would be more comfortable sending my own people," said Norris, no compromise in his voice.

"He means no offense," Otto said, smiling in a friendly way. He'd dropped his arms enough to rest his hands on the horse's flank. "But his men will better know what he's looking for, and how to report back to him, you know."

Gisela frowned, all her suspicions returning. Could he tell that she'd found a perfect opportunity for escape? Was he trying to thwart it without letting on that he knew her plans?

Or had her years on the run simply made her distrustful? The prince had once again extended his arms, and Gisela allowed herself to slide warily into them, letting Otto lift her down from the horse. He was surprisingly strong given his lean frame. When her feet were solidly on the ground again, she hurried to Haiden, who'd clambered awkwardly down from his own steed, barely avoiding landing in a heap on the forest floor.

"A word?" Gisela muttered.

With a nod, Haiden moved slightly away from the rest of the group. The head guard had already sent his men scouting, and others were industriously pulling out supplies, apparently ready to start preparing a meal.

"He's the prince!" Gisela hissed, after checking no one was immediately beside them.

"Yes, I heard that," said Haiden shortly. "Bit of a shock, wasn't it?"

"I knew this was a bad idea," said Gisela. "Should we slip away now, or wait for darkness?"

"Slip away?" Haiden demanded. "Gisela, I'm still going through with this. Nothing's changed."

"Nothing's changed?" she repeated in disbelief. "How can you say that after what we just learned? Have you forgotten your own words just before, about dungeons and all that?"

"What I mean is, nothing's changed from their perspective," Haiden said fairly. "We already weren't planning to tell them any of that. As far as *they're* concerned, their identity shouldn't make a difference."

"But it makes every difference to us," Gisela all but moaned. Of course her brother was going to be difficult about this.

"Think about it, Gisela," Haiden said seriously. "They don't appear to be suspicious of us at all right now. If we sneak off and disappear, on the other hand, they'll become very suspicious. And they know our real names, as well as the general direction we were heading. It wouldn't be a smart move."

Gisela bit her lip, unable to deny the sense in his words.

Why had they let themselves get into this situation in the first place? They were usually so good at avoiding notice.

"Come on," Haiden said, walking back toward the rest of the group. "We should help prepare our rabbits, at least."

As it happened, however, the guards in charge of the food waved them both away, insisting they didn't need assistance. Gisela hovered, uncertain, until Otto—Prince Otto —approached.

"Water, Gisela?" he asked pleasantly.

"I have my own water skin, thank you, Your Highness," Gisela said awkwardly.

He sighed, lowering the offered water and studying her. "I could tell you were uncomfortable when I introduced myself properly. There's no reason my title needs to make any difference, you know. I'd be happier if no one in the group even used it, honestly."

Gisela couldn't think of a reply to this, but at that moment Monty joined them, backing the prince up.

"He really means it," he informed Gisela. "We just call him Otto."

"Not all of us." The dry voice belonged to the middle-aged woman who seemed out of place among the rest of the group. She appeared alongside Monty, studying Gisela with shrewd eyes. "I prefer to call everyone by their accurate names." She pointed what appeared to be a closed wooden slat fan at Gisela in a purposeful way. "Is Gisela your true name?"

Swallowing nervously, Gisela nodded.

"You may call me Lady Louisa," the older woman said graciously. "I have accompanied the prince as a representative of King Ryker's Council of Nobles."

On the words, the older woman snapped the fan open, to reveal that only the two outer slats were made of wood, the rest of the fan consisting of white feathers. It was possibly the most out-of-place item Gisela had ever seen in the forest, and it took her a moment to realize that in staring at it, she'd failed to respond politely to the lady's introduction. Feeling something was required of her, Gisela dipped her head in what she hoped was a respectful gesture.

"Come on, Lady Louisa, don't make her think she has to be all stiff and proper," said Monty in a wheedling tone. "It'll just make the trip dull."

"I don't have the smallest interest in influencing her as to what to call Prince Otto," the older woman said, her voice calm. "But I've lived a few more years than the rest of you, Lord Montague, and believe me when I say time will teach you caution." Her eyes bored into Gisela's. "It will also teach you how to tell when someone is hiding something."

Gisela forced herself to meet the other woman's eye without fidgeting, but she didn't feign bewilderment. Superfluous finery notwithstanding, something told her Lady Louisa wasn't one to be easily deceived. After a moment of silent consideration, the older woman's face relaxed slightly.

"Not that I blame you, of course, child. You're no doubt hiding many things, as well you would, given we're strangers to you. But know that if those things include any nefarious intentions, you won't get far with them, not in this group. We may seem novices to you, given your mastery of the forest. But we're more capable than you realize."

"I mean no one any harm," said Gisela cautiously. "And it certainly wasn't by design that I encountered your group. I'll be frank, and tell you that my preference would be to part ways as continued strangers." She glanced over to where Haiden was in cheerful conversation with Valerie, the singer from the city. "But my brother wishes to see the elf settlement, which makes this a rare opportunity."

"Very commendable of you to take his preferences into

consideration," said Monty cheerfully. "I'm sure I'd never do half as much for my little brother."

"That I believe," said Lady Louisa wryly, causing Monty to flash her a charming grin. Gisela ignored them, turning to the prince instead.

"We gave our catch to your guards, Your Highness, but they won't allow me to assist in its preparation."

"They don't need assistance," Otto assured her. "It was generous of you to share your catch. That's more than enough."

"But you can't just feed us for the whole duration of our journey," Gisela protested.

"I don't see why not," said Otto lightly. "In a group our size, the addition of two people won't make any substantial difference."

Gisela shifted her feet on the forest floor, finding it hard to meet his eyes. "I don't like to be indebted to you," she admitted. "To anyone."

There was a moment of silence, stretching long enough that Gisela snuck a look up at the prince's face. He didn't look offended, as she'd thought he might. He was watching her seriously, with... not sympathy, precisely, but understanding. She realized suddenly that they were alone, Monty and Lady Louisa having moved back toward the cleared ground where Valerie and Haiden were sitting.

"I don't consider you indebted," Otto told Gisela. "I'm expecting that you and your brother will provide valuable insight for us, since you know Ilgal as none of us do." He must have seen that Gisela looked unconvinced, as he added, "If you really wish it, I could speak to Norris about you and your brother joining the hunt and foraging rotations. I'm sure they would appreciate the experienced assistance."

She nodded. "That we could certainly do. We've been living off the forest all our lives."

"Excellent," said Otto brightly. "It's settled. So you see, the agreement we've reached is perfectly fair, no indebtedness on your side." He grinned. "To tell the truth, I'm well pleased to have the opportunity to make an agreement with a human guide. We were starting to worry we'd need to try to retain an elven one, and attempting to make a bargain with them would probably have cost me my firstborn child or something."

Gisela laughed weakly. "I see it's not only forest folk who are aware of the pitfalls of dealing with elves."

"Far from it," Otto assured her. "My father treats with them regularly, and I've often been called upon to be part of those discussions." His smile faded as he glanced northward. "Although in recent years we've had very little interaction with the Imperator, or any other elves from Ilgal. The longer I'm in the forest, the more I realize I'm out of touch with the politics of the region. That's a large part of why I wish to meet with the Imperator in person."

"What's the other part?" Gisela asked, following as he started to walk back toward the central area where the others were waiting for food.

"I hope he can help me with my original purpose in coming to Ilgal," Otto explained. He tapped one gloved hand over his chest. "Do you feel the pressure of the magic growing wild, or are you acclimatized, given that you live in the forest?"

"No, I feel it," sighed Gisela. "It wasn't an issue when I was a child. It's been slowly growing for years, but recently it's become acute. It must be very strong for you, since you come from outside."

Otto nodded, and Monty chimed in from nearby. "It's blasted uncomfortable," he informed her cheerfully. "It's getting worse the deeper we go. It's almost tipped over from discomfort to pain, honestly."

"I didn't think outsiders would be willing to put up with it for any length of time, to be honest," said Haiden.

"Most aren't," Valerie informed him. "There's a reason we're a small group, except for the guards. And they have to do as they're told and don't really get a say, poor things."

"My men are just fine, Miss Valerie," Norris said gruffly, happening to pass by at that moment.

"Ah, Norris." Otto flagged him down. "Would Gisela and Haiden be of use to you in the hunt and forage rotations?"

"Perhaps, Your Highness," Norris said guardedly, glancing at the two newcomers. Likely he wanted to watch them for a while before deciding whether to trust them with any role. Gisela didn't blame him for this sign of excellent good sense.

"You're putting our guests to work, Otto?" Monty demanded, once Norris had walked on.

"Gisela requested it," Otto informed him. "She was concerned about our deal being unequal. And although I don't agree, I can sympathize with her position."

"It's far from unequal," said Monty, flashing Gisela an especially charming smile. "Speaking for myself, I couldn't be more delighted to expand the number of beautiful young women in our party."

Gisela just blinked at this unexpected gallantry, but Valerie let out an unladylike snort, and Lady Louisa a long-suffering mutter of "spare us."

"What?" Haiden spluttered around the water he'd been drinking, staring at Monty in bewilderment. "Did you really just say that to my sister?"

"Why should you be surprised?" Monty asked staunchly. "If you try to tell me that a woman as beautiful and intelligent as your sister has never attracted admiration from men, I won't believe you."

"Oh, no, she has, all the time," Haiden said. "It's been near unmanageable for the last couple of years. It's one of the reasons we rarely venture into human villages. But usually it's forest men who say that, often ones who've seen too many summers, more likely than not missing a few teeth. I thought they acted that way because they couldn't do better. I never imagined an educated, titled, *young* man would need to resort to those tactics."

For a moment, Monty looked affronted, but any response he might have given was drowned out by a gleeful guffaw from Valerie. Even Gisela, who'd told herself to make a point of not offending these wealthy, powerful people, couldn't hold back a giggle. It was irresistibly entertaining to see her fifteen-year-old brother put the over-confident young lord in his place. After a charged moment, Monty's face relaxed, and he joined the general laugh at his expense.

"You impudent little pup," he said lightly, ripping an acorn from the branch above him and chucking it at Haiden. "I see I'll have to watch my behavior now I'm under such wise scrutiny."

Gisela exchanged a laughing glance with Haiden, her opinion of Monty increasing considerably at this evidence that he could laugh at himself.

"He's really not as bad as he seems," Otto murmured from beside her, as Valerie continued to tease Monty for his humiliation. "He's been playing it up ridiculously on this trip in a misguided attempt to get Valerie's attention. He's a bit of a charming dog, but not usually outrageous or anything. He was one of the only ones able to help himself from fawning over my stepsister for her title, for example. She's very fond of him for it."

Gisela looked at the prince in surprise, wondering why he was confiding any of this in her. To her consternation, he looked right back, his eyes searching as they studied her face.

"Do the men around here really all hassle you?"

"Hassle is a bit strong," said Gisela quickly. "We prefer to keep to ourselves anyway. We do just fine."

"But you won't forever," Otto pointed out. "It doesn't sound like a sustainable life even without the magic growing wild, but when you add that...no one will be able to stay in Ilgal forever unless we do something about it."

"Do you really have a plan to help with that?" Gisela asked, barely noticing the way she'd turned toward him in her eagerness. It was amazing how easy it was to forget he was a prince, and just speak to him like a normal person.

"We have the possibility of a plan," said Otto. "But to be honest, it's not going well at all. I'm hoping the Imperator will be able to help me with it."

"Hm." Gisela pursed her lips. "The question of whether he's able to will be secondary to whether he's willing to. He's an elf, after all."

Otto sighed. "Yes. I'm aware."

Guards approached with their food at that moment, and the group settled themselves on handy rocks and branches. Gisela noted with approval that with the exception of those standing watch, and the three scouting ahead, the guards also ate with them. Since the men seemed to be serving the roles of both guards and servants, it spoke well of the prince that he didn't hesitate to share a meal with them.

He certainly wasn't how she'd pictured royalty. As she ate the first meal she hadn't personally prepared in years, she found herself reflecting that it would be a shame if Haiden brought down this prince's kingdom.

She was only too happy to shake the thought from her mind when it was time to get back on the move. If she wasn't careful, she'd become like her mother.

To Gisela's relief, she wasn't asked to remount Otto's horse.

The scouts returned as they finished eating, reporting that there was no lightening of the dense foliage ahead. They would have to proceed on foot, leading their mounts.

That suited Gisela excellently, and when the group began moving again, she found herself shifting naturally to the edge of the clump. She didn't even realize she was doing it until a guard directed her back inside the protective ring he and his fellows had formed. Apparently Gisela's instincts still hadn't fully accepted her decision not to slip away altogether.

By the time darkness approached, however, Gisela had to admit that there were advantages to traveling in a group. And it wasn't just the fact that scouts had gone ahead and found a good place to camp, or the hot food cooked without her involvement. It was the company. The others were friendly and pleasant, and conversation flowed readily between the group members. No one even complained in spite of the difficult terrain and slow going, with the exception of Monty's expressions of dismay, which Gisela quickly learned to recognize as good-natured attempts to lighten the mood rather than grabs for sympathy.

She also couldn't help feeling satisfied at the look of contentment on Haiden's face as he watched Valerie light a fire with her songcraft. It must be nice for him to have another singer to bear the burden of the tasks that usually fell to him. Although she could practically see him itching to ask Valerie all the questions crammed in his head. There was so much about songcraft they didn't know, and it was rare to have the opportunity to learn about it. Hopefully Haiden would be smart enough to ask questions without making his vested interest obvious.

In spite of her pleasant reflections, Gisela slept uneasily. It was too much to expect of herself to fully relax around strangers after so many years avoiding everyone but her brother. Her thoughts flew to their current home, a simple hut they'd constructed themselves, not too far from the western edge of the forest and the seaside cliffs beyond. Had it been discovered in their absence? They didn't have much of value, but it would still be a setback to lose their additional clothes and other supplies. And they would be unlikely to make it back for a long time, given they were currently traveling in the wrong direction.

In spite of these disheartening thoughts, she saw nothing to concern her during the night hours. The guards were organized and diligent, swapping shifts regularly, and keeping a close eye on their surroundings. And as strange as it was to be without her usual privacy, there was something comforting about sleeping in a circle around the large fire, so many others in her line of sight. They had to sleep that way—the nights were too cold now to allow anyone to sleep further out from the fire. More than once she saw the eyes of some creature watching them from outside the circle of light, but none were daring enough to approach a group of their size.

Yes, there was a great deal to be said for company.

The group got going early the next morning, everyone optimistic after the night's rest. By the afternoon, however, the good mood had definitely dipped. It had started to mist early in the day, and the rain settled into a steady drizzle by lunch time. Gisela and Haiden were used to it, and were thankfully dressed for an Ilgal winter. But the city-dwellers were noticeably dampened by the constancy of the rain.

Worst of all, they were barely making progress. The foliage was so thick they had to hack their way through constantly, and Gisela couldn't even tell if they were still going northward. Every now and then they would stop for Valerie to conduct a direction-finding song—a process both Gisela and Haiden watched with avid interest—but their sense of direction would desert them soon after. By mid-afternoon, they'd hardly covered any ground.

"Gisela." Haiden's murmur drew her attention. The group had stopped to shelter miserably under the insufficient cover of the canopy while scouts tried to figure out the best way forward. "Maybe I could help us find our way. If I...you know."

"Haiden, no." Gisela's voice was firm. "You agreed not to reveal your singing."

"They seem trustworthy to me," Haiden argued.

Gisela made a noise of protest. "As if you could be sure so soon!"

"But we'll never get to the elves' settlement at this rate," Haiden coaxed. "We need to use path-finding magic."

"You can't do path-finding magic," said Gisela brutally. "Not reliably, anyway."

Haiden gave her an aggrieved look, but she didn't back down.

"You made it work one time. Every other time, it's fizzled out or led us into a dead end. It's not your fault," she added quickly. "I'm sure it's not an indication of your strength or capacity. You just haven't had the chance for the training it requires."

"But Valerie has," Haiden argued. "And she's strong, I can tell. I really think that if we combined our singing, we could harness the paths."

"If she's so strong, she should be able to do it by herself," said Gisela flatly.

"But she doesn't know how," Haiden said. "She probably doesn't even know it's possible."

"And I don't see any reason you can't tell her about it without revealing that you're a singer," Gisela told him. "I know you know how to be careful with your speech."

"I know how to be careful with everything," grumbled Haiden. "That's *all* I know, thanks to you."

Gisela tried not to let the reproach sting, especially as Haiden didn't fight further. He looked disappointed, but he made his way over to Valerie compliantly. Gisela followed at a distance, curious to see if the singer from Terenford could really harness the paths of Ilgal.

"Valerie." Haiden's nonchalance didn't sit naturally on a fifteen-year-old. "You're a singer, right?"

Gisela wanted to roll her eyes.

"I am," said Valerie, sounding amused at the teenager's attempt at casual conversation. It was very well established by this time that Valerie was the group's singer.

But she was too kind to openly laugh, for which Gisela was grateful. Like everyone else, Valerie must have noticed Haiden's fascination with her. Not knowing he was a singer, they probably thought him infatuated with the pretty older girl. It was safer to let them believe that.

"You trained at the Academy of Song?" Haiden pressed.

Valerie nodded.

"Did they ever talk about trail-finding?" Valerie looked confused, and he hurried on. "I've seen you find north with your songcraft, that's why I ask. I wouldn't have guessed that the academy covered that kind of topic. I assumed the studies there were more academic than practical."

Valerie frowned. "The academy covers both academic and practical training, but I admit, I didn't learn the direction-finding song at the academy. I did some research of my own when I was invited to join this trip, and concluded it might be useful."

"It clearly has been," Haiden commented. Gisela could see her brother itching to ask Valerie to teach him, but he mastered himself. "Did your research mention path-finding?"

Valerie shook her head. "Not that I can remember."

"It's probably not in any books in the city," Gisela commented. "I think it's specific to Ilgal."

"But what is it?" Valerie asked, as Haiden nodded slowly.

"Well, we don't know all the details," Gisela hedged. "But we've heard people talk about it. It's supposed to be one of the first songs learned by singers of Ilgal." She couldn't quite help a glance at Haiden, whose face looked glum. There was so much he'd been unfairly denied. "Anyway," Gisela went on quickly, "it's a way for singers to harness the paths of the forest."

"Harness the paths?" Valerie repeated the words slowly, starting to look excited. "So the paths themselves are magical? I suspected as much when the path changed on us, back before we ran into you. A new path appeared, and the old one disappeared completely."

Haiden nodded. "That means it was a forest path, rather than one built by humans. It happens more and more the deeper into the forest you get."

"They say that even human-built paths are prone to shift in the heart of the forest," Gisela said. "Nothing is immune to the magic if you go deep enough in."

"And singers can create these paths?" Valerie pressed.

"No." Gisela shook her head. "They're forest paths. Ilgal creates them, or the magic of Ilgal does. But singers can supposedly harness them, and get them to temporarily bend to the direction the singers want. They can find safe passage through the forest. In theory."

"That would be amazing," said Valerie, her eyes alight with the same enthusiasm Haiden always showed at the prospect of learning a new skill. "I wonder if I could do it."

"It would probably be harder for someone from outside of the forest," said Gisela cautiously.

"But not impossible," Haiden encouraged. "Why don't you try? I heard the words of the song once. Apparently it takes a lot of power, but you seem strong. The singer who was talking about it also referred to it as a sort of heart magic...whatever that meant."

Gisela could only hope his bafflement wasn't as obviously fake to Valerie as it was to her. The other woman didn't comment if so, just frowning thoughtfully.

"Heart magic? That will probably be very difficult for me to achieve, since I'm a stranger to Ilgal. But tell me the words anyway. There's no harm in trying."

Haiden readily did so, Valerie listening closely. With a nod, the singer from Terenford cleared her throat and began to let out a low, simple melody. At first she sang without words, getting her bearings, magically speaking. Gisela had heard Haiden do it many times.

Speaking of Haiden...

Glancing around, Gisela realized that instead of supervising closely as she'd expected, he'd stepped back, melting into the tree line. And he was avoiding her eye. Suspicious, Gisela took a few steps toward him, alarmed to hear his familiar low voice join Valerie's just as she started on the words of the song. She should have known he wouldn't be able to resist joining in. A quick glance around showed that no one else was paying them any attention, but it didn't make Gisela feel better about the risk her brother was taking. Haiden's voice mingled softly with Valerie's, and although Gisela couldn't feel it herself, she'd heard Haiden dissect his craft with her enough times to imagine how he was combining his magic with Valerie's, using his innate knowledge of Ilgal to steer the volume of power he couldn't have achieved on his own. Gisela understood his plan. Valerie would provide the extra power needed; Haiden, born of the forest, with Ilgal in his blood and heart, would provide the heart magic that the forest would respond to.

Valerie's song faltered, then picked up speed, accompanied by an excited gesture. Stepping forward, Gisela saw that a shimmering path had appeared at the singer's feet, wending northward through the trees. A moment before, the forest ahead of them had been relentlessly thick, but now she was looking at a thin cleared ribbon, one that would be easy for their horses to traverse.

"Look!" It was Monty who first noticed the phenomenon, and he was at Valerie's side in a moment. "Valerie, did you do this? It's incredible!"

Valerie broke off, and Gisela heard Haiden's song quickly die down now that its cover was gone. If Valerie heard anything, she gave no sign. She turned to Monty, her excitement at the achievement for once eclipsing her usual irritation with the young lord.

"It's a forest path. Apparently singers can harness them with something called path-finding magic. Haiden and Gisela told me about it." She beamed at Gisela. "And it's still there. I didn't know if I'd have to keep singing constantly for it to stay."

"No, now you've summoned it, it's here," Gisela said, less enthusiastic than the other woman. Otto had hurried to join them, along with a number of the others, and he listened with interest as she continued. "But be wary. Forest paths have their own priorities. Just because you've sent it in a certain direction doesn't mean it will continue in that direction. They're fickle things, and can absolutely lead you astray if you displease them."

"You talk about them like they're sentient," Lady Louisa commented mildly.

Gisela shrugged. "I don't really know how else to explain it. But everyone in Ilgal knows that forest paths can be both help and hindrance." She nodded at Valerie. "And if one singer can control them, so can others. And no doubt the elves, with the right talismans. You can never be certain that you're on a path of your own choosing rather than one someone else has chosen for you."

"So that's what that elf leader meant," Otto mused. "She said that neither human roads nor the forest's paths will take us to the Imperator's settlement."

Gisela sighed. "I don't even want to hazard a guess at what kinds of protections the elves might have around their central settlement. We would be wise to assume it will be harder to find than just following a road."

Otto nodded, seeming thoughtful but undeterred. Gisela couldn't help liking that about him. He wasn't one to rush into things foolishly—he considered his actions well before taking them, unlike his friend Monty. But at the same time, he didn't seem easily daunted. His presence here, deep in Ilgal, was testament to that.

"Well, what are we waiting for?" Otto said suddenly. "Let's make the most of it while it's here." He turned to the head guard. "What do you think, Norris?"

"As you think wise, Your Highness," the older man said. He called an order to his men, who all quickly started into motion. As the group moved toward the horses, Haiden emerged from the brush. Heart flopping uncomfortably, Gisela saw Valerie looking at him with a little too much interest. Apparently Monty saw it too, judging by the way his eyes passed between the pair.

"Come on, Haiden," said Valerie brightly. "Looks like we'll be riding again, and I think my mare is familiar enough with you now that she might consent to carry you as well as me, at least for a while."

"All right," said Haiden, unable to hide his enthusiasm as he hurried after her.

Monty, on the other hand, looked far from pleased at this development. And Gisela had a feeling his disapproval had nothing to do with losing Haiden as a passenger.

She bit her lip, even her unease at Haiden's proximity to the too-observant singer unable to completely banish her amusement at Monty's expense.

Until a low voice sounded right behind her, causing her nerves to once again overwhelm any sense of humor.

"And you'll ride with me again, I hope, Gisela?"

# CHAPTER SEVEN

# Otto

Gisela froze, her expression looking so much like a deer in a hunter's sights that Otto felt his lip twitching. Some might have felt dismayed by her reaction, but he didn't. He'd been able to tell from the start that Gisela was wary of him—of all of them, but especially of him since learning his identity. And he didn't take it personally any more than he blamed her for it. It was evident that she and her brother were all alone against the world out here in the treacherous forest, and he didn't need to know her story to acknowledge that she probably had good reason for her caution.

Taking offense would be a fool's response to her mistrust of him. The only approach that made any sense to him was to try to earn her trust by showing himself trustworthy.

Perhaps backing off and leaving her alone completely would also be a sensible response. But he didn't want to. Something about Gisela drew him in, and he was determined to win her good opinion.

"Bullion won't mind carrying us both for a bit," Otto tried again, when Gisela still didn't respond.

"Oh...all right," she said, endearingly flustered. She watched silently as one of the guards brought Bullion to Otto's side.

Waving the guard off, Otto cupped his own hands, offering them to Gisela to help mount the horse. She clambered up, and he used a nearby branch to vault up behind her. She fit very comfortably between his arms, he couldn't help reflecting. But he'd be wise not to dwell on that particular reaction, for a myriad of reasons.

Bullion, long-suffering creature that he was, plodded forward in line, behind Monty and in front of Lady Louisa. Valerie was the first in the group, excepting guards, and it was quite entertaining to see how avidly Monty was watching the singer and her passenger. Otto would have to give him a hard time for that later. It wouldn't be the action of a friend to fail to tease Monty for being openly threatened by a fifteen-year-old.

Otto glanced down to see that Gisela was also watching Valerie and Haiden. He couldn't see her face, but he could sense that she was ill-at-ease. He wished he dared ask her why. He couldn't see anything about the interaction that would bother a sensible person—thereby excluding Monty, at least where Valerie was concerned.

"This path is incredible," Otto said, hoping to lift some of the tension from Gisela's shoulders. "We're all indebted to you for explaining the phenomenon to Valerie."

"Anyone from Ilgal could do that," said Gisela, a little too quickly.

"I hate to be contradictory, but I don't think that's true, actually," Otto informed her, trying to speak pleasantly to show he meant no criticism. "I'm not from Ilgal, but I've lived on its doorstep all my life. I've spoken to plenty of people from Ilgal, and my own stepsister was born in the forest. I've never heard her mention these forest paths. We hear all sorts of rumors about the forest's magic, but few people near Terenford have stories of anything as concrete as what I've just witnessed."

"Really?" Gisela seemed genuinely surprised. "I didn't realize the forest was so different near its edge, but I suppose that makes sense. The magic gets more potent the deeper in you go, doesn't it?"

"So all the experts tell us," Otto agreed.

He reached out to brush a low-hanging branch out of the way, keeping his hand in place as they passed another. The path was very handy, but not as wide as the human-built roads they'd traveled on in the first few days of their time in Ilgal.

His eyes traveled ahead, noting that there were a number of encroaching branches coming, all of them laden with dark berries. Otto recognized them as a type of berry native to the forest, which the group's foragers had included in their meals numerous times. They looked especially appealing for some reason, and he found himself reaching out for one as they passed under the next branch. He pulled a whole clump off, and was about to grab a berry from it with his teeth when Gisela suddenly drew in a sharp breath.

"Stop," she said swiveling so quickly that she almost lost her balance.

Otto steadied her, lowering his arm in the process. He could see Gisela's profile as she stared at the clump of berries in the hand that was now supporting her elbows.

"Is that what you were about to eat?" she demanded. "Where did you get those?"

"From a branch back there," said Otto, nonplussed. "Are they dangerous?"

"Of course they're dangerous!" Gisela said, rattled.

"But..." Otto trailed off, feeling more than usually stupid. "But we've eaten them lots of times. I thought they'd been approved as safe by the forest tracker who trained these guards."

"They are safe, normally," said Gisela. "But it's not safe to eat *anything* you harvested or caught on a forest path. It's almost definitely going to be affected by magic, and there's no saying what that will mean for the person who eats it."

"I...I didn't know that." Otto felt both chastened and grateful, but most of all just foolish. "Thank you for warning me. How did you know?"

"I saw you pick the berries," said Gisela, her sudden discomfort raising Otto's suspicions at once.

"No you didn't," he contradicted boldly. "You went all stiff before you looked back at me, and you didn't seem to have any idea what I was about to eat when you asked me. And you asked where I'd gotten it."

Gisela remained silent, her form once again stiff in front of him.

"Gisela?" he pressed, determined to get a straight answer.

She let out her breath in a soft sigh. "The talisman I carry on me," she said reluctantly. "The one Valerie sensed when we first met you all. It warns me if I, or one of my...companions...is about to eat something dangerous enough to kill or seriously harm us. It sent a sort of shockwave through my body all of a sudden, and I realized you must be eating something, or trying to."

Otto's mouth fell open. He couldn't figure out which part of that revelation to respond to first.

"Thank you," he said at last. "It seems I was at much greater risk than I realized."

"Yes." Gisela's voice was stilted. "Ilgal is fickle and unpredictable. When it seems innocuous is when it's at its most dangerous. The journey has been smooth so far. Too smooth. We should expect more trouble."

Otto swallowed. "We should warn the others not to eat anything from the forest path." He looked around, seeing that no one else appeared interested in swiping berries from the trees. Embarrassing that he'd made such a blunder. "I suppose our hunters and foragers will need to go further afield for food when we stop."

"We'll all need to go further afield when we stop," Gisela said firmly. "Sleeping on the road is no safer than eating from it. Whatever romanticized stories people like to spin about it in the city, magic doesn't inherently seek to protect or help people. It's a strong and unpredictable force, and I don't know anywhere it's more potent than here, in the heart of Ilgal." She tilted her head. "Except Selvana, of course, if rumors are to be believed. But thankfully we haven't reached that level of crisis here."

"No," Otto agreed soberly. "Not yet, anyway."

Gisela didn't answer, but the reflexive way she rubbed her chest told Otto that she didn't need reminding of how dire the magic situation in Ilgal was growing. None of them did. It was remarkable how much he'd adjusted to the constant pressure thanks to relentless exposure, but he was still very aware of it. It was always there.

"Did the berries call to you?" Gisela asked abruptly, recapturing his attention.

"I don't know," Otto said, taken aback. "I wasn't aware of being hungry before, but I suddenly was. They looked very good, even though I wasn't particularly fond of them when we had them previously."

"Hm." Gisela sounded grim. "You probably need to be even more careful than the rest of us. You're a target, with your position and all."

"I am?" Otto asked faintly. "The magic can tell who I am?"

"It's not as simple as that," Gisela said. "It's not really sentient...exactly."

"Thanks for clearing that up." Otto's voice was dry, and he was rewarded with a rare laugh.

"I'm sorry. I really don't know how to explain it better."

Otto waved her apology away. "You can forget all about your earlier qualms, anyway. It sounds like you may have saved my life—I'm the one who should be wrong-footed in our agreement, since I'm now deeply in your debt."

Gisela disclaimed with every sign of discomfort—a refreshing response after dealing with the unscrupulous elves—and Otto deftly turned their conversation to lighter topics.

The afternoon wore quickly away, their progress ten times as quick now that they had a path to follow. Valerie continued to regularly employ her direction-finding song, and Otto was gratified each time to see that the path was still leading north. For now, at least, the forest path seemed to be cooperative.

For the most part, he and Gisela didn't speak, Bullion bearing their combined weight with impressive fortitude. Valerie and Haiden chatted cheerfully ahead, and Monty continued to shift irritably in his saddle, but Otto found the silence on his own mount companionable rather than awkward. Gisela seemed to be relaxing marginally around him, quite an impressive feat given their forced proximity on the horse.

It was much like holding a woman close in the movement of a dance in his stepmother's ballroom, but so much more prolonged. Otto found himself picturing the forest-dwelling girl at a royal ball and smiling. It was hard to imagine—his life in the castle felt increasingly far away, and he continuously surprised himself by how little he missed it. Mostly he missed Rosa—his stepsister would be an excellent addition to this adventure. But she was newly married and living far away in a new kingdom, with her own challenges to overcome, no doubt.

Evening was drawing near when Norris called the group to a halt. A scout had obviously been sent ahead, although Otto hadn't even noticed the man leaving, and he'd now returned with a proposed site for the night's camp.

"Is it far enough off the road?" Gisela asked, leaning forward across Bullion's neck to get the scout's attention.

The man's eyes flicked to Otto, silently seeking approval, and Otto gave a quick nod. If Gisela and Haiden were to be of use to the group as local guides, the men needed to respect their expertise.

"It is, miss," the guard said. "Perhaps ten minutes' walk."

"That's good." Gisela settled back in satisfaction, the warmth of her back once again brushing Otto's chest. The space had felt almost chill in the emptiness when she'd leaned forward. He was becoming far too used to riding double.

Otto noticed Haiden nodding ahead. "Should be far enough not to agitate the magic of the path."

"But will the path wait for us while we sleep?" Valerie asked, sounding fascinated.

Haiden let out a guffaw, and Otto felt the rumble of Gisela's silent chuckle against his chest.

"Don't ever expect magic to wait around for you," Haiden informed Valerie. The fifteen-year-old was clearly enjoying having information the adults around him didn't. "Your best bet will be to try again tomorrow to harness a path. This one won't hang around once we're off it."

Following the scout's lead, the group directed their horses off the path, moving eastward. After only a minute of ducking under overhanging branches, Gisela spoke.

"Stop, please," she said, and Otto pulled Bullion up at once.

"What is it?"

"I'd like to dismount and travel on foot," Gisela said. "May I?"

"Of course." Otto swung his leg around Bullion's rump, sliding down into the undergrowth. "Let me help you down."

Gisela studied him for a moment, her expression hard to

read. Otto found himself holding his breath. He felt like he was facing some kind of test.

"Thank you," she said at last, and he let his breath out. She lay forward on the horse, swinging awkwardly around and sliding down with Otto's assistance. Otto took Bullion's reins, ready to walk with her, but she shook her head.

"No offense, but you'd be more hindrance than help."

"Help with what?" Otto asked, trying not to sound put out.

Gisela didn't answer, instead letting out a soft whistle that sounded like a bird call. From a few horses ahead, Haiden turned his head at once, his posture instantly alert. Gisela motioned to him, and without even asking Valerie to stop, he squirmed his way off her mount. He was lucky they were moving at a slow walk in the difficult terrain, and even so he scrambled to his feet with a wince.

The two siblings moved together into the trees, leaving a perplexed Otto to remount Bullion as best he could.

"What are they doing, Your Highness?" Norris asked suspiciously.

"I don't know," said Otto. "But I'm sure they'll explain soon enough."

"Are you?" Norris didn't sound convinced, and he remained on edge all the way to the clearing the scout had indicated.

Otto was also surprised, having expected the pair to reappear much more quickly. When the two slight figures emerged from the tree line just as Otto slid from his saddle, he felt a definite sense of relief.

"We shouldn't camp here," Gisela said, her words directed to Otto rather than Norris.

"Why not?" he asked.

Gisela gestured behind her, and he followed her gaze. All he could see was foliage.

"What is it?"

"Someone's come through here recently." Haiden spoke up. "There were signs of their passage most of the way along our route from the path."

"I didn't see any signs," said the scout, frowning.

Gisela shrugged. "They were there. I can show you if you like."

The man moved forward, and so did Otto. He watched with fascination as Gisela pointed to apparently bruised leaves, and indents in the moss on a fallen branch. The guard looked nonplussed.

"Those are very faint. It's probably an animal."

Gisela shook her head. "I thought that at first, but the path isn't right for that. It wasn't a group or anything. Most likely a single human, I'd say."

"You think this person is lying in wait for us?" asked Norris suspiciously.

"No." Haiden shook his head as well. "There's no reason to think that. There are plenty of recluses spread across the forest, living as we do. But we'd still be wisest to pick a different spot."

"I don't see why." The scout sounded affronted. "One person shouldn't be a threat to us even if they did come back here."

"That's not the point." Gisela pushed past them all, emerging back into the clearing. "Everyone hold still, before you trample the signs further," she called. The group paused, most looking bemused at being ordered around by the usually withdrawn forest girl. "Look here." She pointed to what appeared to Otto to be a perfectly normal patch of grass. "And here. Whoever it was, they considered camping here as well, but then decided to move on."

"Why?" asked the scout.

Gisela shrugged. "I don't know. And that's the point. He or she knew or suspected something we don't, and that something led to the decision not to camp here after all. We don't need to learn whatever it was the hard way when we can just learn from the other person's example."

Norris frowned. "That's quite a leap," he said. "Even if you're right that someone was here, maybe they just rested here during the day, or decided to move on out of preference rather than fear of danger. Deciding that we all have to relocate seems overly cautious."

"That's more or less Gisela's thing, to be fair," Haiden chimed in.

Gisela threw her brother a dark look. "Being overly cautious is what keeps you alive in Ilgal," she informed Norris. "And I would prefer not to camp here."

"Do you know of another equally suitable spot close by?" Norris asked.

Reluctantly, Gisela shook her head, as Norris must have known she would. She and Haiden had acknowledged that they didn't know the area.

"Then I think moving on would contain as much risk as staying here," the head guard said, not unkindly. "It's near dark, now, and time for us to be settled in a defensible position."

Gisela bit her lip. "But isn't it better to avoid conflict than defend against it?"

"Of course," said Norris. "But I don't consider there to be enough evidence that we're courting conflict by camping here. I appreciate your input, but this is the most secure option we have."

"Very well." Gisela didn't sound angry, but nor was she convinced. "Haiden, we can find another spot before dark without too much difficulty, I imagine."

"What?" Haiden started, staring at his sister. "No way. I'm staying with the group."

"Haiden." For the first time, Gisela looked distressed. "It might not be safe."

"Gisela."

Otto paused, trying to find the right words. He felt torn. He had no hesitation acknowledging the pair's superior knowledge of the forest, and he would have been willing to look for another place to camp. But he'd put Norris in charge of the expedition's safety, and it wouldn't be fair—or wise—of him to undermine his head guard's authority, especially not in favor of near strangers.

"I know there's always a risk out here," he said delicately. "But don't forget that traveling with a group this size really is different from your usual situation. The threats we need to worry about aren't the same ones you usually face."

"He's right, Gisela," Haiden said quickly. "If we go off on our own, we'll be in unfamiliar territory in the dark. We might not even be able to find the group again."

She gave him an incredulous look, and he raised his eyebrows, not backing down.

"What? I'm right. We don't have all our usual means of finding our way."

Gisela held his gaze, and Otto watched the silent standoff in fascination. Haiden was referring to more than just the familiarity of their usual surroundings, he was certain. But he didn't pry.

"Fine."

It was the second time Otto had witnessed Gisela giving in to her brother's defiance of her guidance, and she didn't look any happier about it this time than she had the previous. One thing was clear, though. If Haiden was staying with the group, Gisela wouldn't be going anywhere. Otto could only be glad. However capable she was, he couldn't help but think she was safer with the group, watched over by armed guards.

Sensing that the siblings needed some space, Otto moved

away, setting about the task of removing Bullion's saddle and rubbing the horse down himself.

"Thanks, old boy," he told the stallion, visiting the group's food stores and returning with an apple. He crooned to the creature for a moment, laying one hand on the horse's flank. "You've gone above and beyond today, carrying the two of us." He glanced toward Gisela's slight figure. She was standing with her arms crossed, looking like a tightly coiled spring. "Not that she's very heavy, is she?"

Some of the guards were already at work building a fire in the center of the clearing, and Otto joined the others in searching for promising logs and large rocks. Soon they had a ring of makeshift logs set up, and Otto found himself perched on a branch alongside Monty.

"Well, I like this paths trick," the young lord said brightly. "We made much better progress, didn't we?"

"Seems like it," Haiden chimed in, apparently suffering from none of the qualms that still kept his sister quiet in her place beside him on a large boulder. "But it's so hard to tell when the foliage is this thick. I might go for a climb, see if I can get a sense of how far north we've come."

Knowing how protective she was of her brother's safety, Otto expected Gisela to protest, but she nodded slowly.

"It's a good idea."

"How will climbing help you do that?" Monty asked, interested.

Haiden gave him a pitying look which caused Otto and Valerie to exchange grins. It was hard to decide what was more entertaining—Monty feeling threatened by Haiden or Haiden's assumed loftiness around the lord.

"Can *you* see the stars from here?" Haiden gestured at the canopy overhead. The clearing wasn't large, and even at its center, only a thin band of sky was visible. "I didn't realize you had some kind of magical extra sight."

"No, I'm afraid I don't." Monty leaned back, quite at ease. It was only where Valerie was concerned that he gave Haiden any reaction whatsoever. "I'll leave that to the royal elves."

"What do you mean by that?" Lady Louisa looked over at him.

"Don't you know the stories?" Monty asked comfortably. "They bandy these kinds of legends about at the academy. The ruling elves have some kind of mystical power in their blood. Extra sight, some call it. They can predict things, like the future."

Out of the corner of his eye, Otto saw Gisela and Haiden exchange a look. His attention caught, he watched them. Both were suddenly very alert to the conversation, trying inexpertly to hide the tension that had them sitting rigidly on their rock.

"Oh yes, I've heard that one," Valerie said reminiscently. "In my class, it was the stories of the giants most people were obsessed with. I think half the students had grand dreams of fighting off an invasion with the power of their songcraft alone. The elves came into those stories too, though, that's how I heard about the extra sight."

"Elves came into stories about giants?" Otto asked, surprised. "I thought the two races despised each other, even more than they hate humans."

"I think they do," said Valerie. "There was just some story about the royal elves of the Vadolisian tribes making a prediction with their extra sight. They said the giants were plotting to breach the wall and suck the life from the rest of the continent."

"Sounds grim," Monty said lightly.

"Sounds like the kind of dramatic tale people love to tell without basis in fact," Gisela chipped in with a cynical twist to her lips. "I can't say I'm surprised to hear that city folk sit around telling stories about things they don't understand, as if they can bottle the magic of places like Ilgal into simple bedtime tales."

"So it isn't true, then?" Otto challenged, watching her carefully. "About the royal elves and their extra sight?"

Gisela shrugged, instantly uncomfortable again. "Don't ask me. I'm no expert on elves."

"Hm." Otto let his eyes dwell shamelessly on her face. What exactly had her and her brother reacting so notably to this discussion?

"Never mind about the elves, though," Valerie said. "Can you really tell where you are from the stars?" Her question was directed to Haiden, and she sounded impressed.

"Not with as much certainty as he's implying." Gisela spoke shortly, apparently not having completely forgiven her brother's defiance.

Haiden shot her a look. "No need to be sour because I'm better at reading the stars than you are, Gisela."

She snorted. "You wish."

Otto found himself smiling, the interaction strongly reminiscent of his spats with Rosa, but Haiden's next words drew him up.

"You know it's true. Even Papa said I have more of a natural affinity for it."

Gisela bit her lip, her eyes darting around the group at what was evidently a slip. It was the first time Otto had heard them mention any family.

"Did your father teach you all these survival skills?" Monty asked, displaying a painful lack of tact. "That's handy. Where's he? Also in Ilgal?"

"He's gone," said Gisela flatly.

"Both our parents are," Haiden chimed in, his voice hard, and not in the usual condescending way he adopted with Monty.

"It's just us," Gisela added. "Like we told you."

"I'm sorry," Otto told her sincerely. "It's not easy to lose a parent, and I can't imagine losing both. My mother died when I was very young. I barely remember her."

"Count yourself lucky." The muttered aside from Haiden trailed off as Gisela nudged him.

Otto looked between the two of them thoughtfully. Clearly his words regarding his own experience hadn't softened them as he'd hoped they might. He exchanged a look with Monty, seeing both his sympathy and his curiosity reflected in his friend's eyes.

"I think I'll go for that climb now," said Haiden, standing abruptly.

No one said anything in response, and after an awkward moment, he strode into the tree line. At that moment, a guard appeared with a pot which he placed over the fire, ready to start making stew. The group devolved into smaller conversations, and Otto found himself rising.

A few quick strides took him around the circle, until he stood in front of Gisela. "Do you mind?" he asked, gesturing to Haiden's vacated seat.

She gave a non-committal grunt, which he figured was as good as he was likely to get. Lowering himself onto the boulder, he leaned forward, putting his elbows on his knees and holding out his hands to the fire in an attempt to drive away the chill of the night air.

"Will Haiden be all right by himself?" Otto asked.

Gisela unbent slightly, nodding. "He can climb a tree better than you can ride a horse. He won't go far. He just needed a minute."

"I'm sorry," Otto said sincerely. "I didn't mean to upset or offend him."

"You didn't," Gisela told him. "It wasn't you."

"It sounds like you haven't had an easy life," said Otto softly. "I'm sorry memories of your mother aren't happy ones."

Gisela sighed. "They're not all unhappy," she said quietly, her eyes staring unseeingly into the fire. "But she was...complicated."

Otto waited in silence, figuring she would elaborate if she wanted to. After a long moment, she pulled her gaze from the flames and turned it to his face.

"Her ancestors came from the Reviled Lands."

She said the words with a definite note of defiance, and Otto studied her face. He had the sense she was testing him, and he didn't feel at all concerned about the outcome. He truly believed himself to be trustworthy, regardless of her clear wariness. He didn't anticipate giving a poor reaction to anything she might share.

"Amazing that she knew that," he commented. "Of course I realize there must be many descendants of the original refugees across the continent, but I was under the impression that most probably couldn't even trace their ancestry. The lines have been intermingled so much by now that anyone with ancestors from those kingdoms must have many more ancestors from Providore."

Gisela held his gaze, her shoulders lowering the tiniest amount.

"Yes, I think that's generally true," she acknowledged. "But my mother's family held their heritage more closely than most. It was a point of great pride for them. I think her grandparents were part of a community of mainly refugee descendants, hiding in plain sight among the residents of Ilgal."

"It's a shame they had to hide," Otto commented. "But I'm not surprised. I've heard of how generations past had strong prejudices against the survivors from the war that ripped the Reviled Lands apart."

"I think those prejudices only served to galvanize those who'd banded together," Gisela said quietly. "By the time my mother married my father—who didn't share that ancestry at all—the community had already intermingled plenty with the Terenans around them. But they didn't act like it. They still raised their children to think of themselves as exiled members of the old kingdoms, and to revere their history."

"Were you raised that way?" Otto asked curiously.

Gisela's face was hard again. "For a short time. But Papa didn't support it, and it never meant much to us. Not like my mother hoped. It's so long ago and so far away, and like you said, more of my ancestry is Terenan now. I think I would have taken more interest in it if I found any joy in my mother's inherited memories. But it seemed all she could focus on was what had been lost. I don't think I can ever remember her being truly, unrestrictedly happy."

Otto let out a long breath. No wonder she'd called her mother complicated. What a strange weight to carry after so many generations.

"Thank you for sharing that with me," he said. "I can tell you're unsure if it's wise to do it, but I don't know anyone now who would hold that ancestry against you. What happened in the Reviled Lands was terrible—and I'll admit that as royalty, I've been raised to think very negatively of a place where monarchs were violently overthrown and their supporters all murdered. But no one blames the descendants who live among us now. After all, the ones who fled to Providore weren't exactly those in support of the uprising."

"No," said Gisela softly, something in her voice Otto couldn't read. "They were...vehemently against it."

A guard approached at that moment, handing Otto the first steaming bowl of stew. He thanked the man quietly, then presented the dish to Gisela.

She shook her head quickly. "No, that one is yours."

Otto smiled. "We're in the middle of the forest, Gisela. I don't see any reason my consequence needs to be pandered to by feeding me first. I hope I was raised to be more considerate than that."

Gisela stared at him, seeming taken aback by his attempt at chivalry. But after a suspended moment, she accepted the bowl, her fingers cool where they brushed against Otto's.

"Thank you," she said softly.

Otto nodded, withdrawing his hands quickly from the warm dish. He'd been strangely reluctant to let it go, but he didn't want her to think he regretted offering it. A moment later the confused guard brought another bowl for Gisela, which Otto intercepted. The others were chatting cheerfully while they ate, but Otto and Gisela sat in silence. The sadness of her tale—particularly all the things she'd clearly left unsaid—hung between them.

"I'm tired," Gisela said abruptly, when her bowl was empty. "I'd better find Haiden."

"You go sleep," said Otto, taking her bowl from her hand and shaking his head. "We'll direct Haiden to your spot when he gets back."

Gisela hesitated, clearly unsure about settling for the night without her brother at hand, but just as clearly exhausted.

"You said yourself he'll be fine," Otto reminded her gently.

Deflating a little, she nodded, making her way to the far side of the large ring of firelight. She and her brother had rejected bedrolls the night before, refusing to take them from the guards who'd offered their own. It was a little painful to see her curling up on the grass underneath a thin cloak she'd pulled from her own pack, but Otto supposed she knew what she was doing. She'd likely slept like that many times before.

He got up from the boulder, moving around the circle to join

Monty, Valerie, and Lady Louisa. They were speaking in muted tones, Gisela's move toward bed apparently having changed the mood.

"Is Haiden still not back yet?" Valerie asked Otto quietly, as he sat beside Lady Louisa. "We'll have to be sure to save him some stew."

"No need to mother the boy, Valerie," Monty said with unconvincing airiness. "I'd say he gets enough of that from his sister."

"Can you blame her for protecting all she has?" Otto asked curtly. "Some of us know how much family means to those who don't have it."

Monty fell silent, chastened, and Otto turned to Valerie.

"He's still climbing, as far as I'm aware. We should definitely save him some food."

"If they're truly all alone, as they say, they're very vulnerable, aren't they?" Lady Louisa flicked her fan open and shut in a reflective gesture as her eyes lingered on Gisela's still figure, just out of earshot. "So young to be just the two of them against the world."

"Yes, they are vulnerable, I think," Otto said, his eyes going the same direction. "In spite of their capability, I don't think they have much to fall back on."

"Not nothing, though," Monty commented. "They have some kind of access to magic, don't they, Valerie?"

"What do you mean?" she asked cautiously.

"You said you sensed a talisman on them, when we first met," Monty explained. "Didn't you?"

"Oh." Valerie nodded slowly. "Yes, that's right."

"So they have some kind of protection."

Otto debated explaining the nature of the talisman, and the fact that it offered only very limited protection. But he was too distracted by Valerie's reaction. She was industriously finishing her stew, a little too blatant about her desire not to engage with the conversation. Did she know something he didn't about Gisela and Haiden?

Aware of his words to Gisela, Otto kept an eye on the tree line as everyone began to wind down, waiting for Haiden to re-emerge. But there was no sign of the truant, even by the time everyone else had settled for sleep.

Frowning, Otto glanced from his empty bedroll next to Monty to the still form of Gisela, on the other side of the fire. He suspected that she'd never actually intended to fall asleep without Haiden having returned, but she must have been exhausted, because to all appearances, she was out to the world. He couldn't also go to sleep while Haiden was still absent. Quite apart from wanting to demonstrate to Gisela that she could trust him, he felt concerned about the teenage boy himself. Haiden had been gone a long time now.

Otto moved into the trees, unsurprised when a guard materialized at his side, giving him space but keeping within easy hailing distance.

"I'm not going to relieve myself," Otto informed him, recognizing the indicators of a guard assigned to shadow him.

"Then where are you going, Your Highness, if I may ask?" The guard drew closer as Otto continued through the trees, the glow of the fire fading from sight.

"I'm looking for Haiden," Otto said. "He hasn't come back yet."

"He's snuck off?" The guard seemed uneasy at this information. "We should notify Norris at once, Your Highness."

"No, I'm not suspicious of him," Otto said quickly. "I'm concerned for his safety."

The other man seemed unconvinced, but at that moment, a shuffling sound drew both of their attention. The noise came from the opposite direction to the camp, and Otto peered hope-fully through the darkness.

"Haiden?"

Instead of a human voice, his call was met by an alarming chorus of sounds somewhere between grunts and growls. The noise seemed to stretch all around them, and it made the hairs on Otto's neck stand up. The guard drew his sword and leaped in front of the prince, calling a warning over his shoulder as Otto reached for his own weapon.

It had barely cleared its scabbard when a wall of dark, hairy shapes burst from the undergrowth, heads lowered and tusks gleaming in the moonlight as they charged.

# CHAPTER EIGHT

# Gisela

Gisela awoke with a start, horror quickly overtaking confusion as awareness returned. How could she have fallen asleep with Haiden still absent? And what was going on?

There was uproar all around her, and she sprang to her feet, forcing back the grogginess of her interrupted sleep.

"Gisela! Over here, quick." Lady Louisa's voice drew her attention to where the older woman stood with Valerie and Monty, as close to the fire as comfort allowed.

"What's going on?" Gisela demanded, hurrying over to them.

"I was hoping you could answer that," said Lady Louisa. She was brandishing her fan as if poised for action, although what action Gisela couldn't imagine. "We seem to be under attack, but I haven't figured out by what."

"All right, stay here," Monty said briskly, his hand traveling to the hilt of a sword as he attempted to shoulder past the guards standing in a clump around the group.

"I don't think so," Valerie said flatly, the firelight dancing on her blazing hair as she tossed it over her shoulder. "I'll be more use than you, Monty, you should stay here to look after the others."

"If you think I'm staying here while Otto's out there—" Monty started, and Gisela's eyes widened. The prince wasn't in the clearing? A glance around confirmed it. No wonder the guards were in such a frenzy.

Her sluggish mind finally caught up with the sounds she was hearing, and she spun in a quick circle, letting out a groan.

"Galboars," she said. "Sounds like a big herd, too."

"Those violent pigs you mentioned?" Monty asked, his eyes flying to Valerie in alarm. "You're right about your magic being useful, Valerie. You should stay here to protect everyone from within the clearing."

"Nice try," she growled, but Gisela cut her off, uninterested in their petty dispute about who should hang back.

"Where's my brother?" she demanded.

"Uh…" Monty looked around, confused. "I don't know," he admitted.

"Neither do I." Valerie sounded concerned. "I don't remember seeing him after he went to climb that tree."

"What?" Gisela felt the panic rising. "That must have been hours ago."

"I believe His Highness went looking for Haiden," Lady Louisa chimed in. "I saw him slip into the trees when the rest of us were settling for sleep."

Gisela's breaths were coming too quickly now. How could she have been so careless as to let Haiden go alone? He was more than capable of safely climbing a tree in the darkness, but she hadn't counted on a territorial galboar herd. And now both Haiden and the prince were in danger because of her lapse in judgment.

"I have to go find him," she said, her mind in a panic as she thought of her brother alone in the darkness, surrounded by enraged boars.

The others protested, but unlike them, she didn't hang about to argue over it. She was already sprinting toward the edge of the clearing, stooping to retrieve her bow from beside her sleeping spot as she went. She could hear Lady Louisa telling the others in no uncertain terms to stay put, but the grunts of the galboars soon drowned out her words. Their ire was rising, and she could tell they were preparing for an attack.

The borders of the clearing were manned with armed guards, weapons raised in determination. Fear clawed at Gisela. If they took on the galboars head to head, there would be casualties.

"We need to retreat!" she called. "It's not necessary to fight! If we leave, they won't follow us."

"Get back to the fire," Norris bellowed at her, his eyebrows drawn together in disapproval. He was striding toward her, three other guards following close behind, weapons drawn.

"Listen to me!" she pleaded, turning to face him. "They're gearing for an attack, and they won't use logic. They'll fight in a frenzy, and they won't stop until we leave their territory or they're all dead." She paused. "Or we're all dead."

The head guard continued to glare at her, but she thought she saw a couple of the others exchange uneasy looks.

"Even if that was true," Norris told her, "leaving is not an option while the group is split. The prince is out there, with only one guard."

"I understand," said Gisela quickly. "My brother is out there as well. And I'm not going anywhere until I find him. But please at least tell your men to prepare to retreat to safer ground." She gestured behind her. "Listen to the grunts. They haven't surrounded us in a ring, only a semi-circle. They want to drive us out rather than eliminate us. They're not our natural predators—this is a territorial display."

Norris hesitated for a moment, then barked an order over his shoulder. Three of the guards broke rank from the inner ring near Monty and the others, moving toward the packs and the loosely tethered horses that stood among the trees nearby.

Relieved, Gisela started moving toward the line of guards, but Norris grabbed her arm.

"Not you, miss. You stay here with the others. We'll find the prince and your brother."

Gisela tugged her arm free, shaking her head. "There's no way I'm staying here."

Norris ignored her, already passing through the line of guards with his companions. "Don't let her or any of the others through," he told the defenders curtly.

Gisela was seething, but she mastered the emotion. Arguing with Norris would only waste time. Once he was out of sight between the trees, she ran her gaze along the line, looking for a weak point. There, that overhanging branch.

"Sorry, miss, but we have our orders," said one of the guards. "You're to stay here."

Gisela ignored him completely, shifting back a step as she slung her bow over her back. Then she sprinted forward, taking the guards by surprise as she leaped upward just in front of one of them, seizing the overhanging branch and swinging herself up in an experienced motion. Their cries left her unmoved, and she took care to travel from branch to branch across several trees before dropping to the ground.

Only to immediately clamber back up again as she was met with the sight of a full-scale galboar charge.

"They're coming!" Gisela screamed back toward the clearing. She barely pulled her feet up in time to avoid the tusks of the enraged galboar trying to gouge its way through the tree in which she'd taken shelter.

Gisela looked around frantically, spotting a promising route into the next tree. She moved through the branches, her heart in her throat as the stream of galboars passed below her, heading for the clearing.

"Haiden!" she screamed, straining her ears to hear her brother. "Haiden, where are you?"

Her thoughts flew to Otto as well, but she told herself to focus. The prince had three dozen guards. Haiden had no one but her to protect him. He'd never had anyone but her.

"Gisela?"

She turned hopefully toward the sound, dropping once more to the ground after checking that she'd cleared the charging herd. For better or worse, they were now between her and the group in the clearing.

"Haiden, is that you?" she called, sprinting toward the sound.

But she hadn't gone far when she heard a terrifying snuffling. She spun wildly, confronted with the sight of a huge female galboar, its beady eyes fixed on her. Gisela gulped, her hands reaching behind her for a helpful trunk to scale, or branch to swing up with. But she found only empty space, and heard only the alarming sound of a low, sustained grunt. She turned slowly, her heart doubling its pace at the realization that there were not two, but three of them. And they had her surrounded, no trees in reach. They were too close for her to even use her bow.

Moving slowly, she leaned down and drew a knife from her boot, aware of how poor a defense it would be against the huge creatures. But she couldn't just do nothing. The thought flashed through her mind that she would die without knowing whether Haiden was safe, and sudden defiance coursed through her.

No. Protecting her brother was her job. It was the only role in her life with any meaning. She couldn't let these creatures take her away from him.

"Haiden," she called, her eyes never leaving the galboars who were circling her now. "If you can hear me, get out of here! They seem to be trying to herd everyone south. Go that way."

"Gisela!" The voice was closer now, and Gisela realized with a start that it wasn't Haiden at all. She turned her head to check, but that was a mistake. Seeing their opening, the boars lunged forward, and Gisela barely brought her knife out in time to cause the closest one to duck to the side. Not before its tusk grazed her arm, however.

Gisela let out a grunt of pain, resisting the urge to grasp the oozing wound with her other hand. She needed to keep her blade brandished. It was the only thing she could think of that would buy her any time.

It wouldn't be enough, though. Not with three of them. She adopted a fighting stance, letting out a guttural grunt that was the closest approximation to the galboars' cry that she could manage.

It didn't work. Far from deterring them, it seemed to raise their ire. All at once one lunged at her from behind, its tusk catching at her tunic before she could fully turn. She braced herself for pain, but it didn't come. Instead she heard a very human cry that mingled horribly with the galboar's high-pitched squeal. The other two galboars pivoted quickly, Gisela spinning around with them to see Otto pulling a long sword from the twitching flank of the galboar which had tried to gut her.

"What are you doing out here?" he roared, spinning to face the next galboar. Seamlessly, he raised his sword with one hand while the other arm shot out to sweep Gisela behind him. She was so taken aback, she didn't even resist, barely keeping up with events as a guard came sprinting into sight behind them.

"Your Highness!" the man cried, looking panicked to see the prince facing off against two furiously snarling galboars.

"What are *you* doing out here?" Gisela cried in belated response to Otto's question, watching in a daze as the two men moved in a deadly dance around the boars.

"Looking for your blasted brother, what do you think?" Otto panted.

He lunged forward, his blade locking with the galboar's tusks. Alarmed, Gisela started forward with her knife raised, but the prince managed to disengage his sword without assistance. The sound of their cries had obviously attracted attention, because Norris and his companions came bursting through the foliage a moment later, taking in the situation at a glance and racing to the prince's defense.

The humans were panting heavily, the effects of the magic's pressure on their chests no doubt amplified by their exertions. Supposedly to outsiders, it was like trying to run through a bog.

But even so, with six humans and only two galboars, it was over quickly. One of the guards sustained an injury to his leg, but it didn't look serious. Gisela was still staring blankly at the downed galboars when a hand took gentle hold of her chin, tilting her face up to the weak moonlight as Otto searched her features.

"Are you all right, Gisela?"

She nodded mutely, overwhelmed by the gentleness of his fingers, and the concern in his eyes. She hadn't been touched so caressingly since childhood. The prince's forehead glistened with sweat, and a wayward strand of hair curled over it, drawing Gisela's eyes as her mind tried to make sense of what had just occurred.

"You saved my life," she said stupidly.

Otto didn't respond at once, the intensity in his eyes softening slowly as his panting breaths also steadied.

"I guess we're even now," he said at last.

Gisela blinked at him, struggling to comprehend how he could think his own actions just then equated to her warning about the berries. That had cost her nothing, required no heroics. He'd just charged a trio of enraged galboars to protect her. And why? What reason did he have to care if she lived or died? She couldn't remember the last time anyone unrelated to her had acted selflessly to protect her. Even those who *were* related couldn't be depended on.

Worse, she didn't know how to make sense of a situation where she was the one being protected instead of doing the protecting. She couldn't decide if it made her feel glad, or deeply uncomfortable.

Stowing her dagger at last, she brought her hand up to grip the wound on her other arm, which was dripping blood onto her breeches. The sting of it was starting to intrude on her consciousness as the sense of crisis faded.

"You're hurt." Otto sounded alarmed.

She shook her head, full awareness returning. "I'm fine," she said. "But the others!" Their little patch of forest was still now, but the sounds of chaos could be faintly heard through the trees.

Comprehension flared in Otto's eyes as well—apparently he'd been as detached from reality as she had—and he turned.

"Come on!" he said, seizing Gisela's uninjured arm and tugging her forward. The guards surged around them as they ran back toward the clearing, Gisela searching the dark trees fruitlessly for any sign of Haiden.

The ground was easier to pass than it normally was in the dark, the undergrowth having been trampled flat by the galboars' charge.

When they reached the clearing, they were met with pandemonium. The guards had retreated into a smaller semi-circle, Lady Louisa and Valerie at the center. Everyone seemed markedly out of breath, some of the guards actually clutching at their chests. The singer was letting out a frantic song in the faintest voice Gisela had heard from her, the purpose of the melody unclear in the melee. Monty had joined the ring of guards, taking his position right in front of the two women, but Gisela could see at a glance that the defenders were struggling to hold their line.

"You were right." Norris's voice was low and urgent beside her, and she turned to him in surprise. "They're not surrounding our people. They're trying to push them back."

Gisela studied the scene again, confirming his assessment. She could see that some of the guards had gathered the horses as instructed, and loaded most of the supplies into their saddlebags. Even the bedrolls were no longer on the ground.

"The clearing must be a territorial mating ground," she said quickly. "It's probably been vacant since last year, so it's no wonder Haiden and I didn't pick up the signs of it when we first got to the clearing. Galboars aren't as common in our area, and we're no experts. Seems like the lone traveler who was here before us was more familiar with their ways...that's probably why he abandoned the site as a camp."

"I should have backed you," said Otto, sounding stricken. "I'm sorry."

Gisela shook her head. She didn't feel any need for apologies, or any sense of pleasure in being proved right. She just wanted to see the group get to safety, especially Haiden.

She glanced at the dark trees behind her. Where was her brother?

"Come on, Your Highness." Norris grabbed the prince's arm, dragging him toward the edge of the clearing. He was obviously trying to get around the line of attacking boars, to reach the horses and the rest of the group.

"Gisela."

Her eyes flew to Otto, and she realized he'd planted his feet against Norris's efforts, his eyes narrowed as he observed her hesitation.

"I have to find Haiden," she told him desperately.

"Gisela, we're going back to camp. Come on," he said, no compromise in his voice. Just as Norris had done to him, he took firm hold of her arm, pulling her behind him. They plunged back into the trees, giving the clearing a wide berth then arcing back around to enter it from the south.

"Retreat!" Norris's voice brought the defenders' heads whipping around, every eye finding him. "Head south!"

"How?" Monty called desperately, even as his eyes lit with relief at the sight of Otto.

"To retreat quickly enough and still stay together, we'll need a road," Lady Louisa agreed crisply. She turned to the young woman beside her. "Valerie?"

Valerie's battle song faltered and broke off. "I...I can try," she said desperately. She closed her eyes, raising her voice again. It sounded weary and brittle, and nothing happened.

"It's not working," she said, wringing her hands. "I can tell that the magic isn't responding to me."

"Valerie." Monty's quiet voice cut across the continued clash of metal on tusk, the grunts of the galboars, and the cries of the guards. "Focus. You can do this. I know you can."

The panic died from Valerie's eyes as she visibly steeled herself, but Gisela's heart sank. Touching as the sentiment was, Monty was wrong. Valerie couldn't do it alone. She needed Haiden, and he was nowhere to be found.

Fear clutched at her heart, souring the melody Valerie was releasing. But before it could take hold, she heard a low voice from behind her, and spun to face the tree line. She could see nothing in the darkness, but the delighted cries from the others told her that something was working. The song from the trees stopped at once, and Gisela stumbled forward, her eyes searching the darkness for Haiden.

He emerged from the foliage, looking rumpled and tense, his eyes taking in her blood-soaked clothes and the way her hand still gripped her arm.

"Gisela!" he cried, starting forward.

"I'm all right," she told him. "What about you?"

"Yes, I'm fine," he said quickly, casting a glance over the group. Gisela turned to see that about half of the guards had formed a deeper front line, holding it while the rest of the party frantically started mounting horses. A road, shimmering faintly in the darkness, stretched out southward from the edge of the clearing.

"Not ideal to travel a forest path at night," Haiden commented. "But unavoidable in the circumstances. I guess we know why that other traveler didn't want to camp here, hey? You were right, Gisela."

"Never mind that!" she cried, annoyance rising now that the first relief had passed. "Haiden, where were you?"

He grimaced apologetically. "I'm sorry. I was upset, and I wanted space. I did climb a tree to check the stars—we must be close to the center of the forest, by the way—but I walked a long way before I did. I headed back as soon as I heard the sounds of the galboars, but it took me ages to get here, since I obviously kept to the trees."

Some of the tension drained from Gisela's frame. Of course Haiden knew the smart thing to do in a galboar attack. Getting into the trees was always their first strategy, since the creatures couldn't climb.

"Haiden!"

Otto's cry made them both turn to see the prince riding toward them, his horse's hooves churning up the ground. Behind him, the line of humans was thinning as more and more were released under Norris's oversight to mount their horses.

"There you are!" Otto was still addressing Haiden, his voice tight. "What are you two doing? You need mounts!" He came to a stop beside them, Monty right behind him. "She's hurt, Haiden, can you help me get her up?"

"I can manage," said Gisela, embarrassed by all the attention.

Otto ignored her protest, reaching out an arm to grip her elbow. Haiden gave her a boost, and the next thing she knew, she was planted behind Otto, her good arm around his waist and her face pressed into his back to keep her balance. She glanced back just long enough to see Haiden scramble onto Monty's horse, then buried her face in Otto's tunic again as he sent his mount cantering forward on the newly formed path.

Gisela could no longer see the method by which Norris was extracting his men, but after no more than ten minutes of hard riding down the road, the head guard appeared, calling the group to a halt.

"They're no longer pursuing," he told Otto curtly. "It seems we've left their territory."

Gisela let out a long breath of relief. A glance back at the group made her heart flop at the sight of a few empty horses. But she relaxed again when she saw that their riders, although injured, were very much alive, riding double on their fellows' horses to allow them to be supported. She wondered idly how much stuff the group had lost. Personally, she'd lost nothing. She kept her rucksack with her at all times.

She suddenly became aware of Otto disengaging her arm from his waist, and she let go quickly, embarrassed that she'd had to be prompted. Screwing up her eyes against the pain in her other arm, she started to swing her leg around, ready to slide off the horse.

"Whoa, easy there!" Otto said quickly, hastening to dismount first. "Let me help you."

He eased her down, and she submitted far more tamely than was wise. Now they were no longer in motion, the pain was intense, and she realized she was feeling faint. Her feet found the ground, and she swayed for a moment before forcing her weary legs to take a step back from Otto.

"What were you thinking, Gisela?" The prince's voice sounded angry, an emotion she'd never heard from him. Surprised, she blinked up into his face, wishing her swimming vision would clear. "Why did you go charging alone into the trees in the middle of an attack?"

"I...what do you mean?" she asked stupidly. "My brother was out there."

"I know you care about your brother, but you should care about yourself as well," Otto said curtly.

Gisela couldn't think of a response, and the next thing she knew, Haiden was in her range of vision, frowning at Otto with a terrifying disregard for the risks of offending the prince.

"What's going on? Why are you berating my sister?"

"Because she completely disregards her own safety in her determination to maintain yours," Otto said bluntly. "Do you realize she left the protection of the clearing to hunt for you, after the galboars were already attacking?"

"Gisela," Haiden moaned. "Why would you do that?"

She frowned groggily at him, once again confused. "Why do you think?" she asked, putting a hand to her spinning head. "I always protect you. That's my job. That's my one job."

"It's not." She could see from Haiden's face that he was embarrassed, but she didn't have the energy to pander to his feelings.

"Even when she was surrounded by the creatures, all she could think about was to call a warning to you," Otto said, sounding exasperated.

It was all very confusing to Gisela, and she closed her eyes, trying to marshal her thoughts. It wasn't that Otto's words didn't make sense. He was right, and she knew it. Now it was all over, and Haiden was fine, she realized that she should have trusted her brother to be safe instead of losing her head and running after him. He'd known what to do. But what she couldn't understand was why Otto seemed personally affronted by her foolishness. She couldn't see any way it affected him at all.

"Quite the exciting evening, wasn't it?" Monty's voice had joined the conversation, his cheerful tone forced and brittle.

"Where's the medic-trained guard?" Otto asked, still sounding uncharacteristically curt. "Gisela is hurt and needs attention."

"I'm fine," she murmured in a protest that everyone ignored.

"He's tending to the wounded," said Monty. "Valerie is helping him. No serious injuries, thank goodness."

"I'll tell them about Gisela's injury." Gisela hadn't even realized Lady Louisa was nearby, and she kept her eyes closed. The pain was hard to think through, and it was growing more difficult to calm her spinning head.

"Enjoy your evening walk, Haiden?" Monty's voice took on an edge that Gisela didn't like. "Nothing like a solitary nighttime wander, never mind it forced the crown prince to sacrifice his safety to look for you."

"Monty. No one forced me to do anything." Otto's voice was weary, and Gisela had to agree with him. She couldn't see how anyone would gain from an escalation of the situation.

"I'm sorry, I didn't realize His Highness's safety was my responsibility." Haiden's gruff voice told Gisela that he was still mortified, but trying desperately not to show it. "I also didn't realize I needed your permission to go for a walk in my own forest."

"And such a lovely, pleasant forest it is," said Monty sarcastically. "No wonder you're so proud of it."

"You think we don't know how dangerous it is?" Haiden demanded. "You think we like being chased by galboars, and dumped days from home without shelter, and forced to eke out a living on the barest scraps, while the likes of you feast in castles?"

"If you don't like it, you're more than welcome to leave," said Monty tightly. "Why stay if it's so dangerous and miserable? I can't for the life of me think why anyone would choose to live in this ghastly place, with boars attacking when you sleep, and magic crushing your heart from the inside out."

"Oh, we should *leave*." Haiden's tone was unnatural now, and he gave a brittle laugh. "What an excellent idea. Why didn't we think of that, Gisela? Shall we just hop along to the forest's edge now, resettle in the city?"

"Leave it, Haiden," said Gisela tightly. She squeezed her eyes open, overcoming her exhaustion enough to send him a silent warning. He was straying very close to topics that shouldn't be touched in present company.

Haiden raised his hands in an angry gesture of surrender, half turning away.

"No, what does that mean?" Otto demanded, his eyes too shrewd as they settled on Haiden. "Why don't you leave if you want to? Can't you?"

"I've just about had enough of this," Haiden said angrily. He cast a glance at his injured sister, and Gisela could see the emotion quivering below the surface of his surly expression. "A bunch of rich, titled, city-dwellers coming into our forest and telling us how we should live and what we should do, as if you have any idea how our lives work."

"You're the one who wanted to travel with them," Gisela reminded him, increasing the pressure on her arm. She hated to complain in front of them all, but she was struggling. "Do you think that medic-trained guard might be free soon?"

"Gisela?" Otto's attention was instantly on her, his presence suddenly warm and near as he stepped close. "Are you all right?"

She swayed forward a little, not fully in control of herself. The next thing she knew, Otto had drawn her against his chest and was supporting her there, his voice anxious.

"I think it's worse than we realized. Monty, get the medic, now."

Gisela didn't fight it, leaning her head gratefully against Otto's shoulder and letting him take her weight. The fuzziness was pulling at the edges of her consciousness, tempting her to give in.

"Stay with me, Gisela," said Otto firmly. "You need to stay awake."

"Look at her clothes." Haiden's voice was scared, making him sound young again. "Look how much blood she's lost. I couldn't see it properly before."

"I'll be fine," said Gisela reassuringly, hating to hear her brother worried. "It does sting, though."

A tutting sound announced the approach of the medic, his unfamiliar voice reaching Gisela through the growing fog.

"Why is she still upright? Lie her down over here. We need a tourniquet on that arm." The guard clucked his tongue. "I don't like the look of that."

"What do you mean?" Otto sounded almost as alarmed as Haiden had. "Is it a bad wound?"

"The wound itself doesn't look serious," said the guard. "Although it's not a clean cut at all—those boars have brutal tusks. It must sting like wildfire."

"It does," Gisela confirmed, keeping her eyes shut against the spinning in her head.

It took her a moment to even realize that she was being carried, and she'd hardly grasped that fact when the motion stopped, and someone laid her flat. Otto, she was fairly sure. There was something different about his touch from anyone else's. It was warmer, somehow. More comforting.

She gave her head a little shake. What nonsense was she thinking?

"The issue is the blood loss," the medic went on. "It should really have been treated straight away, but...well." He sighed. "We were fleeing a pack of savage boars, so there's only so much you can do."

"Herd," Gisela corrected vaguely.

"If you say so, love," said the medic. He was a middle-aged man, and she found his confident tone comforting.

Gisela let her mind drift as he worked on her arm, reassuring the prince as he did so that no members of the party had suffered lasting injuries. The medic was about her father's age, probably. With his pale skin and close-cropped hair, he didn't look like her father, but if she closed her eyes, she could almost imagine the capable hands tending to her wound belonged to Papa.

What would he think if he could see her now? He'd be worried, but he wouldn't fuss. He never fussed. He'd tend to her injuries in a business-like manner, then set about teaching her better, showing her how to more successfully defend herself next time. Perhaps he'd finally make her a bigger bow, as he'd promised to do.

"Haiden," Gisela said vaguely.

"Yes, I'm here, Gisela." Her brother's hand was suddenly gripping hers.

"We should tell Papa, don't you think? He'll want to make sure the boars are clear from the area."

"Gisela..." Haiden hesitated, and Gisela frowned. What was he reluctant to tell her? "Gisela, Papa's not here. Remember?"

"Oh." Gisela stilled as memory crashed back in. "Oh. Of course. I don't know what I was thinking. I thought...I thought maybe he was coming for us. He used to always come and find us when—"

"Gisela." Haiden's voice sounded a little desperate as he cut her off. "Gisela, I think you're confused. You shouldn't try to talk. You should just rest."

"Yes." Gisela let her mind relax, slipping toward the blissful oblivion tugging at her. "Haiden, are you safe? Are we somewhere safe now?"

"Yes, Gisela." Her brother's voice was soft and very sad. "We're safe for now. You can rest."

With a deep sigh, Gisela succumbed at last.

# CHAPTER NINE

# Gisela

Gisela woke in dappled light, blinking up at the sky in confusion. She didn't recognize the area, and her first thought was for her brother. Where was Haiden? She had a vague sense of him being missing, or not safe. With a groan, she pushed herself to a sitting position.

"Whoa, easy, easy." Monty's friendly voice greeted her from one side, and she looked over at him anxiously. Where were the others?

"Monty? Where's Haiden?"

Monty shook his head, a wry smile playing at his lips. "Otto was right," he muttered.

"What?" Gisela asked, confused, and Monty smiled at her.

"Never mind. Haiden is fine. He's right over there, with Lady Louisa. I think she's put him to work, helping to make more arrows for the hunters."

"Ah," said Gisela, following his pointing hand and recognizing her brother's frame, seated on a boulder and bent over something. "That was a smart idea. He's very good at making arrows."

"Is he?" Monty asked brightly. "That's a bonus, then. I think the main purpose was just to occupy him. He's been very anxious about you, and driving us all crazy in the process."

"About me?" Gisela asked, putting a hand to her aching head. "Why..."

She trailed off as she remembered the night before. Looking down, she realized that her arm had been neatly bandaged, and now looked clean. The same couldn't be said for the rest of her.

"Yes, I'm afraid you're still in your blood-soaked clothes," Monty said apologetically. "Haiden assured us you'd have spares in your pack, but Valerie has also offered to give you some of hers if you have a need."

"That was very kind," said Gisela uncomfortably. She moved her arm experimentally. "It barely stings."

"That's also Valerie's doing," said Monty, sounding as proud as if he'd done it. "She's quite good with healing magic. Top five in her class, I've heard."

"Oh." Gisela couldn't think of anything to say, her mind too busy going over the events of the night before. Her eyes widened as certain things came back to her. "Monty, I remember getting pretty confused from the pain last night. Did I say anything embarrassing?"

"Last night?" he repeated sympathetically. "That wasn't last night. You've been unconscious for two weeks."

"WHAT?" Gisela sat straight upright, her mouth falling open in horror.

"I'm only teasing you," Monty laughed. "I'm sorry. Otto told me not to be annoying, but I couldn't help myself. It *was* last night. You slept through breakfast, but not by much."

Gisela relaxed, glaring at him. "Don't think I didn't notice that you failed to answer my question."

Monty gave a low whistle. "You're sharp, I'll give you that."

"Or maybe I'm just not as easily distracted by your supposed charm as city girls," said Gisela.

He laughed. "Ouch. You and Valerie should team up. I'll have no ego at all by the time this expedition is over."

Gisela couldn't help smiling. "I don't think it'll do you any great harm. Now answer my question."

"You said some strange things, but nothing too embarrassing," Monty said. "I guess you should ask your brother, since he's more likely than I am to know what will embarrass you."

Gisela winced, but didn't press the point. Bringing Monty's attention to the more dangerous parts of her rambling speech was the opposite of what she wanted to do.

"You mentioned Otto," she said instead. "Where is he?"

"He joined a scouting party," said Monty. "They should be back pretty soon, but he asked me to keep an eye on you while he's gone."

"He asked *us*," Valerie corrected, appearing behind him and shooing him away. "And I'm sure Gisela has had more than enough of your company." She took his vacated place, smiling at Gisela. "Sorry. I wasn't paying attention, or I would have taken over from him as soon as you woke."

"I appreciate the thought, but I don't need constant supervision," said Gisela, amused.

"Actually, according to the medic, you do," Valerie said matter-of-factly. "He wasn't too pleased when you passed out last night, and we're all under strict instructions to keep an eye on you." She waved a hand. "And the others, of course." Gisela followed her gaze to see a few guards with bandaged limbs or torsos, sitting together under a nearby tree, stringing bows and sharpening swords.

"But they're allowed to do something useful," Gisela protested.

"Well, life's not fair," said Valerie cheerfully. "I say you should take every opportunity to embrace it being unfair in your favor."

"Well, there's something in that," Gisela acknowledged, leaning back against a stump. "It's not often I get to lie around after the sun's risen."

"So I imagine," said Valerie. "But enough chitchat. I'm glad for the chance to talk to you, Gisela, because there's something I particularly want to ask you."

"Oh?" Gisela asked, watching idly as a leaf floated down from a nearby tree. "What's that?"

"Are you a singer?"

"What?" Gisela sat fully upright again, trying to keep her alarm inside as she searched the other girl's eyes. "A singer? Me? Why would you ask that?"

"That's not an answer," Valerie pointed out. "Are you?"

Gisela hesitated for only the fraction of a second. If Valerie was onto them, she'd rather the other girl think Gisela the singer than find out it was Haiden. But if there was any chance she didn't know, Gisela should do all she could to keep it that way.

"No, I'm not," she said. "Not even the tiniest bit."

Valerie laughed. "You either are or you aren't. There's no way to be a little bit a singer."

"Well, how should I know that?" Gisela demanded. "I've answered your question, now you answer mine. Why would you ask if I'm a singer?"

"Because of something that happened before we met you," Valerie said, in her refreshingly straightforward way. "We passed through an elf settlement further south. Otto was after information on where to find the Imperator, and the leader of the settlement wanted to make an exchange in order to answer his question."

"Of course," Gisela muttered.

Valerie smiled. "We expected that. What none of us expected, however, was for the elf to ask for information about me."

Gisela felt her forehead crease as she studied the singer's face.

"You? I thought you were from the city. What interest would elves of Ilgal have in you?"

"None at all, I'm fairly sure," Valerie responded calmly. "I was just as confused by their questions as anyone. Or at least, I was then. After we met you and your brother, I started to wonder if I might have my answer."

"I don't understand what you mean," Gisela said warily. She couldn't see where the other girl was going with her comments, and she didn't like it.

"The information the elf wanted was whether I'm a singer, and whether I have a brother."

"And do you?" Gisela asked blankly, still lost.

"I don't," Valerie said, seeming amused. "But that's not the point. The point is that you do have a brother."

"Maybe it's the blood loss, but I don't follow," said Gisela flatly.

Valerie shifted into a more comfortable position. "I don't think the questions had anything to do with me at all. I think they were just trying to figure out if I was someone else. Someone they're looking for." She gave Gisela a pointed look. "Someone who's a young woman, a singer, and traveling with her brother."

Gisela's heart sped up, but she fought to keep her expression politely confused. "If that's so, it's not me," she said. "Because I'm most definitely not a singer. And there's no reason I can think of that the elves would be interested in me."

Valerie considered her for a long moment before nodding.

"All right. I'm not sorry to be wrong. It didn't strike me as a good thing to have the elves making clandestine inquiries about you."

Gisela mustered a smile. "Definitely not a good thing."

"Well, I'll give you some space," Valerie said. "I'm sure you want some time to gather your thoughts after what you went through last night. And I'm guessing you want to change. There's a small brook that way, not far through the trees."

"Thank you," Gisela said, trying to speak naturally.

Valerie nodded. "In the meantime, I'll let the medic know that you're awake."

Gisela stared unseeingly after the other girl as she walked away. Was it possible that Valerie's interpretation of the elves' request was correct? The very possibility made sweat bead on Gisela's forehead.

Of course, what she'd told Valerie was true. She wasn't a singer, and technically speaking, there was no reason for the elves to be interested in her. But the words were misleading. If they were interested in Haiden, then they might be interested in her as a means of getting to him. But why would they be interested in Haiden? He was a singer, sure, but the elves didn't care about that. They had their own means of harnessing the power of magic, by mining it from the ground and distilling it into talismans. It was a practice no other creatures were allowed to undertake, so elves had total monopoly on mined magic. And there was certainly no shortage in Ilgal.

The only thing Gisela knew of that might set Haiden apart from other singers was the prophecy about him made by Asivah, of the royal elves. She didn't understand what interest the reclusive creatures would have in a prediction regarding the human kingdom in which they arguably lived, but then, she didn't pretend to fully understand Asivah's words. Could the tale have been garbled in the telling, so that anyone searching for the pair of now-grown children might think it was the sister who was a singer, or perhaps both of them?

The idea that her exiled existence with Haiden might be targeted by not only the unscrupulous humans their parents assured them would want to exploit a singer, but also the powerful, inscrutable elves, terrified her.

If the elves were searching for them, their plan of approaching the Imperator's settlement was madness. She didn't need to know the reason they were being sought to know that they didn't want to be found. She would have to speak to Haiden.

Her eyes traveled across the clearing to where her brother sat chatting cheerfully with Lady Louisa.

Gisela struggled to her feet, wincing at the stiffness in her limbs. She realized as she rose that she'd been laid out on a bedroll. She wondered who among the party from Terenford had given up their bed for her. It made her uncomfortable to have benefitted at the cost of someone else, but she pushed the thought aside. Her immediate priority was getting into clean clothes. The ones she wore were so covered in her own blood, she feared they might be beyond recovery.

Having retrieved her pack, she hurried through the trees in the direction Valerie had indicated. To her relief, the brook wasn't far and it was, for the moment, abandoned. Gisela didn't dare attempt a full wash with the camp so near, but she took the chance to wash the blood from her hands and arms before completing a rapid change of clothes.

Feeling much better, she returned to the camp, moving through the trees until she emerged near Haiden and Lady Louisa. She passed three guards on the way, all of whom nodded to her while barely taking their eyes from the foliage in front of them. Clearly the head guard didn't intend to be taken by surprise for a second time, an attitude Gisela approved of.

"Gisela!" Haiden rose as soon as he spotted her, embracing her in a tighter squeeze than he'd given her in years. "How are you feeling?"

"I'm fine," she told him. "Nothing a bit of rest and a few good nights' sleep won't fix."

Haiden didn't look convinced. "I'll accept that when I hear it from the medic."

"A wise course," Lady Louisa approved. She dipped her head in greeting to Gisela, not shifting from the boulder where she was sharpening arrows with surprising deftness. "Good morning, Gisela. I'm glad to see you upright and with us again."

"So am I," Haiden agreed. "You looked pretty bad last night, Sis. I've never seen you pass out like that before."

She made a face. "I'm sorry I gave you a scare. My memory is a little hazy. Did you carry me, Haiden? When did you get so strong?"

"That wasn't me." To Gisela's embarrassment, Haiden seemed to be watching her face closely. "It was Prince Otto. He picked you right up and carried you across the clearing."

"Oh."

Gisela couldn't think of anything else to say, painfully aware that her cheeks were heating. He was right. She could recall it now, the sensation of safety and her vague awareness that it must surely be out of place given who had her in his grip.

"Monty told me that a scouting party is out right now," she said, trying valiantly to salvage the conversation. "Why are we all waiting for them, instead of moving while they scout ahead, like usual?"

Haiden looked at her like she'd lost her mind. "Because you were unconscious, for one thing."

"It's not just that," Lady Louisa chimed in. "We can't easily move forward as a group, because it seems we don't quite know where we are."

"The forest paths led us a merry dance, did they?" Gisela asked grimly, settling herself beside Haiden as he resumed his seat. "I can't say I'm surprised."

"Yes, they do seem to have been fickle," said Lady Louisa, showing no great signs of concern. "We're not entirely sure we were going as northward as we might have wished. The scouting party is hoping to ascertain that."

Gisela's eyes drifted thoughtfully to Haiden. He'd returned to his task and didn't seem aware that she was trying to get his attention.

"So why did you bring the fan into the forest, Lady Louisa?" Haiden asked, probably continuing whatever conversation she'd interrupted. "They might be common in Terenford, but they're much too delicate for the forest. It doesn't even get very hot here!"

Lady Louisa just smiled. "A lady should never be without her fan."

"If you say so," Haiden said doubtfully, still oblivious to Gisela's attempt to catch his eye.

"Lady Louisa," Gisela said, "I apologize for my rudeness, but could I please speak with my brother alone for a moment?"

"Certainly, child," said Lady Louisa. "Nothing rude about that." She laid her arrows aside, brushing off her skirts as she rose. She alone among the women present seemed to prefer to wear gowns, even in the forest.

"What's up, Gisela?" Haiden asked, when the older woman had moved away. "Is it your injury? I knew you couldn't be as all right as you're pretending."

"Nonsense, I'm fine," said Gisela dismissively. "It's not that. It's just that I'm worried, Haiden."

"There's a change," he said, although he spoke with less than his usual snarkiness. There were some benefits to getting injured and alarming everyone, it seemed.

Ignoring the quip, Gisela quickly outlined what Valerie had said, watching as her brother's frown grew.

"I don't see the cause for concern," he told her. "That could be about anyone. There's no reason to connect the elf's questions to us."

"And yet, Valerie did," Gisela pointed out.

Haiden didn't seem troubled. "That's because we're the only brother and sister she's met in Ilgal." He must have seen she wasn't convinced, and he shrugged. "I guess we'll find out one way or another when we get to the central settlement."

"That's what has me worried," Gisela said. "I don't think we should go there, Haiden. Maybe it's for the best that we're off course. We never promised to go all the way there with them."

"No way." Haiden's response was predictably strong. "I'm going, Gisela. I want answers. I don't want to go back to how it was. I can't live the rest of my life that way."

"What other choice is there?" Gisela demanded. "We weren't living as hermits for fun, Haiden!"

"The other choice is to stop hiding and running, and face whatever comes our way," Haiden insisted. "We're strong enough to take it."

"Strong?" Gisela stared at him. "Haiden, we're more vulnerable than we've ever been."

"We're not," he scoffed. "We're traveling with the crown prince and three dozen armed guards."

"All of whom could turn on us at any moment," Gisela murmured. "We're completely in their power, Haiden."

Her brother shook his head. "You have serious trust issues, Gisela."

She bit back the retort that started to rise. That was easy for Haiden to say. She'd shielded him from the ill intentions of others for as long as she could remember. She knew none of it was really his fault, but it was hard not to feel resentful when he threw it in her face.

"Can you still feel the stones?" she asked instead.

Haiden nodded. "Of course. But I'm not going home, Gisela. I want to see this through."

"Maybe you should call them," Gisela said. "Can you leave one at the site where we hid our gear, but bring the rest to you? We can find our way home from that spot. But it might be worth having the others, in case we need to use them."

Haiden closed his eyes, frowning in concentration. Gisela watched uneasily as his brow furrowed further. Something was wrong.

"What is it?" she asked.

He opened his eyes again, his gaze apologetic. "I've been ignoring them," he said. "I assumed they'd all be where we left them. But they're not. Most of them still form a sort of trail in my mind, between our hunting location and where we left our gear. But one—I think the one that was with the gear—is somewhere else entirely. I think someone took it. It could have been picked up by an animal..."

He trailed off, and Gisela sighed.

"More likely someone found and stole our gear, and accidentally took the rock as well.

"Yes." Haiden grimaced. "That's what I think, too."

"Oh well," Gisela said heavily. "None of it was irreplaceable. We'll just have to hope they didn't scout far enough around the gear to find our current home and take the rest of our stuff. When we finally make it back, we'll have to go in with caution. Would we be able to find our way back home from the last rock in the trail you can feel?"

"I'm sure we would," said Haiden. "I'll leave that one, and call the rest. Should I call the one that's all on its own?"

After a moment's reflection, Gisela shook her head. "If

someone has it, they might notice it rolling away, and it would lead them right to us. Better to leave it."

Haiden nodded, closing his eyes again and flexing one hand. Gisela knew he didn't need to do the gesture to activate the object control magic. But it must help center his thoughts.

"They're moving," he murmured at last. "But they're a long way away. I'll have to keep calling them for hours, probably."

"It would be good if you could time it so they reach us when no one's likely to see," Gisela commented.

She scanned the clearing the group had claimed. Everyone seemed engaged in their tasks, no one appearing to watch the siblings. But she had no doubt the guards were aware of their location. They must be keeping a close eye on the newcomers to the group. In their shoes, she would be.

"I'll feel better when we have some resources to our names," she commented, in reference to the stones.

"You've still got the talisman, right?" Haiden asked. "Maybe you should go with the foraging party next time."

Gisela nodded. "Maybe I should."

She didn't elaborate, but mention of the talisman sent her deep into thought. It was a useful object, which she'd never regretted spending their limited funds on. And she certainly didn't regret preventing the prince from eating the berries from the forest path. But she was mystified by the incident. The talisman had been cheap partly because it was very limited. No doubt it was possible to purchase more comprehensive warning talismans, but this one only worked for the carrier and that person's close companions. She'd thought, from the description of the vendor, that closeness was defined by connection rather than proximity. He'd said it related to the level of trust and the nature of the relationship she had with the person in question. She'd understood him to be saying it would respond for her or her brother only.

It had therefore been both surprising and unsettling when the magic had prodded her in response to Prince Otto's actions. And she didn't want to advertise its function too widely, because she wasn't at all confident it would cover the rest of the group. She couldn't even explain why it had covered the prince.

Was it the magic that had defied her understanding, or her own heart?

# CHAPTER TEN

# Otto

Otto peered through the leaves, seeing nothing of interest through the dense foliage. It was a very good thing that Norris's guards included much more experienced trackers than him. He'd probably been foolish to insist on coming on this scouting expedition. He knew that Norris hadn't relished it. No doubt the head guard would prefer to be back at camp, directing preparations rather than forced to join the scouts himself. But where the prince went, Norris went. That had been made very clear throughout their journey, and Otto guessed the head guard had received very specific instructions from his father.

He had an uncomfortable suspicion that if saving Otto meant abandoning the whole rest of the party to their deaths, Norris wouldn't hesitate. He'd certainly been quick to leave the group to the mercies of the galboars the night before to come looking for Otto in the forest.

It was all the more reason for Otto to be sensible and cautious, and he probably should have stayed with the main group. But he'd felt the need for some space and thinking time, away from everyone else.

All right, full honesty...away from Gisela. Watching her sleeping form was bringing up all kinds of uncomfortable emotions. Otto's forehead creased in a frown as he once again remembered the night before. Her injury had been distressing, and even he had been taken aback by the panic that had flooded him when she'd collapsed in his arms.

He knew his reaction was heightened by guilt. He'd been lecturing her, and listening to Monty bicker with Haiden, just generally wasting time while she teetered on the brink of consciousness. He should have paid more attention. He'd had no idea how much blood she'd lost, or how deeply the galboar had speared her with its tusks.

But it wasn't just her physical injuries that made his heart ache. Her confusion and distress had been worse. She always seemed so steady, so capable. The walls around her were thick, and nothing seemed to rattle her. But when she'd been fading, a glimpse of vulnerability had shown, and it had speared Otto right through the heart. He hadn't missed the nervous way Haiden had tried to stop her from mentioning their father, either. There was clearly a great deal more to their story than Otto knew. What had they endured, left alone to fend for themselves in the woods since they were children? Through what crisis of tragedy or neglect had they found themselves alone in the first place?

And why did they both seem afraid, not just of the dangers around them, but of exposure? Some part of Otto knew that he would be wise to be cautious of the pair. Whatever they weren't saying, they were hiding for a reason. Some would argue that those with nothing to hide wouldn't fear exposure. But he didn't want to assume the worst of Gisela and Haiden. He preferred to be trusting, even if it meant he had to deal with the consequences when he was wrong.

That was just how he'd felt with Rosa, and it had paid off

there. When his father married his stepmother, gaining him a stepsister his own age, his friends had warned him to be careful of how the fifteen-year-old girl might exploit him and his position. But Otto, heart raw from so many years of loneliness with only his endlessly busy father, had been desperately eager for a family. He hadn't hesitated to take the risk of exposing himself to her rejection. And even when she'd proven resistant to accepting the relationship between them, he'd persisted. Eventually she had overcome her reluctance to embrace her new life, and now he considered her his closest friend.

He just hoped he could get through to Gisela with persistence as well, because she seemed even more desperately in need of a friend than Rosa had.

"What's your conclusion?"

The curt voice of Norris drew Otto from his abstraction. Another guard was descending from the tree into which he'd climbed some minutes before.

"I'm almost sure of it, sir. We're well off course. Miles to the east of where we thought we were."

Norris blew out an irritated breath. "How is that possible?"

"I imagine the forest paths are to blame," Otto chipped in. "Gisela did warn us that they're fickle, and might lead us astray."

Norris frowned. "But we were checking our direction regularly yesterday, and the whole time we were on the forest path, we continued to travel north."

"But we didn't check anything last night, when we used one of these paths to flee the galboars," Otto pointed out.

"That wasn't a long journey," Norris protested. "We couldn't have traveled this far off course in that time." He looked to the scout who'd been up the tree. "Don't you agree?"

The man shrugged. "Not on an ordinary path, we couldn't, sir. But there's magic at work in these forest paths, and I won't pretend to understand it."

"We should ask Gisela and Haiden," Otto said. "As well as Valerie. Maybe they can give us more insight. But I don't think it's outside the realm of possibility that our short flight on the path last night took us a much greater distance than is logical."

"If we could harness that to our advantage, it would be very convenient," Norris grunted.

Otto gave a laugh that wasn't as light as his usual one. "It would, wouldn't it? That could be another question for our new additions. They might have experienced something like this before. Remember the day we met them? They said they'd been out hunting and due to a misadventure had ended up a long way from their intended destination. We never asked how they got so far off course in such a short time. Maybe they wandered onto one of these paths."

"There are a lot of things we never asked them, Your Highness," said Norris, in the disapproving tone he always used when speaking of the siblings. "You know my views on the matter. I don't believe we need their assistance at all."

"Yes, I know how you feel about it," Otto said patiently. "And I take your concerns seriously. But I have no intention of casting them off. To be frank, I'm not sure how you can argue that we don't need their assistance when listening to Gisela's advice last night would have spared us an attack that could easily have cost some of our lives."

Norris closed his mouth with a snap, apparently chastened. Otto felt a little guilty for the older man's chagrin—after all, he could have ordered Norris to follow Gisela's advice, and he'd chosen not to do so—but he didn't take his words back. He thought Norris was unfairly prejudiced against Gisela and Haiden, and it would be good for him to acknowledge his own fallibility.

"It seems we have our answer about our location," Otto went

on. "We should head back to camp and regroup. We'll need to trek west before we can continue north."

The scout who'd gone up the tree nodded. "I think you're right, Your Highness. The map shows a significant swampy area in this region, and I already see the first signs of it. We'll have to go west to skirt to its south, then turn northward again."

Otto nodded, falling into step behind Norris, who was retracing their steps. The head guard had his blade out, and his eyes were constantly scanning the area for threats. Otto had thought him fully focused, and was therefore surprised when the older man spoke.

"I imagine I seem overly suspicious to you, Your Highness," he said, not taking his eyes from the foliage ahead. "But it's that suspicion that makes me valuable to your father. He assigned me to this role because he trusts me to exercise sound judgment."

"I know, Norris," Otto said. "And I'm grateful for your capable protection. But if you'll allow me the impertinence, your suspicion frees me not to be suspicious. And I like it that way."

Norris shot a quick look at the prince, then nodded slowly, his eyes returning to the undergrowth ahead. He looked marginally more relaxed at the realization that Otto's decision to trust the newcomers was intentional rather than oblivious.

"We all have our roles, Your Highness."

The group walked on for several more minutes before Norris spoke again, his voice gruff this time.

"I saw what you did last night, Your Highness. Giving up your bedroll for the forest girl. That wasn't necessary. Any of my men would have given ours if you'd asked, including myself. We'd prefer it over seeing you go without."

Otto smiled wryly. "I'm sure you would, but don't begrudge me the small act of generosity." He gave a small sigh. "One of the many things my father has taught me is that it's the duty and the privilege of a ruler to make sacrifices for his people. He told me that there will be many times when, for the benefit of the kingdom, I must step back and let others take the risks and make the sacrifices in my place, as uncomfortable as it might feel. He also told me that when that's not the case, when there's no barrier to doing it myself, I should never shirk it. On the contrary, I should take every chance, because self-denial is a discipline a king must practice for himself, as no one else can or will teach it to him."

He threw Norris an amused glance. "And I'd say the topic in question falls into that latter category, wouldn't you? Giving up my bedroll so that Gisela could sleep off her injury in the minuscule comfort it offers wasn't exactly riding into battle unnecessarily and risking my life."

Norris was silent for so long, Otto assumed he was trying to think of how to respectfully word his disagreement with everything Otto had said. But the head guard surprised him.

"King Ryker is a good king."

Otto nodded readily. "He is."

"And so will you be, Your Highness, when your time comes."

"I...thank you." Otto could think of nothing else to say. He was taken aback by the praise, but gratified. Norris wasn't someone who bestowed his good opinions liberally.

When the group finally emerged into the clearing, Otto found his eyes drawn at once to the bedroll he'd laid by the fire. His heart thudded strangely when he saw it was empty, and he scanned the clearing swiftly.

There she was, sitting with her brother to one side of the clearing, looking—at least at a glance—none the worse for wear. As he studied her from a distance, she looked up, her eyes finding his, and her form going still.

Otto forced himself to look away, concerned his fixation on her would become obvious to everyone. Norris was already calling some of his other more senior guards to him to share the scouting party's conclusions.

"I'll notify Monty and the others," said Otto, breaking away from the group.

He made his way to where Monty and Valerie were attempting to help prepare food, apparently to the great annoyance of the highly capable guard who usually took charge of the process. As Otto drew close, Lady Louisa appeared, a question in her eyes.

"Yes, we were right." Otto's words encompassed Monty and Valerie as well. "We seem to have been carried a significant distance off course by the forest path last night. We're much too far to the east."

His eyes were drawn once again to where Gisela and Haiden were sitting. They were watching the group avidly, but neither seemed certain of whether they were welcome to join. To Otto's relief, Valerie spoke up.

"Gisela and Haiden will know more about this than we do." The singer followed Otto's gaze and beckoned to the pair. "Oi, come join us!"

The brother and sister rose at once, hurrying over to the group with curious expressions. When Valerie repeated what Otto had said, they both nodded, looking resigned.

"We should probably have foreseen that," Haiden commented. "We were in a state of chaos when we took the forest path last night. Especially vulnerable to the magic's malice. If it was inclined to be malicious."

"Which apparently it was," Gisela chimed in.

Valerie frowned. "We don't know that. Just because it took us on a different course doesn't mean it meant us harm."

"You're all out of your minds," Monty said, a hint of humor in his bewildered voice. "It's just magic—a raw force to be molded and harnessed by those with the ability, and turned to their will. Surely it doesn't have plans and intentions of its own."

"I forgot you were such an expert on magic," said Haiden pleasantly.

Valerie grinned. "Oh yes, didn't you know? When his father donates money to the academy, the learning just trickles straight into Lord Montague's head."

"That's quite enough criticism of the earl's generosity, thank you," said Lady Louisa tartly, giving Valerie's shoulder a light rap with her closed fan. "Especially coming from one who benefited from it throughout years of study."

Valerie fell silent, biting her lip.

"I don't see what difference it makes whether the magic of the paths had good or bad intentions," the older woman went on. "The question is simply what do we do next?"

"You're right, Lady Louisa," Otto agreed, once again grateful to her for cutting short Monty and Valerie's latest battle. "It would make most sense to take a northwesterly direction from here, but it seems that we're near the border of a large area of swamp that falls between us and the center of the forest. We'll need to travel due west until we get around it, then continue north."

"Will we take the paths again?" Lady Louisa asked.

Otto turned to Gisela. "What do you think?"

She exchanged a look with her brother before answering. "I think there are benefits and there are risks. It's simply a matter of deciding which outweighs the other."

"But what would you do?" Otto pressed.

"I'd take the paths, for certain," said Haiden confidently.

Gisela thought for a moment longer before answering. "I think I would, too. We're such a large group, and traveling with mounts. Our progress will be impossibly slow otherwise."

Otto nodded. "I'm inclined to agree. It hasn't escaped me

that although the paths took us away from our desired course, they did safely carry us out of the galboars' territory. I'm not sure we should conclude that the magic meant to harm us. For all we know, this roundabout route will keep us clear of the creatures all the way to the central elf settlement."

"Ah, Otto," Monty chuckled. "Always determined to be trusting, aren't you?"

"An instinct that's proved right much more often than your teasing would suggest," Otto countered calmly. He noticed that Gisela was looking between the two friends with a veiled expression, but he didn't comment.

"Do we have any idea of what's out this way?" Lady Louisa asked. "Other than the swamp, I mean."

"I'm afraid not," said Otto, with a hopeful look at Gisela.

She shook her head. "We've never been this far north before. I've heard of the swamp, but I don't know anything about what we'll find."

"Well, I suppose we'll find out tomorrow," Otto said. "Norris has decided we should stay here for the rest of the day to regroup. He'll send out hunting and foraging parties, and the rest of us can assist with maintenance and restocking."

Everyone murmured agreement, dispersing to their various tasks. Otto noticed that Haiden sidled up to talk to Valerie, causing Monty to follow. Shaking his head, he turned to find Gisela watching him silently.

Fighting down awkwardness, he moved toward her. "How are you feeling?"

"I'm fine," she said, too quickly. She cleared her throat. "Thank you for your help last night."

"I didn't do anything requiring thanks," said Otto. "I'm just glad you're all right. You gave us a scare." His eyes traveled to the bandage the medic had applied after she passed out the night before. "Does your arm hurt a lot?"

She shook her head. "Barely at all. That reminds me, I forgot to thank Valerie. Monty told me that she helped the healing along." She swung her arm in a low circle. "I can tell."

"Oh?" Otto tilted his head to the side. "You've experienced healing song before?"

"I...uh, yes. Once or twice," Gisela said, not meeting his eye.

"From whom?" Otto asked, a note of eagerness in his voice. "Did you pay at a market, or are there singers who do the rounds offering healing? We've barely encountered a single singer in Ilgal."

"Yes, I think many of them have left," said Gisela, glossing over his original question. She seemed ill-at-ease, and, feeling daring, Otto raised a hand to gently touch her shoulder.

"Are you all right, Gisela?"

Her eyes flew to his, and for a moment she stayed in place, their gazes locked. The previous night flashed again through Otto's mind, the memory of her face pressed into his back as they fled from the galboars on Bullion, the feel of her leaning into him when she began to lose consciousness. The remembered sensations created a bewildering mix of awkwardness and elation, and it was impossible to keep them fully separate from the current moment.

Then Gisela shifted slightly backward out of his reach, and Otto quickly let his hand fall. The last thing he wanted to do was press her.

"To tell the truth," said Gisela curtly, "now that I know we're not nearly as close to the elves' settlement as we thought, I'm reluctant to continue further north. Finding the Imperator is not a priority to me, and I'm not convinced you need our help."

"You would most definitely be a big loss to us, but of course I understand your feelings," Otto said, trying not to let his disappointment show. "You're perfectly free to leave at any time."

"If only I was."

The muttered words made Otto frown. "What do you mean by that?"

"Only that my brother doesn't agree with me," Gisela said quickly and unconvincingly. "Haiden is determined to continue, and there's no point me leaving without him."

"No," said Otto lightly, watching her face more closely than ever. "I've heard from your own lips that protecting him is your only job."

The hint of a wince passed across Gisela's face, and Otto silently chastised himself. It had been clear that Gisela wasn't entirely in her right mind the night before. She likely regretted the things she'd let slip, and desperately curious as Otto was about her revelations, it would be unchivalrous to push for information.

"I suppose the gallant thing to do would be to offer to help persuade him," he added, still speaking in the same light tone. "But I'm too selfish to do it. I much prefer having you both with our party, especially as we head into unknown territory off our chosen path."

Gisela gave a rueful smile. "I wouldn't dream of asking it of you. Neither our safety nor my plans are your responsibility. And I don't think Haiden would listen to persuasion, anyway. He's at the age when you know everything."

"Ah, yes," said Otto reminiscently. "I remember it well. I miss that age, honestly. Life was much simpler when I was fourteen, and nothing could dim my confidence."

That earned him a more genuine smile. "Fifteen, actually. Don't let him hear you aging him down."

"My mistake," said Otto gravely. He shook his head, a smile playing around his lips. "And I take it back. Fifteen was right around the age when I rapidly found out that I knew nothing at all. Particularly when it came to girls."

Gisela threw him a startled look, and he laughed.

"I'm not talking about sweethearts," he clarified. "I'm talking about my sister. Stepsister, technically. We were both fifteen when our parents married, and she didn't let my rank slow her down in the slightest in her mission to put me in my place."

"Ah yes." Gisela nodded. "I remember hearing about the king's second marriage, and the stepdaughter he acquired. Five years ago, wasn't it?"

Otto nodded, surprised at the accuracy of her memory.

"It was a...tumultuous time for Haiden and me," she said softly. "We heard about it at a market...the first we'd been to since being out on our own. Every detail of that gathering is vivid in my mind, although it was unremarkable in itself."

"The two of you have been living alone in the forest for five years?" Otto asked. His heart ached for her as his mind performed some calculations. "Since your brother was ten? You must have only been—"

"Thirteen," Gisela said unemotionally. "But we managed all right. It was an improvement in our situation. I still hold to that."

"I'm sorry," said Otto, not knowing what else to say. "You were so young...I can't even imagine how difficult that must have been."

"No, I'm guessing you can't," said Gisela, her tone humorous, but too dry for true mirth.

Otto hesitated, sensing the need to proceed delicately. "I won't pretend to understand your life. But I do sympathize."

"Of course," said Gisela. "I know that it's the duty of a ruler to see to the wellbeing of his people."

Her face was unpleasantly emotionless now. They'd somehow strayed onto uncomfortable ground, but Otto was still determined to persist. He frowned slightly, wondering how to get through to her.

"It is, but it's not just about duty, Gisela. I really do care about Ilgal." He smiled. "Although I'll confess that prior to this expedition, I've been known to shy away from it in a most cowardly way. Rosa used to make fun of me for it whenever I refused to join her on her trips into Ilgal. But habit is hard to break, you know, and I think I became a little too fond of the comforts of life in the castle."

"I don't doubt it." Gisela's voice was unarguably cold now, and Otto could tell that his attempt to lighten the mood by self-deprecation had failed dismally.

"But I do care," he hurried on. "That's why I begged my father to let me lead this expedition." His eyes bored into hers. "I'm sure it must seem absurd to you to see us sheltered city-dwellers tramping through the forest, trying to solve problems we know nothing about. But even though I've never lived in the forest, I'm not completely disconnected. My stepsister was born in Ilgal, and still has a very close connection here. She might not live in the forest anymore, but members of her family still do, and I care about them and their wellbeing deeply. I'm not as removed as you might think. She taught me how important the forest way of life is to all the people of this region. I'll admit I never understood her love for the forest before I came here, but I think I'm starting to understand. In spite of its dangers and challenges, it's mesmerizing, isn't it?"

An emotion was growing behind Gisela's eyes as he spoke, and he couldn't read what it was.

"How pleasant," she said when he finished, her tone stilted. "I'm so glad your father's marriage could give you a taste of admiring our forest from the comfort of your castle."

Otto bit his lip. "I've offended you. That wasn't my intention."

"Not at all," Gisela said quickly, dipping her head in a gesture that was clearly meant to be respectful, but felt colder to Otto than her voice. "You've given me more consideration than I have any right to expect from royalty. I spoke out of turn, and I apologize."

She started to turn away, but Otto's hand shot out, once again gripping her arm.

"No, please speak freely," he said quickly. "I always want you to be honest with me, Gisela. You don't have to tread carefully around me. I swear I'm not prone to royal wrath. And I truly want to understand the thoughts behind your words."

She paused, studying his face for a thoughtful moment, then turned back toward him.

"Like I said, I've heard about the king's marriage. I know that the queen and her daughter came from the forest. I've even heard of your stepsister's paternal grandparents. Everyone has. They're the best known and most profitable timber producers in Ilgal. Maybe in Terenford they seem like forest rustics—I even remember the rumors that the court turned their noses up at the new queen and princess."

Otto felt his mouth set in a thin line. He wished he could deny her words, but he remembered vividly some of the sly insults his stepmother and Rosa had endured after joining the royal family. He honestly thought the memories pained him more than they did Rosa.

"Any who did were quickly put in their place," he said shortly. "The queen has the full respect of her subjects now."

"I'm glad," said Gisela, although she sounded closer to indifference. "And I'm sure it does your father credit. But my point is that in Ilgal terms, they're more like royalty than rustics. Don't they live in a grand old manor that's been passed as an inheritance down the generations? That's the rumor, anyway."

"They do," Otto acknowledged, her meaning gradually sinking in.

"I'm not saying they're not Ilgal folk," Gisela clarified. "And I don't mean anything against them. But they're wealthy and successful, live a stone's throw from the capital, and rub shoulders with royalty. If you'll forgive me for speaking bluntly, it's absurd of you to suggest that your connection with them gives you any concept of the way of life of people like my brother and me. People who survive on what we can hunt and forage, going without food if we don't have success on any given day, moving residences regularly to escape frost or blight, relying on our wits not to be swindled or worse at every market, existing as best we can day to day, with absolutely no hope for any improvement in the future."

She was breathing hard by the end of this rambling speech, and all Otto could do was stare. He felt ashamed of his presumption, but judging by the concern overtaking Gisela's features, she was misinterpreting his silence.

"I apologize," she said quickly. "I had no right to call you absurd. I—"

"Please." Otto held up a hand. "Don't try to take it back. You had every right, and you were absolutely correct. I'm the one who spoke foolishly, and out of turn. And I can only ask you to forgive my insensitivity."

She shook her head, her voice a little thick. "There's nothing to forgive."

"Yes there is." Otto took a step closer. "I fully acknowledge being ignorant, Gisela. But that doesn't mean I don't care. My father and I are both deeply concerned about the growing crisis of the magic here. I'm here to help, or at least to try. I know I'm out of my depth among the trees, but back in Terenford, I really can make things happen. If we find a solution, I can put the wheels in motion, with the full resources of the crown behind me. And that's truly all I'm here for."

Gisela's dark eyes met his, and for a tense moment there was silence. Otto felt like she was trying to read him, and this time he didn't feel as confident of his ability to pass her assessment.

He'd been cocky and foolish, far too convinced of his own merit. He should have seen before now that there was so much he didn't know, and could never comprehend.

"If that's true, I'm grateful to you," she said softly, breaking the spell at last. "We don't have much hope here, and if there's outside help that can improve our situation, I don't think we're too proud to take it."

"Gisela." Otto swallowed, struggling for words. "It breaks my heart to hear you say you have no hope for your future to be any better. You're an intelligent and capable woman with your whole life before you. I don't believe for a moment that things won't get better."

Gisela's smile had a hint of bitterness as she turned away from him. "I became very dramatic in my little speech, didn't I? Haiden and I do fine. We'll be all right."

"I've seen enough of your capabilities to have no doubt you do better than all right," Otto said, refusing to be turned aside. "But that doesn't mean that you don't deserve better. Please, give me an honest answer. Is the growing magic the biggest concern you face?"

Gisela sighed. "It's certainly a big concern. I'll admit, I don't see a way forward."

"Have you ever considered leaving Ilgal?" Otto asked delicately.

There was a long pause before she answered. "We're not leaving the forest."

"I'm not saying I think you should," Otto clarified quickly. "I've never agreed with evacuation as a solution. I understand that for those with Ilgal in their blood, the idea of leaving is almost sacrilegious. I just wondered if—"

"It's not sacrilegious," Gisela cut him off shortly. "But it's not something we're considering."

Her tone made it clear she didn't wish to discuss the matter further. Curbing his raging curiosity, Otto let it drop.

"Well," he said instead, "if you do decide to continue with us, I'll be grateful. And I won't forget your assistance, either. I swear I'll do anything in my power to improve your future and that of your brother."

Gisela gave a wry smile. "You'd best be careful bandying about promises like that. Don't you know these woods are infested with bargain-loving elves?"

"Infested?" Otto said ruefully. "If only. I've been searching for them for days, and I can barely find a single one. They're almost as scarce as singers."

Gisela's smile faltered, her tone becoming more formal. "In any event, thank you for your offer, but Haiden and I have been looking out for ourselves for a long time. As I said, we'll be fine."

And with another dip of the head, she turned and strode away from Otto, leaving him with an empty feeling of dissatisfaction.

# CHAPTER ELEVEN

## Otto

The following day found the party up with the sun, everyone more rested than they had been in weeks, and ready to be on the move again. The medic-trained guard declared his injured fellows well enough for travel, largely thanks to the healing songs of Valerie.

Valerie once again managed to harness a road with her songcraft, a process Otto watched with fascination. It was only after the shimmering trail had solidified, and everyone was mounting their horses, that Otto realized Gisela and Haiden weren't present. A moment later they slipped into sight through the trees, and he thought no more about it. As previously arranged, the siblings were to ride with two of the guards, to give Bullion and Monty's horse a rest. Otto knew it was best for his stallion, but he couldn't help feeling deflated at how eager Gisela had seemed to take up the guard's offer.

He put the matter from his mind, focusing on the road stretching out due west in front of them. Soon the horses had settled into a steady trot, Norris's guards in formation around them. The day was cold but clear, and after an hour or two of riding, Otto could no longer see his breath in front of him.

They stopped regularly to allow Valerie to use her direction-finding song, which confirmed that they were continuing westward. Perhaps the forest paths were more reliable during the day, Otto reflected idly, his eyes on Gisela's dark hair three horses ahead.

On one occasion, when the group started back up after Valerie checked their direction, the singer pulled her horse alongside Otto's.

"So far so good," he commented cheerfully.

She nodded, her eyes thoughtful as they scanned the group ahead of them.

"Is something on your mind?" Otto asked.

She let out a sigh. "Yes, it is, and I'm not sure whether I should tell you."

"Is it a safety concern?" he asked quickly. "Is it about the path, or the direction we're going?"

"No, it's not about the trail." She considered him for a moment. "Forgive me if I'm too blunt, but I saw you and Gisela talking yesterday. And I got the impression that the conversation was intense."

To his annoyance, Otto felt his face heating. "Is there a question in there?"

"I suppose there wasn't, was there?" Valerie bit her lip. "Gisela seemed...worked up. Which is unusual for her. I just wondered...did you explain about what we're doing out here?"

Otto frowned. "That we're trying to develop a plan to alleviate the wild magic? I thought that was common knowledge by now."

"I don't think the nature of the plan is common knowledge," said Valerie. "Have you ever told Gisela—or Haiden—that you're hunting down singers?"

"Hunting down?" Otto raised an eyebrow, amused. "I knew I

should have brought my bow and arrow, but I've never been much good at archery."

Valerie wasn't impressed by his humor. "You know what I mean. Have you explained the details?"

"No, I haven't," said Otto. "It's not exactly a secret, but it was agreed by the Council of Nobles that strategically speaking, we shouldn't advertise the plan until we know whether we can implement it. Reports of their attempts in Selvana are still too preliminary to draw any definite conclusions."

"That's what I thought," said Valerie, nodding. "Well, if you want my advice, don't mention it to Gisela or Haiden. At least, not unless you do it very carefully."

Otto frowned. "Why not? I mean, I wasn't planning to, but why do you say that particularly?"

She drew a deep breath, which she let out as a near groan. "I hope I'm not out of line to tell you this," she muttered.

"Not to pull rank," Otto said mildly, trying to keep his impatience at bay, "but I am the crown prince, and the leader of this expedition. If you know something I don't, you really do need to tell me."

Valerie sighed. "That's what I concluded, and it's why I'm here. But it's a gray area, because it's not something I know. Just something I strongly suspect."

"Which is?" Otto prompted.

She dropped her voice. "That Haiden is a singer."

"What?"

Otto wasn't nearly as successful at keeping his voice low, and several heads swiveled in their direction.

"Sorry," Otto muttered. "But...are you sure?"

"Pretty sure," she said.

"How do you know?"

She raised an arm in a vague gesture. "I can just tell. There are lots of little things. For one, he's fascinated with me, and in spite of Monty's jokes, it doesn't seem to me to be anything to do with romantic interest. For another, I'm fairly sure he's been helping me with the path-finding song."

Otto let out a low whistle. "That's why they were out of sight when you called the path this morning. I thought the forest almost seemed to be singing along with you." His eyes darted to Valerie's. "Gisela?"

She shook her head slowly. "I don't think so. But I get the sense she's as dedicated to keeping his secret as if it were her own."

"It is her own," Otto said absently, his eyes once again on the back of Gisela's head. "She has trouble separating herself from Haiden's wellbeing. I think she's forgotten she exists outside of him."

"Yes." Valerie sounded sad. "They clearly haven't had an easy life, and I think she's shouldered most of their burdens."

Otto nodded, his heart heavy. "Why are they keeping it a secret?"

"There could be a lot of reasons, but the most obvious one is fear," Valerie said. "Fear of exploitation, perhaps. Him being a singer doesn't do as much as you might think to reduce their vulnerability. He obviously hasn't been trained, and I don't think he's very adept at his craft. You should see the way he watches when I sing. It's like he's trying to drink in every detail."

"Thank you for telling me this," said Otto seriously. "I'd much rather know than be in the dark." He ran his mind back over his conversations with Gisela, seeing a number of tense silences and terse answers in a new light. "If nothing else, so that I don't put my foot in it."

"What are you going to do with the information?" Valerie asked.

Otto considered for a moment, his eyes unseeing as they gazed up at the canopy above. "I think I'll just sit on it for now.

I'd prefer to earn their trust enough for them to raise it than confront them with it."

Valerie visibly relaxed. "I think that's wise," she said. "I'm sorry I delayed so long telling you. I didn't want them to be cornered with it, or to make you suspicious of them. I really don't think they pose any threat to us."

"Neither do I," said Otto readily.

Valerie nodded. "I'm glad, not least because it makes me feel less treasonous for keeping it to myself before. I realized that I shouldn't really be making the decision as to whether the information was a security risk."

Otto smiled. "I'll hold off charging you with treason for now, Valerie. But I can't speak for Norris."

"No." Valerie chuckled. "I don't think any of us would dare speak for Norris." She cast a sideways glance at him. "Will you tell him?"

"Not at present," Otto said comfortably. "But you don't need to worry. The information is with me now, and I'll take full responsibility if our silence causes any issues."

Valerie nodded gratefully, letting her horse fall behind his. Otto appreciated the space to think. Valerie's revelation was certainly eye-opening. Although the information related to Haiden, Otto couldn't keep his eyes from Gisela as he pondered it. No wonder she was so protective of her brother, and so wary of giving out information. What part had Haiden's songcraft played in the circumstances that had left them adrift and alone as children? He longed to tell her that she didn't need to hide her secrets from him, that she had nothing to fear from exposure. But he wasn't confident that she trusted him enough yet for that to be wise. He knew from his experience with Rosa that he had a tendency to push too hard. He would do better to let her come to him, difficult as that might be.

The day passed uneventfully, the group setting up camp

before sunset well off the path. The scouts had found an excellent site, next to a small waterfall that tinkled into a forest pool. In fact, Otto had noticed significantly more creeks and ponds throughout the day than in their previous travels. Probably due to their proximity to the swamp.

"It's too bad of us to camp here, really," Haiden commented as evening approached, lying back against a bedroll. Otto had noticed that while Gisela seemed to always feel compelled to find a way to help—whether needed or not—Haiden apparently reveled in the chance to be idle. Not that he blamed the fifteen-year-old.

"Why's that?" Otto asked, studying the boy's face curiously. Was there really songcraft hidden behind that casual expression?

"Don't step there." Haiden's voice was sharper, and Otto froze. He followed Haiden's gaze to see a snake slithering away through the grass, having just passed right under where Otto was about to walk.

The prince watched it nervously. "Do we need to catch it?"

"Catch and kill it, do you mean?" Haiden asked, eyebrow raised.

Otto shrugged uncomfortably. "Only if it's necessary for our safety."

Haiden eyed him. "I've never been in favor of pre-emptively attacking," he said. His face relaxed into a friendlier expression. "It's not necessary in this case. It was just a wisp adder. They are venomous, but not especially dangerous. They're more averse to company than my sister."

Otto gave his head a wry shake as Haiden chuckled at his own humor.

"Anyway, now we're here, it won't come looking for trouble. It'll disappear into the undergrowth."

Otto nodded, content to take the forest-dweller's word for it. "So why did you say it's too bad of us to camp here?"

Haiden shifted into a more comfortable position, his voice still casual.

"Well, there are probably a lot of animals who usually drink at this pool," he explained. "And like the wisp adder, they'll be too scared to come close with us all camping here." His eyes strayed to the pool behind Otto, his tone growing distracted. "I imagine they'll just drink downstream, though."

Otto looked back over his shoulder to see what had captured Haiden's attention. Valerie was kneeling by the water's edge, assisting a few of the guards who were filling large pots with water from the pool. As they watched, she began to sing, a fierce, angry sort of song. Before his eyes, the water in the pots bubbled, to the evident satisfaction of the guards holding them.

"She's good," Haiden commented. "She doesn't seem to realize how skilled she is. Apparently there are songs to purify the water directly, but she said she doesn't know them. Instantly boiling the water seems just as good to me, though. Much faster and easier than doing it over a fire."

Otto said nothing, smiling as his eyes lingered on Monty, hovering some distance behind Valerie and casting dark looks at the obviously interested Haiden.

Otto followed his friend's gaze back to Haiden. He could see it now. Knowing the truth, he found Monty's jealousy even more comically foolish. To be fair, he had also believed Haiden to have developed a youthful infatuation with Valerie, but now that he was paying attention, it seemed so obvious that the boy's fascination was with her craft. How desperately Haiden must have longed for proper training, growing up in isolation with only a sister who was determined to protect his secret at whatever cost. Otto couldn't imagine Gisela encouraging her brother to seek training from strangers. It was a shame, because if she was allowed to, Valerie could probably teach him a great deal as they traveled.

The night passed peacefully, interrupted only by the normal noise of the darkened forest. Bats swooped overhead, but even the horses were used to them by now, and nothing interrupted the sleep of those fortunate enough not to have sentry duty.

In the morning, Valerie summoned a path again—an activity for which Haiden was noticeably absent—and all seemed well. However, they'd barely been on it for an hour when the shimmering trail began to fade right under their horses' hooves. Before long, it had disappeared completely, and they found themselves picking their way through dense undergrowth.

"Well, that's unfortunate," sighed Monty, riding alongside Otto. "But we did have a good run."

"Not good enough to get us near the central settlement, I'm guessing." Norris sounded grim, but then, that was his usual demeanor.

Unconcerned, Otto stretched out his arms, then started to slide one leg back, preparing to dismount. "Seems a good place to stop for a break."

"I don't know about that," said Haiden warningly. "It may be random, but if the trail brought us here on purpose, we should be cautious. We have no idea of the magic's intentions."

"He's right," Gisela agreed. "We should keep moving."

"Very well," said Otto pleasantly. "But you two, it's time for a change in mount. Those two horses have been carrying double riders for long enough."

Gisela shot him a suspicious look, which he met with his most open smile. He did feel a tiny twinge of guilt a few minutes later, when one of the guards helped boost Gisela up onto Bullion in front of him. She wasn't entirely wrong to suspect him of scheming, but after all, he meant no harm by it.

They continued for only a short time before a scout appeared at the front of the group, returning from the path ahead. Norris called a halt while he spoke to the man, and Otto prodded Bullion forward to hear.

"Apparently there's an elf settlement not far ahead," the older man told Otto, swiveling in his saddle. "No more than an hour's ride."

"Could it be the central one?" Otto asked excitedly. He felt Gisela tense slightly in front of him, and locked the information away for later. "Could the path have taken us further than we thought?"

"It's possible, I suppose." Norris sounded reluctant to pin any hope on it.

"One way to find out," Otto said brightly. He turned to the scout. "Please, lead on."

The man nodded respectfully, swinging his horse around. The fact that he didn't suggest dismounting gave Otto hope that the way forward wasn't too dense.

His optimism was well-founded. The foliage thinned out considerably as they progressed, the thick undergrowth giving way to the rockiest ground they'd encountered in Ilgal. Soon the trees were interspersed with huge boulders, and the group passed a number of sinister looking caves.

"Nice spot to camp for the night, don't you think?" Monty muttered, as they approached a particularly forbidding entrance, hung over with vines.

"The elf settlement is through there," the scout said from up ahead, pointing to the very cave Monty had mentioned.

The nobleman groaned. "Of course it is."

"How do you know?" Otto challenged.

The scout looked sheepish. "I encountered an elf, and he told me as much."

"He was very likely lying," Norris said, scowling at this sign of ineptitude from one of his men.

"I don't think so, sir," the scout said. "He didn't give the information freely. We struck a bargain. In exchange for telling me the location of the elf settlement from which he hailed, he wished to know the size of my group." He inclined his head to Otto. "I hope I didn't err in agreeing to the bargain, Your Highness. I deemed it to be within the role I'd been given."

"You didn't err at all," Otto reassured him. "Our travels aren't secret from the elves, and little as they might regard us, I don't believe any formal elf settlement is so oblivious to the political ramifications as to attack my party outright. You did well. If the elf struck a bargain with you, he'll be bound by its magic same as you are, and I think we can trust the information he gave us." He looked down at the dark hair cascading in a braid down his passenger's back. "Do you agree, Gisela?"

She nodded. "Yes, he can't tell you an untruth in fulfillment of a bargain. Not without triggering the magic, and we'd know if that had happened."

"Very good," Otto said decisively. "Let's proceed."

Norris didn't look entirely convinced, but he gestured for the scout to obey the prince, and soon the group was riding into the cave. It was plenty high enough for the horses to walk into. Almost at once they were swallowed by darkness, only the weak light of the scout's lantern leading the way. Otto could still feel Gisela's tension, and he had to sternly suppress the impulse to put a reassuring arm around her. Something told him she wouldn't welcome it, and there was no point offering comfort that would only make her *more* uncomfortable.

A moment later, a small circle of pale light appeared ahead, and the riders directed their horses toward it. The circle grew until it became an opening, daylight trickling into the cave and revealing it to be more of a tunnel.

When the group emerged, blinking, it was to find an array of elves waiting for them, ranged across a rocky shelf at varying heights. Otto pulled Bullion up, swinging around to allow him to better search the gathering of elves. One stood prominently at the front, perfectly positioned on the rocky wall so that he looked Otto in the eye. He must be the leader.

Otto repeated the words he'd used at the last settlement.

"Greetings. I am Crown Prince Otto, son of King Ryker who rules this kingdom, and I have come to speak with the leader of this settlement, if he or she will welcome me."

"I am the leader of this settlement," said the elf Otto had addressed. "And you give me no gift with this information. I already know who you are. Rumor of your errand precedes you."

"Warm bunch, aren't they?" Monty muttered from behind Otto.

He ignored his friend. "My words were motivated by manners rather than generosity," Otto responded. "Will you respond in kind, by engaging in speech with me?"

The leader considered him through narrowed eyes, clearly not pleased that Otto had phrased his words carefully enough to avoid triggering a bargain or asking a favor.

"You may enter," the diminutive elf said at last, the slight wiggle to the tips of his ears the only sign of his continued irritation. "And I will speak with you, Crown Prince Otto, provided you come alone." His eyes passed to Gisela, sitting straight-backed in front of Otto. "With your companion, if you wish. The rest of the group may wait here."

"I would be glad to meet with you alone, as first suggested," Otto said firmly.

Norris made a noise of protest, but Otto waved him down. Lowering his voice, he spoke for Gisela's ears only.

"Monty's horse can take you for a while, Gisela."

She nodded mutely, her eyes sliding back to the nobleman behind them. At a sign from Otto, Monty prodded his horse forward. With a strength that belied his feigned indolence, he placed his hands on Gisela's arms, taking care to avoid her injury as he helped her slide from Otto's horse onto his own. Otto tried not to feel disgruntled as he watched his friend settle her basically in his lap. He'd asked for Monty's help, after all. And protecting Gisela from unwanted attention was the main priority.

"Your Highness, I must object." Norris had approached as well, his eyes on the elves still watching them silently from the rocks. "I at least should accompany you, preferably with several of my men."

"It's not ideal," Otto conceded. "But it's an acceptable risk, in my view." He followed Norris's gaze, dropping his voice. "Feel the air, Norris. These elves aren't as inclined to meet us with friendship as those in the last settlement."

"That cool indifference was friendship?" Norris asked skeptically.

Otto smiled. "For elves, close enough. These ones, however…"

He trailed off, noting that the elf leader was watching, his expression giving the uncomfortable impression that he could hear every word. It wasn't necessary to say more, however. Norris must have felt the frostiness as well as he did. Ignoring the head guard's scowl, Otto dismounted, handing Bullion off to Norris. At once, the elves began to descend from the rocky shelf, their leader coming last of all.

# CHAPTER TWELVE

# Otto

Two of the elves came to flank Otto, directing him with gestures but saying nothing. They only reached his middle, but walking between them, his height didn't feel like an advantage. He felt awkward, like his limbs were suddenly too long, and he wasn't sure what to do with them.

Following the group across grassy ground interspersed with rocks, Otto looked curiously around him. This settlement was nothing like the one inside the rings of trees. He couldn't see any dwellings built from wood, either on the ground or in the canopy. Caves yawned at him from all sides, some with wisps of smoke curling up from holes in the rock. Other dwellings were more obvious, built on the ground rather than hidden inside caves, but these also were of stone.

The further into the settlement Otto went, the louder grew a series of metallic sounds. They came from all sides, and as they passed a particularly large rocky mound, Otto glanced over to see several elves at work among the stones. He'd rarely had the opportunity to watch elves mining, and would have liked to linger. But his guides led him inexorably on. He knew a moment of surprise that there was still an active mine inside such an established settlement, but on reflection he realized that unlike most mines, these ones could probably continue to produce almost endlessly. It wasn't really the rock they were accessing, but the magic. And given the rate of growth of Ilgal's magic, it probably replenished constantly.

He brought this gaze forward in time to see the elf leader disappear into a large cave. Most of the group of elves came to a stop, but the two on either side of Otto continued into the dwelling with him. Because dwelling it was. To Otto's surprise, the cave—which had looked dark from the outside—proved to be flooded with light as soon as he stepped inside. There was a hole in the ceiling, but the light didn't come through there. That appeared to serve as a chimney, with smoke rising up to it from a fire in the middle of the space. The light—faintly blue in nature—pulsed from what appeared to be precious stones arrayed in brackets around the rock walls.

It wasn't a rough cave either, but beautifully hewn, with smooth sides and decorative alcoves. Woven mats of moss were placed around the floor, and elf-sized furniture gave the space the feel of a grand home. Otto looked down to see the elf leader waiting, and at a sign from him, the others prodded the prince toward a low bench placed on one side of the fire pit.

"You may sit, if you choose," the elf leader said.

Otto sank down, his legs stretched lopsidedly in front of him as he perched so close to the ground. He was glad to see the elf take a seat himself. Awkward as it felt to tower over the smaller creatures, he didn't especially wish for the reverse situation. The two elves who had escorted Otto across the settlement stood on either side of the bench, silent and watchful. They had the demeanor of guards supervising a prisoner, and Otto had to stop himself from reassuringly feeling the hilt of his sword. He would of course defend himself if necessary, but all he knew of elves suggested it was unlikely to come to that, and he didn't wish to imply that he was expecting violence.

"What brings you to our settlement, Crown Prince Otto?" the elf leader asked.

Otto tilted his head in polite inquiry. "I thought you said that rumor of my errand had preceded me."

The elf regarded him steadily. "It has. I understood you to be searching Ilgal for singers, with the intent of forming them into a force that could attack the growing magic and fight it back."

Otto didn't respond. The description was basically correct, but he was surprised by the choice of language. The elf made it sound so...combative.

"It does not seem to me that this errand would bring you to our settlement," said the elf leader. "And yet it is clear that you approached us intentionally."

"Not as intentionally as you seem to give me credit for," Otto told him with a candor that might be unwise. "I am seeking the central elf settlement where the Imperator can be found, and I had hoped I might have reached it. Evidently, I have not."

The elf exchanged a sharp glance with one of his fellows standing by the bench. When he turned back to Otto, there was humor in his voice, although Otto found it unconvincing.

"Did you believe me to be the Imperator, Crown Prince Otto? A flattering but deeply inaccurate assessment."

"No." Otto permitted himself a smile. "I realized when we entered the settlement that my hopes were unfounded. Do you know how much further I will need to travel to reach the Imperator's settlement?"

"I do not," said the elf leader, leaning back in his chair and lazily surveying the prince. "Had you asked if I know its location, I could not honestly give you the same answer. But the question of how far you must travel is more complex. The forest has its own trails, and its own ideas of distance. I cannot tell you what route it may require you to take, or what destination it may choose for you."

"Yes, so I've discovered," said Otto dryly.

"Indeed?" The elf's increased interest told Otto that he'd erred. "You've experienced the forest paths since your arrival in Ilgal, have you? If you've done so without ending up at a dead end, one might infer that you found a way to direct them."

"We have a singer in our group," said Otto carefully, painfully aware of the information Haiden and Gisela thought secret even from their own party. "As I'm sure you know, since you seem so well-informed as to our party."

He didn't have a clear idea on the methods by which the elves of Ilgal communicated across great distances, but he strongly suspected that this leader had received a full report from the leader of the other settlement with whom he'd bartered information previously.

The elf remained at ease, folding his fingers together. "A singer from the city, however. It would be quite a feat for a stranger to our parts to harness the forest paths. That's heart magic, generally requiring a connection with the land."

"I can't comment on that, not being well-versed in matters of magic," said Otto flatly.

The elf regarded him shrewdly. "Why are you seeking the central settlement?"

Otto frowned at him, trying to hide his surprise. Had he been wrong to think this elf knew the details of his interactions with the other elf leader? He'd been open with her about his purpose in seeking out the Imperator.

"How about I tell you that information in exchange for your guidance as to the best route to reach the Imperator's settlement from here?" he countered.

"Do you propose a bargain along those terms?" the elf asked. Otto nodded. "I do."

The elf's eyes narrowed in thought, the silence stretching out.

"I decline," he said at last. "I would prefer to barter for other information."

"What information?" Otto asked warily.

"There are two members of your party dressed as forest-dwellers," the elf said abruptly. "Who are they? For information about them I would be willing to strike a bargain."

Otto frowned. They wanted information about Gisela and Haiden? He could understand the elf leader being curious—the siblings' garb certainly marked them as out of place among the party from the capital. But if the elf was willing to trade for answers, there was more than idle curiosity at work.

"That is an odd request," he said slowly. "And I must decline. I do not feel I could in all honor trade information that is not my own."

"Does your position as crown prince not entitle you to some claim over your subjects?" the elf asked, his lip curling in apparent disdain. "It seems I have misunderstood human politics."

"It seems so indeed," Otto said, his dislike for the miniature leader growing. The elf who had run the other settlement had been shrewd in her own way, but nothing like this. "I do not consider my subjects my property, to barter at will."

One thin eyebrow went up, a strange glint in the elf's emerald eyes. "Barter them? I did not ask you to give them to me in their entirety. I wish only for information."

"I understood your request," Otto said. "And my answer hasn't changed."

"So confident in your decisions for one so young," the elf commented. He studied Otto's face. "If you feel your authority cannot support such a small step, perhaps you should call them in here. You could ask them if they wish to enter into the proposed trade."

"I'd rather not." Otto's voice was flat now. Did the elf truly expect to manipulate him by insulting his authority, as if that would make him want to prove he had power as prince? He wasn't so weak-minded. "I don't wish to waste your time or my own," he went on curtly. "If you are interested in the bargain I proposed, very well. If not, I will be on my way."

"I do not consider that bargain beneficial to me or my people," the elf leader informed him. "I know your purpose in Ilgal, and I doubt I will have difficulty discovering your intention in speaking to the Imperator." He frowned. "Focused consideration will probably provide the answers. Am I to conclude that the Imperator has agreed to assist you to locate singers within the forest, or in some other way to provide you with the access to magic that you need?"

"If you were to reach that conclusion, you would do so entirely on your own," Otto said calmly. "I made no such claim, as we're both aware."

One of the elves standing alongside the bench shifted, irritation radiating out from both him and his fellow. The leader kept his face impassive, but Otto could see a spark in his green eyes. They didn't like him much, that was perfectly clear. Sensing there was nothing more to be gained from the conversation, Otto stood. The elf leader did the same, his eyes never leaving Otto's.

"It would be inhospitable to send you away with nothing, Crown Prince Otto," he said, his tone bordering on impudent. "So I offer you some advice as a gift freely given. You are out of your depth here. Your domain does not extend to the forest. You would be wisest to remain within your territory."

Anger flashed over Otto, but he kept it in check. He could

see in the elf's eyes that he hoped to bait the young prince, but he'd underestimated Otto. It wasn't the first time Otto had encountered powerful players who expected him to be hotheaded due to his position. But his ego wasn't fragile. He felt no personal offense at the elf's blatant disrespect. His anger was all for his father, and the knowledge that the king would counsel caution helped him to speak calmly.

"Unsound advice is not a gift I value," he said.

On the words, he turned, feeling justified in dispensing with the usual formalities given the elf's insolent comments. His opponent said nothing, but Otto could feel the elf's narrowed eyes on his back as he strode from the dwelling, still flanked by the other elves.

Word of his arrival seemed to have spread since he first passed through the settlement, because many more curious eyes watched him this time. He ignored them all, feeling no compunction about sparing them any friendliness.

The rest of the group were right where he'd left them, and Otto's indignation grew as he realized they were being watched over by armed elven guards. Arrows bristled at their backs, and a few even clutched spears.

"Back already," Monty said, as soon as he was within hearing range.

Otto saw his friend's surprise as he took in the prince's demeanor, but he made no reply.

"Ready to depart?" Otto asked, once he'd rejoined them. His eyes flicked to Gisela, still settled in front of Monty, looking uneasy as she watched him approach.

"We're leaving?" Monty asked. "Already?"

"Yes." Reclaiming his reins from Norris—who, unlike Monty, looked relieved that they were departing—Otto swung up onto Bullion's back.

Perhaps reading his face, no one questioned him as they

turned their mounts and headed back through the tunnel. The elves accompanied them to the cave's edge, and Otto forced himself to muster some politeness.

"Well met," he said, dipping his head ever so slightly.

The elf standing at the front of the group—one of the ones who'd flanked Otto into the leader's dwelling—returned the gesture, his emerald eyes cold, and the tips of his ears stiff.

Otto nudged Bullion into a trot, heading in what he hoped was a westerly direction through the rocky patch of forest.

"What was all that about?" Monty asked, drawing alongside him, Gisela still riding double on his mount.

"Wait." Gisela's voice was so soft Otto barely caught it. "Elves have excellent hearing. Much better than ours. Give it a few minutes."

The nobleman waited obediently, only trying again after several minutes had passed.

"I take it the leader wasn't especially helpful? Given you seemed cross with the whole settlement."

Gisela looked surprised at this assessment, and perhaps sensing it, Monty grinned. "For Otto, that stiff formal look is as close to rude as he gets. He's far too easy-going. Frankly, it's not like him to punish a whole village for the leader's rudeness. Assuming he was rude to you."

"I doubt any of them would consider it punishment," Otto said dryly. "And from what I know of elf culture, they're loyal to their leaders, even to a fault."

"That's true." Gisela nodded. "Although loyalty doesn't mean quite the same to an elf as to a human. It's not necessarily a matter of emotion. It's an official position, more about honor and propriety than actual preference. The elves are very partic-ular about their ways of doing things. And those ways don't include questioning a ruler's right to respect."

She shifted slightly in the saddle as she spoke, some thought in her mind that Otto couldn't read.

"That's what I've been taught," he agreed. "And it's why I find the behavior of that settlement's leader incomprehensible. I thought that in Ilgal, the Imperator was considered by all the elf groups to be their...I don't know, overlord. The leader of the last settlement was quick to direct me to his authority, but this one seemed bent on preventing me from finding him."

At that moment Norris, riding on Otto's other side, called a halt. Apparently he felt they'd gone far enough to regroup.

"Do I take it, then, that you didn't receive helpful directions, Your Highness?" he asked. "We're none the wiser as to how to reach the central settlement?"

"That's correct," Otto said regretfully. "He wasn't in a hurry to give me information."

"Couldn't you barter for it?" Monty pressed.

"I tried. It didn't work."

"He wanted an unreasonable exchange, did he?" Monty asked sympathetically. "What was it?"

With great self-discipline, Otto prevented his eyes from flicking to Gisela. "Something I was unwilling to give. That's not what troubles me, though. I expected aloofness...I certainly didn't expect any elves to go out of their way to help us. But this was more pointed than that. He was actively trying to block me. They all were."

"Did he understand the nature of our errand?" Valerie demanded. During Otto's absence, Haiden had wound up riding double with her.

"He did," Otto said. "He was well-informed. I think he'd received word from the other elf settlement."

"Strange that his response was so different from that other leader's, then," Valerie pointed out. "She didn't seem to have any hesitation in directing you to where the Imperator could be found."

"Perhaps the Imperator's orders regarding our presence here have changed," Norris said grimly. "Are you sure it's wise to seek him out, Your Highness?"

"Not entirely," Otto told him candidly. "But the more I interact with the elves of Ilgal, the more determined I am to speak with the one in charge. I knew they had their own hierarchy, and their own views regarding forest laws. But this one openly spurned my father's authority in Ilgal."

Monty's eyebrows jumped upward, and Norris's lips pressed into an even thinner line than usual.

"Do you think the Imperator could be planning to seize full control?" Lady Louisa asked sharply.

"The thought occurred to me," Otto acknowledged. "In light of the elves' obedience to their leader, I don't know what else to conclude from such brazen comments from the head of a formal settlement."

Haiden cleared his throat, bringing several pairs of eyes to him. But the teenager didn't speak, his gaze fixed meaningfully on Gisela.

Otto's eyes traveled the same way, noting that she'd mashed her lips together, her expression displeased.

"Gisela." Haiden's voice sounded like a parent prompting a recalcitrant child. Coming from the fifteen-year-old, it was almost enough to break Otto's heavy mood and make him smile. "Gisela, it might be important."

"We don't know anything, Haiden," murmured Gisela.

"We know what we saw and what we heard," he argued.

"What are you two talking about?" Norris demanded. "What haven't you told us?"

For another moment, the silent standoff between the siblings held, then Gisela deflated with a sigh.

"I was hoping not to get involved with...whatever this is, but Haiden's right. For all we know, it might be important." She glanced at her brother, who nodded encouragement. "The day we met you all, we stumbled across a group of elves we'd never seen before. *Someone*," she sent her brother a glare, "thought it was a good idea to follow them through a gate, landing us in the middle of nowhere. And we saw them meet with a lone elf, and give him a message to take out of the forest."

"Take where?" Otto asked sharply, locking away this second mention of *gates* to seek clarification later. "Who was the message for?"

"No idea," said Gisela. "They talked about a shipment of gold following by some other means. It was all very clandestine. We didn't get the impression that it was an official message going through proper channels."

"Although it had the Imperator's seal," Haiden chimed in.

"That was your guess," Gisela corrected quickly. "I didn't think that. It was an elf seal of some kind, but we don't know enough to recognize whether it was a royal one."

"Looked royal to me," muttered Haiden.

"I don't think it was," Gisela insisted. She hesitated, then met Otto's eye. "I heard them mention the Imperator, and they didn't sound at all respectful."

"You think there might be a group of elves in Ilgal who aren't loyal to the Imperator?" Otto asked slowly.

Gisela shrugged uncomfortably. "I don't think anything. I don't have an opinion on the matter, and I don't really want to form one. I'm just telling you what we saw and heard, like Haiden said."

Otto ran his hand absently over Bullion's reins, thinking it over. "What would be the motive of a group like that? Who would they be communicating with—sending gold to—outside the forest?" And, the unspoken but obvious question: how did it affect his own mission in Ilgal?

Haiden sighed. "We could probably have found out if we'd been able to return to the place. They were all going to meet back up in a week."

"Could you find it again?" Norris asked quickly.

Haiden shook his head. "No. We had no way to mark the location, and we ran straight through another gate after the elves. Besides which, the week has elapsed by now."

"Well." Otto thought it over. "If nothing else, it's information that might be of interest to the Imperator. You never know when I might need something to barter." His eyes passed from Haiden to Gisela. "Thank you for sharing it."

She nodded tightly, still seeming uncomfortable with sharing more information than strictly necessary. He could guess which sibling had been the one to decide to eavesdrop on the elves. For his part, Otto was with Haiden. He was inclined to think that the more information he had on hand when dealing with the shrewd elves, the better. He only wished the siblings had overheard more.

"What next, Your Highness?" Norris asked, in a practical spirit.

"We continue on the course we were on before we encountered that settlement, I suppose," Otto said. "West, and then north once we skirt the swamp."

"Should I call the forest paths?" Valerie asked.

"I don't think they'll come," Gisela said, sounding weary. "Not this close to an elf settlement. The elves usually have their own magic in place."

"Through the undergrowth it is, then," Otto said bracingly. "We'll ride while we can, and be ready to proceed on foot as needed."

The group let out a collective breath, but no one protested.

They knew him well enough not to bother. Easy-going he might be, but he was also determined when he set his mind to something.

And each day spent in Ilgal made him more determined to get to the bottom of what was really going on in the forest.

# CHAPTER THIRTEEN

# Gisela

Gisela stepped over a patch of brush, wincing as her foot snapped a twig on impact with the ground. She was getting careless to be making noises like that.

Not that it really mattered, given the group in which she was traveling. There were over forty of them—they couldn't move silently through the trees. And like the rest of them, she was exhausted, and not at her sharpest. She and Haiden had never had idle lives, but they weren't used to the pace of travel they'd sustained since joining the prince's expedition. Usually they had a home base to return to, even if that home changed every few months. Now, it felt like they were always moving.

Always moving, and never getting anywhere.

Right on cue, she heard a soft song from behind her, and turned to see Valerie wearily lifting her voice. Frowning, the singer closed her eyes, stumbling over a log as she lost track of her physical surroundings. Monty reached out from beside her, steadying her before she could lose her footing altogether.

"Thanks," she muttered, not meeting his eyes as her own flew open.

"Checking our direction?" he asked.

She nodded, blowing a strand of hair out of her eyes. "It makes no sense, though. I think we're going in a circle."

He groaned. "That sounds about right. It's certainly how it feels."

"Which way is north?" Otto asked, apparently determined to remain positive.

Valerie pointed, and the prince gave a decisive nod.

"We'll head that way."

"Are you sure we're clear of the swamp?" Haiden asked doubtfully.

"It's been days since we left the elf settlement," Monty chimed in wearily. "Surely we've passed it by now."

Haiden didn't look convinced, and Gisela agreed. "The air feels damp to me, and there still seems to be a lot of water in the area."

"Well, if we head north, we'll find out," Otto said. "If we have to backtrack and continue west, we can always do that." He turned to Norris. "Is there any reason we can't change course?"

The head guard scanned the area in his habitual way before answering the prince. "If there's a chance we're near the swamps, I'd prefer not to send the whole group into them. The main force can rest here while we send scouts."

"I wouldn't say no to a rest," Monty said, leaning against his horse's flank. They'd been walking the mounts all morning, given the terrain.

"All right," said Otto. "We can send out multiple groups, and hopefully we'll find a better way forward. I wouldn't mind the chance to scout ahead without Bullion in tow."

"No, Your Highness." Norris's objection was predictable. Ever since Otto had blithely thrown himself into the elves' power at the last settlement, the head guard had been set against allowing the prince to leave the main group for any reason. "You should stay here, as will I."

Otto looked faintly mutinous—an unusual demeanor for him—but Lady Louisa came to Norris's support.

"I agree, Your Highness. We have no idea what's ahead. You shouldn't be going anywhere without a dozen guards at least. Not if there's any possibility the elves are contemplating rejecting the king's authority outright."

Under their combined insistence, Otto submitted, leading his horse over to a grassy patch of ground.

Gisela knew it would be more sensible to keep her distance, but she was touched by his dejected attitude. Chastising herself for getting involved, she moved to stand beside him.

"Never mind," she said sympathetically. "You can get lost in a bog next time."

Otto laughed, although the expression turned into a grimace. "I must seem absurd. A prince allowed to lead a meandering expedition through the forest, still complaining about being too restricted."

"You didn't complain," Gisela pointed out.

He sighed. "In my head I did. I'm just eager to reach the Imperator. I have this growing sense of crisis, like we're on the edge of disaster, and we have to attain our goal quickly, or it will be too late. Does that make any sense, or do I sound mad?"

"No, it makes sense," she said slowly. "I feel it, too. There's something very intense about this part of the forest, and it increases the deeper into its heart we go. It's like the sense of foreboding in my mind grows at the same rate as the pressure on my chest."

"It's not the direct journey to the central settlement that you signed up for," Otto said remorsefully. "If I hadn't pressed you, you'd likely be well and truly back to your home by now."

"Probably," Gisela agreed, surprising herself with the smile that tugged at her lips. "But I can't say I regret the change in our trail."

Otto's face softened in an answering smile, the expression warmer than it had any right to be.

"You're not missing your home, then?"

Gisela shrugged. "Not really. We haven't lived there long. There's no sentiment attached to the place. We were probably going to move on in a month or so. It wouldn't be any great catastrophe if we never make it back to that particular dwelling."

"Really?" Otto looked surprised. "I'd thought you were very fixed in your home here." He hesitated. "If you're considering a change, then maybe...maybe you should consider coming back to Terenford with us."

Gisela swallowed. The suggestion had taken her completely by surprise, and she was unable to pull her eyes from his.

"To the capital? With...with you?"

"I know Ilgal is important to you," Otto said quickly. "And I know you said a while ago that you weren't considering leaving. I'm not trying to drag you away. I just thought it might be a good experience for you both, to see what city life is like as well."

Longing rose up in Gisela, fierce and unexpected. She'd known this wasn't a trail that was open to her, and she had never let herself get wrapped up in the idea. But having it laid out before her made it hard not to indulge in daydreams. How much easier life would be if they could leave the forest. And Otto was inviting her, welcoming her to follow him back to his world. They wouldn't be friendless. He'd probably be able to set them up with somewhere to live, help them find employment. They wouldn't even have to abandon Ilgal altogether, because Teren's capital was right on the forest's edge. They could come and go as they pleased, like the prince's stepsister had apparently continued to do after moving to the city.

*Stop,* she told herself. Daydreams like that would only make reality harder to endure.

She cleared her throat. "It's kind of you to think of us, but that's not an option."

"Why not?" Otto asked, once again taking her by surprise. She'd expected him to politely accept her answer, and she didn't have an explanation ready. "Are you so attached to the forest that you can't stomach the idea of leaving, even temporarily?"

"No!" The word burst from Gisela before she could stop it. Drawing a breath, she tried to moderate her tone. "I do love the forest—I think those of us with Ilgal in our blood can't help it. The forest takes hold of us, and we can never fully separate ourselves from it. But that's not why we won't be joining you in Terenford. We're just...not able to."

An honest answer, even if not a very open one. Of course she knew that Otto wouldn't understand what she meant, but it was the truth, plain and simple. They were quite literally incapable of leaving the forest, after all.

Otto's eyes were both bewildered and sympathetic. "You're not able to, or you're not willing to?" he pressed. "Gisela, what can I say to convince you that you deserve more than what you've condemned yourself to?"

To her dismay, Gisela felt her eyes filling with tears. She was surprised by the longing she felt to unburden herself to Otto, to share all her fears and struggles with him. As much as he might be at sea in the world of Ilgal, he'd projected solidity and security since the moment she'd met him. Sensations she didn't experience much in her life. If only she could explain to him that she wasn't refusing out of a misguided determination to keep herself sequestered. That she wasn't condemning herself to the bleak future before her—someone else had condemned her to it, and there was nothing she could do.

Perhaps seeing her wavering, Otto stepped forward. He lifted a hand, hesitating for only a moment before touching his fingertips briefly to her cheek.

"Gisela, I want to help you. If there's a way, please tell me how."

She shook her head mutely, not trusting herself. A tingling feeling radiated out from where he'd touched her, engulfing her whole face in a warmth that was terrifyingly intoxicating.

"I don't think the forest brought our trails together by chance," Otto persisted. "I know it makes no sense, but I can't help believing I was meant to enter your life. And I don't intend to leave it without a fight." He lowered his voice. "I don't want to go back to Terenford without you. How could I go about my life, not knowing whether you and your brother were all right?"

Gisela swallowed. "The same way you went about it before, I imagine." She could hear the hint of sadness in her voice, try as she might to hide it. No good could come of him knowing how desperately she wished she could follow him out of the forest.

"Impossible." Otto's voice was a murmur. "You've come out of nowhere and changed everything."

He reached out more confidently this time, brushing the back of his hand against her cheek before letting his fingers tangle in her dark hair. It was tied loosely back at the top, with most of her tresses flowing freely down over her shoulder.

The gesture was intimate, and yet somehow it felt incredibly natural at the same time. Gisela had to remind herself to breathe. It would be so easy—and so dangerous—to lose herself completely in the open warmth of his gaze. Otto was so unlike the person she'd been forced to become. There were no secrets in his eyes, no wariness. He didn't hold anything back, and something buried deep within her longed to respond to his invitation in kind.

But she couldn't afford to do that. On so many levels.

She shifted backward in a minute movement that was still enough for Otto to immediately lower his hand from her hair. He'd never pressed her, and she knew him well enough to realize he wouldn't start now, whatever he might want. A contrary part of her regretted it.

"It's kind of you to be so concerned for us," she said through dry lips. She could feel the inadequacy of the words, the absurdity of pretending they were speaking of her and Haiden's safety instead of matters of the heart. But she didn't know what other answer she could give. "But we were all right before we met you, and we'll be fine after you have to return home."

An honest part of her, deep in her core, screamed that the words were a lie as far as her own heart was concerned, but she forced it into silence. The crown prince of the kingdom was the last person she could afford to entangle hearts with, for a myriad of reasons.

"Don't worry about us." She took another step back, forcing an unnatural smile onto her lips. "And I don't think you need to worry about the feeling of crisis you mentioned earlier, either. It's probably part of the elves' defenses, to keep curious strangers away. With any luck it means we're close. I'm sure we'll find a good route ahead when we scout."

"We?" Otto asked quickly. He seemed disappointed by the abrupt return to an impersonal tone, but he didn't try to recapture the moment Gisela had cut short.

Her smile became a bit more natural. "Oh, *I* have every intention of scouting ahead. I'm the least important person on this expedition, and I therefore have the luxury of doing what I please."

"You're not the least important," Otto contradicted, his eyes regaining a fraction of their earlier intensity as they searched hers. "Far from it."

In spite of herself, Gisela felt her cheeks heating again, but she refused to be drawn back onto dangerous ground. "Very diplomatic of you. Must come with being a prince."

"I am good at being diplomatic when I choose," Otto said

unashamedly. "But that wasn't what I was doing. I meant what I said." He took the smallest of steps toward her, closing the gap again and causing Gisela's breath to catch. "I think you've made a lifetime habit of underrating your own importance, Gisela."

"Not at all," she said, struggling to maintain a light tone. "I'm important to my brother, for one thing. Without me, he has no one."

For some reason, that only made Otto's frown grow. Gisela wasn't sure she wanted to know what was behind the expression, and she couldn't help but be relieved when Haiden appeared at that moment, interrupting the conversation.

"Should we join a scouting group, Gisela?"

His eyes passed to Otto, his expression shifting slightly as he took in the prince's proximity to his sister. Otto stepped smoothly back, but it didn't do much to ease the tension. Haiden was still looking between them, his expression uncomfortable and his manner expectant.

"Yes," Gisela said briskly, irritated with her traitorous heart for its increased pace. "I was thinking the same thing." She nodded to the prince before ushering Haiden toward the head guard.

"We can take a direction," she told Norris, who was gathering some of his men. "We'll cover the ground at least as effectively as your scouts."

Norris regarded them. "Just the two of you?"

Gisela shrugged. "Are you sending the scouts out in groups?"

"Pairs," he admitted. It was clear he still wasn't entirely sure he trusted them, but after a minute he just nodded. "All right, form up."

Soon there were five pairs awaiting instructions. Gisela could feel Haiden's tension beside her, and she found herself strangely nervous about being alone with him. She didn't like feeling that way about her own brother, to whom she was closer than anyone, but she could feel the interrogation building inside him, and she didn't know what to tell him about her charged interaction with the prince. She didn't know what to make of it herself. She could hardly dare to believe what her heart had been trying to tell her in the moment, that Otto was as affected by her nearness as she was by his. It was too absurd. And yet, she'd never seen him touch anyone else's face like that, or heard him use that low murmur with the others in the group, even his closest friends.

When Norris finally gave them directions, Haiden half sprinted into the trees, his long legs making it hard for Gisela to keep up.

"Slow down, Haiden," she said. "We won't scout very effectively if you run straight past every marker and animal trail."

"I know," said Haiden. "But scouting isn't my main concern right now."

Gisela swallowed, wondering how much he'd seen of her discomposure around Otto. It took her a moment to realize that Haiden's attention wasn't focused on her at all.

"It's almost here," he muttered. "We should get a bit further from the group."

"What's almost here?" Gisela asked, bewildered.

"The last stone." Haiden shot her an incredulous look, as if she should have been able to read his thoughts all along. She let out a long breath. So that was what had him so impatient.

"Oh, the stone! That's good." She chuckled to herself. "That's a relief, actually."

"Why?" Haiden demanded.

"No reason," she said quickly. "Which way is the stone coming from?"

"There." Haiden pointed.

Gisela swiveled to face the indicated direction, peering

through the trees. She couldn't see any sign of it yet. "This is the last one, you said?"

Haiden nodded, and for a moment neither moved, just waiting. Since their discussion about recalling the white stones they used for marking their trails, Haiden had been slowly drawing them to himself. Although he didn't need to harness fresh power to activate the object control magic that allowed him to make the stones move from afar, he'd still found the process of drawing them over such a vast distance to require sustained energy. After a short while, they'd decided the wisest thing would be to pull them to him one by one. It required a smaller amount of energy and focus, spread over a longer period of time. They also hoped that individually the stones would be less likely to attract notice on their travels than if they were moving unnaturally in a clump.

Of course, the downside was that instead of just once, there had been multiple occasions when Haiden had needed to find an excuse to get away from the group to receive the stones. It was too much to hope that no one would notice or ask questions if an apparently inanimate object flew out of the brush and into his hand.

"There you are." Haiden sounded like he was fondly addressing a pet, and Gisela's lips twitched as she watched the round stone trundle into sight. It rolled through the moss, bounced its way up a boulder, and levitated into Haiden's outstretched hand.

"It's a good thing you have pet rocks, Haiden, since Papa never did let you get that cat you wanted."

"Or the pigeon," Haiden said mournfully. "That one was particularly disappointing. The vendor made an excellent case for its usefulness, I thought."

Gisela snorted. "You were about eight years old, Haiden. You thought every vendor was convincing."

"To a boy who had nothing, they all were," Haiden said.

"Nothing?" Gisela couldn't help the wistful tone to her voice. That had been back when they'd still lived with their parents, in a solid home, with someone else putting food on the table every night. She didn't think of that as a time when they had nothing.

"I suppose we had more then than we do now," Haiden conceded. "But even though I know I complain, I prefer our life together, Gisela. Less to eat, but also less to fear. I've slept soundly just about every night we've been on our own. I never used to sleep soundly in that house."

Gisela gave him a sad smile, squeezing his arm for good measure. "I know what you mean." She didn't say more, since she couldn't honestly claim to agree. She felt like she'd been sleeping with one eye open for the last five years, but she thought of that as the cost of Haiden sleeping soundly, and she didn't begrudge it.

"Speaking of pigeons," Haiden said, stowing the stone in his pocket where half a dozen others waited, "have you noticed the one in the cage attached to one of the guard's saddlebags? Apparently it can take a message all the way to the castle!"

"Yes, Valerie was telling me," Gisela said, slipping a hand into her own pocket to touch the rocks she was looking after. "Remarkable if it's really true. I'm inclined to think it would get eaten by a hawk before it ever made it out of the forest."

"Very possible," Haiden agreed. "So since we're out here anyway, should we do this scouting thing?"

"Of course," Gisela said. She grinned at her brother. "Should we use the stones to mark our trail, just in case we can't find the main group?"

He let out a bark of laughter, as she'd intended. "Somehow I don't think it will be a problem. Not the stealthiest of parties, are they?"

"Not quite," Gisela agreed. She moved forward, peering

through the trees. "You were right earlier, when you were talking to Monty. The air is quite damp."

"Yes, the swamp isn't far," Haiden said, plucking a leaf from in front of his face and twirling it idly. "I don't think this is the way to the elf settlement."

Gisela grunted. "Well, I suppose ruling out a direction is helpful in itself."

"If you say so," Haiden said. "So are we going to talk about the other thing?"

"What other thing?" Gisela asked vaguely.

"You and the prince." Haiden's words were blunt, and Gisela cast him a quick look.

"What about the prince?"

"Don't play dumb, Gisela," Haiden said disapprovingly. "There's something funny there. He was looking at you like... well, like Monty looks at Valerie."

"I wouldn't say that," said Gisela, amused. "I've never seen him be jealous someone else was talking to me, or hover near me all the time for no reason."

"Haven't you?" Haiden asked flatly. "I've seen both."

"You have not!"

"I have," he insisted. "When you ride on anyone else's horse, he looks depressed. And every time we stop to rest, he's suddenly there. Have you really not noticed it?"

"I haven't noticed it because it's all in your head," Gisela told him firmly. A part of her conscience squirmed at the strict denial, but surely it was true. Otto couldn't be romantically interested in her, not truly. In spite of what had just passed between them, she didn't believe it. She couldn't allow herself to believe it.

"And that's without even talking about how *you* act around him," Haiden said, as if she hadn't spoken.

Gisela came to a stop, making a noise of protest. "And how do I supposedly act?"

Haiden turned to her, frowning slightly. "It's hard to explain, but not like you usually do. And you tell him things, don't you? You never tell anyone anything."

"If you're talking about your songcraft, I most certainly haven't told either the prince or anyone else," Gisela said hotly.

"I wasn't talking about that. I know you told him about our ancestry from the Reviled Lands. I heard him mention it to you the other day."

Gisela bit her lip. She felt defensive and cross, while her brother remained calm. It was a role reversal that had her wrong-footed.

"I'm sorry if you preferred me to keep that private," she said stiffly. "I should have asked first."

"Don't be absurd, I don't care," said Haiden dismissively. "You're the one who always insists on keeping everything secret. My point is just that it's not like you to share that information if you didn't have to. Admit it, you trust him. And you don't trust anybody."

Gisela let out a long sigh, trying to expel her defensiveness with it. "I want to trust him," she admitted. "He's very good at seeming trustworthy, and he's the crown prince of our kingdom, so of course I want to believe his intentions are good. Otherwise we're not the only ones who'd be in trouble. But wanting to trust him is not the same as trusting him."

Haiden considered her. "The trouble is, Gisela, well...exactly that." He saw her confusion and added, "He's the crown prince of our kingdom."

Gisela closed her eyes for a moment, giving a curt nod. "I know. He's the last person we should be forming any kind of friendship with." *And definitely not anything more than friendship,* she added silently. "If we were smart, we would have avoided ever interacting with him, let alone traveling with him."

"Maybe it's not us failing to be smart, but him," Haiden said darkly. "There's a certain irony in us discussing whether we should be trusting him when the truth of it is he shouldn't be trusting us as far as he can throw us."

"That's not true," Gisela said firmly. "We're not going to hurt anyone. *You're* not going to hurt anyone."

Haiden just shrugged, turning away from her to scan the forest again. "Maybe if we reach the central elf settlement, and get the chance to speak to Asivah, we'll find out if that's true."

"We don't need any elf princess to tell us who we are and what we are—and *aren't*—capable of," Gisela said defiantly.

"Speak for yourself." The words were muttered, and before Gisela could respond, Haiden pushed on. "We're the worst scouts in Ilgal right now. Our chatter will notify every creature in the vicinity of our presence. Come on."

Gisela pressed her lips together, tempted to argue the point further. But she got the sense he wouldn't appreciate it, and he was right about the scouting. Falling in beside him, she turned her attention to their surroundings.

The going was slow, and it got worse the further afield they went. The trees were sparser, their branches seeming sad and defeated, but the ground was marshy, making it difficult to find good footing.

Still, neither sibling suggested turning back. They'd traversed worse sections of forest than this, after all. And in light of their conversation about Otto, Gisela was in no hurry to rejoin the main group. It would be hard not to be aware of Haiden's eyes on every interaction she had with the prince from now on.

They'd been scouting for close to an hour when Haiden suddenly paused.

"What it is?" Gisela breathed. She stilled, listening carefully. She heard nothing but the normal sounds of the forest.

Haiden frowned. "I sense magic. It's faint, I think because it's not that close. But it's definitely magic."

"Another elf gate, do you think?" Gisela asked. "Because if so, I refuse to go through it this time."

Haiden didn't spare a smile for her attempt at a joke. "It's not an elf gate. It's something else. Come on."

Moving silently, Gisela followed him, her bow in her hand now. The worst part of the marshy ground was that it was harder to avoid leaving tracks. Still, it was far from a true bog, for which she was grateful. And, to her surprise, as Haiden wended his way between the trunks, following the invisible trail only he could sense, the ground became firmer.

"It seems there's a natural path through here," she murmured.

Haiden nodded tersely, his eyes fixed ahead. A few more steps, and he stopped abruptly, flinging out a hand in a familiar gesture.

Following his silent command, Gisela melted into the undergrowth and found a spot to conceal herself. Haiden did the same, his figure soon hidden from view. Peering through the leaves, Gisela waited. A minute later, she heard movement, followed by the sight of a tall woman emerging from between the trees ahead.

The woman walked confidently, a sack over one shoulder and something grasped in her other hand. A talisman perhaps? Could that be what Haiden had sensed? It would have to be strong if he'd identified it from so far away, though.

The stranger came to a pause some distance from Gisela's hiding place. Carefully, she shifted slightly to keep the woman in her sight. The stranger was looking down at a severed stump, and at first Gisela wondered what she was waiting for. Then the woman raised whatever was in her hand and waved it over the spot. Before Gisela's astonished eyes, the stump melted away completely. From her vantage point, she couldn't get a good look at what was there in its place. Whatever it was, it was flatter than the stump had been.

Gisela thought she heard something issuing from the spot, something that didn't sound like it could come from the woman. But before she could figure out what she was hearing, the woman dropped the sack onto the ground where the stump had been, and it suddenly fell from sight, emitting a soft thud a moment later.

"It's a hole." Haiden's murmur drifted to her, suggesting his hiding place was closer to hers than she'd realized.

The woman looked up suddenly, her eyes scanning the area. Swallowing, Gisela held completely still, knowing Haiden would do the same. After a moment, the woman turned back to the patch of ground in front of her, waving the talisman again. The stump materialized again, its hazy edges becoming firm and solid within seconds.

With a final swift glance, the woman turned away, hurrying back through the trees and out of sight.

# CHAPTER FOURTEEN

# Gisela

For a few minutes all was still, as Gisela and Haiden waited to ensure the woman was out of hearing.

Haiden was the first to emerge. "Where do you think that hole leads?" His voice was much too eager for Gisela's liking.

"To a storehouse for stolen talismans, most likely," she said, her tone intended to dampen his enthusiasm.

It didn't work.

"Imagine if we could get our hands on whatever's in there," said Haiden, his eyes glinting.

"No." Gisela's voice was so sharp, she clapped her hand over her mouth, for fear the woman hadn't traveled as far as they thought. "We're not getting involved, Haiden. We're already in too precarious a position. We don't need to take on whatever this is as well."

"Speak for yourself," he said. "I want to know what's in there. I think maybe I should follow her and see where she goes. I can always come back to examine the stump."

"Don't you dare," Gisela said, alarmed. "Haiden, we have no

idea who she is or who she's with. You can't go off after her alone. You could be walking into danger."

"Do you really want to ignore this, Gisela?" Haiden asked incredulously. "Because I'm telling you now, that's not going to happen."

She let out a moan. "Why are you so stubborn?"

He smiled innocently at her. "Probably the way I was raised."

Gisela ignored this dig at herself, running a hand through her hair as she thought. "If you're determined to pursue this, we should do it right this time. We should tell Otto about it, and let him decide how to investigate."

Haiden raised his eyebrows. "Tell me again about how you *haven't* broken your prevailing principle and decided to trust someone other than ourselves?"

"Enough," Gisela said, sending him a dark glance. "This has nothing to do with us or our secrets. Tell me one good reason we should keep it from Otto."

"Oh, I don't think we should," Haiden said. "I'm perfectly willing to tell the others." His eyes searched hers. "I'm glad we told them about the elf meeting we witnessed. Otto's all right. I don't like the idea of him going into negotiations with the elves without all the information."

Gisela studied her brother. Apparently she wasn't the only one who'd warmed to the prince. She was glad to think the heir to their kingdom was someone worthy of respect. But she could understand her brother's discomfort. Given the prophecy hanging over Haiden, the prince's worthiness wasn't entirely a relief.

"Let's go, then," she said. "It will take us a while to get to the group. Even if we go now, we may not be able to make it back before dark, and I doubt Norris will allow anyone to come here at night."

"Shouldn't we just have a quick look at that stump first?" Haiden asked hopefully.

"Absolutely not." There was no compromise in Gisela's voice. "Haiden, we have no idea how far that woman went. We also don't know what kind of protections she has in place. That talisman must have been powerful for you to sense it from a distance. She could have some kind of alarm magic set up to notify her if anyone approaches."

"Actually," said Haiden thoughtfully, "I don't think the talisman is what I sensed from way back there. I think it was the magic from the hole. When it was open, I could feel it much more strongly. It was like there was a treasure trove of magic in there."

"All the more reason not to approach without backup," Gisela said flatly. "You can come back with Norris and his men."

Haiden looked frustrated, but to Gisela's relief, he didn't argue. She knew the days when he would blindly obey her guidance were gone now, but she could only be grateful he still retained some respect for her leadership of their two-person tribe.

"We'll leave a stone here, to make sure we can find our way back," Gisela said, pulling one out from the half she had custody of. "But I think we should move further away before doing that. We wouldn't want her to sense anything."

"I don't think she was a singer," Haiden commented. "Singers don't usually need powerful talismans, do they? But there's no harm in a bit of distance, as long as we're sure we can find our way from the stone to the stump."

Gisela nodded vaguely as she searched the forest ahead for a good hiding place for the stone. It gleamed white in her hand, the sight deeply linked with safety. When she saw that glimpse of white through the trees, it meant she was almost home. Almost secure.

"It's handy that I can sense them so well now," Haiden commented idly, when she knelt to secure it in a rotting log. "Now we don't have to place them visibly enough to follow the trail. Do you remember the first time we used them to find our way home?"

Gisela stared at him, surprised by the question. Was he genuinely asking? Did he really think she would ever forget that night?

"Of course you remember," he said, as if reading her mind. But his tone stayed conversational, showing none of the emotion she felt at the memory.

Emotion he was surely also feeling, although she didn't blame him for wanting to hide it.

"I thought we were done for," Haiden went on. "Do you remember how much I cried? You seemed like the cleverest person in the world when you found the way home. I thought you were brilliant for having the stones ready just in case. It was only years later that I realized how horrifying it was that you were already carrying them with you all the time."

Gisela stood slowly, staying silent as her brother continued. He'd never shared these thoughts with her before.

"How many times do you think she tried to leave us that first year?"

"I don't know." Gisela's voice was soft and sad. "Five? Ten? They blur together. It felt like a lot because we were young and scared, but it probably wasn't that many. Her efforts increased as we got older, when you started to develop your singing."

Haiden nodded, the pair of them remembering in silence for a moment. "And every time, your stones saved us," he commented. "You'd think she would figure it out and confiscate them."

"I don't think she was ever thinking clearly enough to be

that strategic," Gisela said wearily. "She acted from the impulse of the moment, usually."

"The panic of the moment, more like," Haiden said.

"I think Papa might have known about the stones," Gisela said. "He was always relieved when we made it home, but he stopped being surprised. I think that's why he didn't search for us as much as we got older."

"Do you?" Haiden raised an eyebrow. "You're more generous than I am." His eyes traveled to the log where the stone was concealed. Gisela wondered what it felt like in his mind, his awareness of it sitting there, separated now from its fellows. "Come on," he said. "Let's get moving."

Gisela followed his lead as he forged ahead, retracing the route they'd taken from the group. It was technically Haiden's role, since he was in front, but she counted the trees in her head anyway. She couldn't help it. The habit was too ingrained. The mood was somber after their unusual moment of reminiscing, and they traveled in silence. It wasn't unusual for them to go hours in that manner, but it didn't feel comfortable this time. Too many things were changing in their world, and Gisela couldn't keep back a fear that those things would come between them.

When they'd well and truly cleared the marshier ground and were nearing the area where they'd left the group, Gisela put a hand on her brother's arm.

"Are you all right, Haiden?"

He came to a stop, turning to face her. "I never actually asked. When *did* you start carrying the stones, Gisela?" he demanded, ignoring her question.

Gisela searched his eyes, trying to understand what had brought on this mood in her brother. "The night of the festival," she said calmly. "The one where Asivah the elf princess said the prophecy, and Mother..."

Haiden nodded, finishing the thought she was reluctant to say aloud. "And Mother panicked, and made her very first attempt to abandon us in the woods." He paused. "Not us. Just me."

"Us, Haiden," Gisela said firmly. "It's always us. There is no you and me, just us. We're one entity."

"We're not, though," Haiden said unexpectedly. "We're two entirely separate people."

"Of course we are, but you know what I mean," Gisela said impatiently. "We're in it together, I promise."

Haiden shook his head, apparently taking no comfort from the words that used to soothe him so reliably when he was a child. "You're the one choosing not to understand what I mean. We've shared our lives to an extent most siblings don't have to, but that doesn't mean we can't have different trails ahead of us, Gisela. The prophecy isn't attached to you, and it doesn't have to dictate your future. If we could find a way around Mother's magic, you could have a full, free life. I have no doubt you'd prosper in the capital, for example."

"Haiden, what are you talking about?" Gisela demanded, upset. "I'm not going anywhere. Why are we even discussing this?"

"Because it's time," Haiden said simply. "You're eighteen now, Gisela. You need to think about your own future. I already told you, I've seen the way you are around Otto. I know you'd love to leave the forest when he does, discover what his world is like back in Terenford. And there must be a way for us to make it possible."

"It doesn't matter what's possible, because that's not my trail," Gisela said, starting to feel angry. "Haiden, I can't believe you think I'd ever consider abandoning you. It's like you don't know me at all."

"I know you too well," he contradicted. "Better than you know me."

Gisela spluttered a protest, but he barreled on with all the brutal honesty of a fifteen-year-old. "I know you enough to know that you'll miss out on living your own life if I don't push you into it. And you think you know me, but you still see me as a child. You don't even know me well enough to see that I'm desperate to live *my* own life. You still react to me as though I'm that crying four-year-old who's been abandoned by his parents in the forest."

"That isn't true," Gisela argued, frustrated.

But Haiden wasn't hearing it. "It is. You know I appreciate everything you've done for me, Gisela, but you can't keep treating me like I'm your son instead of your brother. I'm basically grown up now, and I want to make my own decisions, and forge my own path. If you never let me take any risks, how can I?"

Gisela bit her lip, unable to help feeling hurt at his words. He was trying to temper himself, but his frustration came through all too clearly.

"I'm trying to keep you alive, Haiden."

"It's not much of a life, though, is it?" Haiden demanded. "I don't want to spend the rest of my days following the stones down safe paths. I want to follow adventure when I encounter it, not run away from it."

"What do you think we're doing now?" Gisela said angrily. "*You're* the one who wanted to join this group. We're here so you can have your adventure. Do you think I want to be exposing ourselves like this?"

Haiden was clearly ready to retort, but a sound made them both pause. Putting their argument on hold, they exchanged a warning look and backed into the trees. A minute later, someone came into sight, moving through the undergrowth with a passable attempt at stealth.

Gisela let out a breath of relief when she recognized one of the guards, coming out of her hiding place just as Haiden did the same.

"Greetings," she said, causing the man to jump. "Were you sent to scout this way because we took too long to return?"

The guard blinked between them. "No, I'm not scouting. I'm just on close patrol. Camp isn't far." He pointed in the direction they'd been traveling.

"Oh, we're closer than I realized," Gisela said. "We'd better report to Norris, I suppose."

"He's not at camp," the guard informed them.

Gisela paused mid-step, frowning back at him. "I thought he was going to stay with the prince."

"He did," the man said. "The prince isn't in the camp, either. They both went through the gate, with most of the others."

"Gate?" Gisela asked, alarmed. "What gate? Do you mean an elf gate?"

The guard nodded, looking faintly envious. "Quite something to behold, seeing them disappear into nowhere. Don't know how it feels to step through it."

"Not as exciting as you'd think," Haiden informed him, his voice betraying the same impatience Gisela felt. "Why did they go through an elf gate?"

"To attend the festival," the guard said. He looked between them, confused. "How long have you been out? Is this your first return from your scouting? You must have gone a long way. It only took maybe a quarter of an hour for one of the scout groups to discover a gate."

"How did they sense it?" Haiden demanded. "Was Valerie with them?"

"They didn't sense it," the man explained. "They saw it. Said they could see a random patch of light in the forest, and when they approached, they found themselves looking into a clearing filled with stalls and people. Like looking through a window, apparently. Anyway, they came right back and told the rest of the group. The chief and His Highness figured out quickly enough that it must be one of these elf gates you two had mentioned. Exploration suggested it was a market with music and dancing and whatnot, nothing sinister, so most of the group have gone to explore."

"Probably a full moon festival and market," said Gisela, glancing at Haiden. Predictably, he looked excited about the prospect of mingling with more people. "I wonder where the gate leads."

"To the market," said the guard. "I told you."

She shook her head. "No, I mean I wonder what part of the forest the market is in. Whether it's closer to our destination or further from it."

"Let's find out," said Haiden, bouncing on the balls of his feet. "We might recognize the area, you never know. We'll have a better hope of doing so than the others, probably."

Gisela nodded slowly, unable to share his enthusiasm. Markets could be very useful, but they were also a risk. A number of risks, actually.

"Let's go, then," she said.

At the guard's direction, they passed through the camp and continued on its far side. As he'd said, most of the group were absent, only a handful of guards remaining to keep watch on the area. Clearly Monty, Valerie, and Lady Louisa had joined Otto in exploring the market.

"Do you think we should have told that guard what we found?" Haiden asked, as they moved through the forest. They didn't need the guard's directions now. Gisela could tell from Haiden's confident stride that he could sense the gate with ease.

She shook her head. "I'd prefer to make the report to either Norris or Otto. It sounds like we'll find them both at the market. I suppose we just tell whichever one we find first."

Haiden didn't respond. He'd picked up the pace, and Gisela could see that she'd lost his attention. She didn't blame him. Even she could locate the gate now, the lights of the festival spilling out into the darkening forest, and the forms of many market-goers visible between two tree trunks ahead. The sound wouldn't carry until they'd actually passed through the gate, she knew, but she could almost hear the music of the elven instruments.

Haiden went first through the portal, Gisela close behind. She took a moment to get her bearings, disoriented by the flood of light and deluge of sound. The market was bustling, suggesting that whatever new restrictions the Imperator had placed on the trade of talismans, they weren't absolute. Plenty of humans had flocked to the market, and elven vendors could be seen at many stalls, offering their talismans.

"Not as much magic here as usual," Haiden commented. "The talismans don't feel very strong. Maybe they're only allowed to sell minor ones."

Gisela looked around, trying in vain to see what he could sense with his extra ability. But of course the talismans looked unremarkable to her. She had no way to judge their strength.

She turned around to find that Haiden had taken off while she was distracted, striding across the space toward a stall hung with colored lanterns. Gisela wended her way through the crowd after him, frustrated that he wasn't waiting for her. His earlier words rang in her ears, about how she wasn't letting him live his own life. She had no idea what to do with the accusation. She could understand his frustration, but leaving him to fend for himself was unthinkable. As grown up as he felt, he was still only fifteen. And he was doubly vulnerable due to his undeveloped but desirable singing ability.

Catching up to her brother at last, Gisela seized his arm, just as a high voice caught her attention from just by her elbow.

"...you'd need a singer for that, a talisman won't suffice. And you'll not find a singer here. Not one with any sense, anyway."

Haiden looked sharply around, his expression telling Gisela he'd also heard the comment. She looked to see an older elf manning the closest stall. He was in conversation with a young woman who looked crestfallen at his pronouncement.

"You're sure you don't have any talismans that can help?"

"Nought," the elf said, showing neither sympathy nor pleasure at her dismay. "No one here will. Even if a talisman could do that, it would be too powerful for me to sell you under current regulations. But in any event, that type of power requires magic that's sung, not mined."

"There must be *some* singers here," the woman said, scanning the crowd hopefully. Gisela felt Haiden twitch beside her as the stranger's eyes passed over them. "I thought they often frequented markets to offer their services for a fee."

"Not lately." The new voice heralded the approach of an older human woman, bearing every sign of being the classic market busybody. Gisela knew such people well—they came to trade in gossip as surely as in wares. "At least not around here. What part of the forest are you from, lass, that you're unaware of the rumors? No sensible singer would show his or her face in this part of the forest, not with their kind being rounded up for harvesting."

Cold horror washed over Gisela as she felt Haiden stiffen beside her. Rounded up? Harvesting? What did that mean? What could the woman be talking about?

"Dramatic, as humans always are." The elf spoke dismissively, but the young woman looked intrigued.

"What do you mean *rounded up*?"

"La, I don't know, child," the older woman said comfortably. "It's been happening for some time, though. Every village in the region seems to have been affected. Folks have taken to hiding their singers, if not sending them out of Ilgal altogether. Rumor is the ones who've been taken are all being held somewhere, but who's to know the details? The point is, they're taken, and they're not seen again. And even if there were singers here, they'd be hiding amongst us, not making themselves known, and certainly not offering their services."

"Come on, Haiden," Gisela murmured, prodding her brother into motion. "We need to get out of here. You can't be here."

"Gisela." Her brother's voice sounded dazed, her own horror reflected back at her in his eyes. "Gisela, that's what we found."

"What?" she asked, still chivvying him through the crowd. "What are you talking about?"

"The hole. The stump. The place we saw, where something's hidden, with a potent concentration of magic leaking out when it's uncovered. That's it. That's where the singers are being held."

"What?" Gisela came to a halt, staring at him. "You think that hole we saw the woman access was—"

"A prison," Haiden finished eagerly. "Or a cage, or whatever you want to call it. That sack she dropped down it was probably food."

Gisela bit her lip. "It's just a guess, Haiden."

"A good one," he argued. "I felt it, Gisela, from ages away. I don't know how else to explain the quantity of magic I could sense." His eyes lit up. "And we can find our way back there! We left a stone." He turned in a full circle, searching fruitlessly through the throng. "We need to find the others. With the might of the prince and his guards, we can liberate everyone!"

"Slow down," Gisela said, alarmed by the light in his eyes.

No doubt his every heroic dream was coming to a head, but all she could see was danger. This rumor was everything she'd ever feared, everything that had led her to keep Haiden's ability quiet all these years.

"I think I see Norris," said Haiden, disregarding her words completely. "Come on." He seized her hand, pulling her through the crowd. His jostling was forceful enough that the strangers around them parted quickly, allowing them a clear passage toward the group of familiar-looking guards.

They'd barely gone ten steps, however, when Haiden came to an abrupt halt, almost causing Gisela to run into his back.

Her protest died on her lips as she followed her brother's gaze to see another figure frozen not a stone's throw away, staring at them with wide eyes that swirled with too many emotions to name.

The years fled from Gisela, and for the briefest of moments she was a child again, looking into a face that made her feel loved and protected. Then all the events between that time and the present dropped on her in a crushing deluge, and she felt Haiden's hand clench in hers.

Even knowing all that had passed, she couldn't stop the whisper that escaped her lips.

"Papa."

# CHAPTER FIFTEEN

# Otto

Otto turned, surveying the brightly lit clearing. It was a mesmerizing sight. What a windfall to have inadvertently camped so close to one of the market gates Gisela had told him about. Not only was it fascinating to witness a forest market, but his chances of discovering exact information about the location of the Imperator were probably better here than anywhere else. Gisela had told him how markets were protected by order of the Imperator. No bargains could be entered into other than those relating to the sale of wares, and the regulatory magic placed over the gatherings usually prevented elves from tricking humans into bargains they didn't realize they were entering. He could ask for information more freely, and even if he didn't get the answers he wanted, he wouldn't find himself accidentally giving away half his father's kingdom.

A small group of elves were set up on the far side of the clearing, making music on small wooden flutes. It was an enchanting sound, haunting and captivating in a way no melody made by a human voice ever could be. Although of course it also lacked the magic that was drawn out of the earth by human song. And no voices swelled the melody.

Otto moved toward a nearby stall which was filled with the types of fabrics Gisela and Haiden's clothes were made of. Perhaps acquiring forest clothes would make their group less conspicuous.

"Your Highness." Norris's low voice drew Otto's attention, and he turned to see the head guard hovering close at his shoulder. The man had barely left his side, his every move showing that he was on high alert in the presence of so many strangers.

"Yes, Norris." Otto turned away from the stall, abandoning the idea of new clothes with a wry smile. He didn't think a change of outfit would do much to prevent them from drawing attention.

"I think we should consider returning to camp," Norris said tightly. "We're attracting a great deal of attention."

"Nonsense," Otto said. He glanced around, noting how many pairs of eyes were lingering curiously on the well-dressed young stranger and his escort of uniformed guards. "I mean, not that we're attracting attention. Obviously we are. But we'd be mad to return to camp without making the most of this opportunity for information. For all we know, this location might be closer to the Imperator's settlement. The gate might be providing us with a shortcut."

"Yes, Your Highness, I have men making those inquiries already," Norris assured him. "There's no need for you to ask the questions yourself. In fact, it's better if you don't."

Otto strolled to the next stall, where a keen-eyed elf was selling some kind of toffee apple. "Oh, I realize that," he assured Norris. "But that doesn't mean I should leave. I want to explore the market." He nodded at the elf, his eyes flicking back to the coated apples, which glowed faintly in the dancing lantern light. "Are they enchanted in some way?"

"Why don't you find out, good sir?" the elf asked with a grin. "Only two coppers a piece."

Otto laughed. "No thanks. I'd rather not risk it." He turned to Norris, who was still frowning. "Didn't you say the scouts haven't all returned yet?" he challenged the head guard. "The camp may not be any safer than here, for all we know."

"They've almost all returned," said Norris. "Only one pair is yet to report in."

Otto frowned as his eyes passed over the crowd, spotting Valerie's fiery hair at a nearby stall, Monty hovering predictably close.

"That pair is Gisela and Haiden, isn't it?"

He stared unseeingly at the market, his mind lost in memories of his last conversation with Gisela. Had she understood what he wasn't saying? What he hadn't even found a way to acknowledge to himself? Surely she had. She was far too intelligent not to read him. Which made it all the more depressing that she'd pulled away from him. But on the other hand...she hadn't seemed entirely unaffected by his nearness.

Shaking his head, he forced his attention back to the present, a hint of concern lacing his thoughts. "I wonder what's taking so long. I thought they'd be here by now."

Norris made a noise of acknowledgment, but before he could speak, Otto caught sight of two familiar figures fighting their way through the throng in the center of the clearing, and he brightened.

"There they are. They're probably looking for us to make their report."

He hurried toward the pair, Norris close behind him. The prince's eyes were on Gisela as they came into hailing distance, so he missed whatever made Haiden stop abruptly. But he saw Gisela stiffen, her eyes widening and her face contorting for a moment in the most vulnerable expression he'd ever seen her wear.

Otto was close, but not close enough to hear her quiet whisper. He didn't need it, though. The resemblance between Haiden and the tall man standing ramrod straight in the center of the clearing was marked.

"It's their father," he breathed, taking another step forward.

"What?" Norris's voice was sharp enough to reach the siblings, but neither of them seemed to hear. They were locked silently in the gaze of the man Otto had never seen before. "I thought their parents were dead."

"So did I," Otto murmured.

"So they lied to us." Norris's voice was dark, but Otto felt none of the older man's suspicion. He made a shushing motion, his eyes still riveted on the scene in front of them.

"Gisela. Haiden." The man's voice sounded choked. "You're here. Are you...are you all right, then?"

"We're still alive, as you can see." The hard voice sounded nothing like Haiden's usual tones.

"You've both grown so much," the man said, coming closer to the pair. Neither moved toward him, but neither backed away either. Otto watched, spellbound, as the stranger's eyes passed wistfully over his daughter's face. "Gisela, you're all grown up now. When did you become a woman?"

"Sometime in the last five years, I suppose," she said. Her voice was softer than Haiden's, and not as angry. But it was infinitely sadder, and it made Otto's heart ache in response. "It seems we'd best leave. It's no longer safe for us to be here."

"No, don't leave," he said quickly. "You're safe."

Haiden let out a derisive snort, and the man hurried on.

"What I mean is, she's not here. She's at home."

"Home? How nice to still have one of those," Haiden said

pleasantly. "I'm sure home is very cozy now it's only the two of you. Plenty of food to go around."

"Haiden, you know I never wanted this," the man said, anguished.

"You didn't fight to stop it, either," Gisela cut in. "How long did it take you to realize we weren't coming back? When did you grasp that we'd left on purpose?"

"I looked for you," he said, his voice weak. "I searched everywhere. But when I found your things gone, I realized you'd planned for it. And I knew I had no right to call you back."

"Well, that's one thing we agree on," Haiden said coldly.

"I knew you were strong enough," the man insisted. "Both of you. I taught you how to be strong, to survive, to overcome every obstacle. I knew you'd be all right. If I'd left your mother alone, she wouldn't have fared as well."

"All right?" Haiden repeated incredulously. "Is that how you think we've been all these years? I'm sure you slept as peacefully as a baby, with such unassailable knowledge of our welfare." His lithe frame quivered with tension, his anger barely held in as he turned to his sister. "Come on, Gisela, let's go."

"Yes," she agreed, looking weary and suddenly much older. "We need to leave."

"No, you can't just go."

The man stepped forward, seizing her arm. Otto watched in surprise as Gisela twisted her arm rapidly, yanking it downward toward her father's thumb and wrenching herself immediately free of the stronger man's grip.

Far from being angered by this defiance, the man broke into a smile. "You remember the tricks I taught you."

"And I've learned plenty more, so let's not make this into a scene," Gisela said coldly. She glanced around and, doing the same, Otto realized how many people were watching the reunion. The immediate area had fallen quiet.

Gisela met the older man's eyes as she continued. "I know you had your reasons for what you did...and what you didn't do. But you also know that we have our reasons for keeping our distance." She stepped back decisively.

Gisela didn't appear to have noticed Otto and Norris, but he moved toward her anyway, driven by an impulse to range himself by her side rather than see her stand alone. Haiden apparently felt a similar urge, because with two quick steps, he put himself between his father and sister.

"Don't you dare lay a hand on her. You have no right to tell us what to do or where to go. You surrendered that right years ago."

"Please, I just want to talk with you," the older man said, raising his hands in a placating gesture.

Otto stepped forward again, placing himself just behind Gisela. Still not sure if she actually knew he was there, he reached out and put a hand on her shoulder. Gisela's slim form sprang instantly into motion, and before Otto realized what she was about, she'd grabbed his hand in a viselike grip, thrust an elbow back into his stomach, and smashed her foot down onto his. He let out a grunt, releasing her at once, and Gisela whirled around. Norris appeared at Otto's side, his expression furious, but Otto waved him back.

"Otto!" Gisela gasped, clearly startled by his identity. "I'm so sorry, I—I thought—I mean, I acted on instinct, and—"

"It's all right." He waved a hand, hoping it wasn't obvious how much she'd winded him. He shifted his weight off his injured foot. "I'm the one who should apologize, I didn't mean to scare you."

His eyes passed to Haiden and their father, who'd been startled out of their standoff. Otto felt his hand clench a little, and forced himself to relax. He didn't know what had passed between the members of this family, and it wasn't his place to insert himself. But he couldn't help but feel critical of the father whose presence had sent Gisela into her most defensive, most suspicious state. It was clear that the encounter with the man who should have made her feel safest of all had instead brought back memories of being in a constant state of vulnerability. Her demeanor was reminiscent of how it had been when Otto had first met her. He hadn't even realized how much her attitude had changed, and seeing her revert was painful.

"Sir." The stranger moved forward, as if to take charge of Gisela. "Please allow me to apologize. I assure you she meant no harm."

"Don't speak to him on our behalf," cut in Haiden scornfully. "We know him, unlike you." His voice took on a formal tone that dripped with irony. "Father, allow us to introduce you to our new friend. His Highness, Crown Prince Otto, heir to the throne of our fair kingdom."

Norris's quiet growl told Otto that the head guard wasn't impressed about this public pronouncement, but for his part, he was more interested in the stranger's response. Gisela and Haiden's father had gone completely still, his eyes wide and horrified as they passed from Otto to the others.

"Pleased to make your acquaintance," Otto said calmly, inclining his head slightly.

"What...what are you thinking?" The man didn't even respond to Otto, his eyes still on his children. "How is this possible?"

"Having left us to our own devices, you must trust us to take care of ourselves," Gisela said crisply. "We're fine, which is all you need to know. I suggest you leave."

"But...but surely you..." The man trailed off, apparently either unable or unwilling to say more.

"Goodbye, Father," Gisela said, turning away in a clear dismissal.

The older man obviously wasn't satisfied, but by this time a number of Otto's guards had gathered around him. Valerie and Monty had joined the group as well, along with Lady Louisa. In face of so many observers, he seemed to lose his nerve.

"If you're sure you know what you're doing," he said to his children, looking miserable. Then, with a final bob of the head, he turned to stride away. He'd only taken two steps before he turned back, however, his eyes sad as they rested on Gisela and Haiden. "If you ever...I mean, you know where to find us. We haven't moved."

"Don't hold your breath," Haiden said in clipped tones.

The man didn't respond. With a final glance between his children, he hurried from the clearing.

"I really am sorry," Gisela said to Otto, looking mortified. "I shouldn't have—"

"No apology necessary," Otto assured her. "It'll teach me not to assume someone knows I'm there."

"Some apology might be necessary," growled Norris under his breath.

Otto ignored him. "So I take it that was your father," he said delicately, his eyes on the stranger's retreating back.

Gisela gave a short nod.

"The one who you told us is dead," Norris said flatly.

"I never said dead," she contradicted. "I said he was gone, which was true. He's gone from our lives and has been for a long time."

"Can you believe him?" Haiden's angry voice cut across the conversation. He didn't appear to have been listening at all. "Acting like it's some kind of emotional family reunion?"

"That's what it seemed like to me." Monty's mutter earned him an elbow to the ribs from Otto.

"I need some air." Still ignoring the rest of them, Haiden strode off into the crowd.

"Haiden!" Gisela made to chase her brother, but Otto stopped her, taking the risk of seizing her arm again.

"Give him some space," he advised her. "He'll be all right."

Gisela bit her lip, clearly not liking it.

"Trust me," Otto pleaded with her, his heart moved both for her and for Haiden.

As good as Gisela's intentions were, she was as bad with Haiden as Norris was with Otto. He jerked his head toward the guard, dropping his voice for Gisela's ears only.

"I know what it's like to be always followed by well-meaning protectors. And if Haiden is anything like I was at fifteen, he'll find it unbearable in moments like this. Privacy is something a prince has to sacrifice, but I don't see any reason Haiden has to be subjected to the same indignity."

Gisela deflated slowly before his eyes, raising one callused hand to the side of her head.

"You're right," she said reluctantly. "I know he doesn't want his sister hovering at times like this. But..." Her eyes were pleading as they met Otto's. "All we have is each other."

"And he knows that as well as you do," Otto assured her, his heart wrung all over again. "I'm sure he won't go far."

"He shouldn't really go anywhere without making his report," said Norris in an undertone. "This is what comes of sending civilians as scouts." His voice was dark, and Otto suspected it had more to do with Gisela's accidental attack on him than on Haiden's desertion. It must sting the guard's pride to have allowed a teenage girl to get past his defense of the prince.

"Our report," Gisela said, sounding dazed. "Yes. We were looking for you, to tell you what we found."

"Never mind that," said Otto. His hand was still on her arm, and he led her gently away from the center of the clearing, hoping to reduce the number of eyes gawking at them. "It can wait. You must be as much in need of room to breathe as your brother is. That didn't look like an easy confrontation."

"It wasn't," Gisela acknowledged. She was still far from her normal collected self, her eyes continuing to dart around the clearing. Probably looking for Haiden. Otto had the sense that she felt his absence like an agitating splinter. "But I should still make my report."

Otto frowned, but before she could elaborate, they were interrupted by a high-pitched voice.

"Are you really the human prince?"

Frustrated, Otto turned to see an elf watching them, perched on the branch of a nearby tree. Swallowing his irritation, he forced himself to nod his head respectfully toward the elf.

"Good evening. I am."

"Unusual for you to be wandering the forest all alone, isn't it, Your Highness?" the elf persisted.

"His Highness is not alone."

Norris's voice was hard as he materialized at the prince's side. Otto could see that all Norris's misgivings about coming to the market were solidifying. The elf's interruption was inconvenient, to say the least.

"We've heard of your mission, of course," the elf went on, unconcerned by the tension radiating from every member of his audience. "I think all the elves have. But I don't know what brings you to our market. You won't have any success in rounding up singers here. None are willing to show their faces."

Otto made no answer, distracted by Gisela's demeanor. She'd stiffened under his touch at the elf's words, and when he looked down at her, she was staring at him in shock. He could see the color draining from her face.

"What is it?" he asked her. "Are you all right?"

"It's...it's you?" she whispered.

"It's me what?" Otto tightened his grip as she tried to pull her arm away, fighting a horrifying feeling that if he let her go now, she'd never return to him. "What are you talking about?"

"You're the one who's...who's *rounding up* singers?" Gisela's voice was growing stronger, the revulsion in her tone hard to take.

"I wouldn't say rounding up," Otto said defensively. "I mean, I am looking for singers, yes. That's why I'm in Ilgal. I told you that."

"No, you told me you were looking for a solution to the magic crisis," Gisela said, her face still ashen. "You never said that solution involved rounding up singers like animals."

"Hang on," said Otto, indignant. "Let's not get carried away. No one said anything about rounding them up—"

"Yes they did," Gisela argued. "Everyone's talking about it! The rumor is running wild in the market, and all across the forest."

"It's true," the elf chimed in, most unhelpfully, Otto thought.

"Rumors are never the full truth," Otto said impatiently. "I'm not trying to round anyone up. I'm trying to convince them to join me and help."

"I love the way humans twist and bend words to make them say whatever they wish rather than what they actually mean," the elf said smugly.

"Like elves can talk," Otto snapped, losing his temper. "You're masters of manipulating words."

The elf grinned at him, the pointed tips of his ears wobbling as he bowed his head as if in acknowledgment of a compliment. Irritated with the interfering creature, Otto pulled Gisela further away, Norris following in his usual unshakable way.

"Gisela, you know me," Otto said. "You can trust that I—"

"I don't know you," she contradicted, her voice taut and her face strained. "Not really. I was a fool to convince myself I did.

I've seen with my own eyes what your idea of *convincing* the singers is, and if you think I—"

"What are you talking about?" Otto asked, searching her face. She fell silent at his interruption, and now her lips were pressed shut. Did she know he knew about Haiden? Did she suspect him of trying to influence her brother without her approval? "Is this about Haiden?" he asked, so quietly he hoped even Norris wouldn't hear. "I know you want to keep his abilities a secret, but—"

"You know about Haiden?" she asked, her voice a strangled whisper. "How long have you known? Who else—?" Her eyes darted to Norris, and another thought seemed to occur to her. "Where is he?" she demanded, her voice instantly rising in her anger. "Where is my brother?"

"I...I don't know," said Otto, taken aback by her change in demeanor.

"Yes you do!" Gisela cried. "You convinced me not to follow him. You said to give him space, when all along, you were just trying to get your hands on his power."

"Gisela, that's madness," Otto protested. "No one's trying to exploit him. Surely you can trust that I—"

"No. I can't trust you." Gisela wrenched her arm free of Otto's hand at last. Her eyes were wild, unreasoning. Otto could see that in her mind, all her worst fears were playing out, and he had no idea how to convince her that it wasn't true. "I should never have let myself trust you," she said.

Before Otto could say another word, Gisela took off, running through the crowd in the direction Haiden had taken.

"Should I bring her in, Your Highness?" Norris asked, looking taken aback by the turn of events.

Otto shook his head quickly. "No. She's not thinking clearly at all, and that will only reinforce all her fears. We're not holding them against their will, Norris. They've always been free to leave at any time." His heart ached at the thought. "We'll just have to hope they come back to us when their emotions have cooled down."

The head guard's expression suggested his hopes didn't run the same way as the prince's, but Otto ignored him. He knew that Gisela's outburst might seem absurd from the outside, almost like she'd lost her mind. But he knew her well enough now to see that wasn't the case. She'd been carrying a weight all alone for far too long, and far before she was ready for it. Those types of burdens left their mark. And now everything she'd fought for was at risk, and she felt powerless to protect the brother whose safety had been her sole purpose most of her life. It was enough to make anyone lose their head for a moment. But he had faith that she'd find her way through it. And as much as he wished he could help her do it, he suspected she would need to face that monster on her own terms.

As for his own part in it all...he'd just have to have faith that when she'd had a chance to collect herself, the effort he'd put into building her trust wouldn't be wasted. Surely she'd realize he couldn't be doing anything nefarious.

"What was all that about?" Monty and Valerie hurried up to Otto, their eyes on the point where the crowd had swallowed Gisela up.

"I don't entirely know," Otto said helplessly. "Gisela believes we're after Haiden, I think. She's afraid of us exploiting him."

"Does Gisela know that we know about Haiden, then?" Valerie demanded.

Otto grimaced. "She does now. I think I bungled that particular revelation, too."

"What revelation?" Monty demanded. "What do we know about Haiden?"

Otto sighed. "That he's a singer."

# CHAPTER SIXTEEN

# Otto

"What?" Monty and Norris's exclamations came in unison, and another voice followed soon after.

"Haiden is a singer, is he?" Lady Louisa sounded thoughtful as she appeared from the crowd in company with a pair of guards. She ranged herself alongside Valerie, tapping her closed fan against two fingers of her other hand. "That helps explain Gisela's overprotective attitude toward him."

"How long have you known, Your Highness?" Norris demanded, looking irate.

"A while," Otto admitted. "But I didn't have any proof. Although I think we can consider Gisela's reaction confirmation."

"With respect, Your Highness, that was very unwise of you to keep that information from me," Norris said, his lips a thin line. "To properly protect you, I need all the information regarding any possible threats."

"I don't believe Haiden is a threat to me," said Otto calmly.

A high snort drew Otto's attention to the branch above his head, and he frowned to see the elf who'd so unhelpfully inserted himself into Otto's conversation with Gisela earlier. He must have followed through the branches when Otto pulled Gisela away from him.

"Don't consider him a threat, hey?" the elf asked, sounding amused. "How wise you must be, to see all ends."

Otto narrowed his eyes at the miniature eavesdropper. "This conversation is private," he informed the elf flatly.

The stranger just blinked his emerald eyes lazily, his smile suggesting he had no intention of moving on.

"He has a point, Your Highness," Norris muttered. "You can't know for certain that Haiden's ability posed no threat to you."

"I'm sorry to have offended you, Norris," Otto said shortly, "but I made my decision intentionally, and not without reason." He gestured to his body. "And as you see, no harm has come to me as a result."

Norris looked far from pleased, but he said nothing further. Otto's eyes flicked back to the elf, who was not only continuing to hang around, but looking unpleasantly smug in the process. What did the elf mean about Haiden being a threat? Did he know something Otto didn't, or was it idle chatter, intended to cause trouble? The young elf seemed a particularly impish example of his kind. Certainly nothing like the dignified elderly leader who'd admitted that she was tempted to exploit Otto's youth, but must instead refer him to the authority of the Imperator.

"Come on."

With a final dark look at the elf, Otto led his group around the edge of the clearing. They were attracting attention from the crowd—unsurprising after Haiden's announcement of his identity—and he was becoming increasingly uneasy. The whole mood of the market had changed, everything seeming less orderly and more chaotic by the second. Otto could see Norris eyeing a clump of interested-looking humans nearby.

"I think we might be wise to return to our camp, Your Highness," Lady Louisa said, with her usual unruffled dignity.

"Yes, you might be right," Otto agreed. "But I'd be more comfortable if Gisela and Haiden returned in time to accompany us."

"They can find their way back, Otto," Monty told him easily. "They know their way around better than any of us do."

Otto bit his lip, not satisfied. Before he'd marshaled his thoughts to make an argument that would convince Norris to let them all wait, his eyes were drawn to a trio of elves approaching across the market clearing. They were moving toward the group with purpose, and it was too late to avoid speaking to them without obvious rudeness. Norris had already spotted them, and at a subtle signal, he sent his guards to form a loose ring around Otto and the others. The conversation petered out, and everyone in the prince's group watched silently as the three elves reached their position and came to a stop in a line before bending into synchronized bows.

"Greetings," said the elf at the center of the trio. "Do I understand correctly that you are Crown Prince Otto of the human kingdom?"

"Of this kingdom, you mean," Monty said disapprovingly.

"Peace, Monty," Otto murmured, before dipping his head slightly to the elves. "I am Prince Otto. To whom do I speak?"

The middle elf bowed again. "Well met, Your Highness. I am Josper. I understand that you passed through my own settlement not long ago. Regrettably, I was not present and missed the opportunity to make your acquaintance then."

Otto studied the elf thoughtfully. He was immaculately dressed, his snow-white clothes suggesting he felt no need to camouflage himself in the forest. He was confident in his protection, then, which probably meant he had a position of respect. He certainly wasn't young and impish like the elf who'd eavesdropped. In fact, he was more conciliating in his speech than any elf Otto had so far encountered in Ilgal, but it didn't make him warm to the stranger. On the contrary, he found himself less inclined to trust the elf. His eyes were too sharp for his polite words.

Otto was aware that it made no sense to conclude that the elf was showing him a false front. Their kind were generally considered shrewd to the point of being unscrupulous, but they weren't often accused of outright duplicity. And yet, Otto found himself reflecting that this elf was of a different kind from the ones he was used to.

"You find yourself with that opportunity now," he said smoothly. "Was there a particular matter that caused you to wish for my acquaintance?"

"Merely that I have heard rumors of your quest in our forest, and wished to understand what I have heard," Josper responded. His eyes flicked to Otto's companions, lingering on both Monty and Valerie. "I have been led to believe that you travel with a singer of Ilgal in your party. I would be delighted to have speech with this person."

"Not this again," said Monty impatiently. He shifted so that he stood at Valerie's side. "She's not from Ilgal, and she's not interested, so you can leave her alone."

Otto half expected Valerie to chastise Monty for speaking on her behalf, but she seemed to be in agreement with him this time.

"I'm the singer in the group," she said, looking unflinchingly down into the elf's eyes. "But there's some misapprehension, and it's followed us for some time. I'm not from Ilgal. Whoever it is you're looking for, I'm not that person."

Josper regarded her steadily, his shockingly green eyes unreadable. "Is that so?" he said at last. His eyes passed over the rest of the group. "And are you the only singer in your company?"

"It strikes me that we'd be unwise to give information away without return," said Otto lightly. "Are you seeking to make a bargain with us?"

The elf showed no sign of emotion other than the tiniest wiggle of the tips of his ears. "Such bargains are not allowed at public markets," he said. "As I suspect you know, Your Highness."

"Then it doesn't seem that we're in a position to assist with your inquiries," Otto said blandly. "Perhaps we shall meet again, Josper."

The elf inclined his head deeply. "If the trails deign to bring us together," he agreed. He moved back, but he clearly wasn't satisfied. His eyes kept searching the group, always coming back to rest on Valerie.

Monty took a half step forward, ready to jump, unasked, to Valerie's defense. But the elves turned away as another of their kind joined them. With a frown, Otto realized that it was the impish elf who'd been irritating him earlier. Josper asked his younger fellow something Otto couldn't hear, in response to which the impish one shook his head, the tips of his ears wobbling with the motion. He glanced at Valerie, muttering something indecipherable, then gestured out at the crowded market.

"I meant what I said, Otto." Valerie's voice was quiet in Otto's ear, drawing his attention away from the elves' interaction. "It's not me they're looking for. But they are looking for someone. Two someones, I think."

Otto looked sharply around. "You think they're looking for Gisela and Haiden?"

She nodded. "I've suspected it for a while. I think their information is incomplete, though. I don't think they know for sure which of the siblings is the singer, or perhaps they think it's both. And I can't believe it's just that he's a singer, because we haven't seen any other evidence of the elves being unduly interested in singers. They're seeking these particular ones for some reason, this brother-sister hermit pair who've been living out of reach of civilization for years. Remember how the elves in that first settlement wanted to know if I had a brother? I think this one wondered the same about Monty and me just now, judging by the way he looked between us."

"He thought you and I were brother and sister?" Monty sounded more outraged by this than everything else.

Otto ignored him, his voice hollow. "And in the second settlement, they wanted to trade information about Gisela and Haiden."

"They did?" Norris joined the conversation, his brow furrowed. "You never said as much, Your Highness."

"It was immaterial, given I refused," said Otto flatly. "But Valerie is right. Everywhere we go in Ilgal, there's no sign of any singers. Haiden is the only one we've encountered. And he was doing his best to keep that fact hidden. It makes sense if someone's looking for him."

"The thing is," Valerie said slowly, "I don't think they know the elves are looking for them. I think they're just cautious anyway. I hinted something to Gisela about the elves looking for her and her brother, and although she seemed alarmed, I got the sense she was genuinely surprised."

"I'm not sure," said Monty skeptically. "I think they must be hiding something. Did you see their father's reaction when he found out they were running with a prince? I thought he'd try to take advantage of the connection, but he didn't respond that way at all."

Otto grimaced at the understatement. He wasn't inclined to read too much into it, though. It wasn't uncommon for his elevated status to unnerve people. Either way, the situation looked bad, he reflected, his eyes lingering absently on the two humans who still remained of the gawking clump from earlier. They were hanging back out of hearing range, but still watching with great interest.

"It seems we have all questions and no answers," he said grimly. "Do I have this right? The elves, or at least some of them, have Haiden and Gisela in their sights, and we don't have any idea why. And we don't think Gisela and Haiden even know they're being sought. *And* we currently don't know where Gisela and Haiden are, because they ran off in a state of distress, and still haven't come back."

"That seems to cover it all, yes," Monty said.

Otto groaned. "I don't like this at all." He nodded at Norris. "You were right, we shouldn't have let Gisela just disappear. It's time to split up and search for them. I'm not going back to our camp without them."

Norris protested, but Otto stood firm against the head guard's attempts to get him to return to camp and leave the search to a contingent of the guards. Their impasse was only broken by Valerie's interjection.

"Otto, why don't we head back toward camp together? I'm not saying we go all the way back through the gate," she added quickly, seeing he was about to argue. "But if we get away from the crowd a bit, into the trees, I can try to harness a seeking song. I'm not amazingly experienced at them, but I've spent enough time now with Gisela and Haiden that I might be able to get a sense of which direction they went. Personally, I think they probably made for the camp, and with any luck we can follow them there."

"An excellent suggestion," said Norris briskly. "It's settled." Giving Otto no time to argue, he turned to give instructions to his guards, sending off two groups of three to look for the missing siblings in opposite directions.

Apparently keen to put her song to use, Valerie struck off toward the out-of-sight gate, Monty following close behind her. Otto hurried to keep up, his ears catching a soft hum of melody from the singer. He could only hope that it would work. His anxiety for Gisela and her brother was growing by the minute.

Two guards flanked Otto, and a glance back at where Norris was still issuing orders showed that even the last of the fascinated onlookers had dispersed. Otto looked ahead to realize that Valerie had passed out of sight, and Monty was rapidly disappearing between the trees. He increased his pace, his minders doing likewise.

They hadn't gone far into the trees when a sharp cry rang out.

"Valerie?" Otto called, breaking into a run. The word had barely left his lips when he heard an angry shout that he recognized as Monty.

"Let go of her, you—"

Both the words and the metallic sound of a weapon being drawn cut off abruptly, and fear clogged at Otto's throat.

"Monty?" he called, sprinting around a thick trunk. "Valerie?"

His friend came into sight, bent double and looking winded, and Otto threw himself down at his side.

"Your Highness, this area isn't safe," said one of the guards tightly. "We need to retreat to—"

Otto waved him into silence, gripping Monty's shoulders. "What happened?" he demanded. "Where's Valerie?"

The name seemed to recall Monty to his surroundings, and his head snapped up. Otto could see fog clearing from his friend's vision, and a moment later, Monty had launched himself to his feet, Otto jumping up with him.

"Valerie!" Monty screamed. There was no reply, and he turned to Otto. "They took her! Two men, they came out of nowhere, one grabbed her, and the other covered her mouth. And when I tried to come at them, they threw something at me."

"They threw something?" Otto repeated, confused. "What did they throw?"

"I don't know how else to describe it," Monty said, frustrated and impatient. "But it wasn't anything I could see. I think it was magic. One of them was holding something, and he sort of swung it around her and then threw...nothing...at me."

"We can figure that out later," said Otto quickly. "We need to find them."

"Yes, they can't be far." Monty picked up his sword from the grass, his eyes wide and panicked. "Valerie!" he called again. "Valerie, we're coming!"

"I'll go this way," Otto said, sprinting forward amid protests from his guards.

"No, not between those trees!" Monty called frantically. "That'll take you through the gate back toward camp, and miles from wherever they ran to!"

Otto dodged around the gate, which he hadn't even noticed approaching, his eyes searching the darkness fruitlessly.

"They can't have gone far," he called to Monty. "We can surely find them!"

In spite of these words, they could find no sign of Valerie or her abductors. Their shouts had attracted Norris and the guards still with him, and soon there were a dozen of them scouring the area. The singer had simply vanished. And the guards searching the surrounds for Haiden and Gisela came back just as unsuccessful. Norris sent some of his men through the gate to check the camp, but the guards there had seen no sign of the truants returning.

"They took her because she's a singer," Monty said, his

hollow voice cutting into Otto's rising panic. "It's coming back to me. She was singing as she ran, and a man appeared out of nowhere. He had a sack, like he was going to put it over her head. He planned this. I think whatever group he's part of came to the market hoping to find singers."

"And they found more than one," Otto said, horror creeping over him as he remembered Gisela's words about the market being rife with rumors of someone rounding up singers. Why hadn't it occurred to him that the culprit might be someone other than himself?

It certainly hadn't occurred to her. She'd instantly assumed it was him. Anguish gripped his heart as he remembered the disgust and betrayal in her eyes when she'd accused him. She'd run from him as though he was a charging galboar.

"What do you mean?" Monty asked, clearly struggling to think of anything beyond Valerie. His eyes focused laboriously on Otto. "You think they took Haiden as well?"

"And Gisela, most likely," Otto said miserably. "I can't imagine her letting her brother be taken without her."

Monty looked as anguished as Otto felt, and he belatedly realized that his friend would receive that comment as a criticism. But Otto didn't blame Monty for Valerie being taken, any more than he blamed Gisela for her own capture. He was the leader of their group. He was the one who'd failed to protect those under his command.

"What are we going to do?" Monty asked hollowly.

"Find them," Otto said, his eyes sparking. "And destroy whatever group thought they could get away with this."

# CHAPTER SEVENTEEN

# Gisela

Gisela ran blindly through the crowd, her panic rising as she searched the throng for Haiden. She was so overcome with fear, she could hardly think straight. She and Haiden had faced their share of danger, but she hadn't felt this truly vulnerable in a long time. Whatever had come at them, they'd faced together. And now she was alone with the crushing weight of Otto's betrayal. So much for the prince holding no secrets, she thought bitterly. And worse than her own disillusionment, Haiden was alone somewhere, driven to his most reckless state by the unexpected encounter with the father whom he'd once adored.

It was a recipe for disaster, and Gisela knew only one thing for sure: she had to find Haiden, and fast.

"Are you looking for your brother?"

The voice came from Gisela's elbow, and she looked down, expecting to see an elf. But it was a human child who blinked up at her.

"The one you were with before, who ran off into the trees?"

"Yes, where did he go?" Gisela demanded.

"He's a singer, isn't he?" the girl said, by way of answer. "I heard him singing when he went into the forest."

Gisela bit her lip, habit making her reluctant to acknowledge it.

"If he is, I don't think you'll see him again," the child said matter-of-factly. "Singers disappear, at least near my village. Most of them move to the city, but the ones who don't eventually just go missing."

Gisela pressed her lips into a thin line, her anger with Otto defying reason. How could he do it? How could he pretend to be so gentle and affable, and all along be orchestrating mass abductions?

The girl spoke again, pulling Gisela from her sense of betrayal. "You know, if he's your brother, you should run away."

"Why would I do that?" Gisela demanded.

The girl shrugged. "Bad things happen to the families of missing singers. They get sick, or hurt. Some of them even die."

Gisela hesitated, deeply uneasy about these revelations. Just what kind of operation was Otto overseeing? It was hard to believe that the genial prince would approve of such tactics. Was it possible that he didn't know the extent of it? Were his underlings taking matters into their own hands? An inkling of hope prodded at her, and she pushed it down. It was terrifying to realize how desperately she still wanted validation of her desire to trust the prince.

She put a hand to her head, trying to settle her thoughts. Her head and heart were completely at odds, and she had no idea what to think. It didn't help that she knew herself to be rattled by the encounter with her father. Her judgment was likely not at its most sound.

Lowering her hand, she gave her head a little shake. The girl's warning raised a lot of questions, and in other circumstances, she would want to ask more. But she didn't have the luxury of time now, not if Haiden had run alone into the trees and marked himself as a singer in the process.

"Which way did he go?" she asked.

The girl pointed, but her expression suggested she thought Gisela was crazy. "You're going after him? Nice knowing you, I guess."

Gisela ignored these dire words, calling a hasty thanks over her shoulder as she ran in the direction indicated. Moments later, she plunged into the trees, the light of the market's lanterns dropping rapidly away.

"Haiden?" she called, scanning the dark foliage for any sign of her brother. "Haiden, where are you?"

It hadn't been long since he'd stormed off, she told herself as she plunged deeper into the trees. He couldn't have gone too far. Would he have gone back through the gate to camp? It seemed unlikely—the gate was on the other side of the clearing. More likely he'd wanted to strike out alone to clear his head. Maybe he'd climb a tree again. He seemed to find it easier to think nearer the sky.

Gisela looked up, ducking as a bat swooped suddenly above her head. She shuddered. There was very little light now, and the sounds of the market were muted and distant. Something moved in the undergrowth, and Gisela swung around in a slow circle, scanning the area for threats. There was a reason she and Haiden usually avoided moving through the forest at night. Actually, there were lots of reasons. She'd gotten lax during her time with Otto's group, but she wasn't surrounded by thirty guards now. She was all alone.

Which meant Haiden was, too.

Galvanized by that thought, Gisela forced herself to go on, calling her brother's name. She wasn't deep in the trees—she could still faintly hear the market—when she caught a definite human tread behind her.

"Haiden?"

She spun around hopefully, but her optimism died at the sight of a burly man she'd never seen before, stepping purposefully forward with a sack in his hands.

Gisela's first instinct was to run, but a noise behind her told her that the man wasn't alone. She was quite possibly surrounded. Changing tack, she brought her fists up at once, dropping into a defensive stance.

"Oh ho, a fighter, are you?" the man chuckled, advancing unconcernedly. "None of that, lass, let's not make it harder than it needs to be."

He reached out one thick hand, grabbing her wrist in an iron grip and tugging her toward him.

Gisela let him pull her a couple of steps, letting him think he had her. When he pulled her closer and therefore gave her some leeway to work, she sprang back into motion, planting her feet and yanking her hand down toward his thumb. His grip was strong, and it took her two tries to wrench her hand free, her skin burning from the friction. But she didn't pause. Quick as a flash, she brought up both hands, palms flat, to connect with his ears.

The man staggered back with a cry, his hands flying to his ears. With any luck, she'd ruptured his ear drums.

Gisela swirled, ready to face whoever had been lurking behind her. What she saw, however, made her freeze at once.

"You *are* a fighter." The speaker was a tall man. She couldn't make out his expression in the darkness, but his voice sounded amused. "But I think you'd better give it up now."

Gisela's eyes passed to the limp form slung over the man's shoulder. She'd know that figure anywhere. For another moment, she held herself tense, then she deflated, all the fight going out of her. They had Haiden in their power, which meant they had her cornered. Her brother was clearly unconscious, and it would be far too easy for the stranger to end his life with the wicked looking blade held in his other hand. It took all her willpower not to fight back when the first man grabbed her from behind, locking her arms in place with his stronger ones.

"You didn't sing, though." The man who had Haiden considered her thoughtfully. "Are you smarter than your brother in keeping it hidden, or are you not a singer after all?"

"I thought the rumor in the market was that there was a pair of singing siblings," said the man holding Gisela, his voice uncomfortably close and much too loud.

"That's rumor, though, isn't it?" the other man said impatiently. "We don't want to drag her all the way there if she's no good to us."

"Works for me," growled Gisela's captor, still speaking too loudly. "Let me be the one to run her through. She's done destroyed my ears, little vixen!"

"Serves you right for being bested by a waif," spat the other one contemptuously. "No one's running her through, not here, anyway. Better bring her and let the boss decide. She'll have our hides if we get it wrong."

"Yeah, I guess that's true," muttered the disgruntled one. He gave Gisela a shake for good measure. "But if she decides you're useless, I'll be doing the honors myself."

"Enough chitchat," said the one still holding Haiden. "We gotta get out of here before anyone else comes this way." He nodded to his fellow, who was binding Gisela's hands together. "Gag her as well, just in case."

Gisela struggled instinctively as the man forced a rough band of material into her mouth. Seeing her resistance, the armed man held his blade suggestively against Haiden's exposed back, and Gisela subsided at once.

"There's a good girl," the man crooned, making her long to

pound his jaw with her fist. "No need for anyone to get hurt, now."

The next thing she knew, Gisela was slung over her captor's shoulder, and the pair of men were moving through the forest at a quick pace. To her surprise, they didn't strike deeper into the undergrowth, instead skirting around the edge of the clearing, leaving a solid distance between themselves and the markets all the way. It was agonizing to realize that help was close, but still just out of reach. Whoever they were, these men were familiar with the forest. They moved carefully, making little noise and leaving barely a trail. Any signs of their passage would be obscured by the imminent exodus of many market-goers.

Gisela stiffened when she realized that they were drawing near to the very location where her group had entered the market. Her breathing quickened as she struggled to draw the cold air through her nose, her mouth still blocked by the revolting gag. They were going through the gate back toward camp. She'd begun to question her assumptions about Otto's involvement, but all her suspicions returned.

That was, until the men passed through the gate and immediately took a sharp turn, heading in the opposite direction from the camp. Gisela's sense of direction was hampered in various ways, but she was fairly certain they were going north.

The men drew close enough together for her to see her brother's face, and she squirmed in position, trying to get a better look. Haiden didn't look injured, which was a relief. But why didn't he wake? This was too long for him to be unconscious if nothing was seriously wrong with him.

The journey began to feel interminable, Gisela losing all sense of time. Her panic grew as Haiden remained unresponsive, even when the terrain became rough, and she knew he must be getting as jolted as she was.

After another incalculable stretch of time, the ground

became marshy. The men were moving on a firm path, but around them, the forest floor was looking less like dirt and more like bog. Gisela realized with a sharp intake of breath that she recognized the surroundings. The scraggly trees, the damp air... they were close to the area she and Haiden had scouted, which meant...

The hole. Haiden had been right. The hole must be a prison for all the singers who'd mysteriously disappeared from Ilgal in recent times. And she and Haiden were about to join their number.

But their captors trudged right past the small clearing she and Haiden had observed. Gisela stared fruitlessly around, looking for the stump. One of their stones was nearby. A lot of good it would do them, since Haiden was the only one who could feel its location, and he was here anyway.

"I'm about ready for something hot," grunted the man carrying Gisela. "And someone to check my ears. They're killing me."

Gisela allowed herself a silent surge of vicious satisfaction.

"We'd better get a hot meal at the very least," the other one agreed. "Two in one night? That's better return than any market's given in months."

Gisela's captor made a noise of agreement in his throat. "They've all gotten too smart to show themselves." He jiggled Gisela painfully against his shoulder. "Except these ones, apparently."

"Ah, they're little more than kids," said the one in front. "Wonder why their parents didn't get them out of the forest, like most others've done."

A tangle of emotions went over Gisela at the words. She could hardly believe she'd seen her father that night, for the first time since she and Haiden had left their home in the dead of night five years before. There'd been no chance to process the encounter given what had followed. Even now she resisted her mind's attempt to dwell on the night they'd last seen their parents. She'd been only thirteen, but she'd understood what was happening by then. And she'd learned to read the signs of her mother's growing unease. Neither she nor Haiden had been surprised when their mother woke them with a story of harvesting mushrooms by moonlight. They'd let her think she was taking them into the forest to abandon them, all the while ready for this to be the time they struck out on their own, and didn't leave any stones to guide them home. Had she ever figured out their role in it? Or did she still think she'd succeeded in abandoning them to their deaths? Their father would correct her on that impression if so.

"Here we are."

The satisfied voice of one of the men drew Gisela from her thoughts. She twisted around to see that they'd entered a large clearing. Nestled against the trees on the far side of the space was a wooden cottage, its thatched roof illuminated by the moonlight that flooded the open ground. She'd had no idea a dwelling was so close to the point where she and Haiden had seen the false stump. The men strode across the clearing, knocking twice before pushing the door open and lugging their burdens through into a spacious room. A single lamp burned on a table in the middle of the space, and Gisela could see at a glance that the room was used for food preparation. It was empty of people, but the sound of muted voices issued from behind another closed door.

"Sounds like the meal's still going," said Gisela's captor brightly. He dumped her unceremoniously onto a chair next to the table. "Now don't make trouble if you know what's good for you. Or what's good for your brother, I guess I should say."

Haiden was deposited on the ground in the corner, and the two men hurried through the door, affording Gisela a brief glimpse of light, and the sound of conversation. The moment the door closed behind them, Gisela slid from the chair, hurrying to her brother. Her attempts to shake him awake produced no response, and anxiety threatened to overwhelm her.

"He's fine."

The feminine voice was much softer than the two men's had been, and Gisela spun around to see a woman leaning against the scrubbed table. Gisela blinked in the lamplight, trying not to let her recognition show on her face. It would be better if this stranger didn't know that Gisela had watched her clandestinely before. But there was no doubt this was the woman who'd turned the stump into a hole.

"Your brother," the woman said, as if there had been any doubt whom she was speaking of. "He hasn't been knocked out by force. His sleep is magically induced. He'll wake when I'm ready for him to wake. And as I said, he'll be fine."

Gisela studied the woman cautiously, trying to keep her anger at bay. She was painfully aware of her powerlessness.

"Ah, but of course you can't answer me," the woman said pleasantly. "I don't think there's any need for that gag, do you?"

She pushed herself upright, walking across the room with a mincing, unhurried step. Gisela couldn't help flinching as the woman produced a blade with an abrupt motion Gisela was sure was intended to intimidate her. But the stranger just sliced through the gag, her movements precise enough not to cut Gisela's skin.

Relieved, Gisela drew in a long breath. The foul taste of the gag lingered, but that was the least of her concerns.

"Who are you?" she demanded. "What do you want with us?"

"It seems you really aren't a singer," said the woman thoughtfully. "Or you're being very strategic in hiding it. It wouldn't do any good, you know." She raised a small item, carved to look like an acorn, but clearly made of solid wood. "Doesn't look like much, does it? But it's arguably the most powerful talisman I have. Magic-draining talismans are rare, you know. If you sing, this will absorb the power and release it harmlessly. None of your songs will affect me."

"I can't sing," Gisela said flatly, wondering if the talisman could really be that powerful. "I've never been able to."

"I'm inclined to believe you," the woman said, with every appearance of politeness.

"So there's no reason to keep me and my brother here," Gisela went on. "You can let us go."

The woman chuckled. "What's your name, child?"

Gisela kept her mouth clamped mulishly shut.

"If it helps, I'll go first. Mine is Lorraine." She twisted a strand of graying hair behind her ear. "An ordinary name for an ordinary person. There's nothing magical or especially intimidating about me, you know. You can relax."

"Hard to do, when I'm bound and my brother is unconscious on the floor at your orders," said Gisela angrily.

Lorraine gave a delighted laugh. "Well done, child. I'm delighted at how quickly you've recognized who's in charge. You were indeed intercepted at my orders."

"Abduction is hardly something to boast about," Gisela said.

"Ah, but it is merely a means to an end," Lorraine said comfortably. "And that end will certainly be worth boasting about, I promise. Now. Your name, please. Purely for the purpose of more convenient conversation."

Gisela regarded her uncertainly, but she could see nothing to be gained from pointless defiance. For all Lorraine's talk of being unintimidating, Gisela got the sense she would be wise to choose her battles with this woman.

"My name is Gisela," she said stiffly. "And I don't want any trouble. All I want is for me and my brother to be left alone to live our lives in the forest in which we were born."

"An admirable desire," Lorraine said approvingly. "And in a broad sense, it's exactly what I want as well. And what I'm working hard to achieve. But unfortunately, in a more specific sense, I'm not able to grant that request. Because your brother is a singer—don't bother denying it, my men heard him sing with their own ears—and therefore I need him."

"For what?" Gisela demanded.

"To save our forest," said Lorraine, as if it was obvious.

Gisela made an angry noise in her throat. "I'm sure you think you're above reproach, with the support of the royals behind you. But if you think I'm going to agree that the way to combat the growth of the magic is to round up singers and cage them like animals—"

"The growth of the magic?" Lorraine interrupted, bewildered. "I don't care about that." She pounded her chest with one fist, indicating the place where everyone in Ilgal felt the growing presence of the building magic. "That doesn't bother a true child of the forest. It's only outsiders who can't handle the pressure that we've learned to live with as a normal part of life. Why should I care about that?"

Gisela frowned. "So...so your purpose in getting your hands on the singers isn't to somehow use them to clear the magic?"

"Of course not," Lorraine said, sounding offended. "My plans are much more concrete than that." Her eyes were keen as they looked Gisela over. "And I'd love to know what made you think we had royal support in our scheme. I'm delighted that the rumor has taken hold."

"But...but don't you?" Gisela asked, shifting her hands uncomfortably under their bonds. She was getting the sense that Haiden had been grabbed opportunistically. If this woman didn't know they'd been traveling with the prince, she'd prefer to keep it that way. "Everyone says the prince is looking for singers all through the forest, and—"

"Ah, yes, that." Lorraine sighed. "It's a pain, really. Competition we don't need. But I haven't heard that he's actually found any." Her face suddenly split in a grin that Gisela found unnerving. "We've gotten there ahead of him. We've been operating for months, after all. He's barely begun his doomed mission."

Misery washed over Gisela as the last ounce of suspicion as to Otto's motives evaporated. Of course he wasn't behind this. She should have realized that the rumors about singers being rounded up couldn't relate to his quest. He would never have anything to do with the type of operation she'd stumbled into. With every interaction for weeks past, he'd shown her that he was too honorable for that. And yet she'd been ready to deem it all a lie on the merest accusation.

She felt doubly foolish because, if she was being completely candid, Otto was incapable of this type of plot in more ways than one. The woman before Gisela oozed wily strategy. She was cunning and sharp and completely at home in the forest. Otto, on the other hand, had been fumbling his way through Ilgal without even a clear idea of where he was going. How could she have let herself believe he was playing some deep game all along, with all the evidence suggesting the contrary?

But she knew how. It was nothing to do with Otto, and everything to do with her. She'd been letting herself believe that she could learn to trust again, but it had just been living a lie. And she hadn't even been circumspect enough to keep her suspicions to herself. Instead she'd thrown them immediately in Otto's face. How could he forgive that? She didn't expect him to. Her inability to trust anyone had destroyed her relationship with someone who was not only incredibly powerful, but— more to the point—dearer to her than she dared to admit, even to herself.

"I have other reasons for not wanting the prince to succeed, though," Lorraine went on. She was of course oblivious to Gisela's inner misery, her brow furrowed like a complaining child's as she thought only of her own schemes. "Which is why I've encouraged the rumor that he's behind the disappearance of all the singers. An idle chat in a market here, a gossip with a traveling peddler there...half of Ilgal probably believes it by now. Sensational rumors spread so much more quickly than the truth."

Gisela ground her teeth together. "So you've found a convenient scapegoat for your activities. Never mind that he's the crown prince of our kingdom."

"It's not just about finding a scapegoat," Lorraine informed her reasonably. "It also serves my purposes to have everyone think that the prince is behind my plans. If the elves think the crown is plotting against them, so much the better."

"You're trying to stir up trouble between the prince and the elves?" Gisela could only stare at her. "Don't you have *any* fear of consequences?"

"The prince is the one who should fear the consequences," said Lorraine, her voice suddenly sharp and angry. "He's the one who's failed us. Or his father, at least. How dare he come in here, meeting with elf leaders, openly seeking to treat with the Imperator, recognizing the elves' authority as though their presence here is legitimate?"

Gisela raised her eyebrows. "You don't think the elves have a right to be in Ilgal?"

"Ilgal belongs to us," said Lorraine, bringing her fist down on the corner of the table. "I didn't care about the little freaks when they kept to their own areas. But now they've taken what's mine, and they'll regret it."

"I don't understand," said Gisela blankly.

Lorraine was breathing hard, but she must have seen

Gisela's genuine confusion. She lowered her hand back to her side, taking a few deep breaths before speaking again in a much calmer tone.

"You're not from this part of the forest, are you?"

Gisela shook her head.

"Well." Lorraine nodded. "That would explain it. I am from this area. My family has lived here for generations." Her face hardened. "Will live here for generations to come." Her eyes traveled to Haiden's still form. "I see you understand family loyalty, Gisela. So you'll understand my feelings when I say that not so long ago, my family were the wealthiest and most influential leaders in the heart of Ilgal, a region my ancestors have held dear time out of mind. Then, several years ago, the elves decided they wished to distance themselves from the human capital. They decided to move their central settlement to the heart of the forest. Not build a new one, you understand. To move the one they had, by use of magic. And they did move it— right where my village used to be. We lost everything. It's all gone, obliterated, wiped from existence. My family became little more than beggars."

"I'm sorry," Gisela said quietly. "That's awful. But it doesn't justify you taking my brother."

"My motivations might be personal," Lorraine said briskly. "But my goals are for all of us. When the elves have been driven out of Ilgal, all the humans will thank me."

"I doubt the king will," Gisela said dryly. "Once you've pitched him into conflict with all the elves of Ilgal."

"He can take care of himself," Lorraine said dismissively. "He's not my responsibility. It's supposed to be the other way around, and he's failed at that, so he can take whatever consequences come. Now." She brushed her hands together meaningfully. "Let's see what we have here."

She bent down beside Haiden, and Gisela moved quickly to put herself between the two of them.

Lorraine sighed. "Don't be tiresome, please." She made a complicated whistle, and at once the door to the other room opened. A broad-shouldered young man strode into the kitchen, looking inquiringly at Lorraine.

"Thank you, my dear," the older woman said, smiling fondly at him. "Restrain the girl, please."

"Yes, Mother." The man stepped up to Gisela, grabbing her bound hands and tugging her awkwardly up before wrapping her in a bear hug which hardly allowed her to wiggle. "She's secure."

"Not much on the boy," Lorraine commented, pulling a knife from Haiden's boot before feeling around his garments for pockets. She pulled the half dozen white stones out, studying them curiously. She didn't say a word, however, placing them on the table beside the knife before turning to Gisela. "Your turn, child." In a businesslike fashion, she reached for Gisela's pockets, unearthing some twine, Gisela's knife, some dried meat wrapped in a leaf, and, of course, her stash of rocks.

"How curious." Lorraine pulled the last item out of Gisela's pocket, and the captive glared at the sight of her most valuable trinket in enemy hands. "This is a talisman, isn't it?" Lorraine asked curiously. "They have a kind of weight to them." She turned it over in her hand. "What does it do? And is there something special about these stones?"

Gisela glared at the older woman, her mouth firmly shut.

Lorraine chuckled. "No matter. I can see that you're not ready to trust me yet, and I won't push you."

"I will *never* trust you," said Gisela fervently.

She meant it. She'd made the mistake of withdrawing trust where it had been genuinely earned, and the results had been disastrous for both her and Haiden. If only she'd been fair to

Otto when he still had the chance to help her, they might have been able to rescue her brother, and whoever else was in that hole. But she'd let her suspicions take over, and made him into a villain he'd never deserved to be.

She wasn't about to make the opposite mistake and give trust to this woman who clearly didn't have a right to it.

"That would be a shame," Lorraine said, her voice pleasant. "I would prefer to have both you and your brother join my cause willingly. But it's of no great significance. The good news is that you can still be of use to me, even if you're not a singer."

"How delightful." Gisela couldn't hold back the sarcastic retort.

"I'm glad we're of the same mind," Lorraine said placidly. "Now, I'm sure you'd like me to wake your brother, but that really wouldn't be wise until he's properly secured. My primary assistant hasn't yet returned, but when he does—"

A knock sounded at the external door on the words, and Lorraine beamed at the lithe man who walked through it.

"We've got another one, Boss," he said brightly. "And this one's strong, I reckon. She almost fought off my paralysis magic. But we got there in the end."

Gisela's eyes passed in alarm to the figure slung over the man's shoulder. A sack slipped down from her head, revealing a strand of fiery hair, and it was all Gisela could do to hold in her gasp. Valerie! This was doubly bad. Not only for the singer, but for Otto and the others. They had no magical protection now.

"Well done," said Lorraine, rubbing her hands together. "From the market? What a fruitful night!"

"Yes, and she was traveling with the prince," the newcomer said gleefully.

"Excellent." Lorraine's lips curled in a smile that bordered on cruel. "Did you manage to deploy the defensive magic, by any chance?"

"I did," the man said, a regretful note to his voice. "But not against the prince, I don't think. It was another member of the party, a young man. Someone important though, from the look of his fancy clothes and his presumptuous air."

"Well, that will have to be good enough," said Lorraine. "Perhaps for the best. The prince isn't the safest target, after all."

Gisela longed to demand more information, but she was afraid of giving away her connection to the prince and his group.

"Do you have energy left for a binding song of some kind?" Lorraine asked the man. "This one isn't a singer, but I'd like to keep her around to help anyway. She's still in need of some persuading, though."

"No problem." The man turned to Gisela, his eyes narrowing in concentration. The next moment, a strong, baritone voice issued from him, the wordless melody twisting around Gisela. Lorraine's son let go of her and stepped back as the bindings fell from her wrists.

There was no relief, however. As soon as they were gone, Gisela felt something else wrap around her, something invisible. It felt like cold chains, but she could see nothing. And it was around her ankles as well as her wrists. She could shuffle, but she wouldn't be able to run.

"That should keep her close," the man said, nodding in satisfaction. "And notify you if she strays too far."

"Thank you." Lorraine's voice was warm and motherly, and anger rose in Gisela.

"How do you sleep at night?" she spat at the newcomer. "You're a singer—how could you betray your own?"

"My own?" He snorted, unmoved by her accusation. "The people of Ilgal are my people. Most singers don't deserve my loyalty. They run to the city the moment they let out their first song, abandoning Ilgal. Abandoning all of us."

"I'm grateful that you're not as faithless as most of them," Lorraine said approvingly. "But don't lose heart. We can still hope that many of them will come around in time. Now, let's get these two into the pit."

"The pit?" Gisela repeated, aghast. "You think that approach will bring anyone around?"

"Oh, we have other ways as well." Lorraine's bland smile was unnerving.

With a gesture of her head, she had both her son and the singer hefting one of the unconscious prisoners up on their shoulders and following her out the door. Gisela shuffled after them, enraged by her own powerlessness but determined to at least see where Haiden was taken.

The group passed out of the clearing, and as Gisela had expected, they quickly reached a familiar stump. Lorraine pulled out the talisman she'd used last time, and Gisela glared at it.

"And I suppose that's a singer-made talisman, is it?" she said scornfully. "Since of course you'd *never* have purchased it from the hated elves."

"I've already made my views clear on using a distasteful means to a worthwhile end," Lorraine said shortly.

Gisela's eyes widened as she realized something. "The elves know you're a threat, don't they? You're the reason the Imperator has set limits on the talismans to be sold to humans within the forest."

Lorraine made a scornful noise. "The elves don't know half of what they think they do." A smug smile crossed her face. "But if they're getting nervous, so much the better. Now quiet. You'll disturb the others, who are likely trying to sleep."

She waved the talisman, and the stump melted away before Gisela's eyes. She did her best to feign astonishment in case anyone was watching, but Lorraine's eyes were on the hole, and the other two seemed occupied with their burdens.

"Drop them in," said Lorraine indifferently.

Deaf to Gisela's protests at the rough handling, the men dropped Haiden and Valerie onto the stone landing which was the only thing visible just inside the hole.

"May as well wake them up," said Lorraine. "I would have preferred to speak to them individually before the others poison their thinking, but judging by the sister's reaction and the fact that the girl was traveling with the prince, there's probably not much point. If we leave them unconscious too long and addle their brains, they'll be no use to us."

Horror washed over Gisela at this cold way of speaking of living human beings. Lorraine's civilized veneer made her feel even more dangerous, somehow.

Neither of the underlings seemed troubled by Lorraine's tone. The singer had already begun to hum softly, the sound growing quickly to a melody, its words mostly meaningless to Gisela. Before her eyes, the still forms of Haiden and Valerie stirred on the ledge below, both of them sitting up and looking around groggily.

"Haiden!" Gisela cried, hoping to cover any evidence the two captives might give of their acquaintance with each other. "Are you all right?"

"Gisela?" Haiden blinked up at her, his eyes widening. "Gisela! Are you all right? What's going—"

"That's enough talking," said Lorraine brutally.

She nodded at her singer assistant, and he pulled a palm-sized red stone out of his pocket. Singing quietly, he stroked it, as if rousing a beloved pet from sleep. He then pushed his fingers along its surface and out, doing the gesture once toward Haiden, and then again toward Valerie.

Both of them gasped, then fell silent. Searching their

features in alarm, Gisela tried to figure out what was wrong with them. Both were clutching at their throats.

"You won't be able to use your voices while you're down there," Lorraine informed them unemotionally. "For now, I suggest you try to sleep. You have a great deal of work ahead of you."

As she spoke, she raised her own talisman, and Haiden's and Valerie's forms were obscured by the rapidly solidifying log.

"No!" Gisela cried, throwing herself forward. "No, open it up again! Haiden!"

"Relax, I didn't put him in there to die," Lorraine said dismissively. "He's too valuable for that. Now if you don't want to be thrown in there with him, I suggest you fall into line."

"I do want to be thrown in there with him!" Gisela cried passionately. "I'd rather be in prison with my brother than free while he suffers."

"Very touching." Lorraine's voice was dry. "But completely pointless. You're no use to him in there, and you can be of some use to me out here."

She made a random tugging motion at the air in front of her, and to her dismay, Gisela felt her invisible chains respond. She was tugged forward, forced to shuffle a few steps toward the older woman.

"That's better," Lorraine purred. "Now, let's put you to work."

# CHAPTER EIGHTEEN

## Otto

Otto strode back into the clearing, his anger barely under control. He couldn't remember the last time he'd felt so enraged, and so powerless. That Gisela had been snatched from his protection so brazenly—not to mention Haiden and Valerie—was bad enough. That she'd done so while angry with him, and believing him some kind of monster, was even worse.

Where was she? Was she hurt or worse? Did she still believe him at fault for whatever was going on?

"Norris!" he called, and the head guard moved across the group to his side.

"Your Highness?"

"Our first priority—our *only* priority—is finding them," Otto said grimly. "Understand?"

"I understand, Your Highness," said Norris. He hesitated. "But if you'll forgive the liberty, Prince Otto, my priority must remain your protection. It's the only purpose for which your father entrusted me with this task."

Otto ground his teeth together. He knew the head guard was right, but he didn't want to hear it.

"What are you saying?"

"That you need to stay in the clearing, Your Highness," Norris said. "Or return to camp. Others of us will continue the search."

Again, it wasn't what Otto wanted to hear, but he knew the older man was right. Reluctantly, he went with a pair of guards through the gate, Monty accompanying them. When they returned to the camp, Otto could barely keep his countenance. All he could see around him was the absence of those they'd lost. They had to find them. They had to.

But hours trickled by without any progress. Norris had been mainly coordinating the search from the camp, determined to stay close to the prince. But he received regular updates from the guards, and after one such update, he made his way to Otto's side. Monty hurried to join them, his face drawn and anxious. He'd handled the hours of waiting no better than Otto had.

"What news?" the young lord demanded. "Any sign of them?"

"I'm afraid not," Norris said. "The market is emptying. There's no point in continuing to search. They're long gone from the area, and any sign of their passage will be covered as the crowds leave."

"We can't give up," Otto said determinedly. "They're counting on us, Norris. They have no one else to search for them."

Norris hesitated. "With regards to Miss Valerie, Your Highness, certainly. I don't wish to return to Terenford without her any more than you do. But as for the others..." He trailed off, perhaps quelled by Otto's glare.

"Well?" the prince demanded roughly. "What about Gisela and Haiden? If you have something to say, then say it, Norris."

The older man met him look for look. "No one saw them taken, Your Highness. For all we know, they simply chose to leave. And as you said, they were free to do that all along. We have no reason to assume they're in need of our rescue." He paused, then pushed on. "For all we know, they were part of the group that took Miss Valerie."

"That's nonsense," said Otto angrily. "I don't believe any of that for a moment. They wouldn't leave forever without telling us, and they certainly wouldn't have anything to do with capturing Valerie."

Norris remained silent, not giving any sign either of agreement or dispute.

"For what it's worth, I agree completely with Otto," Monty chimed in. "I saw no sign of Gisela or Haiden when Valerie was grabbed, and I don't believe it of either of them."

"We're wasting time arguing about it," Otto said, grateful for his friend's support, but unable to bear the frustration of idleness. "We should be searching."

"Your Highness." Norris's steady voice should have been calming, but Otto just felt chafed by this evidence that the head guard felt none of his desperation. "You've made your orders clear, and I intend to follow them to the best of my ability. But my considered opinion is that we'll gain nothing by continuing to search the area. If we wish to discover where Miss Val— where *they* were taken," he corrected at Otto's glare, "then we need to pursue other means."

Otto frowned, thinking this over. Norris was likely right.

"Have the guards turned up anything useful when questioning witnesses?" he asked.

Norris sighed. "They've asked many questions, but there don't seem to have been any witnesses. Or at least, none that were still at the market by the time we started asking around. Most of the market-goers have left now. It's mainly the vendors remaining, and they're beginning to pack up."

"I'm going back to the market," said Otto suddenly. "I want to speak to that impertinent elf if he's still there. He knew something, I'm sure of it."

Norris looked reluctant, but in face of Otto's determination, he rallied an escort of half a dozen guards. Soon they were passing back through the gate, returning to the light and bustle of the festival. Not that there was much bustle left. As Norris had said, the clearing was mainly occupied by vendors now, all of them engaged in packing their wares.

Otto scanned the area for the impish elf, disappointed to see no sign of him. His eyes fell on a stall nearby, where a female elf was boxing up pottery that had been fired in such a way that it gave the appearance of water moving constantly across its surface.

"Do you think the magical regulations regarding bargains in the marketplace are still in effect?" he asked Monty, who'd followed him through the gate.

His friend shrugged. "I would assume so. The market isn't over until it's over, surely. I mean, the gates are still active, so that means it's still open to the public, right?"

Otto nodded. He would have to hope they were right. Striding up to the elf, he dipped his head.

"Greetings. May I have a word?"

She looked up, surprise flashing through her green eyes before she lowered her torso in a bow.

"You may, Your Highness. But your guards have already spoken to me, and I spoke the truth when I told them I saw nothing. I do not know where the missing members of your party are."

"I understand," said Otto shortly. "And I'm not doubting your words. I want to know where your central settlement is, and how I can reach it."

"Do you?" The elf seemed taken aback. "Why?"

"Because I need to speak with the Imperator," said Otto. "I'm answering your questions frankly, I'd appreciate if you did the same. Is it close to here?"

"No, it's not," she told him. She didn't elaborate.

Otto drew a deep breath, mastering his impatience.

"We're camped through that gate." He pointed through the trees. "Is it close to that location?"

She squinted in the direction indicated, apparently making mental calculations. "I think that's fairly close," she said. It's not far north of there, but it's difficult terrain." She hesitated. "I assume you know I can't strike a bargain with you, Your Highness."

"I do," said Otto promptly. "I am willing to offer you gold as a gesture of goodwill, however."

A crooked smile curled her lips. "Sales were down tonight, thanks to all the commotion. But I have no right to request or expect any such thing from you."

Otto refrained from rolling his eyes. He didn't care about the elf finding a workaround for the restriction on bargains. He was very happy to pay for information, and didn't begrudge her the gain. He just didn't want to be bound by the magic that accompanied bargains.

At a nod from Otto, one of the guards stepped forward, placing several gold coins onto the case the elf was halfway through packing.

"The central settlement is just through that gate," the elf said, pointing to the far side of the clearing. "The gate will close soon, and it's not freely accessible to the public like the others. There's a temporary password."

She paused, and Otto nodded to the guard, who added more gold to the stash on the case.

"Which I believe is *moonrise bloom*," the elf finished, as if there'd been no break in the sentence.

"May the canopy shelter you and the trails remain straight under your feet on your journey," Otto said crisply, repeating the traditional blessing of Ilgal that Gisela had taught him.

He turned on his heel and strode across the clearing, his eyes searching the trees for the gate the elf had mentioned.

"Norris," he said, and the guard materialized beside him. "Go back to camp and pack up as quickly as you can. Leave anything that can't be packed in a hurry. "Have someone assist Lady Louisa in gathering her things. We're going through that gate."

"What if the elf was deceiving you, Your Highness?" Norris asked quickly.

"Then we'll find ourselves stranded in a random patch of jungle, likely no worse off than we were before we found the market," Otto said. "But if she was telling the truth, I'll finally be able to negotiate directly with the Imperator, instead of wasting even more time dancing around whatever's really happening out here."

"Hear hear," said Monty. Otto could tell his friend was as eager for action as he was.

None of them having magic, they couldn't easily sense the gate. It took several minutes of careful searching to find a place where the view between two thick trunks didn't look right for the rest of the surrounds. It was quite a small opening—probably because it was designed for elves—and it would be a squeeze to get the horses through. But they would manage.

"I suppose we should wait for the others," Monty said, shifting his weight with all the impatience Otto felt.

The prince glanced at him. "Which of us is going to talk sense into the other?" he asked, with a touch of grim humor. "I'm as eager to move as you are."

A cleared throat made them look around. One of the more senior guards was watching Otto with an uncompromising look.

"I'll serve that function, Your Highness. My orders are clear—no one is to go through that gate unless the whole party is assembled."

"But what if they all take too long, and it closes before they get here?" Monty argued.

The guard's steely tone didn't waver. "Then by staying here we will have avoided our group being separated."

Otto sighed, gesturing at Monty in a *stand down* sort of way. "There's no point arguing with him when he's right, Monty." He saw that his friend didn't look convinced, and he clapped a hand on Monty's shoulder. "Don't think I don't understand. I feel just as frantic as you do."

His friend stilled, searching the prince's eyes. "Do you?" he asked quietly. "Have you really thought about what you're saying?"

Otto threw him a sharp look, surprised to hear the normally flippant Monty asking such a shrewd question. But he shouldn't be. He and Monty had been close for a long time. Of course his friend would have noticed Otto's feelings changing toward Gisela. Quite possibly Monty had realized it before he had.

He was saved from the need to reply by Lady Louisa, who appeared behind them, leading both her own horse and Valerie's, her fan tucked under one arm.

"One of the guards can do that, Lady Louisa," said Monty quickly, moving to intercept her. His face seemed paler than usual as he took in Valerie's things, strapped onto the horse's saddlebags.

"Better if they have as many hands free as possible to protect us all," the countess said unemotionally. "Given we apparently have no idea what we'll be walking into."

"I'm sorry to rouse you from your sleep in the middle of the night like this, Lady Louisa," Otto said, belatedly realizing how little he'd considered the comfort of the older woman, or anyone else in the group.

"First of all, it's not the middle of the night, Your Highness," Lady Louisa informed him. "It's just about morning, surely. Secondly, if you think I was sleeping, you're far off. I could no more sleep than you. As the only other woman in our expedition, I've considered Valerie under my protection from the moment we left Terenford." She pinned him with a shrewd look. "And you're not the only one who's grown fond of Gisela and Haiden, either."

Otto just nodded, unable to find words around the lump in his throat. Whatever the countess said, none of the missing trio were under her protection. They were all under his. And he'd let them be snatched by kidnappers for who knew what sinister purpose.

His eyes returned to the gate, relieved to see the incongruous scene still visible between two trunks. Lady Louisa was right—in the patch of woods on the other side of the gate, the first hint of dawn could be seen. The canopy must not be as dense there as it was on the edge of the market clearing.

"All right, Your Highness." Norris's gruff voice held only the barest hint of his lingering disapproval. "We're ready."

Otto turned as the head guard strode past him. The whole group was gathered behind, leading their horses. The gate wasn't tall enough for them to ride through mounted.

Norris hesitated when he reached the gate, extending a hand toward it. His fingers stopped mid-air, and after pressing his palm against what appeared to be an invisible wall, he glanced back at Otto.

The prince nodded. "Moonrise bloom," he said with more confidence than he felt.

Nothing visibly changed, but when Norris tried again, his

hand passed cleanly through. After sweeping his eyes across the group one more time to assure himself all was in order, Norris stepped through the gate.

Otto was quick to follow, maneuvering Bullion forward before any of the other guards could beat him to it.

The strangest thing about passing through the gate was how unremarkable it felt. If he hadn't known he was going through a magical doorway, he wouldn't have guessed it. Each step felt just like the one before. Only his surroundings changed.

And those certainly did change. The trees that ringed the market square had seemed large and tall when among them, but they were saplings compared to the ones through which gray dawn light now filtered. These forest giants had undoubtedly been around for generations longer than Otto had. Ten men holding hands wouldn't be able to reach around the bases. No branches sprouted from the trunks until well above Otto's head, creating a sense of space that he found calming after being confined in the thickest part of the forest for so long. For the first time since he'd entered Ilgal, he felt as though he could really breathe.

It helped that the undergrowth wasn't nearly as thick in this part of the forest, the earth covered in scattered twigs and the odd fern rather than a tangle of brush. Glancing up, Otto saw that the enormous trees continued in all directions.

"Look, Otto."

Following Monty's gaze, Otto saw a path start out of nowhere not far ahead of where he was standing. It consisted of a weaving line of smooth, polished stones, each as flat as the stone floors of Otto's own castle.

"Do you think it leads to the central settlement?" Monty pressed.

Otto shrugged. "Presumably."

"I'll send some scouts ahead," said Norris gruffly.

"That won't be necessary—it leads to the central settlement." The new voice sounded amused. Turning, Otto saw the elf vendor who'd given them directions to find the gate. She was pulling her wares behind her on a small cart. A few others trailed through the gate behind her, the darker patch of forest behind them lightening slightly. The sun was reaching the market clearing just as it was rising on the majestic scene into which the group had stepped.

"You didn't say you hail from the central settlement yourself," Otto said, frowning a little.

"You didn't ask," the elf replied.

"Didn't offer anything in exchange for the information, more like," grumbled Monty.

"Indeed," she agreed unashamedly.

"Come on," said Otto, turning back to the path. His companions looked as exhausted and disheveled as he felt, and the sooner they reached their destination, the better. In the quiet calm of the new area, his sleepless night was catching up to him rapidly.

They moved quickly along the path—or rather, alongside the path, as the horses made it impractical to fit on it, even single file. It was clearly designed for elves. The ones who'd returned from the market slipped past them, showing no great interest in the human prince and his group. After a short distance, they came to a thicker clump of smaller trees, into which the path dove. Otto was surprised—he'd assumed the elf settlement would be in the more open, spacious section of forest.

The foliage was thinning ahead when they encountered a pair of elves standing on either side of the path. They were wearing what appeared to be a uniform, and were openly armed, two circumstances very unusual among elves in Otto's experience.

"To whom do I address myself?" asked one. His eyes picked Otto out immediately, roving over his form with detached interest. Otto had no doubt they knew exactly who he was.

"I am Crown Prince Otto, heir to the throne of this kingdom," he said, his words a little short. "I have come for an audience with the Imperator."

The other elf raised an eyebrow as if he found Otto's boldness impertinent. Otto could feel Monty's disapproval beside him, and he was inclined to agree. He'd started the journey with what he thought was an undemanding ego, but the consistency of the disrespect shown by elves to his position as his father's heir was starting to grate on him.

"Does the Imperator expect you?" the first elf asked.

"I can't speak to what the Imperator expects," Otto said flatly. "But as my father's representative, I certainly expect an audience."

For a moment there was silence, neither elf seeming quite sure how to respond to this direct demand. They exchanged the briefest of looks, then the first elf dipped his head.

"I will show you into the city, Your Highness, and inform the Imperator of your presence."

Otto said nothing, tilting his head slightly in acknowledgment. Soon the group was in motion again, and Otto's observation about the thinning trees was quickly confirmed. The denser patch was apparently just a band, out of which the path soon emerged. Otto glanced once along the tree line, noting that the band of trees curved away inward, as if part of a huge circle around the settlement. Then his gaze passed back to the path ahead, and his eyes widened.

He heard Monty catch his breath, and he had to agree. The sight of the central settlement was an impressive one. It was easy to see why the elf now leading them had called it a city. The space was vast, enormous trees once again dominating the scene. The path wove between them, with tracks branching frequently off, either worn into the dirt or lined with plants. These tracks all led to enormous trees, and Otto had to crane his neck and look up at the forest giants to see why they warranted paths.

Like the first elf settlement he'd visited, this one had many —perhaps all—of its dwellings in the trees. Unlike that settlement, however, they weren't wooden structures built on the branches. Although some were reinforced with wooden platforms and supports, they were carved into the trees themselves, a feat only possible because of the sheer size of the trunks. A few of these carved dwellings were on ground level, but most were up well above their heads, with spiraling steps cut into the trunks.

Lights gleamed from lanterns hung in the trees, some golden, some the greenish light of sunlight through leaves. Dawn was properly breaking now, and Otto suspected the lights would soon be extinguished.

"Where do you think the Imperator lives?" Monty asked.

Lady Louisa stepped up beside the pair. "My guess would be at the center of the spiral. Knowing how grandiose elves are."

"Spiral?" Looking ahead through the trees, Otto realized she was right. The path of polished stone curved inward in a spiral.

Their elf guide had paused to let them all admire the settlement, but now he moved forward with a hint of impatience. The group followed him, Otto noticing that Bullion seemed more at ease than he had in a long time. He could understand his horse's reaction. This part of the forest certainly felt safe from predators or accidents. Of course, Otto was no fool. He knew that treating with the elves brought its own kind of risk. But it was a risk he would have to take. Finding Valerie, Gisela, and Haiden was the priority now.

As they traveled down the path, Otto was aware of being watched by many pairs of eyes. It was a sensation he was used to —curious onlookers observed him everywhere he went in his own city, after all. But it was particularly unnerving when the watchers were perched high in the trees above. He felt surrounded on all sides, and not at all sure how warmly they welcomed him. The settlement had been mostly still when they first entered it, but the activity of the morning was rapidly unfolding. Even so, it was nothing like the bustle of a new day in Terenford. The elves moved with a quiet grace that he rarely saw in the capital's residents. They went about their tasks in a manner that was somehow both efficient and unhurried.

They had some things in common with their human fellows, however. More than once, Otto looked up to catch an elf watching him, only to have the stranger slip away, green eyes glinting with the unmistakable excitement of information. Gossip was universal, apparently. He had no doubt their arrival would soon be known throughout the whole city.

The spiral continued steadily inward for long enough that Otto's steps began to lag with weariness. His heart lifted when at last he saw the path changing ahead. The individual stones were placed steadily closer together, soon giving way to a fully paved stone courtyard of sorts. Otto pulled his exhausted gaze from the polished smoothness of the ground to blink at the structure ahead of him. He'd expected the center of the spiral to contain the most gargantuan tree of all, and in one sense he was right. The tree before him didn't look as tall as those around it, but its trunk was by far the stoutest he'd ever seen. It put to shame his previous thought about requiring ten men to circle it—he doubted fifty of him could reach around this trunk. If it was even one trunk. It might have been many close together—it was hard to tell. The natural structure was buttressed, the line of the wood undulating in and out in waves, with elves flitting between the strips of trunk. The section right before them had been carved away to form an elaborate doorway, revealing an enormous space surprisingly flooded with light.

"That's not a house," Monty murmured. "It's more like…"

"A castle," Otto finished unemotionally. No one elaborated. They were all thinking the same thing. The nature of the Imperator's position and authority went beyond anything they'd expected.

"What kind of tree is that?" he asked, glancing at the guard to his left. The man was the most knowledgeable arborist among them. At least since Gisela and Haiden's departure.

"I'm not sure," said the guard. "It looks like some kind of cypress. Except…bigger. Much bigger."

At a word from their elf guide, others in the same uniform approached and offered to take the group's horses. The guide then ushered them across the stone courtyard toward the large opening.

"You will be shown to a room where you may wait while a message is taken to the Imperator," he began, but a new voice cut him off.

"That won't be necessary."

Otto turned with the rest of them to see a stately elf striding toward them, surrounded by a startlingly large retinue. He was elderly, judging by the deep lines in his face, and the pure silver of his hair. But his voice was commanding—high, like all elves' voices, and as cold and clear as a mountain stream—and his emerald eyes were piercing. He wore no crown on his head, although a carved wooden circlet was fastened around one upper arm.

Not that Otto needed the marker to know he was meeting the Imperator at last.

"Greetings," he said, stepping forward and dipping his head more respectfully than he had to any elf yet. He felt awkwardly tall, and debated for a moment about whether to kneel down to better address the diminutive elf. Thinking better of it, he straightened. "I am Crown Prince Otto, son and sole heir of His Majesty King Ryker, ruler of Teren and all its territories. I come unannounced, but I trust you will receive me."

The Imperator studied him gravely for a moment, his upward gaze shrewd but not openly disapproving. "Indeed I will, Crown Prince Otto. I have heard rumors of your presence in our forest. It is with pleasure I learn that you have reached our city in safety."

It was on the tip of Otto's tongue to say that not all of their group had arrived safely, but he held his peace. It would be wiser to establish amicable communication with the elf leader before diving into the question of rescuing their missing companions.

"I have been seeking your city for some time," Otto acknowledged. "Or, more accurately, yourself. I wish to speak with you on my father's behalf."

"Indeed?"

The Imperator's politely curious tone didn't fool Otto for a moment. There was no way the elf leader could fail to comprehend why it would be helpful, even necessary, for him to discuss the forest's future with the monarch of the kingdom.

Otto noticed movement behind the Imperator, and his eyes passed down the line of the elf's attendants. It was easy to see them all, given how well he could see over the head of the Imperator, who was, after all, about half Otto's height. He'd assumed at first glance that they must all be servants or guards, but closer inspection suggested that wasn't the case. Not only were some dressed as elaborately as the Imperator himself, they didn't all look fully grown.

In particular, the two walking immediately behind the Imperator—one male, one female—weren't as tall as their leader, and their faces bore the signs of youth. They must be close to adulthood, though, whatever age that was for elves. Otto knew they aged considerably more slowly than humans, so he was aware that even with their teenage appearance, the elves were probably in their twenties or thirties.

Behind them strode four other elves, these ones noticeably older, although without the ancient appearance of the Imperator. Were they his family, perhaps?

It was the youthful male whose fidgeting had drawn Otto's gaze. He was watching the prince with eyes that were harder than the Imperator's, and his expression wasn't as diplomatic. Ignoring him, Otto turned back to the leader.

"Is there somewhere we could speak more comfortably, and perhaps more privately?"

"There are many such places." The Imperator's tone was placid. "But you speak as though our wish to treat with one another is mutual, when it has not been so established."

Otto's patience, already worn very thin from a night of sleepless anxiety, threatened to disappear altogether. "Barring some duplicity on your side, I find it hard to think of a reason you would be unwilling to speak with me."

"Do you?" The Imperator raised his eyebrows, and a number of elves behind him let out disapproving murmurs at Otto's tone. He didn't care. "And yet humans are fabled to be creatures of great imagination...often to excess."

Otto narrowed his eyes, but before he could decide how to answer, the Imperator spoke again.

"There are legitimate reasons for me to hesitate to treat with you, Crown Prince Otto," the elf said in that high, clear voice. "Chief among them being the rumor that has reached my ears. If I am to believe what is being spoken within the forest community, you have entered Ilgal for the purpose of rallying singers to your cause, with the eventual aim of driving our kind out of our ancient, ancestral home."

"What?" Otto didn't have to feign anything this time. The blank astonishment that crossed his face was authentic, and the Imperator's searching gaze suggested that he knew it. "That's not at all my purpose." Otto frowned. "I didn't come here with any intention of hiding my activities in Ilgal. I am rallying singers—or at least, attempting to—but the cause I wish them to assist with has nothing to do with driving your kind away."

"Is that so?" The Imperator's voice still held no particular emotion, although the young male behind him was watching Otto with narrowed eyes. "For what purpose have you been removing singers from their homes, then?"

"First of all, I haven't removed any singers from their homes," said Otto grimly. "Someone else has been doing that, and it's got nothing to do with me. That's one of the matters I wished to discuss with you, and urgently. As for my own purpose, it's nothing more or less than seeking a method for easing the growth of magic in Ilgal before it reaches the level it reached in Selvana, and the ground becomes toxic."

"Toxic for *humans*," the Imperator corrected. "Our elven brethren in Selvana were never in danger of death from the wild magic there, any more than we are here."

Otto drew in a long breath, telling himself not to lose his temper. "In any event, I did not enter Ilgal as part of a scheme against you or your people."

"So you claim," said the Imperator dispassionately.

Monty made an angry noise beside Otto, and the prince felt his own irritation flare.

"Do you truly accuse me of lying to your face?"

"I accuse nothing," the Imperator said, one fine, silver

eyebrow slightly raised. "But you are unknown to me, and therefore so are your intentions."

"I could say the same of you," said Otto shortly. "If we're to base our assessment of one another on rumors, you have your own questions to answer. I've come to request assistance from Ilgal's singers, but at least I'm not hunting anyone down. That's more than I can say for the elves, in spite of your kind supposedly taking no interest in humans."

The Imperator frowned, and Otto got the sense that for the first time, he'd truly confused the elf leader. "To what do you refer?"

"To the numerous encounters during which elves have asked us about a human brother and sister with some kind of singing ability," said Otto.

He tried to speak as if the matter was purely impersonal, but someone else reacted visibly to his words. Two someones, in fact. Otto's eyes traveled to the young elves behind the Imperator as he went on.

"It seems the elves are seeking these siblings, whoever they are, far and wide. And I need hardly add that as Terenan humans, they are beyond argument my father's subjects. So I have just as much reason to suspect you of designs against my people as you have with regards to me."

The Imperator said nothing, his expression hard to read. Otto's gaze strayed again to the younger pair. The male elf looked calculating, but the female one merely thoughtful. She'd been the one to look up with interest when Otto mentioned the brother and sister with singing ability, and her gaze was clear and unflinching as it passed between Otto and the young male elf.

"I trust neither of us will base our assessment of the other on rumors, as you've said," the Imperator said smoothly. His gaze followed Otto's. "It seems you take an interest in my grandchildren, Crown Prince Otto. Allow me to introduce them to you. This is Lonik, my grandson and heir." The young male elf bowed. "And this is Asivah, my granddaughter."

"I am glad to meet you both," said Otto, inclining his head again.

He turned back to the Imperator, but was distracted by Monty beside him. At first he thought his friend's grunt was intended to signal disapproval of the elves' presumption, but Monty's face was twisted in what looked like pain.

"Monty?" he asked, concerned. He placed a hand on his friend's shoulder. "Are you all right?"

"Your party is understandably tired after your journey," the Imperator cut in. "You will be shown to rooms where you can rest. I would like you to join us for our evening's gathering at sundown. There will be further opportunity for speech between us."

Otto barely heard the dismissal, and only nodded vaguely in response to the Imperator's departure. He hadn't even probed for information regarding where their missing companions might be, but that would have to wait. Monty was trying heroically to hide it, but it was clear to Otto that he was in considerable pain.

"What's going on?" Otto murmured.

Monty shook his head, his eyes screwed tightly shut. "I don't know," he panted. "Just sudden, sharp pain."

"Come on." Otto steered his friend toward the edge of the room, their own guards hovering uncertainly around them, and a number of milling elves watching them in bemusement.

Monty's teeth were clenched, the odd grunt of pain escaping them. His arms were taut with the effort of holding himself together, the muscles defined through his tunic. Otto couldn't remember the last time he'd seen his friend in such pain.

"Monty, talk to me!" he said frantically. "What's happening?"

He looked at the closest guard. "We need help. Ask the elves to—"

"Uhhhh..." Monty let out a long breath of relief, his figure slumping. "It's gone. Whatever it was, it's stopped."

"All of a sudden?" Otto demanded.

Monty nodded.

"But what caused the pain?"

"I don't know," said Monty, wincing slightly as he massaged his chest. He cast a dark look at the ethereal beauty of the scene around them. "But I don't trust this place."

"No," Otto agreed grimly. "Trust is a commodity we can't afford when it comes to elves, I think." His eyes searched Monty's face in concern. "Are you sure you're all right?"

Monty nodded. "Right as rain now. It was intense while it lasted, but when it stopped, it was all gone at once."

Otto slowly blew a disheveled tuft of hair out of his eyes. "Something else to add to the long list of things going on that we don't understand in the least. One thing is for certain. I intend to be at that gathering. There's plenty more to learn here. Did you see the reaction of the younger elves when I mentioned...?" He trailed off with a significant look, knowing Monty wouldn't need him to finish the thought aloud.

"I saw," Lady Louisa interjected quietly. "I'm not sure the Imperator has any idea of that particular search, but at least one of his grandchildren knows something about it. Probably both of them."

Her words made Otto's thoughts swirl, trying to piece it all together. It seemed that while the Imperator's authority was more established and further-reaching than he'd realized, it wasn't absolute.

He raised a hand to his head, his weariness making his thoughts sluggish. The main thing he was conscious of was a nagging anxiety that blossomed into acute distress when he let his mind picture Gisela's face as she turned from him in the market clearing. Where was she now? Was she safe? Or was she lost, or alone, or in pain...or worse?

Knowing such thoughts wouldn't help him find solutions, he tried to banish them. There were so many forces at work in Ilgal. And if he was going to find the missing members of the group, it was past time for him to start understanding what he was up against.

# CHAPTER NINETEEN

# Gisela

"Up, Gisela. Time to get up. Come on, I'm not feeding and clothing you to lie about." The no-nonsense voice roused Gisela from a sleep that had been uneasy at best.

She blinked up at the expectant face above her, returning painfully to her new reality. From the quality of the light, dawn had barely broken, but Lorraine was apparently in full swing already. It seemed she didn't feel the late night as acutely as Gisela did.

"I didn't ask you to feed or clothe me," Gisela said, pushing herself upright. She didn't like the feeling that she'd been asleep and vulnerable with the other woman present. How long had she been hovering in the small room to which Gisela had been directed when she was finally allowed to sleep the night before? "Just let my brother and me go, and you won't have to do either."

"Not today, Gisela," said Lorraine, with a hint of indulgence.

Gisela studied her through narrowed eyes, running a hand through her disheveled brown hair. "And you're not clothing me, are you? Feeding me you can hardly get out of, if you're going to physically force me to stay here."

"I am clothing you," Lorraine contradicted briskly. "The clothes you're wearing were no doubt practical once, but they're in a shameful state now. I run a tight operation here. I won't have you wandering around the place looking like a beggar."

Gisela glanced down at the tunic and breeches that had served as her primary clothes for the entirety of the time she'd been traveling with Otto's party. Lorraine was right. Her clothes were in sad need of replacement. When she and Haiden had left their home, they hadn't expected to be gone for weeks, and hadn't stocked their packs accordingly.

"You can wear this," said Lorraine, tossing a dress onto a chair next to the pallet where Gisela had slept. "It belongs to one of our party, but she won't miss it."

"A willing member of your party, or one in the pit?" Gisela demanded.

Lorraine just strode from the room with her usual purpose.

"Up!" she reiterated over her shoulder. "There's work to be done, and none of us slack off here. You're no exception."

Gisela didn't need to be told twice. As unwilling a player as she might be in Lorraine's plans, the last thing she wanted was to lie around. Ensuring that the door was shut, she slipped out of her dirty, frayed tunic and worn leggings and into the dress. The task was made difficult by the invisible shackles on her wrists, but at least the dress passed through the magic unhindered. Its only function seemed to be to keep her hands from reaching too far apart from each other.

The dress was of a pleasant forest green, and Gisela couldn't help admiring it in spite of its source. She hadn't worn a dress since childhood—since she and Haiden had been on their own, she'd adopted the same practical clothes he wore. Even when she'd lived with her family, however, she'd never worn anything with fabric of such high quality as the green gown. Perhaps it was from one of Lorraine's voluntarily conspirators after all—

the older woman had claimed that she'd been part of a wealthy group of foresters.

The gown sat well on Gisela, the fitted waist hugging her form before the skirt flowed down, wide enough to feel feminine, but not so much as to be impractical. A darker patch of fabric was sewn around the neckline, providing a stylish collar, and the fitted sleeves boasted an embroidered strip just below her elbow before the sleeves fanned out and fell to her wrists.

Naturally she intended to escape with her brother, and as soon as possible. But...could she take the gown with her when she did?

Returning to her senses, she told herself off for caring about frivolities when Haiden was being kept in a pit like a caged animal.

Her gait restricted by the shackling magic, Gisela shuffled her way into the main part of the forest cottage. Passing into the room from which Lorraine had come the night before, she was confronted by a long dining table lined with people. Everyone was eating efficiently, and someone passed Gisela a bowl without any sign of interest. Did they think she was a new recruit, or did they all know she was being restrained?

Once the smell of hot food reached her nose, she didn't much care. It had been far too many hours since she'd eaten, and she shoveled the food down hungrily, her face close to the bowl to satisfy the shackles. She needed strength if she was going to find a way to run for it. Once she got Haiden out, of course.

While Gisela was still debating whether to try to get information out of the person eating next to her, the stranger finished eating. The table was clear of people by the time Gisela was halfway through her food. They all left the room looking full of purpose. The purpose of hunting down Ilgal's singers, probably.

"Boss says it's your turn for clean up," someone told her, as the last of the stragglers left the room. "Here."

He threw a washcloth at her, then left as well. For a moment, Gisela just sat, looking around her at the twenty or so bowls and spoons, and picturing the cooking mess she'd noted on her way through the central kitchen area.

Well, cleaning up from a meal she could handle. She'd never had the luxury of someone else to do chores for her. Wolfing down the last of her breakfast, she set to work at once. She was considerably slowed by the restrictions on her hands, but even so, by the time Lorraine came striding back through the central area, Gisela was finished. The older woman looked at her thoughtfully, clearly not having expected her to be so efficient.

"Gisela." Lorraine cast her eyes over the neat kitchen, and the scrubbed table visible through the doorway. "In need of another task, I see. You can help me deliver food to our guests."

Looking behind Lorraine, Gisela saw that the man who'd called Lorraine "Mother" the night before was accompanying her, clutching a sack similar to the one she and Haiden had watched Lorraine drop into the hole the first time they saw her.

Gisela decided not to comment on the farcical use of the word *guests*. She was too eager for the chance to see Haiden, and didn't want to anger Lorraine enough to be left behind. So she silently followed as the pair made their way out of the building and across the swampy ground.

She watched as Lorraine waved the talisman over the stump, revealing it for the illusion it was and bringing the hole into view. Gisela could see nothing but the empty stone platform, but a scrabbling sound reached her ears at once, and a moment later, Haiden came into view.

"Haiden!" she cried, relieved that her brother didn't look injured, or as rattled by a night spent in a dark pit as she would have expected.

He opened his mouth, his lips forming her name, but no sound came out. The scowl that descended on his face matched Gisela's own thoughts.

"Remove the gag," she said angrily, directing her words to Lorraine's son, although she knew it was actually the absent, traitorous singer who was behind the silencing. "What right do you have to muzzle him?"

The man ignored her, his eyes remaining on Haiden. Gisela was still glaring at him when she felt the cool tip of a blade against her throat and stiffened.

"None of that, thank you, boy." Lorraine's smooth voice was closer than Gisela had expected. "Stay where you are if you want your sister to see the sunset."

Gisela stayed as still as stone, only her eyes moving as her gaze darted back to the pit. Haiden was frozen as well, halfway through the act of trying to clamber out of the hole. His eyes were wide with fear, and the lines of his lean form were stiff in his anger. Moving slowly, he eased himself back onto the stone platform.

"I'm so glad I kept you around, Gisela," Lorraine said pleasantly, lowering her blade enough to allow Gisela to shift position. "I knew you'd have your uses."

Haiden's face was furious now, but of course he said nothing, still silenced by the magic.

Another familiar figure appeared at his side, and Gisela kept her expression blank. Hopefully Valerie and Haiden would have the sense not to reveal their connection.

"Ah, our other new recruit." Lorraine beamed down at her. "How nice to see you again."

Valerie's expression was as defiant as Haiden's, and Gisela could feel her frustration at being denied use of her singing gift.

"I'm curious, child," Lorraine went on. "How strong is your

singing ability, would you say? Show me on your fingers, on a scale of one to ten."

Valerie pressed her lips together, her hands remaining obstinately at her sides.

Lorraine tutted disapprovingly. "There's nothing to be gained from resisting me, you know. And more to be lost than you realize." She nodded to her son, and her tone turned businesslike. "We've brought your rations, but we're also going to organize an assessment." She saw Haiden and Valerie's confusion as they dodged the sack being dropped onto the platform, and clucked her tongue. "Of course, you're new. You, girl, get one of the others."

Valerie didn't move, instead folding her arms in a gesture of defiance.

Lorraine sighed. "So tiresome, doing this process with every single one of you. Can't anyone just be helpful without being pressed?"

She cocked an eyebrow at her son. "Who was the defensive magic for this one used on?"

The man frowned in an effort of memory. "I think he said it was a young man in the prince's party. Well dressed, pompous air. Probably a noble?" He gestured at Valerie with his head. "Maybe he's her sweetheart."

"How delightful," smiled Lorraine. Her tone turned sorrowful as she returned her gaze to Valerie. "He must be missing you terribly."

The fiery-haired young singer held herself tensely, no doubt recognizing Monty from their description as easily as Gisela did. What they meant by defensive magic, however, she had no idea.

"It would be a shame to cause him additional pain," Lorraine went on. She nodded at her son. "I assume you have the talisman?"

By way of answer, he tapped his pocket. "It's all set up and ready to go." He reached out a hand, feeling around as if for an invisible cord. "I suggest you do as my mother says and fetch one of the others like a good girl."

Valerie narrowed her eyes at him, and he shrugged. "Your loss." He tugged on thin air, and Gisela, Valerie, and Haiden all tensed. But nothing happened.

"Is that supposed to do something?" Gisela asked with a hint of scorn.

"Oh, it's doing its job," Lorraine assured her. "We can't see it, but this young nobleman is feeling it, I promise."

Gisela's eyes flew to Valerie in alarm, and she saw that the young singer looked very uneasy.

"You're bluffing," Gisela said. "Why would she believe you without proof?"

Lorraine shrugged. "She doesn't have to believe me. It makes no difference to me. I'm not the one in agony right now with no idea why it's happening or how to make it stop." She nodded into the depths of the pit. "But the others in there can confirm my story if this young lady wishes for answers. Most of them have seen the effects of this particular type of magic firsthand."

Gisela drew in a sharp breath. "That's how you're keeping them all in check? That's how you intend to get them to help you? By holding their families at the end of a magical leash, and inflicting pain on them if the singers don't cooperate? That's despicable."

"Effective, is the term you're looking for, I think," said Lorraine dispassionately. She looked at Haiden and Valerie. "Now, one of you, fetch someone else, please. Before your loved ones pay the price for your rebellion."

Haiden and Valerie hesitated for a moment, both clearly resenting the idea of obeying an order from their captor. But Valerie looked spooked by Lorraine's claims regarding Monty, and after letting his eyes flick once more to Gisela, Haiden disappeared from view at her side.

For her part, Gisela was seething. In addition to her fears for Monty, it was unbearable to watch her brother be controlled out of fear for her safety. That was all wrong. She was supposed to be the one to protect him—he was never supposed to carry that burden. He was still little more than a child.

At the thought, Haiden's own words to her the day before flashed through her mind. *You think you know me, but you still see me as a child.* He'd told her he was desperate to live his own life, away from her overprotective presence. And even Otto had told her—admittedly more gently—that he knew how Haiden felt to be cosseted, and that he likely found it unbearable.

At the time, Gisela had seen the uncomfortable truth of their words. But it was hard to believe that Haiden was ready to look after himself when the moment he'd struck out away from her, he'd ended up kidnapped and thrown in a literal pit.

An unfamiliar figure came into view below them, his expression showing neither fear nor anger, just a resigned irritation. This singer had clearly been in the pit a great deal longer than one night. He stared mulishly up at Lorraine. No doubt his voice was blocked as well.

"There you are," said Lorraine, the hint of indulgence in her voice making Gisela's skin crawl. "You've had three new members added to your number since last we spoke. Time for an assessment, don't you think?"

The man's expression didn't change.

"What's an assessment?" Gisela asked warily.

Lorraine glanced around at her. "How else can we know the volume of magic we can control?" she asked, her voice pleasant. "You'll be delighted to know that we've been on the edge of having enough manpower for some time. The addition of these new singers, if they're of sufficient strength, could well be enough. We'll soon find out. My lieutenant will be back from his errand shortly, and we'll conduct an assessment." She shot a glance at the singer in the pit. "Prepare everyone to present themselves."

"Your lieutenant?" Gisela repeated scornfully, recognizing the reference to the traitorous singer who was working with Lorraine. "Do you think you're some kind of general?"

Lorraine's voice was hard as she waved the talisman to replace the stump. "Are you truly so slow to understand what's happening here? This is nothing less than war. And by the end of it, either the elves will be defeated, or we will." She looked at her son, fierce pride in her voice. "And it won't be us."

He gave an approving nod, and Gisela's heart sank. She wasn't really surprised. They were children of Ilgal, as tenacious as the galboars, who would charge until either they or their opponents were dead. Gisela could see no way out of this mess without bloodshed and loss.

*It's not your job to save Ilgal,* she reminded herself. It wasn't up to her to save these people from themselves, or to save the elves, or to save Otto's kingdom. It was up to her to protect her brother, nothing more and nothing less. She just needed to find a way to get him out of that pit. And she needed to do it immediately, before Lorraine decided she'd gathered enough singers and put her plan into motion.

"Oh, Gisela." From Lorraine's pointedly casual tone, Gisela could almost believe the older woman could read her thoughts. "You'll be looking for something to do." She pointed to a dilapidated wooden outhouse. "The latrine has become infested by a family of wisp adders. As a native of Ilgal, I assume you'll know how to deal with them."

Gisela raised a haughty eyebrow. "If *you* don't know how to deal with them, you're not as much a child of Ilgal as you claim."

Lorraine chuckled. "I was wrangling wisp adders before I

could talk, my dear child. But one of the great benefits of leadership is delegation." She waved a hand carelessly toward the latrine. "Off you go."

Head held high, Gisela shuffled off. She wasn't averse to the solitary task. She'd known how to safely deal with wisp adders since she was a child, and it would give her time to think of a way to free Haiden.

Unfortunately, as she delicately wrangled the normally reclusive snakes, no brilliant schemes came to her. Her mind seemed instead determined to dwell on her unforgivable behavior toward Otto. She'd barely been away from him for twelve hours, and already she'd had ample time to regret not trusting him. She would likely not be in this mess if she'd only given him the benefit of the doubt which he'd so clearly earned. What did he think of her now? Was he angry with her? Disgusted with the ugliness of her inability to trust, now that it had been brought so painfully into the light? How could she make it up to him? Would she ever be able to convince him that she knew the problem was with her, not with him?

By the time she'd finished with the latrine, Gisela was feeling desperate. The sense of impending crisis that Otto had talked about was stronger than ever, and this time it had a clear basis in reality. There was no more time for fancy scheming. She just had to get that talisman, and get Haiden out.

With that in mind, she went to report back to Lorraine. She found the older woman deep in conversation with the singer who'd captured Valerie. With any luck, she might be able to take advantage of Lorraine's distraction.

"I've dealt with the wisp adders," she said shortly.

"Good, good." Lorraine waved a hand. "There's laundry to be washed in that room there. Get onto that."

"All right," said Gisela, her belligerent tone carefully crafted. She swept past the older woman, intentionally jostling her as if in pointless defiance. In reality, Gisela's hand darted out, slipping discreetly into a fold of Lorraine's gown. She and Haiden had never had to resort to thievery to survive, but pickpocketing was still a skill they'd attempted to cultivate when first living on their own. The task was complicated by the magic loosely binding her wrists, but she managed to get one hand inside.

Face flushed with triumph, Gisela felt her fist close around something small. She drew it out of Lorraine's pocket, not pausing in her stride as she continued into the laundry room. Not until the door was safely shut behind her did she open her fist to examine her prize. Again, luck favored her. It wasn't the acorn-shaped item that Lorraine had described as a magic-draining talisman—although removing that from Lorraine's possession would have its benefits. It must be the talisman she used to clear the stump. It was a small metal pendant, embossed with gold, a substance Gisela knew to enhance magic. It probably held a simple enchantment for lifting concealment, crafted to apply to the artificial stump.

It would be enough.

Gisela filled her arms with dirty laundry, carrying it through the next room and into the main area of the house in such a way that her face was hidden from Lorraine and her companion. She didn't want her nerves to show.

Once assured that the main room was empty, she headed straight for a storage cupboard, into which she dumped the armful of laundry. She was just turning back to the door when she caught sight of a sword lying across a high shelf. On the impulse of the moment, she seized it, thinking it was better to be armed. Her bow and arrows had been stripped from her the night before, as well as her hidden blade.

Moving stealthily, she crept back across the main room, heading toward the front door. All those who'd eaten breakfast in the cottage were nowhere to be seen, presumably still out on their hunting trips. Still, Gisela tried to be cautious as she hurried across the marshy ground, heading for the location of the stump. She gripped the sword in her hand, determined not to fail. She had to get Haiden out. That was all that mattered.

The clearing and the cottage were well out of sight behind the sparse trees by the time she reached the stump. A quick glance around showed no sign of anyone near, and Gisela pulled out the talisman.

"Please be the right one," she whispered, waving it over the stump.

To her delight, the stump melted away, revealing the hole. Gisela hurried forward and knelt at the edge, trying to see into the darkness.

"Haiden?" she called, as loudly as she dared. "Haiden, are you there?"

She waited a moment, then a curious face came into view. It wasn't Haiden, but a young woman, probably not much older than he was.

"Can you get my brother?" Gisela asked her. "The one who arrived last night? I stole the talisman that opens the stump. If we're quick, everyone can get out. There's no one else with me."

The girl's eyes widened, and she scampered back out of sight. Gisela hovered, wondering if she should climb into the pit to speed things up. But it didn't seem wise to put herself into the confined space.

Haiden came hurrying into view a moment later, Valerie and a few others in his wake. Gisela expected them to surge for the opening, but they came to a stop just before the stone platform, staring up at her.

The one Lorraine had given orders to that morning gestured for her attention, then mouthed something slowly.

"What?" Gisela frowned, and he repeated the silent movement of his lips.

"Plan?" she guessed. "You're asking my plan?"

He nodded quickly, and Gisela shrugged.

"This is it," she acknowledged. "I've opened the stump, no one else knows I'm here, and if everyone climbs out, we can run for it."

He frowned, clearly not satisfied with this answer, and impatience rose within Gisela.

"Look, if you want to stay, go for it. But my brother and I need to get out of here." She gestured to Haiden. "Come on."

He hesitated for a moment, glancing at Valerie and the others. Before Gisela could argue with him, a hand closed suddenly on her shoulder. The bottom of her stomach seemed to drop out as fear surged through her. She spun awkwardly on her knees, trying to raise the sword, but it was wrested from her grasp by one pair of hands while another seized her and pulled her to her feet. She struggled, but Lorraine's son held her arms pinned in an unbreakable grip, while Lorraine idly brandished the sword. At the confident way the older woman handled the blade, any hope Gisela had of fighting off her captors dwindled.

"That's it?" Lorraine asked. "That's your plan?" She shook her head. "I'm disappointed, Gisela. I hoped for something more. To tell you the truth, I hoped you might reveal a singing ability you'd cleverly hidden until now." Her lip curled, and she leaned forward, pulling the gold-embossed talisman from Gisela's hand. "Did you really think I didn't feel you taking that straight from my pocket? I thought it was an excellent opportunity to see what you were plotting. Turns out you had no scheme."

She sighed. "Throw her in there, I suppose. It's not worth the effort of keeping her up here if she's going to try stunts like this every time my back is turned."

"We can't seal her voice, though," her son pointed out gruffly.

"It doesn't matter," Lorraine said. "We'll get him to do it later. In the meantime, her voice won't break anyone out of there. I'm satisfied she's not a singer."

The younger man nodded, and the next thing Gisela knew, she'd been pushed into the hole. She fell onto the stone platform with a painful thud, barely registering her change in situation before the light above was obscured. The stump must be back in place.

She let out a soft groan, blinking in an effort to overcome the darkness.

"Well, that plan failed spectacularly."

Her words were deadened by the earthy walls around her. By way of response, hands found her, pulling her gently to her feet and tugging her onward in silence. To Gisela's surprise, her questing eyes quickly found a point of light in what she'd expected to be total darkness. She had her answer as to why no one seemed to be near the stone platform whenever the stump was open. It was merely a landing point leading to a tunnel, one with much more light than she'd expected. And it didn't take long for her to traverse the tunnel in company with her silent guides and emerge into the so-called pit.

It was far from the primitive prison she'd imagined. For one thing, the space wasn't dark at all, in spite of clearly being underground. Lanterns burned on all sides, bathing the huge cavern in warm, yellow light. There must have been air intakes somewhere as well, because the air didn't feel unduly stale. Looking around in wonder, Gisela saw that the area was much larger than she'd imagined, and comfortably fitted out. Sleeping spaces were carved into the earthen walls, furnished with blankets and cushions. There were a few tables around the place, each surrounded by half a dozen chairs. An underground spring provided water in one corner, and crates of various food supplies were piled near it.

There were more people in the pit than she'd guessed, as well. She didn't do a proper headcount, but she would guess it was about forty. A formidable number of singers for Lorraine to have at her disposal.

"How long have you all been here?" she asked, awed.

No one answered, and it took her a moment to remember that they were silenced by magic. She turned to the man who'd asked about her plan, and he gestured toward a rocky section of cave near the spring. Before following him, Gisela turned to Haiden and Valerie. She itched to throw her arms around her brother in relief that he was in one piece, but she refrained, and not just because her invisible bindings prevented it. Her brother had reached an age where he didn't appreciate hugs from his sister. Hopefully he'd grow out of it.

"Are you both all right?"

They nodded, although Valerie still looked pale. Perhaps she was thinking about the threats regarding Monty.

"This place is...not what I expected," Gisela added. They both nodded in agreement, chivvying her toward the spring.

When Gisela caught up with the man who seemed to be the unofficial leader, she realized why he'd led her there. Next to the spring, the wall boasted a large, smooth patch of stone. A pair of younger singers were currently positioned next to it, one scratching words onto the stone with a small, sharpened rock while the other read silently.

"You've made a writing wall, for communicating," Gisela said. The markings were faint, and clearly the progress of the writer was frustratingly slow. But it seemed to be passably effective. As she watched, the writer used a small pitcher to get water from the spring, and washed the words away. Apparently the writing stone wasn't scratching deeply into the wall, just leaving a surface mark.

The man beside her was nodding in response to her observation, even as he gestured for the writer to give him the rock. Placing the implement to the wall, he wrote, *What can you tell us?*

Gisela sighed. "Not a lot, I'm afraid." She glanced around, seeing that she'd attracted the attention of everyone in the space. It was no wonder. How long was it since they'd heard a human voice down here? "Lorraine is gathering you all to use in some kind of attack on the elves, to try to drive them out of the area they've chosen for their new central location."

The man nodded impatiently, clearly already aware of all this.

"She seems to think she's close," Gisela went on. She glanced at Valerie and Haiden. "She's guessing that these two might make it enough for what she has planned. I don't know what that is, though."

She grimaced. "And she's learned that the prince is traveling through Ilgal and looking for singers. She's trying to make it look like he's the one gathering singers to attack the elves, in the hope she'll create real conflict between the crown and the elves. I suppose she hopes the king will turn on them and help do her job for her. Or at the very least, that the elves won't turn to him for help."

A rustling around the space suggested that for some at least, this was new information.

"Are you all singers?" she asked. Heads nodded all around the room. "And are you all bound by threats against your loved ones?"

Again, nods.

Gisela bit her lip. "Does that mean her threats are real, about being able to cause pain to someone if you resist? She isn't bluffing?"

Heads shook vehemently on all sides, and the leader scratched into the stone wall.

*Not bluffing. We've seen.*

"What happens if you don't yield, and they keep going with the magical attack?" Gisela asked, horrified.

His reply was two simple words, and the haunted faces around her told her that some of those present had seen the truth of his words for themselves.

*They die.*

"I'm so sorry," Gisela said hollowly. She saw that Valerie looked paler than ever, no doubt thinking of the fate that awaited Monty if she pushed her captors too far. Something occurred to Gisela. "That's why you didn't race to get free when I opened the stump just now? Even if you escape, she can still inflict pain on them?"

He nodded heavily.

Gisela looked around at all the somber faces. "How long have you all been here?"

The leader scratched out words again, the process slow and painstaking. *Varies. Some recent. Me longest. Almost a year.*

"A year?!" Gisela said, aghast. She fought down panic as she took in the defeated expressions around her. "We have to get out," she said. "We have to do it now, today. You can all access power, can't you? There must be a way to use that."

Valerie gestured in frustration to her throat.

"I know," Gisela groaned. "But that only applies inside the pit, right? If we can break some out somehow, they can—"

She cut her words off as the leader shook his head, turning back to the wall. *Power we show is power she can use.*

Gisela frowned. "But she's going to use it anyway." She put her hands to her head, trying to force her tired mind to think. "We need more time to come up with a plan, but that singer will come any time now to assess how strong you all are. If Lorraine thinks there's enough power in here, she'll move against the elves." She bit her lip. "Is there a way to mask the amount of power, perhaps? To make it seem like you're all weaker than you are?"

The man frowned, pausing to wash the wall clean before writing again. It was even harder to make out his scratches on the wet stone, so Gisela followed the movement of his writing implement carefully with her eyes.

*Magic-draining talisman?*

Gisela shook her head. "Not a magic-draining talisman. That takes magic as it's released and redirects it harmlessly. I mean more like some way to repress the magic in the first place, so it can't be detected."

He raised his hands helplessly. Another singer came forward, taking the stone from him and scratching her own message.

*None of us experts in repression songs. Moot point—can't access magic.*

As the woman wrote, Haiden let out a snort. Apparently that sound wasn't blocked like his voice was. Gisela turned to him inquiringly, and he strode to the wall, seizing the stone. His movements were quick and jerky, but even so, it took ages for him to angrily scratch out his message below the woman's.

*Someone here expert in magic repression. Maybe she can help.*

"Who?" Gisela asked, bewildered.

Haiden held her eye for a moment, his look charged with some meaning she couldn't read. Then he turned and strode abruptly away from her. She watched in confusion as he reached into a sleeping area and pulled someone out by the arm. His victim came unwillingly, wringing her hands as he tugged her forward to the center of the space and fully into Gisela's sight.

She froze, shock washing over her at the sight of the stooped, miserable-looking woman before her. A scratching sound met her ears, and she turned in a daze to see the message someone had scrawled on the wall.

*How can she help? Not even sure she's a singer.*

"She's a singer," said Gisela grimly. "She might be in denial, but I assure you, she has songcraft in her blood."

*How do you know?* It was the leader who scratched this message, his brow creased as he stared expectantly at her.

Gisela let out a long sigh, forcing herself to meet the older woman's eye. "Because she's our mother."

# CHAPTER TWENTY

## Otto

Otto straightened his tunic as best he could, aware he didn't look his best. It would have been nice to attend an event hosted by the elf leader in a better state, but under the circumstances, he had to make the most of things. At least he'd managed to get a few hours of sleep since the morning.

The afternoon was drawing toward evening, and he knew they were expected at the sundown gathering. Apparently they'd conveniently arrived on the day of a weekly dinner hosted by the Imperator for his...court wasn't quite the right word, since the Imperator wasn't a king. But Otto didn't know how else to describe it. From what he'd seen, the so-called settlement was more like a capital city, and the Imperator appeared to operate like a monarch. As the heir to what he'd believed to be the only throne in Teren, it was unsettling, to say the least.

Norris left a few of his guards behind to watch over their belongings, in addition to the two who'd been sent to check on the horses. But the rest of the group was led to a large clearing not far from the Imperator's residence. From what

Otto could see, it was right in the heart of the city, cleared from trees and surrounded instead by a loose ring of wildflowers.

"Remember," Lady Louisa murmured to him and Monty as they stepped into the circle, "this isn't a market or a festival. It's not like the market clearing—there's no magical protection against binding bargains."

They both nodded tersely. Otto hadn't needed the reminder. He'd been feeling on edge since the moment they entered the city, and he knew Monty wasn't much better. The pair had been shown to a shared room for their rest, and Otto had heard his friend tossing and turning on the far side of the space. He had no doubt Monty was as unable to relax as he was, and that wouldn't change until their missing companions were recovered.

"Valerie is tough, Monty," he murmured reassuringly to his friend as they looked about the clearing. It was hung with many colored lanterns, and a long table stretched down the middle of the space. "She'll be all right."

"She's tougher than I am," agreed Monty. "And yet, somehow, that doesn't make me feel less anxious." He threw the prince a look. "Gisela is as tough as they come. Do you feel relaxed?"

Otto grimaced, not bothering to respond with words. Monty's point was sound. They would just have to find them, and quickly. If the elf leader knew anything of their whereabouts, Otto would simply have to do whatever it took to acquire that information.

"Greetings, Crown Prince Otto."

The cool, clear voice of the elf in question cut across Otto's thoughts. He turned to see the Imperator approaching, followed by his usual retinue.

Otto gave the appropriate greetings, trying to overcome his

anxiety to present an amicable front. His best tactic would probably be to win the leader's favor.

"Please accept my compliments on the beauty of your home," he said politely. He cast a glance around him before looking back down at the diminutive leader. "When I learned that your central settlement had moved several years ago, I didn't expect to find such an established community." He looked up at the ancient trees. "You certainly moved to an auspicious spot."

The Imperator smiled. "We did not happen upon these surrounds," he told Otto. "They were carefully selected."

"I'm sure," said Otto politely. "But how did you build this grand city in only a few years?"

The Imperator's grandson—Lonik—interjected, his voice unpleasantly amused. "We didn't build it in a few years. We moved it."

"Moved it?" Otto repeated blankly.

The young elf eyed him with a faintly disrespectful expression. "You don't know much about Ilgal, do you?"

"Peace, Lonik," said the Imperator calmly. He returned his gaze to Otto. "Lonik is correct that we did not reconstruct our city. We moved its location. The dwellings you see have stood for generations."

Otto frowned. "I don't understand."

The hint of a smirk crossed the Imperator's grandson's face. He murmured something inaudible to his companion, but the Imperator's granddaughter gave no response. Her eyes stayed fixed on Otto.

"The city you see is the same city our ancestors have lived in for time out of mind," the Imperator told Otto. "When we chose to relocate, we simply relocated the city. This location, at the very heart of Ilgal, seemed ideal for our purposes."

Otto stared. "But how is that possible? How can you uproot and shift huge, ancient trees?"

"We did not uproot the trees," the Imperator said, the tips of his ears wobbling disapprovingly. "They are our brethren, who have stood longer than we have, and worthy of respect. It is difficult to explain to the limited minds of humans. Think of it as changing the trails by which the city can be reached. Moving its location involved a more sophisticated form of the gate magic, of which we are justifiably proud." He certainly looked proud. "It was a feat that would not be possible anywhere but Ilgal. Here, the magic is so plentiful, many things can occur which would be mere fantasy elsewhere."

Otto tried to wrap his mind around this explanation, still not at all sure he understood. That was likely the elf's intention. For a creature whose head came to Otto's midriff, the Imperator certainly had a way of making him feel small.

"Was no one living here before?" Lady Louisa asked, the shrewd question shaming Otto for not having thought of it himself.

The Imperator's face was devoid of expression as he turned to the countess. "No one more deserving of the location than our ancient community."

Lady Louisa looked neither impressed nor convinced, and Otto had to agree with her silent disapproval.

"I'm not sure precisely what that means," he said frankly, "but it sounds harsh to me. I feel compelled to remind you that any human residents of Ilgal are my father's subjects, and under his protection."

"None of us operate at our best when we act based on feeling compelled," the Imperator commented, clearly untroubled by the criticism. "Your words, Prince Otto, appear to belie your claim that you have no part in any scheme to round up singers to use against our city."

Otto opened his mouth to protest, then reminded himself he needed to be careful what he said. He was frustrated, though. Elves were supposed to be matter-of-fact creatures, so it seemed absurd for the Imperator to make the leap from Otto's comments to a conclusion that he was underhandedly working to oust the elves from their home.

"I must greet other guests, Your Highness," said the Imperator, inclining his head. He sailed away, his silver hair flowing majestically around his small form.

"You didn't ask about Valerie and the others," protested Monty.

"I know, Monty," Otto responded, frustrated. "Trust me, I didn't forget." He frowned after the Imperator. "I don't think he knows where they are."

"I agree," said Lady Louisa. "In my experience, elves are sly in their dealings, but not generally given to prolonged deception. I think if he knew where they were, he would say as much, and use that information to reach a bargain to his advantage."

Their conversation was cut short as a long line of elves entered the clearing, carrying polished wooden dishes full of food. The long table was soon covered, and a series of unfamiliar but tantalizing smells reached Otto's nose. They were invited to join the elves gathering at the table, and they all moved forward.

"Where are the chairs?" muttered Monty.

Otto glanced along the length of the table, now lined with elves. "I don't think they're going to use chairs. Look, the table is the right height for them when standing."

As he spoke, the Imperator took his place at the middle of the table, raising a small wooden bowl in front of him.

"We partake of the forest's bounty," he said solemnly.

At the words, everyone else raised their own empty bowls before them, then brought them down and began to fill them with food. Otto watched with interest as they tucked into steaming meat stews, platters of forest fruit, even a huge bowl of what looked like cooked snails. With no other option, the humans had to kneel at the table to make the height work. Otto felt foolish, and although the food was delicious, he ate quickly, eager to resume his feet.

The others in the group did likewise, and they were among the first to move back from the table. They'd barely all congregated again when Lady Louisa cut into Otto and Monty's conversation, inclining her head toward the other side of the table.

"Time to watch what you say."

Otto followed her gaze to see that Lonik had broken away from his grandfather and was approaching them once again. Asivah, the Imperator's granddaughter, was watching his progress, although she made no move to leave her position next to her grandfather at the table. As he moved toward them, the elf heir gathered a retinue of his own, several elves materializing out of nowhere to follow in his train.

"Greetings once again," Otto said, when the elf drew close. He knew he'd be wise to be polite to his future counterpart, but he'd taken an instant dislike to the elf, and it was difficult not to let it show. Especially as he had the distinct sense that the feeling was mutual.

Lonik didn't bother to respond with a greeting of his own. "Your companion was correct earlier when she said that my grandfather is not one to operate via deception," he said instead, his eyes flicking to Lady Louisa. "Although she seems less informed on the vastly superior hearing of my kind."

His words were met with silence, no one finding an appropriate response. Otto looked up at the Imperator, seated a considerable distance away. He got the sense that Lonik was confident he wouldn't be overheard.

"I am not like my grandfather in all ways," Lonik went on,

his focus now on Otto. "For example, my information is considerably better. This morning you mentioned two siblings with singing ability. You were right that elves have sought their presence. They've done so on my orders."

He gestured, and one of his companions stepped forward, producing a satchel.

"We had hit a dead end in our search, however," Lonik went on. "We had found their belongings, as you see. But there was no further trace of them." His eyes were piercing as they rested on Otto. "Until we learned that they were traveling with your party."

Stunned, Otto could only stare between the elf and the satchel, unable to comprehend why Lonik was telling him this.

"Go ahead, have a look," Lonik said. "Test my words for yourself."

Numbly, Otto reached out, passing his fingers over the items in the satchel. There was nothing to prove they belonged to Haiden and Gisela, but they certainly could. A deerskin jacket in about Gisela's size, a large slingshot he could picture Haiden using, an empty water bladder. He lifted the jacket slightly, a lump rising in his throat at the thought of Gisela out there somewhere, unprotected and perhaps feeling abandoned. Something fell from the jacket's pocket into the satchel, and Otto's fingers brushed over its cool surface. The smooth white stone was small and unremarkable, but he picked it up anyway, examining it.

He looked up slowly, finding the elf's keen emerald eyes on him. "Why are you telling me this? Why acknowledge that you were the one searching for them?"

Lonik's lips curved in a smile. "Because I know what you've been so careful not to say, Your Highness. As I said, I now know that they've been traveling with you. And I believe I know why. You see, I know about the prophecy. I was there when it was made. And I understand the game you're playing. If you're working against your own father, you have plenty to lose, and more need of my help than I have of yours."

Otto stared at him, his mouth slightly open. "I've never worked against my father in my life," he said.

Lonik looked amused. "Do not imagine I am fool enough to think humans as disdainful of outright dishonesty as elves, Your Highness. As I told you, my information is better than my grandfather's. I know how you've been shielding the brother and sister, attempting to conceal both their identity and their abilities. A little inconsistent with your father's mission to gather singers to your cause, isn't it?"

Otto closed his mouth, confused and wary. Lonik was obviously trying to gain the upper hand by demonstrating his knowledge of what Otto had chosen not to say, but the elf was acting on false assumptions. Lonik must know what Otto wanted, although he noticed that the elf had been careful not to say outright that he knew Gisela and Haiden's whereabouts. Desperate as Otto was to find them, he was extremely reluctant to make any kind of bargain with the Imperator's heir.

"What do you want from me?" he demanded.

Lonik nodded to the companion with the satchel, who withdrew. The elves didn't seem to care about the white stone, however, as no one protested Otto's possession of it. It remained clenched in his fist, the warmth of his hand seeping into it.

"I wish to work together," said Lonik smoothly. "But this is not the time and place to discuss the matter. Think on what I've said. I believe we could be of great use to one another."

Otto could think of no reply, and Lonik didn't wait for one. He withdrew with his retinue, leaving the humans staring dazedly after them. As they turned away, Otto belatedly noticed that he recognized one of Lonik's companions. It was Josper, the elf who'd approached him at the market. He'd claimed to live in the rocky elf settlement, and Otto frowned at his retreating form, wondering what he was doing in the Imperator's city.

"What was that about?" Monty demanded. "What prophecy?"

Otto shook his head, glancing around to make sure no one was nearby. There was a large ring of space around them. Unlike attendees at one of his father's functions, the elves were all avoiding the human group as though they carried a plague.

"I have no idea about any prophecy," he told Monty. "But did you hear what he said about his people seeking the siblings?" He nodded toward the now-distant group. "That elf, Josper, approached us in the market just last night, asking about them. Either he was playing some complex game, or they were still looking for Gisela and Haiden then. That was just before they went missing. I think they might be the ones who snatched them last night."

"Then let's make a deal with him," said Monty urgently. "Let's get our people back."

"Not so hasty, Lord Montague," said Lady Louisa warningly. "Unless my instincts are completely addled, that is one dangerous elf."

"I agree," said Otto. He looked apologetically at Monty. "And we have no reason to think they're interested in Valerie, Monty. You saw humans take her, remember? None of us saw who took Gisela and Haiden. I just assumed it was the same ones who took Valerie, but maybe it was actually..." His words trailed off, his eyes drifting out across the gathering of elves.

Monty let out a groan. "You think Valerie isn't even with them? You think she's all alone?"

"Forgive me, Your Highness," cut in Norris, his tone not at all apologetic, "but if you're suggesting that Gisela and Haiden were taken by the elves rather than snatched by whoever took

Miss Valerie, how do we know they were taken at all? Maybe they went willingly with this Lonik."

"Not this again," said Otto, scowling. "They wouldn't leave without a word." He narrowed his eyes as he studied the elf's small form across the clearing. "And they wouldn't go with him."

"He certainly seems slippery," Lady Louisa commented. "I'm not entirely sure what he's up to, but it seems safe to say he's not doing it with the Imperator's authority."

Otto let out a groan, running a hand down his face. "I have less idea than ever of the politics controlling Ilgal," he said. "I came here hoping to save the forest from the wild magic, but it seems my father's at more immediate risk of losing it to the elves." Frustration rose within him. "I can't even protect my own traveling companions, let alone protect my kingdom from the danger Ilgal presents."

"I understand your frustration, Your Highness," said Lady Louisa in a firm but quiet voice. "But this isn't the time to show weakness."

"You're right." Otto straightened his back determinedly. "This is the time to take control." His eyes scanned the space, noting that the Imperator had left the table, and was now seated on a carved wooden chair at the far end of the space, his usual companions scattered around the clearing rather than clumped with him. Otto's eyes settled on one elf in particular. "There's someone else here who I'm pretty sure knows something. And since she's the only one who hasn't approached me with attempts to intimidate or manipulate, she's probably the most worth talking to."

Without pausing to explain himself, he strode off around the edge of the clearing, his companions hurrying after him. The Imperator's granddaughter was speaking with another young elf, but her sharp eyes caught Otto's approach well before he reached her. Apparently she wasn't averse to speaking with him, because she dismissed her companion, receiving him alone.

"Asivah, isn't it?" Otto said, disregarding the tedious etiquette of greetings. He'd reached his limit with civility.

"That's right," the young elf said, eyeing him with interest. "And you are Crown Prince Otto." She glanced behind him, her expression casual. "You look agitated, Prince Otto. You are unwise to wear your heart on your sleeve in the way humans so often do."

"Perhaps I should be the judge of what is wise in human terms," said Otto tersely.

"I wish to speak with you as surely as you wish to speak with me," Asivah responded in the same calm tone. "But we cannot do so with true privacy here. I will find you tomorrow."

With the words, she turned away, strolling toward a group of nearby elves.

"That's put you in your place, hasn't it?" said Monty dryly.

Otto's mouth was set in a grim line. "I have half a mind to search this city myself," he muttered. "If Lonik has Haiden and Gisela hidden somewhere..."

"I doubt you would achieve anything positive that way," Lady Louisa cautioned him. "If you're interested in my advice, I think you should wait and see what this Asivah has to say."

Otto deflated. "Of course I'm interested in your advice," he said penitently. "I think the most productive thing I can do now is sleep." He glanced after Asivah. "And hope she doesn't keep us waiting all day."

None of the elves seemed to pay much attention as the humans departed the clearing. No additional preparations had been made for their accommodation, so Otto retreated to the same room where he'd spent the afternoon, Monty with him. Both men were just as tense as they had been when they'd left for the evening's event, and neither spoke much as they prepared for sleep. There would be no true rest for them, not until they had answers.

Otto woke with the dawn the next day, slipping out of the room while Monty still slept. He made his way out of the Imperator's castle-like dwelling, eager to clear his head with a walk under the boughs of the enormous trees. It was a beautiful and peaceful place. Or it would be if anxiety didn't gnaw at him.

"Prince Otto."

The quiet voice made him start—he'd thought himself alone. It was the high-pitched tone of an elf, but it came from the height of his own head. Glancing around in confusion, he was rewarded with the sight of Asivah, perched on a carved platform that sat atop a doorway in a nearby tree.

"I've been waiting some time," she commented. "You're a late riser."

Otto blinked up at the sky, barely showing the first glints of dawn, then back at her petite features. "My apologies for keeping you waiting," he said blankly.

She smiled as she slid nimbly to the ground. "Careful. That sounded dangerously like saying sorry, which is dangerously like offering restitution."

"Which I've no doubt you'd take full advantage of," Otto said dryly.

"I would," agreed Asivah without a hint of shame.

"I'm not a complete fool," said Otto. "I'm not planning to give you anything for free."

"I didn't expect it," Asivah said reasonably. "You have a problem, and I have a problem. That's why we're meeting to negotiate, isn't it?"

"Is it?" Otto raised an eyebrow. "You tell me—you're the one lying in wait for me here."

"And you're the one who sought me out last night," Asivah

said, her tone brisk. "Let's not waste time, given that our continued privacy isn't guaranteed."

"All right," Otto agreed. "You seem to think you know what my problem is. What do you think I'm seeking?"

"Information about the pair of siblings who've been traveling in your company."

Otto nodded eagerly. "I'm seeking any information you have on them."

Asivah held up a finger, as if to say, *not so fast.* "In exchange for what?"

Otto curbed his impatience, settling in for the inevitable tedium of negotiating with an elf.

"I don't know what to offer as an exchange, because I don't know what you want," he said. "You said you have a problem. What is it?"

Asivah started walking, her gait unhurried. Otto did the same, keeping his steps small so as not to outstrip her.

With a sigh, Asivah glanced at the canopy ahead. "My problem is my cousin. Lonik."

"Your cousin?" Otto repeated. "Not your brother?"

"Lonik isn't my brother," Asivah said, surprised. "Do you know how inheritance of elf leadership works?"

Otto nodded slowly, frowning. "Yes, I've been taught the basics. Leadership skips a generation, giving each ruler a longer reign than humans normally have. The eldest grandchild of the current leader will inherit the role."

"That's right," Asivah confirmed. "The eldest grandchild. Unlike with humans, it's immaterial which of the ruler's children is older. It's simply whichever grandchild is born first."

"I assume that's Lonik," Otto pressed.

She nodded. "It is. And that's my problem."

Otto raised an eyebrow. "You want to inherit instead of him?"

"Not desperately," Asivah said, pausing and plucking a piece of bark from her tunic. "But I'd rather it was me than Lonik. He can't be Imperator. He's unfit for the task."

For a moment, Otto stood silent, unsure what to say in response to this brazen declaration.

"It's my aunt's fault, really," Asivah said conversationally. "She wanted her line to inherit, but she was still unmarried when my parents wed. In her haste to be first to produce an heir, she took a mate without the formalities and deliberations that usually surround royal betrothals."

Otto was a little surprised to hear her call her family royal, but he supposed he shouldn't be anymore. Not after all he'd seen.

"It worked for her purpose," Asivah went on. "She bore her son mere months before my parents had me. But the husband she took was..." Her voice turned dry. "Well, Lonik is just like his father. And her haste shouldn't be inflicted on all the elves of Ilgal."

"Why are you telling me this?" Otto demanded. "Why expose your family's weaknesses to me?"

"Because I fully intend to root out those weaknesses and return my family to its former strength," said Asivah unemotionally. "And I believe you can assist me to do so."

"What makes you think that?" Otto asked cautiously.

"Your position," Asivah said. "I believe I know what you're thinking, Prince Otto, but my grandfather does not wish to repudiate King Ryker's authority over Teren, Ilgal included. And neither do I."

"I'm pleased to hear you say so," Otto commented.

Asivah smiled sardonically, perhaps hearing the undercurrent in his voice. "We have plenty of authority here," she said. "We are content with the level of control we exercise over Ilgal." A shadow crossed her face. "Or we were, prior to Lonik's influence." She shook off the thought. "I for one see no benefit in undertaking either the authority or the responsibility your father holds over the forest's human inhabitants."

Otto held his peace. It was no surprise to him to learn that the elves considered King Ryker to have authority over the human inhabitants of Ilgal. The question of whether the elven inhabitants fell under his authority was much more fraught, but he didn't think his current purpose would be served by entering into that argument.

"My offer to you," Asivah went on, "is that I will give you all the information I have regarding the siblings we discussed in exchange for you persuading your father to recognize me as my grandfather's heir instead of Lonik."

Otto stared at her. "But that's...that's an outrageous exchange. How can I make you the heir if you're not?"

"I didn't ask you to make me anything," said Asivah calmly. "I asked you to convince your father to recognize me. That's the maximum I imagine you can do. Anything on this end is up to me."

Otto made a helpless gesture. "Perhaps I could speak with my father, tell him all you've told me. He might decide to favor your claim."

Asivah shook her head. "Not good enough. You must agree to persuade him."

"How can I guarantee that I'll be successful?" Otto demanded.

She shrugged. "That's for you to figure out. If you aren't willing to commit to succeeding, don't make the bargain. That's the only offer I will consider."

Otto ran a hand distractedly through his hair. How had he stumbled into this political quagmire? Based on what he'd seen and the little he knew, he would much prefer Asivah to become Imperator over Lonik. But he didn't have any confidence that he understood the full implications of getting involved in the inheritance battle.

"Maybe I can get the information I need from elsewhere," he tested. "Your cousin seemed to wish to treat with me in some form. And your grandfather has at least been willing to receive me."

"You can try," said Asivah, unconcerned. "But neither of them know what I know."

"Perhaps I'll search the city myself."

She looked at him, seeming genuinely puzzled. "I don't know what you'd hope to find that way, but I highly doubt you'd discover anything of use to you."

Otto bit his lip. Did she know for certain that they weren't in the elf city, then? He knew she was trying to tantalize him, but it was working. His thoughts flew to Gisela, and the betrayal in her eyes when he'd last seen her. She'd been foolish to let herself believe that he was plotting against her brother, but that didn't lessen the anguish he felt when he remembered it. He had the sense he was the first person she'd let in for a long time, and she thought he'd turned on her.

"All right," he said, the words bursting from him. "I'll speak to my father when I return to Terenford, and convince him that you should be your grandfather's heir, in exchange for you telling me about Gisela and Haiden."

"Agreed," said Asivah promptly, her eyes lighting up. "Is that their names? Gisela and Haiden?"

"You didn't even know their names?" Otto said, alarmed. Had he been conned?

"I didn't," said Asivah. "But I know what you need to know. I gather you've heard the prophecy mentioned?"

Otto frowned. "Lonik mentioned it last night. He said he was there when it was made."

Asivah made a scoffing noise. "Technically true, but misleading. He was present, but not close enough to hear what I said."

"What *you* said?" Otto repeated.

She nodded. "I made the prophecy. It was my first, and I've yet to experience another as potent."

"What was it?" Otto asked.

"It was in a market over ten years ago," she said. "I was still a child by the standards of my kind, and the brother and sister were even more so. They were too young to be all alone, which they were when I first saw them. He began to sing—I think it was his first attempt at songcraft. And when I went to speak with them, I felt the sight move within me."

"What did it say?"

She paused before answering, a dreamy look coming over her face. "That he was an enemy, as his sister feared, and would bring down a rising kingdom. And so I told them."

Otto felt his mouth fall open as he stared at the elf. "You told him that, when he was a child?"

"I did," Asivah confirmed,

Otto ran his fingers along his chin, which could do with a shave. "No wonder she's so nervous of exposure," he murmured to himself.

The new information colored his memory of every interaction he'd ever had with the pair. Not to mention the reaction of their father when he'd learned Otto's identity. Haiden had even seemed to be flaunting Otto's status, but not as though he was boasting. More as if he was trying to be rebellious.

How reliable were elf prophecies? Was it really possible that Haiden had not only the inclination but the power to bring Teren down? To end Otto's reign before it began?

He gave his head a shake. He had no knowledge of Haiden's power, but as for inclination, he didn't believe it of the teenage boy. He refused to believe it. A memory flashed through his mind, of Haiden's words when Otto asked about killing the snake. He'd said he wasn't in favor of pre-emptively attacking. And no wonder. Perhaps the words had always been intended to carry more than their obvious meaning.

"I don't care," Otto said abruptly, coming out of his thoughts and meeting Asivah's eyes. "I don't care if they're prophesied to be my enemies. I refuse to be the type of ruler who eliminates potential threats just in case. They haven't given me reason to distrust them." He gave his head a shake. "This changes nothing."

"An interesting response," said Asivah. He got the sense that he'd genuinely surprised her. She sighed. "If only all leaders shared such noble sentiments."

"So where are they?" Otto demanded. "I'm going to rescue them, regardless of any prophecy."

The elf's delicate features crinkled in confusion. "I don't know where they are. I thought you'd hidden them before coming here."

"What!" Otto stared at her, aghast. "But that was our bargain! You're supposed to tell me where they are!"

"I'm supposed to tell you what I know of them," Asivah corrected. "The prophecy is the main point of relevance. I also know from more recent inquiries that they left their parents' home years ago and have been living alone in the forest ever since. Lonik has been seeking them discreetly for some time, but I don't believe he's had success. And I don't fully understand why he's seeking them."

Otto clutched his hands to his head, horrified by his own idiocy. He didn't believe the elf was deceiving him. She spoke the truth. With a great effort, he stopped himself from hurling recriminations at her. He had no basis to assume she'd been trying to mislead him with careful wording. Fool that he was, he'd just rushed into the bargain, assuming they meant the same thing with regards to the information she held about Gisela and Haiden. And now he was bound by his word, bound by the magic that attached to bargains with elves. He would have to convince his father to take a potentially disastrous political step, and the process had brought him no closer to finding Gisela and the others.

"Your cousin must know where they are," he said, his voice hollow. "Surely he's behind their disappearance."

Asivah frowned. "It would surprise me. I've never known him to do anything as clumsy as abduction before."

"But he openly admitted to me that he'd been hunting them," Otto said. "He even showed me their gear." His hand slipped into his pocket, closing over the smooth white stone he'd kept on him. It made him feel anchored to Gisela, a physical reminder that she wasn't a creature of his imagination. She was real, and she was out there somewhere. And she needed his help.

His fist tightened around the stone.

"Lonik said that he wanted to work together, and that he thought we could be of use to each other. Does he intend to bargain with me for their release?" He eyed Asivah. It seemed she'd been strategic in entangling him in a bargain to help her cause before her cousin could do so.

"I've already told you my views on the unlikeliness of my cousin holding them hidden somewhere," Asivah said, unperturbed. "Your decision not to believe me doesn't change my view."

"But what else would I want his help on?" Otto demanded. "Whatever nonsense he was speaking about me working against my father was purely in his mind. I've never dreamed of..."

He trailed off as something occurred to him.

"What?" Asivah asked, her green eyes bright with curiosity.

Briefly, Otto wondered if he should be seeking an exchange

rather than giving her information freely, but he pushed the thought aside. The elven way of communicating was too tedious for the frantic state of his mind.

"I think it really was in his mind," Otto breathed. "He knew of the prophecy, and he knew I'd been traveling with Haiden, and keeping his abilities quiet. Could he have thought I *wanted* him to bring down my father's kingdom? That I'm plotting to seize control before my time?"

"Now *that* I could believe of Lonik," said Asivah dryly. "That's much more consistent with how his mind works."

"But nothing like how mine does," Otto said. "Which is why it didn't initially occur to me that was what he meant."

"Indeed," Asivah said gravely. "We have a saying among elves. Our assumptions regarding others are a mirror to our own inclinations."

Otto's eyes widened slightly as he met the elf princess's unblinking ones. Several things were falling quickly together in his mind. Chief among them was the information that Gisela and Haiden had shared about a group of elves working clandestinely against the Imperator. He'd thought the elf leader might appreciate knowing he had a hidden enemy. He'd never dreamed the truth of the situation would be so dangerous.

"I know what Lonik wants my help with," Otto said flatly.

Asivah tilted her head in inquiry.

"I'm not the one seeking to overthrow my predecessor and take his kingdom before it's my time. Lonik is. He's planning a coup."

# CHAPTER TWENTY-ONE

# Gisela

An awkward silence settled over the cave at Gisela's words. Not that it had been filled with conversation before. But no one scratched out messages, or continued with their tasks in the wake of her declaration. Instead, many heads swiveled from the middle-aged woman to Gisela and Haiden, searching for a resemblance.

Gisela couldn't see it herself. Her mother looked almost like a stranger. She was...shriveled. Perhaps that was an exaggeration, but it seemed that the last five years had not been kind to the older woman.

"She's our mother," she repeated, unsure why she felt the need to convince anyone. "And we know she's a singer because she cursed us with her voice."

Many eyebrows went up around the space, and the unofficial leader scribbled two words on the stone.

*Cursed you?*

"I know that's not the term singers usually use," said Gisela calmly. "But it's the simple truth." Her eyes searched her mother's face, and her voice dropped in volume. "It's been a long time, Mama." The term of endearment surprised her as it slipped out. She hadn't called her mother that in years, even before she and Haiden left their parents.

The other woman gazed silently back at her daughter, her expression miserable. Gisela remembered distinctly the last time she'd seen her mother, when the older woman had taken her children out into the woods for the last time. She'd seemed to get an inkling once they were in the woods, but when they left the house, she hadn't known that they'd been ready for it. She would never have guessed that they'd packed necessities in their coats, and stashed gear in a pre-arranged place, and had no intention of trying to find their way home this time. She'd thought she was taking them out to abandon them, and Gisela could still remember the conflict in her mother's eyes. It had haunted her ever since.

She didn't see conflict now. Just unhappiness. And, buried in there somewhere, a longing that was painful to see. Gisela didn't want to think her mother missed them and regretted her attempts to leave them to their fate. It was easier to believe the older woman had no love or compassion, that the mother she remembered with such warmth from her early childhood was gone forever.

"How long has she been here?" Gisela asked suddenly, frowning. They'd seen her father the night before, and he'd told them their mother was safely at home.

A scratching noise drew her attention to the stone wall. The leader had answered her question.

*Yesterday. A few hours before them.*

She followed his gaze to Valerie and Haiden. So their mother had been taken while their father was out at the festival, then. Gisela wondered how she'd been recognized as a singer. Someone must have been watching her for some time to pick up the subtle clues, since it was unlikely she'd actually sung. Or perhaps a neighbor had informed on her for gold. Such things did happen, or so she'd heard.

What had their father done when he returned from the festival and discovered his wife's absence? Had he panicked and begun to search frantically for her? Or had he let her go, like he'd let his children go?

Gisela gave her head a shake. There was nothing to be gained from thinking about it. Her frown grew as she considered her mother. If she'd truly only been down there since the previous afternoon, her pitiable state was even more marked. The deterioration Gisela was seeing wasn't the result of being thrown into this pit. It must have started well before then.

"You must have been surprised to see Haiden last night," she commented, her eyes searching her mother's face. It was so strange to be having this reunion with neither her brother nor mother able to speak. Her eyes flicked to Haiden. "Disappointed he was still alive, perhaps?"

The older woman shook her head vehemently, reaching out a tentative hand toward Haiden. He stepped away, and she let it drop.

Drawing a shaky breath, their mother strode over to the wall, holding her hand palm up toward the leader. He placed the stone into it, and she carved three simple words.

*I've missed you.*

Haiden made a noise in his throat that Gisela chose to ignore. Instead, she searched her mother's face, trying to decipher what she saw. True regret? Or only the misery of her own discomfort? Her mother's words weren't exactly an apology. But Gisela didn't know if her mother would ever be capable of a true apology. She'd learned enough of her mother's beliefs to know that the other woman thought herself doing what was right—bitter, painful, devastating, but right—when she did her best to sentence her children to death. She thought she was saving Terenford, preventing her own line from bringing the same disaster on this kingdom as the one that had consumed the land of her ancestors.

The thought made Gisela feel angry and powerless, a lost child all over again. Her emotions weren't made any easier by the fact that she now had very personal reasons for being sympathetic to her mother's desire to protect the crown and royal family of Terenford.

"There's no point discussing the past," Gisela said curtly. "We need to think about our current situation. Haiden could be right about our mother being capable of repressing magic. She's been doing it all her life with her own magic—the only question is whether we can find a way for it to extend to the rest of you as well."

She stared challengingly at her mother. "What? Aren't you going to deny it?"

The older woman drew a shuddering breath, then shook her head, her demeanor inexpressibly weary.

A scratching sound drew Gisela's attention again, the sound niggling at her mind like a splinter in her heightened state. She shifted her gaze to see the leader waiting for an answer to the question he'd carved out.

*Are you sure?*

"Very sure," Gisela told him. She returned her gaze to her mother, her mind slipping back over the years. "I remember the moment I finally understood," she said softly. "I was... what, eleven? I was helping you tend the small garden plot we kept beside the house, do you remember?" She gave her head a reminiscent shake. "It had been months since you'd last tried to abandon us. I was almost feeling relaxed. If I ignored the fact that my heart had become as hard and suspicious as yours, I could almost imagine it was a beautiful, happy moment together. We used to have those once, do you remember?"

The older woman said nothing, of course, just watched Gisela with the spellbound intensity of a starving person watching a feast be prepared.

"Anyway, you were pruning the rosebush, and you pricked your finger on a thorn. It caught you by surprise, I think, and it must have really hurt. You let out this shout that was undeniably melodic, and the stalk in question withered right before my eyes."

Gisela studied her mother's face. It was clear the other woman remembered.

"I confronted you, and you tried to deny it." In spite of herself, pity crept into the memory. Her mother had been so panicked, so terrified. "I think part of you believed your own denial. You'd spent your whole life convincing yourself you couldn't be one of the hated singers and ruthlessly suppressing any sign of it so no one would ever think you had songcraft. It must have been your worst nightmare to see it pass to one of your children."

Out of the corner of her eye, Gisela saw Haiden shift, and she pulled herself together. She was selfish to get lost in this confrontation with her mother, forgetting how much more painful these memories were for her brother. She straightened her back, her tone becoming more brisk.

"You always seemed most vulnerable to the magic when your emotions were high," she said. "It was the same when you cursed us, wasn't it? The day we left for the final time. When you took us into the woods and we struck out on our own instead of aiming for home. You got very agitated, didn't you? Perhaps you realized we had our own plans that you wouldn't be able to control or contain. Did you think we were setting off to under-take the nefarious purpose you'd imagined for us in your mind?

Did you even realize as you yelled after us that your shouts turned into song? Did you know you were using magic when you told us that we were forbidden to leave the forest, that we had to stay within Ilgal?" Gisela shook her head. "It didn't take us long to confirm that you'd placed a true magical restriction on us. We gave up trying to bypass it quickly."

Her eyes hardened, her anger exacerbated by the discomfort of having so many strangers avidly watching this awkward family conflict.

"And here we still are. I'll repeat now what I told you the day of the rosebush incident, Mother. You might have chosen to hate your gift, and hide it at all costs. But I won't let you force Haiden to do the same. His singing is a gift, and he should be able to celebrate it."

Her eyes passed to her brother, trying to convey encouragement, but the challenge she saw there made her pause. He still couldn't speak, but she found that she understood his silent message perfectly. Her own words condemned her. She may not have taught Haiden to deny or hate his gift, like their mother had tried to do, but she had taught him to hide it. Even at the cost of developing it.

Someone else moved forward, taking the stone from Gisela's mother's limp hand and scratching out a message of her own.

*How does this help us?*

"I don't know," said Gisela frankly. "I don't think there's any exact method to it. But I truly have seen my mother repress her magic in a way I didn't know was possible." She glanced at Haiden. "My brother and I have talked about it, and our best guess is that the denial has gone so deep for so long, and she's refused so consistently to use her magic for anything else, that the power that courses into her gets used as some kind of suppression magic. Either that, or she's gained strength enough to push the magic back into the ground rather than letting it enter her in the first place. But I can't begin to guess how to harness that activity."

She noted that the leader of the group had suddenly begun to look very thoughtful, and she addressed her words to him.

"What is it? You looked interested when I speculated about her pushing power back into the ground."

He nodded slowly, taking a minute to wash the writing stone clean before embarking on a painfully slow explanation.

*They test our strength with elven talisman. Tests volume of magic in ground.*

"I see," said Gisela thoughtfully. "So the less magic it detects in the ground, the more you're all absorbing into your bodies." She frowned at him. "Is it uncomfortable for you all, absorbing the magic involuntarily and not being able to release it by singing?"

People nodded fervently on all sides, many raising their hands to rub at their chests.

"It makes the pressure feel more intense, does it?" Gisela guessed sympathetically. She narrowed her eyes, thinking over their predicament. "I assume Lorraine and the others built this pit in a location that naturally releases a high volume of magic?"

The leader nodded.

"Meaning if the talisman detects little to no magic, they can tell they've gathered quite a force," Gisela mused. "A force strong enough to grapple with whatever magic they intend to use against the elves."

Again, he nodded.

"Well, then," said Gisela briskly, turning to her mother. "It seems it's time for you to practice what I once told you to stop doing, Mother. We need you to push enough magic back into the ground to trick the talisman and buy us more time."

Her mother looked alarmed, and in fairness, Gisela couldn't blame her. She didn't even know if the feat was possible. But she found a certain satisfaction in pushing her mother hard for the rest of the morning in her attempts to make the long-internalized process intentional. Haiden and Gisela had suffered a great deal because of their mother's determination to reject her magic. They may as well derive some benefit from it.

When a group prepared a simple noon meal, working according to what appeared to be a well-organized and effective system that Gisela suspected the unofficial leader could take credit for, she paused her efforts. After eating, she handed over to Haiden while she attempted to come up with a plan of escape with several of those who'd been in the pit longest.

Fortunately, time wasn't as short as she'd feared. Whatever errand had Lorraine's right-hand singer absent must have stretched on, because evening fell without any sign of the promised assessment. The reprieve brought little comfort, however, given they'd had no success coming up with a viable plan. For one thing, communication was slow and frustrating. Gisela had been fascinated and impressed to note throughout the afternoon the various ways the singers had found to communicate without their voices. Chief among these was a series of simple signs that everyone but the new arrivals seemed to understand perfectly. But given neither she nor Valerie—who was key in the strategizing—knew the signs, discussion remained hampered.

And of course the idea of escape wasn't new. With months to consider it, the singers had yet to find a way out that didn't endanger their loved ones. Each idea thrown around was more impractical than the last.

In the end, a disheartened Gisela was forced to give up for the night and go to sleep along with the rest of them. She was no closer to finding a way to rescue Haiden from their shared prison, and much further from peace, thanks to the second unexpected encounter with an estranged parent in as many days.

Gisela had no way to tell when the sun rose in the world above. But the inhabitants of the pit obviously had their own methods, because when someone eventually shook her awake, the cave was bustling with all the usual activities of a small community. For a moment, Gisela just watched as wakefulness slowly returned.

A familiar red-haired figure blocked her vision, a wan smile on Valerie's face.

"Join me?" Gisela gestured to the cold stone beside her. "You look like you didn't get much sleep."

Valerie grimaced in acknowledgment, and Gisela studied her face sympathetically.

"Let me guess. Every fiber of your being wants to defy Lorraine and break out of here, and hang the consequences... but at the same time, you're worried about Monty?"

Valerie bit her lip, her expression unexpectedly vulnerable as she nodded.

Gisela sighed, her eyes lingering on her brother, who seemed to have risen more willingly than she had and was now at the writing wall with another young singer, deep in a slow and silent discussion.

"That's a hard place to be in," she told Valerie. "I understand the tension between wanting to take risks and needing to protect those you love."

Valerie shot her a swift look. Belatedly realizing her error, Gisela smiled. "Not that I'm suggesting you love Monty, of course." She paused, then, emboldened by their dire situation, pushed on. "Although I don't see why you don't. He's clearly head-over-heels for you, and unless I've read you wrongly, the only reason you haven't fallen completely for him is because you're adamantly refusing to let yourself."

Valerie's cheeks reddened in the lantern light. Drawing a breath, she shook her head and gestured first to the top of her head, then to her feet.

Gisela stared at her in confusion, and Valerie tried again, more slowly. Exaggerated head shake, tap on the top of her head, pat to each of her two heels, then palm flat against her chest.

"He's not head-over-heels for you?" Gisela guessed.

Pleased with her success, Valerie nodded.

Gisela let out a snort. "You must be as much in denial as my mother because I can't honestly believe you'd be that oblivious."

Valerie sent a curious glance across the space at the older woman, but didn't allow herself to get sidetracked. Once again shaking her head in a pointed motion, she tapped her chest.

"Not you," Gisela translated.

Nodding, Valerie pointed to her throat.

"Your throat?" Gisela asked. "I'm lost again."

Valerie shook her head in frustration, and made a flowing motion with her hand, along her throat and out.

"Your voice!" Suddenly Gisela understood. "You think it's not you he loves, but your songcraft."

Valerie nodded decisively.

"Hm." Gisela studied the other girl for a moment. "I don't think that's true, but I doubt I'll convince you. I imagine you have your reasons for thinking the way you do, just as I have mine."

Her eyes strayed out over the space, taking in both her brother and her mother. Before she could say any more, they heard a strange sucking sound, and most of the inhabitants looked sharply toward the tunnel through which Gisela had entered.

"Do you think that's the sound of the stump being removed?" she asked Valerie nervously.

"Hey in there!"

The sharp, masculine voice came from the direction of the tunnel, confirming Gisela's guess. Her heart sank. They were out of time, and they hadn't come up with a workable plan. None of the previous day's experiments had given her any confidence that her mother could shield the magic absorption of anything like the number of singers present in the pit.

"Come out where we can see you, and bring the redhead."

Valerie met Gisela's eye, startled. Gisela had no doubt that the nerves on the other girl's face were not for herself, but for Monty. It wouldn't be easy for Valerie to curb her instinct to stand up to her captors.

Gisela stood as her friend did, following along the tunnel but staying out of sight.

"It's time to move." The voice came from out of Gisela's sight. It didn't sound familiar. She didn't think it was either Lorraine's son or the singer. "Boss's orders have come through. No assessment—we strike today. Gather your people. I expect all of you to be out of that pit in ten minutes."

Gisela heard the quick intake of breath from the leader, and she didn't blame him. After being forced to make the pit their home for months, they were expected to be ready to leave it forever in a matter of minutes?

"You heard me," said the man above ground, probably reading his listeners' reaction. "And remind everyone what's at stake. If you do your job, you'll all be free to return to your homes. If not, you've all got someone who'll pay the price."

A moment later, the leader hurried past Gisela, back toward the rest of the group. She realized she should go with him, to use her voice to tell everyone what was happening. But she lingered, wondering why Valerie was still near the stone platform below the hole.

"You're coming with me now," came the stranger's voice. "You'll have a special place at the front. Word is we're moving on the elves now because they have a special visitor at the moment. Someone who's a friend of yours."

# CHAPTER TWENTY-TWO

# Gisela

Gisela stiffened. Otto and his group were with the elves? They'd finally found the Imperator's settlement, then! And they were about to be caught up in Lorraine's attack. Fear washed over her, and she wondered if she should run out into the light, try to stop them from taking Valerie. But she couldn't see what that would gain, and there was a great deal to lose. Especially for Monty. Besides, Haiden was still with the main group. She couldn't leave him.

She shuffled back down the tunnel, emerging into the open space to find everyone already in a bustle of motion. It didn't seem her help had been needed to communicate. They must have been holding themselves in readiness for this day for a long time.

One person clearly hadn't fully understood what was happening, however. Haiden appeared at Gisela's side, silent questions in his eyes.

"They've decided it's time to strike." Gisela's words tumbled over each other. "Otto and the others have reached the central settlement, and they plan to unleash the singers on the Imperator." Her eyes widened as she remembered Lorraine's words about using the prince as a scapegoat. "I've just realized—they probably hope to make it seem like Otto called the singers in to attack."

Haiden's expression was grim, and his eyes turned toward the tunnel. Gisela's gaze searched the pit, landing on her mother, huddled in a corner looking confused.

"Wait, Haiden..." She grabbed her brother's arm. "This is our chance to escape. Whoever's gathering everyone up isn't someone I recognize. I wouldn't be surprised if Lorraine and the others are the ones who sent word. They might not even be here. If we stay back, it's possible they won't notice."

A frown descended on Haiden's face as he thought it over, then he nodded.

"We can keep Mother here as well, to shield your magic. In case they check."

People were already starting to move toward the tunnel. Judging by their expressions, many of them were glad to face whatever was coming if it meant they could get out of the pit. Gisela couldn't blame them. Being trapped somewhere you couldn't leave was no way to live a life.

The leader was at the tunnel entrance, counting heads as people passed. Gisela moved to stand beside him, clearing her throat.

"We're going to try to stay back," she told him, deciding to trust him. "They didn't use defensive magic when they captured Haiden. It's worth the risk for us. We'll make a run for it once everyone's gone."

The leader nodded distractedly. It was probably immaterial to him.

The pit was emptied in an amazingly short time. Gisela's mother had given no objection to being held back by her children. She stood by Gisela's side, watching the rest of the group leave. When everyone else was gone, Gisela signaled to the others to stay and crept back up the tunnel.

"Is that everyone?" she heard the unseen man ask.

A shuddering breath met the question, followed by a voice that was gruff and weak from disuse.

"Yes." That must be the singers' unofficial leader. "There's no one left."

"All right, gag him the old-fashioned way, like the others," said the stranger. "And send someone down with the talisman to check." His voice became a growl. "If you've lied to me, someone will pay the price. The silencing magic might not work out here, but the defensive magic works just fine."

Moving silently, Gisela hurried back toward the others. "Hide!" she hissed. She seized her mother's arm as the older woman moved toward a pile of empty crates. "Mother, you have to try to hide Haiden's magic as well as your own. Push back against the magic trying to course into you from the ground. Push as much of it back as you can."

Her mother's eyes were wide and uncertain, but to Gisela's relief, she nodded. A moment later they both dove behind the crates, Haiden hiding himself under a pile of blankets. Gisela could hear footsteps approaching, a rough voice accompanying them.

"Why would anyone *want* to stay down here?"

Judging by the murmur, he was alone. Gisela pressed her eye against a crack in the crate, just able to make out the object the man was raising.

*Now!* she mouthed silently to her mother, and the other woman's face screwed up in concentration.

The man directed the talisman around the area, his eyes squinting. It looked as though he was trying to see the magic in the pit, but magic was invisible to the eye. Although, for all

Gisela knew, a talisman to detect magic might make it visible to the bearer.

To her dismay, the man's roving gaze stopped in the corner where Haiden was concealed. He narrowed his eyes, taking a step forward. Beside Gisela, her mother clenched her fists in the fabric of her gown, beads of sweat standing out on her forehead. As Gisela watched, the man's expression relaxed, and he stepped back.

"All clear down there?" the voice echoed faintly from the world above.

"Yeah!" called back the man in the pit. "Magic's pouring from the ground again, without any gaps I can see."

"Good, then let's go!"

The man didn't need to be told twice, clearly not relishing being underground. The moment he was out of sight, Gisela emerged, her mother behind her. Normally she would have made Haiden count to a hundred with her to ensure the coast was clear, but she was afraid someone might close the stump before they got out.

She didn't need to worry, though. Apparently Lorraine's men considered themselves finished with the pit. No one had thought to enchant the stump back into place. When the trio emerged hesitantly into the fresh air, the scene before them was deserted. They still made their way well into the cover of the sparse undergrowth before anyone spoke.

Haiden was the first. "Thank goodness," he said. "Being muzzled is awful."

"Yes. It is." The quiet voice made both siblings fall silent. It had been many years since they'd heard it.

"Let's go," said Haiden, turning to Gisela after an uncomfortable moment. "If we stay close behind the group for long enough to get a sense of the right direction, we should be able to circle around and reach the elf settlement first."

When Gisela didn't answer, he threw her an impatient look. "Gisela?"

She bit her lip. "Maybe we shouldn't all go."

"What do you mean?" Haiden was almost growling.

"I mean," Gisela insisted, "I didn't go to all these lengths to keep you safe only to throw you straight back into danger."

"No one's *keeping* me anything or *throwing* me anywhere," said Haiden angrily. "Gisela, it's not up to you what I do! You might want to slink away and hide somewhere safe, but I don't intend to desert my friends when they're in trouble."

"That's not fair," said Gisela, stung. "I don't want to desert them. I'm not saying we should both stay back. But if Lorraine gets hold of you, she'll use you to hurt them more. And she won't care what happens to you in the process. Haiden, don't ask me to endanger you to help someone else. I just can't do it."

"But you'd endanger yourself without hesitation," said Haiden, shaking his head. "Gisela, my safety isn't the highest priority in the world! You need to stop acting as though it's all that matters."

Gisela wanted to pull out her hair in frustration. "Haiden, the only reason you're still alive is that I've spent most of my life acting as though your safety is all that matters."

"That just proves my point," said Haiden. "Your obsession with keeping me hidden away is preventing us both from living our lives." He gestured to their silent companion. "Stop fooling yourself that you have to be my mother, Gisela. My *actual* mother is here, and even she doesn't care half as much as you do whether I live or die!"

"That's not true." Their mother's voice was impassioned as she unexpectedly inserted herself into the conversation. "I do care. I've thought about you every day."

"This isn't the time, Mother," said Haiden tersely. He looked Gisela in the eye. "We're both intimately familiar with what happens when people abandon those they love out of a misguided desire to do what they think they have to. Can you honestly tell me you could live with yourself if we didn't do *everything* we can to help Valerie now? And Monty, and Lady Louisa, and Norris?" His eyes bored into hers with uncomfortable shrewdness. "And Otto?"

Something dropped into Gisela's stomach at the thought of Otto vulnerable, oblivious both of the danger stalking toward him and of Lorraine's schemes to implicate him. Of course she would never just leave him to his fate. It was unthinkable.

"You're right," she said, letting out a long breath. "We both need to go. You're the stronger of us, and I can't do it without your help."

A smile flashed across Haiden's face before his serious expression returned. He gave a terse nod. "Let's go." He glanced around him. "What I wouldn't give for an elf gate right about now. Not that we could create one without an elf's help."

"It's more the other way around, actually."

They both turned to their mother in surprise.

"What do you mean?" Haiden demanded.

"The elves didn't always have gates," she said. "My grandmother used to tell me about it. They require a high volume of magic, which Ilgal has always had, but they also require a very sophisticated level of magical manipulation. The elves only figured out the method with the help of singers."

"So...so could Haiden create one?" Gisela asked, stunned.

"I doubt it," her mother said. "The elves claimed the invention, and hoarded the knowledge of the process to themselves. Probably tricked the singers who helped them into a bargain of secrecy or something, knowing their kind."

It was all too likely, Gisela reflected, but of no help to them in their current situation.

"I wonder how many elf innovations belong to the singers as well," Haiden commented, frowning.

"Never mind that," said Gisela. "We need to get moving if we want to overtake the group without being seen." She glanced at her mother. "You're free to go home now. Can you find your way?"

"I'm not going home," the other woman said, surprising Gisela with the strength of her voice. "I'm coming with you to see this through."

The siblings exchanged a look, and Gisela shrugged slightly.

"Suit yourself," she said.

The trail of the large group was easy to follow. In ordinary circumstances, Gisela and Haiden both knew how to move silently but quickly, and their mother would likely have been the one to slow the group down. But unfortunately, Gisela was still bound by the invisible chains placed on her by Lorraine's loyal singer. A quick attempt suggested that Haiden didn't have the skill to remove them by songcraft, and as neither of them wanted to waste time on extensive experiments, she would have to make do. She could move at a steady pace, but she wouldn't be running.

They set off after the group, their saving grace found in the fact that it was no simple task to move such a large group efficiently when they were reluctant captives. They caught up within half an hour.

"Do you think they're really headed toward the Imperator's settlement?" Gisela asked in a murmur, as they started to slow.

"Wherever we're headed, one of my stones is there," said Haiden.

"What do you mean?"

He shrugged. "I've been feeling it for some time. It's the one that we left with our gear, remember? It was removed from that location before I started calling the stones. I can feel the rest of them back near the pit, but whoever found that one took it to the Imperator's settlement. Or at least, to wherever we're going."

"I don't like it," said Gisela uneasily. "Why would our gear be there?"

"One way to find out," Haiden replied.

Taking the lead, he skirted around the huge group ahead of them, getting far enough in front to scale a tree and get a view as they passed below him. When Gisela and her mother caught up to him, he shimmied quietly down the tree.

"The singers are all gagged with cloth," he murmured. "They're herded along with Lorraine's people, and Gisela...there are a lot of them." His face was somber. "They have enough for one guard per singer. And they're pushing Valerie along right at the front."

Gisela frowned. "Is Lorraine there?"

Haiden bit his lip. "I only saw her that one time, from the pit, so I can't be completely sure. But I don't think so. The ground looks pretty swampy ahead," he added. "I think we'll have to wait and follow in their tracks. I can't be sure of finding a safe path through otherwise."

Gisela nodded, and the three of them crept through the trees toward the large trail left by the group. A quick discussion had been enough to convince them they would be foolish to attack on the road. Haiden was only one singer, and many of the captives might be willing to turn on them in order to save their loved ones from being punished for their defiance. It was hard to judge the passage of time, Gisela's mounting tension making every minute feel like an hour. But she thought it was probably close to three hours that the trio moved through the forest in silence. When next one of them spoke, the swampy area was well behind them, the trees large and well-spaced, and the undergrowth lush.

"Who's Otto?"

After so long in silence, the abrupt question from their mother made both Gisela and Haiden start.

"What?"

"Back there." Her mother gestured behind them. "When we first got out of the pit. Your brother convinced you to help by mentioning Otto. Who is he?"

"Gisela's sweetheart," said Haiden, smirking at her.

"He isn't," Gisela protested. Annoyingly, she could feel her cheeks heat. "And keep your voices down, you two. We could be getting close to the settlement for all you know."

"You mentioned a Lady Someone," their mother persisted, ignoring the warning. "That sounds like a noble. Who are you mixing with? Otto isn't...I mean, he couldn't be..."

"Yes, he is that Otto," said Haiden bluntly. "Crown Prince Otto. We stumbled on his group by chance and have been traveling with him ever since."

Their mother stopped walking, causing her children to stop as well.

"You're telling me that whoever threw us into that pit is marching all those singers against our own prince? I thought it was the elves they wanted to target!"

"It is," said Gisela. "The prince is just collateral to Lorraine. I think she hopes to make it look like he's the one who called the singers, because conflict between the crown and the elves can only help her cause."

"But you can't go anywhere near that mess!" The older woman's hand shot out, seizing Haiden's arm. "You know what you're destined to do. Do you *want* to bring down our kingdom?"

"Of course I don't," growled Haiden.

"Then why would you put yourself in the prince's path?" demanded their mother. "Why would you toss your magic into that situation, knowing what you'll probably end up doing?"

"Haiden is in control of what he does," snapped Gisela. "Not some prophecy. And he'd never plot against Otto or the kingdom."

Her mother turned to her. "You're really going to let him go near the prince?"

Gisela's eyes traveled to her brother, whose expression reflected the incredulous anger she felt at their mother's attempt to exert authority after all the years of abandonment.

"As he said earlier, it's not for me to *let* him do anything," she said coolly. "He'll do as he thinks best, and I trust his judgment. Unlike you, I know him."

Haiden's face softened the tiniest bit, and, emboldened, Gisela made no attempt to stem the words trying to burst from her.

"I used to wish we'd never left our beds the night of that festival." Her eyes bored into her mother's unblinkingly. "For years I wished that. Lying in my bed that night, before we snuck out, that was the last time I felt truly safe."

As she said the words—words she'd thought many times before but never spoken aloud—she was hit with a sudden, potent realization. The assertion was no longer true. For a long time it had been, but not anymore. It had been coming on so gradually that she hadn't recognized it until she lost it, but she had experienced that feeling of safety again.

She'd found it with Otto.

With the prince, she'd felt safe, not just from the dangers of the forest, but within her own heart. When he cared for her after the galboar attack, when he drew her out of her shell with that kind patience that always refrained from pushing her too quickly, when he unknowingly made her long to open her heart and share things with him she hadn't shared with anyone before. With him, for the first time since childhood, she'd had a glimpse of how it felt to let someone else share her burdens.

It was more than just warmth or gratitude she felt for him. She remembered the tenderness in his eyes when he'd touched her cheek at camp that last day, when he'd told her with such sincerity that she was important. He'd asked her to come to Terenford with him, pleaded for her to let him help her. He'd even told her he believed they were meant to cross each other's paths. Something deep within Gisela had responded to him in that moment, and even though she hadn't let herself show it, even though she hadn't even admitted it to herself until now, the damage had been done, and it was irreversible.

She was in love with Otto. She'd given him her heart, let him all the way in.

And contrary to the voice of caution in her mind, he'd done nothing to betray her trust. She'd been the one to turn on him, unfairly and without proof.

This realization passed through her mind in a heartbeat, her mother and brother still watching her expectantly. For a moment, Gisela struggled to regain the thread of her point, internally reeling from the truth that had just swept through her like wildfire, burning everything in its path and leaving behind an unrecognizable landscape, ready for new life to grow.

"I don't wish it anymore," she said, a shudder going over her as she wrestled with her emotions. "I don't regret leaving our beds that night, or leaving our home. I'm glad we learned of Haiden's songcraft. I wouldn't change that for anything, and I wouldn't change the trail it's led us down." She met her brother's eye, her resolve growing. "We're not turning back now out of fear. We'll take control of our own destinies."

Her brother gave an approving nod, a light springing into his eyes. It had taken her five years, but she was finally on the same page as him. No more being driven by fear. No more expecting betrayal and disaster around every corner.

Apparently their mother wasn't experiencing the same

transformation. "I can't be part of this," she said, shaking her head.

"No one is asking you to," Haiden responded shortly. Turning, he strode away between the trees, Gisela following close behind.

"You all right?" she asked quietly, as they edged around a large elm. Haiden clearly appreciated her change in perspective, but their mother's insistence on seeing him as a villain must have hurt.

Haiden gave his head a shake. "Let's not get into it. We just need to focus on—"

He never finished the sentence. Distracted by the confrontation with their mother, he walked around the tree and straight into a large figure.

Before Gisela could do more than let out a cry, the man had one thick arm around Haiden's lithe form, the other covering his mouth. Gisela lurched forward, but the next moment she was seized from behind herself.

"Not so quickly, my dear." Lorraine's familiar voice made her stiffen, and another look told her that it was Lorraine's son who had Haiden. Her brother was struggling fiercely, trying to bite the man's hand from the look of it.

But the next moment a low voice joined the confrontation, raised in a song that sounded sinister even to Gisela's untrained ears. Lorraine's faithful singer came into sight, something clutched in his hand. He strode up to Haiden, making a looping motion around the still-fighting teenager with the talisman and then made as if to throw it at Gisela. She flinched instinctively, but nothing actually left his hand.

"Thank you," Lorraine said pleasantly to the singer. "That should simplify things." She smiled sweetly at Haiden. "Feel free to keep resisting, child. No better way to find out what will happen if you don't comply."

Haiden glared at her, attempting again to wrench his arms free. Lorraine gave her singer a pointed look, and the man raised the talisman he'd just used. With it sitting in the palm of his hand, he twitched his fingers, as if hooking them around something invisible.

All of a sudden, white-hot pain radiated through Gisela. She let out a shout and fell to her knees on the forest floor, clutching at her middle in agony.

She heard muffled shouting from Haiden, but she was too blinded by the pain to look up and see what was happening.

"If you want it to stop, all you need to do is stop resisting," said Lorraine in a reasonable voice.

At once, the pain disappeared. Gisela blinked up to see her brother's wide, fearful eyes meeting hers.

"I'm all right," she told him quietly. "It's all right."

"Very noble of you to shield him," said Lorraine, sounding faintly amused. "Even if he knows it's a lie." She looked between them. "Did you really think I wouldn't notice your absence the moment the group joined me at my location? If you were smart, you would have run for it when you managed to slip away. Quite the oversight of ours, failing to activate defensive magic to keep this young man in check." She smirked at Gisela. "An oversight which has now been corrected."

Gisela said nothing, but inside she was seething. All that effort to escape the group, and they'd allowed themselves to be recaptured through carelessness.

"I'm pleased you came back to assist in our cause," Lorraine said pleasantly. "Especially in light of what I heard just now. You were traveling with the prince, were you?" Her eyes dwelled greedily on Haiden, now unresisting in her son's grip. "It looks like I have another singer who needs to be right at the front of our group."

Haiden narrowed his eyes, and Lorraine raised an admonishing finger.

"Now, now." Her eyes flicked meaningfully to Gisela. "Let's not make your sister go through another demonstration just to remind you why you *will* do precisely what I tell you to."

Gisela and Haiden locked gazes, the same panic in both sets of eyes. If there was a way out of the mess, Gisela couldn't see it. They had little choice but to let Lorraine's henchmen shove them back toward the main group.

"That's it," said Lorraine indulgently. "You've arrived just in time, children." Her eyes were now fixed on the trees ahead. "We're almost there."

# CHAPTER TWENTY-THREE

## Otto

"Prince Otto."

Lady Louisa's no-nonsense voice made Otto look up. She'd just appeared at the doorway of the small room Otto was sharing with Monty, her expression that of a nursemaid scolding a child.

"Sit down, Your Highness. You're making me nervous."

"I'm sorry, Lady Louisa," Otto said, continuing his pacing. "But I can't seem to sit still."

"Sitting still is the last thing we should be doing." Monty's scowl was evident in his voice, and the countess sighed as she looked over at him. He was seated on the edge of one of the beds, his foot tapping unevenly on the floor as his eyes followed Otto's progress without really seeing it.

"You're just as bad, Lord Montague," Lady Louisa told him, pointing her fan at him. "Nothing is achieved by worrying."

"Aren't you worried?" Monty demanded. "You're pretty cold for someone who supposedly took Valerie under her wing."

"Monty," said Otto quickly, but Lady Louisa didn't seem offended.

"Of course I'm concerned about Valerie, and about Gisela

and Haiden. But I won't serve their interests by getting myself into a frenzy." Her eyes softened a little as she took in the two young men. "I've been around a lot longer than you two. The first crisis in your life always feels like the most catastrophic."

"We're wasting our time!" Monty burst out. Otto looked over at his friend to see him hunched up with one arm around his middle.

"Monty?" Otto asked, concerned. "Are you all right?" He narrowed his eyes. "Is that mysterious pain back?"

"It doesn't matter," said Monty, wincing slightly. Even as he said the words, however, he bent double, a sharp hiss escaping him as whatever was ailing him intensified.

"Monty!" Otto moved forward, but his friend was already waving him back.

"I'm fine," he said, his features returning to normal. "It's gone now."

"But what's causing it?" Otto demanded.

"I don't know, and it's the last of my concerns," said Monty frankly. He met Otto's eyes. "I just don't understand why we're still here. If you believe Asivah that Lonik isn't the one who's taken our people, why are we lingering here? Shouldn't we be trying to find the group which has been snatching singers?"

"Where would we start?" Otto asked wearily. "We'll have a much better chance of success with the elves' help than without it."

"But the Imperator isn't going to help us," Monty protested. "Not now you've accused his heir of plotting against him. He'll be pretty occupied with that mess for some time, I'd imagine."

"I didn't make accusations," said Otto. "I just told Asivah what Gisela and Haiden told us, and my suspicions. I left it to her to decide what to do with that information. As far as I know, she's still considering."

"I believe she's with her grandfather now," said Lady Louisa.

Her brow furrowed. "I confess, I don't relish being caught up in whatever comes of this family conflict."

Otto ran a hand through his hair. "Nor do I, but I think the dangers of saying nothing would have been greater. After all, my initial purpose in seeking out the Imperator was to learn the true state of affairs in Ilgal. And if there's a power struggle between the Imperator and his heir, that's something my father needs to know about." He frowned, thinking about Lonik. "Not to mention I think it's in all our interests not to have Lonik seize his grandfather's throne."

"Throne?" Monty asked, eyebrows raised. "So you consider him a monarch now?"

"You know what I mean," said Otto impatiently.

The sound of someone running toward them drew all their attention to the open doorway. It was the first time Otto could recall witnessing anyone hurrying within the Imperator's palace-like tree. Within the city at all, actually.

An elf appeared in the doorway, two others flanking him. They all pinned Otto with hard stares, undaunted by the fact that they needed to crane their necks back in order to do so.

"Your Highness," said the elf in front in terse tones. "You've been requested to attend the Imperator immediately."

"Certainly I'll do so," said Otto with dignity.

Monty rose from his position, joining Lady Louisa at Otto's side as they stepped out of the room. Norris and three other guards materialized immediately to accompany them.

"Do you think he's angry about your allegations?" Monty murmured.

Remembering what Lonik had said about elves' superior hearing, Otto didn't respond.

They were taken to a high-ceilinged room dominated by a long table of unpolished wood. Even the surface retained its natural rough bark. Not practical for writing on, Otto thought irrelevantly.

The Imperator was seated at the table, and Asivah was standing beside him with her hands folded respectfully behind her back. Otto's eyes darted between them before he greeted the Imperator. The mood was decidedly tense.

"You wished to speak with me?" he prompted, when the Imperator didn't initiate conversation.

The elf regarded him for another silent moment, making no comment on Otto's decision to bring his entire entourage. Then the elf bent his head, gesturing for the group to sit. Otto, Monty, and Lady Louisa did so, although of course Norris and the other guards remained at attention.

"I have been having a most troubling conversation with my granddaughter," the Imperator said, his eyes hard as they rested on Otto's face. It was impossible to tell whether he was angry with Lonik regarding the alleged treachery, or angry with Otto and Asivah for making the accusation. "But that's not why I summoned you here."

"It's not?" Otto was too surprised to care about the elf's imperious choice of words, although he heard Monty give a small huff beside him.

"No. I have just been notified that two humans, claiming to be singers, have approached our city. They've asked for you by name."

"Who are they?" Monty demanded, rising from his seat.

Otto found himself on his feet as well. "Were they accompanied by another human?"

The Imperator looked at them. "There is a woman with them, yes. I have heard the rumor that you came here in search of missing members of your party. You would have me believe these intruders are they?"

"I don't expect you to believe what I don't yet know myself," said Otto, although his heart was swelling with hope. "Where are they?"

"They remain outside," said the Imperator coolly. "Not satisfied of their identity, I was not willing to allow them entry."

"Take us to them!" Otto demanded.

The Imperator frowned at this means of address, but he didn't comment. Instead he gestured for an elf, who moved forward with a small basin of water. Otto watched, perplexed, as the Imperator received a tiny jar of soil from the serving elf and tipped some into the water. He swirled the water clockwise with his finger, completing one full circuit.

Before Otto's fascinated eyes, the water slowly stilled.

"Soil from the location where the intruders stand," said Asivah helpfully. "The bowl is a talisman bearing a sophisticated enchantment."

The Imperator didn't look entirely pleased with her decision to explain, but he said nothing, merely waving Otto forward. The prince bent over the basin, amazed to see the image of a face swim into view on the nearly-flat surface.

"Is this child part of your group?" the Imperator asked.

"Yes!" Excitement mounted in Otto. "That's Haiden! He's a singer from Ilgal."

"And you trust him?" the Imperator pressed.

Otto's eyes flew to Asivah, who was watching him intently. There could be no doubt she was thinking of the prophecy she'd told him about.

"With my life," Otto said firmly, a silent challenge in his eyes.

"Then it is your life that will be forfeit if he proves traitorous," said the Imperator calmly.

Norris shifted, his expression menacing, but Otto held out a restraining hand. He'd made no bargain with the elf leader that would activate the latent magic attached to elf bargains. If the Imperator intended to kill him, he'd have to give the order the old-fashioned way. And Otto knew that he'd put himself in the elves' power by coming into their city.

"Bring the intruders to the clearing," the Imperator told the elves standing by. "And summon my heir to attend."

Otto saw Asivah give her grandfather a quick look at this addition, but for the moment he had no interest in elf politics. He could barely restrain his impatience as the group made its stately way to the open space where the sundown gathering had been held the night before. They'd barely crossed the ring of wildflowers when three figures were led in by an escort of elves.

"Valerie!" Monty ran forward, throwing his arms around the red-haired singer. She didn't respond to his embrace, her figure stiff and her face pale.

Otto's eyes searched the clearing, landing on another figure. "Haiden!" His relief faded as he saw the unfamiliar woman behind Haiden. "Where's Gisela?"

Haiden swallowed visibly, giving no answer. Something was definitely off in his expression. Like Valerie, he looked ill-at-ease. Monty stepped back from Valerie, obviously noticing the same thing.

"What's wrong?" Otto demanded.

"The elves," said Haiden woodenly. "The elves are what's wrong with Ilgal."

"And their reign is over," said the unknown woman behind the pair of singers.

She raised her fist high above her head, and Otto saw a shudder pass over both Haiden and Valerie. Whatever the woman held must be a talisman of some kind. Distant shouts reached their ears from all sides, and several armed elves rushed at the woman. They never reached her, instead bouncing off an invisible barrier. One of the elves redirected toward Valerie, and Monty sprang forward with a cry.

But the elf fell back, unable to reach either Valerie or

Haiden. They must be included in whatever protection the woman had created.

"Our people surround your city," the stranger said, her eyes resting gleefully on the Imperator. "The shield that protects me connects with each of their positions. No one will be able to pass through our barrier."

The Imperator narrowed his eyes. "Your impudence is unforgivable," he said disdainfully. "And your assertions impossible." His gaze was on the item the woman still held aloft. "I know the type of talisman which could achieve that feat. It's defensive magic of my people's own invention. Few were made, and all are found within my own armory."

"They used to all be in your armory," Asivah said grimly. "No doubt if you check, one will be missing. Grandfather, what more evidence do you need that you've been betrayed?"

Otto saw Lonik look carefully between his cousin and grandfather, seeming uneasy in the realization that something was happening of which he was unaware. Apparently Otto's accusations hadn't yet reached him.

"For what purpose would any of my own people sell such a powerful talisman to our enemies?" growled the Imperator.

"They may not have known or cared to whom it was sold," said Asivah. "If gold was the motivation. It would fetch a hefty price. Remember, the message Prince Otto's people overheard discussed shipment of gold outside of Ilgal."

"What madness are you speaking, Asivah?" Lonik asked tersely.

"Enough!" The shriek of the stranger suggested she wasn't well pleased with the elves' tame response to threats which she'd no doubt expected would throw them into panic. "It's enough that we've acquired it. And it is the least of the magic at our disposal. You think you can come into our home and take whatever you please. Our kingdom belongs to the humans, and so does Ilgal. With the might of the crown we force you out."

She looked significantly at Haiden and Valerie. As they hesitated, waiting for who-knew-what, Monty fell to the ground with a cry of agony.

# CHAPTER TWENTY-FOUR

# Gisela

Gisela struggled fruitlessly against her bonds—both literal and magical—as rage and terror ran riot inside her. From her vantage point, she could see that Haiden and Valerie had entered the elf city, with Lorraine close behind. What would she do to them? What would she make them do to the elves, and everyone else inside the city?

Panic threatened to overwhelm Gisela, her breaths coming short and fast through her nose. A gag stopped her mouth, and it gave her the sensation of being trapped without air in a shrinking space.

*Stop*, she told herself. *Don't panic. Think.*

But no amount of thinking helped her come up with a plan. Only one of Lorraine's lackeys guarded her—the rest were needed for the all-important role of supervising all the singers, making sure none refused to participate in Lorraine's scheme by reminding each one that the lives of their loved ones were at stake. Still, Gisela was fully bound, hands and feet, and had no idea how to intervene even if she'd been free.

She was still searching her mind for ideas when a sudden, crippling pain assaulted her. If her mouth had been free, she would have cried out, but all she could do was curl in on herself on the forest floor. Waves of pain rippled over her body in an attack that would have been unendurable except for one small but powerful truth—it meant that Haiden was defying Lorraine.

*Yes,* Gisela urged her brother silently, even through her misery. *Fight her, Haiden.*

But the next moment the pain was gone, leaving Gisela with a conflicting mixture of relief and disappointment. Her guard didn't even seem to have noticed the bout of pain, his back still to her. She tried to struggle back into a sitting position when suddenly a cool hand touched her shoulder. Jerking her head in alarm, Gisela was astonished to see her mother crouched beside her.

The older woman held a finger to her lips, her eyes flicking meaningfully to the guard. As Gisela watched, her mother started tugging at the bonds on Gisela's feet, using a sharp rock to aid in the effort. As soon as they fell away, her mother stopped, stashing the rock in a pocket and offering her hands. Slowly and silently, she eased Gisela to her feet, and the two of them crept away from the guard. When they were out of earshot, Gisela stopped, heart pounding.

Her mother stopped too, immediately pulling off Gisela's gag.

"Quick, do my hands!" Gisela murmured. "He'll notice any second."

Her mother was ahead of her, already working on the rough rope wound around Gisela's wrists.

"Why are you helping me?" Gisela asked suddenly.

Her mother looked up at her for the briefest moment, then back down to her task. She didn't answer.

"I'm going straight for the elf city," Gisela warned her. "I'm going to help Haiden, not run from him or fight against him."

"I know," said her mother.

The rope fell away with the words, and Gisela turned toward the distant city. To avoid her captor's notice, she'd had to move away from it, so she would need to run fast to get there in time to stop whatever Lorraine was planning.

At the thought, she heard an angry shout from nearby, and her heart doubled in speed.

"Go," said her mother. "I'll try to distract him, and follow if I can."

Gisela studied her mother for a moment, confused by her motivations. But there was no time to ponder it. With a sharp nod, she took off, traveling in a wide arc around the position of Lorraine's lackey.

She was inside the circle of singers she knew Lorraine had positioned around the city—the rebel leader had wanted Gisela close, in case it was necessary to more forcefully coerce Haiden.

She didn't know what she could do. As she crashed through the undergrowth to the best of her still-shackled ability, she only knew one thing.

She had to at least try.

# CHAPTER TWENTY-FIVE

# Otto

Otto turned toward his friend in alarm, dropping to one knee beside the young lord. Monty's face was contorted in agony, his eyes rolling backward and his body convulsing.

"Monty! Monty, what's happening?" Otto grabbed his friend's shoulders, only vaguely aware of Valerie's voice behind him as she unleashed a low, angry song.

At once Monty went still, color returning to his face as his breaths came quickly. Valerie must have released a healing song. But as Haiden's voice joined hers, shouts rose on all sides. Otto whipped his head around to see elves running in all directions as trees trembled and shook. A fissure opened up in the middle of the clearing, one elf barely leaping aside to avoid falling in.

Otto watched in alarm as Haiden and Valerie unleashed a song of destruction on the elven city. Quite apart from being unable to comprehend their motives, he'd had no idea the pair held this kind of power. Even as the thought occurred to him, his ears caught faint sounds of song from the distance. The stranger had said her people surrounded the city. Those people must be singers—no doubt the missing singers of Ilgal who'd been rounded up in recent months.

"What's going on?" The cry came from Monty, who pulled himself to a sitting position as the ground pitched beneath them.

The woman still held her protective talisman aloft, and Otto's eyes widened as they followed her other arm to see her hand buried deep in the folds of her gown.

"She's controlling them somehow," he breathed. "She has more talismans hidden."

"You see, Grandfather!" Lonik's high-pitched shriek cut through the chaos as elven guards raced to surround the Imperator. A nearby tree split with a crack, elven screams filling the air as it toppled. "The humans demonstrate for us how little they are to be trusted! King Ryker deserves no loyalty. He seeks to drive us from Ilgal—it's time for us to expel the humans once and for all!"

"No!" Otto struggled to his feet, staggering across the uneven ground toward the elf leader. "No, she lied when she said the crown was part of this! I know nothing of this plot."

Lonik gave a furious laugh. "You try to claim innocence when your own people lead the charge?"

Otto turned angrily to him, accusations ready on his lips for what he'd assumed was a clever strategy by the elf prince. But the rage in Lonik's eyes made him pause. Unlike his grandfather, he wasn't able to hide his offense behind calm disdain. He looked infuriated beyond control at the attack on his city. Otto realized he had no reason to assume that there was a connection between Lonik's scheming for his grandfather's position and the human group gathering singers for a sinister purpose. It was entirely possible Lonik was genuine in his belief that the crown had turned on the elves. Like Asivah said, he may have sold the talisman for gold, probably through a middleman, with no concept of how it was going to be used. His own culpability in that matter could even be fueling his anger.

"She's controlling them somehow," Otto said, his words directed to the Imperator. "I swear I know nothing of this attack, and I have full confidence that neither Valerie nor Haiden would willingly take part in it."

"Do you think I care how willing their actions are when they're destroying my home?" the Imperator roared, his calm mask slipping as the city continued to be ripped apart. He barked out orders to the elves around them, sending them scurrying toward the palace for whatever defensive talismans were held in readiness there.

Otto looked uneasily around him. It may well be too late by the time they returned. And how could they stop the destruction without harming Valerie and Haiden?

"They're wielding too much power," Asivah cried. "And listen to their song. It's not sophisticated! They're not directing the destruction. They're all just providing the power to fuel something already designed. Someone has a destructive talisman of some kind. Or perhaps a vessel storing raw magic."

Her words were silenced by an ear-splitting crack, and they all turned to see a section of the nearby palace tree fall away.

"We can figure out how they're doing it once we've stopped them," said the Imperator, his eyes furious now. Elves surrounded him, and he snapped out more orders. "Take the singers down. And seize the prince and his escort."

Norris leaped in front of Otto, but the prince stopped the guard with a hand on his shoulder. "No, Norris! We need to show them that we have no part in this."

Before Norris could reply, a new voice carried across the fractured clearing.

"Haiden!"

Otto's breath caught in his throat, relief surging powerfully through him as he at last caught sight of the person he'd been desperate to see for two days. Gisela stumbled into the clearing, her movements oddly restricted and her appearance generally the worse for wear.

Haiden turned as well, his song faltering as fear filled his face. "What are you doing here?" he cried.

The destruction continued unabated in spite of Haiden's silence, supporting the idea that he and Valerie were playing only a small part in what was happening.

"Gisela!" Otto surged toward her, grasping her shoulders and searching her eyes. "What's happening? Are you all right?"

"Otto, we have to stop them!" she gasped. "It's not just here —they're attacking the elves' defenses around the city. We have to—"

Her words were cut off as a battle cry reached them from the far side of the clearing. A group of humans ran into view. The one in front was singing a fast and furious song, but the others didn't appear to be singers. They fell on the Imperator's elf guards with regular weapons. All around the clearing, elves pulled items from their pockets, smashing them in an evident attempt to release power.

Except nothing happened. Consternation was on every elven face as their enemies swept in unopposed, overpowering the smaller creatures with their greater physical strength. Norris and his men rushed forward to engage the attackers, but they were outnumbered, only a few having accompanied Otto to the clearing.

The woman behind Haiden and Valerie spoke suddenly, drawing Otto's attention. "You know your role." The words were directed to Haiden. "It's time. Take out the elf leader!"

Otto let out a gasp as Haiden's face drained of color. The woman held a blade out to him, and he just stared at it.

A soft intake of breath drew Otto's attention back to Gisela.

"It's not the human kingdom he's destined to bring down," she whispered. "It's the elven one."

Otto's eyes widened as his mind tried to catch up. It hadn't occurred to him that the prophecy might refer to the elves. And no wonder—before this trip, he'd never thought of their hierarchy as a kingdom. But he'd seen ample evidence since arriving in the elf city that the role of the Imperator was becoming increasingly royal. Could that be the rising kingdom Asivah's prophecy had spoken of?

He was still wrestling with the question when the woman behind Haiden ran out of patience.

"Now!" she cried angrily.

Haiden swallowed, still not moving. The clearing became slightly quieter as Valerie also stopped singing, gripping Haiden's shoulder in solidarity. The stranger's eyes narrowed, and two things happened at once. Across the clearing, Monty let out a grunt of pain, and right under Otto's nose, Gisela crumpled.

He caught her in his arms, lowering her to the ground as his eyes searched her face in terror.

"Gisela!"

"Haiden!" Gisela gasped out the name, her body rocking in pain.

Otto's eyes darted frantically from Gisela to Haiden, then to Valerie's horrified face and on to Monty on the ground. Suddenly he understood. That was how the woman was controlling them. She somehow had the ability to inflict pain on those they cared about if they defied.

It was diabolical.

Haiden let out a shaky song, the blade rising from the woman's hands and floating magically in the air. He turned his gaze uncertainly toward the Imperator, who was mostly unprotected now. With a gasping song, Haiden set the blade into motion, so that it flew through the air, right above the defending elves' heads and straight toward the elf leader.

"Grandfather!" Asivah threw herself forward as if to shield the Imperator with her body. But Lonik flung his arm out, restraining her. She turned to stare incredulously at him, but Otto had no attention to spare for their family drama. To everyone's surprise, the knife had stopped midair, its blade still pointed toward the Imperator but its forward momentum stopped.

"Haiden," Gisela choked out again. "You...control...your... own...destiny."

With a shuddering breath, Haiden's voice stopped altogether. The blade fell silently to the floor of the clearing, not far from where Monty was on all fours, trying valiantly to crawl toward Valerie through the pain.

The woman Otto didn't know let out a scream of anger, but both singers ignored her.

Valerie ran to Monty, tears pouring down her face as she threw her arms roughly around his hunched form. "Monty," she wept. "I'm so sorry. I'm so, so sorry."

"I'm sorry, Gisela," Haiden echoed brokenly, kneeling at his sister's side. "I'm sorry I can't protect you. But I can't accept that my destiny is to kill and destroy."

"I'm proud...of you," Gisela whispered.

"But how do we save her?" Otto cried frantically. "How do we stop the pain?"

"Him." Haiden's pointing finger identified one of the men still fighting with the Imperator's elves. "He's the only singer who signed up to this venture willingly. The power radiating from him is immense. He has an incredibly powerful talisman that pulls in any magic released in the area, and uses it to fuel a destructive enchantment. It's what all us singers' magic is going into, and it's what drained the magic of the elves' talismans as it was released. It all just makes his destructive power stronger. If we can get our hands on it and smash it, the destruction will cease."

"And what about Gisela?" Otto demanded, terrified at the convulsive way she was twitching in his arms.

"Lorraine has the talismans linked to the defensive magic on both Valerie and me," said Haiden quickly. "But I don't think what she has is the source. I think the singer has that as well. It's all part of one incredibly powerful enchantment, which I think is tied to him. All of the items used to control us are pieces pulled from that original talisman, so if we—"

Haiden's words cut off, Otto letting out a shout as the young singer's head was wrenched violently backward.

"What are you doing?" screeched Lorraine, spit flying as she screamed into Haiden's face. "You *will* do your part! Don't you care if your sister dies? Do you want to kill her?"

"I'm not the one killing her," Haiden growled.

Otto didn't stay to hear their confrontation. He had all the information he needed, and there was no time. Laying Gisela on the grass, he sprinted across the clearing, his sights set on the unfamiliar singer Haiden had identified. He was locked in battle with Norris, holding his own against the experienced guard by use of the low song issuing urgently from his mouth as he fought.

Otto threw himself into the fray, disregarding weapons entirely as he ripped at the other man's garment. The talismans must be concealed within his clothes.

With a roar, the singer turned to him, blade raised.

Before either Otto or Norris could react, another figure lunged in from the side. The singer had no idea what hit him as a flurry of feathers whipped across his face. Lady Louisa brandished her fan with purpose, eliciting an angry cry from the beleaguered man as he raised a hand to defend his face from the bizarre attack.

As if responding to a cue, Lady Louisa snapped her fan closed into a thin line. Seizing it with one hand, she pushed against the base with the other, and Otto watched in amazement as a thin blade emerged from one of the outer wooden slats. The countess stabbed the blade into the singer's upraised hand, causing his cry of anger to turn into a scream of pain.

Seizing the chance offered, Otto plunged his hand into the thrashing man's pocket. His fingers closed around several items, and he yanked them free. The singer tried to grab at him with his uninjured hand, but Norris jumped in the way. Otto dropped the items onto the grass, yanking his own sword free as he did so. He turned the blade in a swift motion and brought the hilt smashing down. A few of the items were wooden, and splintered under his attack. One, however, was made of gold, and it took Otto several savage assaults before it began to crack. When it did, a sharp snap issued across the clearing.

At once, the destruction stopped. Otto looked up to see the singer roaring at him, distracted from his fight by the loss of his magical aid. The lapse in focus cost him, and Otto watched in shock as Norris's blade slid straight into the stranger who was lunging toward the prince, silencing his song forever.

For a moment all was still, before Lorraine's scream of anger split the air. Otto's eyes flicked toward her to see Haiden advancing on the woman, his voice lifted in a song of gleeful fury. Best of all, Gisela was pulling herself to her feet at his side, fists clenched in readiness to assist her brother. Not that it looked like Haiden would need it. Otto could almost imagine he could see the power swirling around Haiden as his song built. Before anyone could intervene, the young singer had his former captive on her knees, her own blade to her throat.

As Otto watched, a group of his guards appeared in the

ruined clearing, wide-eyed with alarm. They'd probably been battling their way toward their prince since the magic-induced earthquake had begun. At a barked order from Norris, two of them hurried to help Haiden subdue Lorraine.

A movement right next to Otto drew his eyes away from the confrontation. Monty was also struggling up from the grass. Far from looking in pain, his eyes seemed to fill with stars as he comprehended who was clutching him in her arms.

"Valerie?" he murmured. He raised a slightly shaking hand to lay against her cheek. "Are you all right? I've been so worried."

To Otto's great surprise, Valerie burst into tears.

"You idiot!" she cried. "Why did you chase after me and get yourself caught up in the defensive magic? They thought we were a couple, and that threatening you would be the best way to keep me in check."

"Which naturally isn't the case, since you hate me," Monty said, his grave voice belied by the way his lips were twitching.

"Exactly." Valerie was hiccuping now. "I can't stand you."

Monty's face wore a tender smile Otto had never seen on his friend before. The young lord raised one hand to gently tuck a strand of fiery red hair behind Valerie's ear.

"They had it the wrong way around," he informed her, no irony in his voice. "Threatening you would definitely have worked on me."

She shook her head, still hiccuping. "You don't mean that, Monty. I know I've been the only singer in our group, but there are plenty of others much more talented than I am. This whole city is surrounded by them."

Monty scoffed. "I don't care about singers."

Valerie cast him an incredulous look, and a hint of his usual cocky grin returned.

"I mean, their craft is very interesting, of course," he said.

"Fascinating to watch. That's why I hang about the academy. But songcraft has absolutely nothing to do with why I hang around you, Valerie. Surely you must realize that."

She shook her head, eyes still streaming. "You said it yourself. You practically live at the academy. It's my magic you want. And you'd quickly realize it's nothing special or unusual and lose interest."

"Valerie." Monty sounded genuinely shocked. He placed a hand under Valerie's chin. "How can you think any of that is true? Listen to me, love."

The term of endearment made her open her eyes in amazement, her gaze passing slowly to meet his.

"I've been haunting the academy for years. I've seen plenty of impressive singers. None of them have kept me awake at night. You're the only one who's ever captivated me." When she still looked unconvinced, he ran a self-conscious hand through his hair. "Oh, hang it, you might as well know. I asked Otto to let me come on this trip only after I heard you were coming."

Valerie's eyes widened. "Is that true?"

"Absolutely true," said Monty. "You're the only reason I'm here. Here," he repeated, his eyes pinning her. "In the middle of a ghastly, boar-infested forest, *away* from the academy and all its impressive singers."

For a shocked moment, Valerie just stared at him. Then she launched herself forward, her lips claiming his very unresisting ones.

Otto looked away quickly, a little stunned at the dramatic about-turn.

"Well, that took far longer than it should have," said Lady Louisa, in an approving tone. She was watching the young couple kiss with a dispassionate air. "Why does it always take some kind of crisis for men to just say how they're feeling?" Her expression softened. "Except my lord, of course. He's delight-fully articulate with these things. I taught him."

Otto ran his hands over his face distractedly as he watched Norris and his men trussing up Lorraine's lackeys. They'd run out of fight once their leader was vanquished.

By a middle-aged noblewoman and her feather fan.

Otto could see how that would make it hard to maintain faith in the leadership of your cause.

"Thank you, Lady Louisa," he said. "I confess I never expected your fan to save the day."

She chuckled. "As I said, a lady should never be without her fan." She jerked her head. "Go on. No need to stand here talking to me when it's not at all where you want to be."

Otto followed her eyes, and immediately forgot all about their conversation. Gisela was on her feet now, her hand on her brother's shoulder, but her eyes straying to Otto.

He propelled himself into motion, his eager strides quickly turning into a run as he crossed the clearing toward her.

# CHAPTER TWENTY-SIX

# Gisela

Gisela's throat felt suddenly tight as Otto hurried toward her. It wasn't any lingering effect of the pain —that had fully lifted when Otto destroyed the talismans. Even the invisible shackles had disappeared, probably because of the singer's death.

No, her heart was pounding not because of magic, but because the look in the prince's eyes made it hard to breathe.

"Gisela!" Otto drew up in front of her, his eyes searching her face intently. "Are you all right?"

She nodded, her cheeks warm. "Thanks to you. You were brave, taking on that singer all alone."

"I didn't feel brave." Otto raised a hand to boldly cup her cheek, apparently past the point of any self-consciousness. "Far from it. I've never felt so afraid in my life. I thought the magic was going to kill you."

"It was," said Gisela frankly. "That's how it works. Some of the other captured singers saw it happen. That's why it was such an effective way to coerce them."

A shudder went over Otto's frame. "Gisela, the thought of losing you...I don't know how I'd survive." A stern look came into his eye. "And don't tell me I'd go on as I was before I met you, because I'm absolutely certain now that it would be impossible. You're much too deep in my heart. You wouldn't doubt it if you'd seen what a mess I've been since you went missing."

Gisela swallowed, hardly daring to believe the moment was real. "I thought of you every minute," she whispered. "I could hardly bear to live with myself, knowing how unfairly I'd treated you. Otto, I'm so sorry that I blamed you for what Lorraine was doing. I spoke in the heat of emotion, and it didn't take me long to realize you couldn't possibly be part of something like that. But I shouldn't have entertained the idea for a moment. I should have had more faith in you."

Otto slid his thumb to cover her bottom lip, effectively silencing her strained apology. In fact, the gentle touch silenced all thought completely as heat blazed out from the contact.

"I don't need an apology from you, Gisela," Otto said, his voice deeper than normal, almost husky. "It was all a very unfortunate misunderstanding, and even at the time I knew it wasn't about me, but about what you've experienced in the past. I just hope, more than anything, for the chance to show you that trust won't always betray you, that those who love you will stand by you no matter what happens. You deserve nothing else."

"You've already shown me," Gisela whispered, tears lingering on her lashes. "You've been showing me since we met, and I should never have doubted you. You must be disgusted with the way I—"

"Disgusted?" Otto cut her off with an incredulous laugh. "That's the last thing I am. Gisela..." His eyes searched hers earnestly. "Do you really not know? Have I really communicated so poorly? I love you, Gisela. With all my heart."

Shock poured across Gisela's senses, for a moment obliterating everything else. She'd acknowledged her own feelings to herself already, and of course she'd sensed that Otto was drawn to her. But she'd never dreamed he'd be so sure, so unashamed that he would declare himself with such vulnerability. He'd been trustworthy even when she gave him no trust, and now he chose to trust her even when she hadn't earned it.

Her heart swelled with love for this unbelievable, incredible man. In addition to being the kindest and most honorable person she'd ever met, he was a prince and future king, born to privilege, with his choice of all the girls in the kingdom. Could it really be possible she'd won his heart?

She didn't pause to question his sanity.

"I love you, Otto," she said, her voice coming out a little choked.

He didn't wait for more of an invitation. Sliding his hand behind her head, he pulled her close, his other arm going around her waist and his lips capturing hers in a kiss more gentle than any caress. Gisela closed her eyes and leaned into him, savoring the feeling of completely abandoning her barriers as her lips moved against his and her hand spread across his chest. She could feel his heart, beating steadily—albeit fairly quickly—under his tunic. The truest heart she'd ever encountered, and it beat for her.

"Whoa, whoa, whoa! I turn around for one minute!"

Gisela pulled back quickly, the moment broken as memory of their surroundings broke into her dreamlike haze. Her brother was standing a few feet away, staring with horror at the sight of the pair locked in an embrace.

"If you're waiting for me to ask your permission for your sister's hand, I'm not going to do it," Otto said, a touch of irritation lacing the humor in his voice. Apparently he wasn't pleased with the interruption. "I don't like to pull rank more often than necessary, but there have to be some perks to being a prince, you know."

Gisela bit her lip, her embarrassment over her brother

witnessing her first kiss fleeing before a much more significant concern. Haiden's eyes flew to hers, and a silent message passed between them. Of course she should have realized what Otto meant when he said he loved her, but she hadn't been thinking that far ahead. How would she tell him that the state of her heart changed nothing, and she still couldn't come to Terenford with him?

"You...you want to marry Gisela?" Haiden asked slowly.

"That's my plan," said Otto brightly. Flame leaped in his eyes as they met Gisela's. The expression faded as he gave a regretful sigh. "But you're right that it's probably not the time. We have a mess to clean up first." He glanced around the ruined clearing. "Do you think the elves will be able to fix all this?"

"Probably," Haiden said, sounding indifferent. "They have plenty of magic at their disposal, don't they?"

"What about all the other captured singers?" Otto demanded. "Are we sure they're free of the magic controlling them?"

Haiden nodded. "Very sure. The defensive magic targeted at a loved one was a physical sensation. I could feel the tether tying me to Gisela as a constant presence. The moment you broke that talisman, they all would have felt it. I have no doubt they'll all have immediately turned on their captors, too," he added grimly. "With their songcraft once again at their disposal, I doubt any of Lorraine's henchmen stood a chance against them." He shook his head. "Being locked up against your will and controlled by threats against those you love makes people very angry."

Otto ran a hand through his hair. "Nothing is certain, though. We'll need to send Norris's men after them. Some may have escaped."

"I can help you find their base," said Haiden. "Most of our stones are there."

Otto looked confused, but didn't stop to ask what Haiden meant.

"Even if some evade us, I doubt they'll be able to do much damage without their leadership," he said. "Not to mention those talismans." He looked toward the ruined items still lying on the grass. "I can hardly believe how much destruction they wrought. No wonder the Imperator restricted sale of talismans to humans if items like that were being thrown about."

His eyes drifted to a pair of young elves. With a start, Gisela recognized one of them as Asivah, the elf princess who had made the prophecy about Haiden.

"I wonder if it really was Lonik who was behind the sale of such valuable talismans. The Imperator's heir," he explained, seeing Gisela and Haiden's confusion. "We think he's been planning a coup and working against his grandfather. I don't think he intended any of this to happen, though. I don't think he realized where the talismans he stole and then sold would end up."

Haiden's eyes lit with comprehension. "The messengers Gisela and I saw were probably working for him! That's why their communication had a seal that looked royal to me, but didn't look like the Imperator's seal to Gisela. The heir probably has his own royal seal."

"You're probably right," said Gisela, impressed. "Which means, based on what we heard that day about a shipment of gold being prepared, his motivation for selling talismans was probably as simple as gold."

"That doesn't answer questions so much as raise more," Otto said. "Such as, to whom was he paying gold, and for what purpose?"

None of them had the answer to those questions, of course, and they all fell silent as the two elves they were watching straightened before the imposing—although miniature—figure stalking toward them. The Imperator appeared to have finished a conversation with some of his attendant elves, and was now primed for a confrontation with his grandchildren.

"Lonik." The Imperator's voice sent a chill down Gisela's spine.

That didn't stop them from inching closer to better hear, however. Monty and Valerie were doing the same, accompanied by Lady Louisa. New figures were appearing at the edge of the clearing as well. Gisela recognized a few of the singers from the pit. Clearly Haiden had been right that they'd evaded their former captors once the defensive magic was lifted. They were all watched closely by a multitude of elves, but no one appeared to be under proper guard.

"You tried to destroy me this day," the Imperator accused, ignoring all the humans infiltrating his damaged city.

"Grandfather!" Lonik protested. "I had no hand in this monstrous attack!"

"You may not have intended it," said the Imperator in a somber voice. "But that does not mean you had no hand in it. I do not refer to the attack of the singers, however. I refer to your own actions. Did you think I would not see what you did when a blade was sent for my heart? Not only did you fail to defend me as you've vowed to do, you physically prevented Asivah from doing so."

The young elf had gone silent at the Imperator's mention of a vow, his alabaster skin starting to look ashen.

"I don't yet have the evidence to prove the accusation that you've been working against me, plotting to overthrow me and take my role before your time. But I have no doubt the evidence will emerge when I investigate what I've been told."

To Gisela's surprise, Lonik didn't try to deny it. His emerald eyes were wide with the fear that had entered them when his grandfather spoke of his vow. He knew something the rest of them didn't, and he seemed to think denials of no use.

"Grandfather, I acted in the interests of our people," he said, even now a wheedling note discernible in his voice. "You would have cooperated with the human prince, and allowed him to gather singers to alleviate the magic's growth in Ilgal. But that only benefits humans. Ilgal is ours—it *should* be ours. If the magic grows out of control, humans will have to leave."

Gisela heard Otto grunt quietly beside her, and she understood his thoughts. It was satisfying in a way to receive this confirmation of his suspicions that someone among the elves was trying to obstruct his goal.

"That's why he wanted me," murmured Haiden. "If he saw humans as the enemy, he must have figured it would help his cause to have the aid of a human destined to bring down the human kingdom."

"That is not your decision to make," the Imperator said to Lonik, his voice still more sober than sad.

"It would have been," Lonik argued. "When my time came. But by then you might have allowed the humans too great a foothold to shake them. I had to act quickly!"

"There is so much you do not understand, Lonik," said the Imperator. "It is not in our interests to drive humans out. Wild, unmanageable magic doesn't help us. Magic is best served with singers to harness it. Some of our best magical advancements have occurred in cooperation with human singers."

Anger crept onto Lonik's face. "I refuse to accept that," he said. "We don't need them. We are superior in every way! They can only hold us back—it was in our interests for me to do what I did."

"I know what you're trying to do, Lonik," said the Imperator wearily. "But it will not serve you. You seek to convince me that your actions did not breach the oath you took regarding serving the interests of our kind. But your greed and lust for power have made you forsake the rest of your oath. You vowed to serve me as your leader and protect me with your life if necessary. You broke that oath today." There was a long and heavy silence during which a frantic mix of anger and desperation rose visibly on Lonik's face. "And I hold you accountable for breaking it," the Imperator finished.

Lonik let out a high-pitched scream, and Asivah drew in a sharp breath. She stepped back from her cousin as his scream cut off, and he toppled to the ground. Along with the rest of the clearing's inhabitants, Gisela stared in shock at his still form.

"Is he...dead?" she whispered.

"Yes." Haiden sounded as stunned as she felt. "When the Imperator said Lonik was accountable for breaching his oath, magic rushed up from the ground into him. It felt..." He shook his head, searching for words. "I don't know how to explain it. It wasn't that it felt evil, exactly. But it was dangerous. It felt hard and inflexible. I think whatever magic bound him to his oath killed him when he broke it."

"Remind me never to mix with elf oaths," Otto said, taking Gisela's shaking hand in his and squeezing it. "Elf bargains are terrifying enough." To Gisela's surprise, he suddenly brightened. "Speaking of which, I think mine just got a whole lot easier."

"Yours?" she asked, perplexed.

"I agreed to persuade my father to recognize Asivah as the Imperator's heir instead of her cousin. Turns out that persuading is going to be a simple matter of providing information. Obviously it's all pretty...awful...about Lonik. But I must say, that turned out well for me."

It was on Gisela's lips to ask how he'd come to make such a dangerous bargain, but her brother's voice distracted her.

"That's what *you* wanted, isn't it?" Haiden's tone was off. "That's what you wished for all along. For the forest to kill me rather than let me wreak the damage you'd decided I would cause."

Gisela looked at him, confused, and realized his attention wasn't on her or Otto. She followed his gaze to see their mother standing nearby, her eyes wide as they rested on the dead elf who was already being covered with someone's garment.

"I don't want that," she whispered.

"It's exactly what you tried to achieve," said Haiden bitterly. "Which means you failed us. We're your children. We should have been your first priority, not a kingdom that isn't even the one you still love in your heart." He gestured toward the Imperator. "Elves might be cold and calculating, but humans aren't supposed to be. Especially not to their own families. They're supposed to be warm and loving."

Silent tears were streaming down the older woman's cheeks, and she said nothing as Haiden turned away. Gisela reached out to grip her brother's arm. She didn't try to find words. Some things went too deep for words.

Unwillingly, Gisela felt her eyes drawn back to the royal elf family. The Imperator's face showed no emotion at the death of his heir and grandson, but he looked older and more weary than he had before. Gisela shuddered. She knew he'd acted consistently with the ways of the elves, but she didn't think she'd have been able to do the same thing. She was glad to be human.

Asivah detached herself from the group, trotting toward the small clump of humans. Valerie and Monty came toward them too, the young nobleman's arm wrapped tightly around the singer, who looked entirely content with the situation. There was no time for Gisela to do more than raise an eyebrow at the other girl before Asivah reached them.

"Well, young singer." The elf princess directed her words to Haiden. "It is many years since we met, but I remember you."

"And I you," said Haiden, the words dry.

Gisela shook her head. Did the elf girl think he would forget the encounter that had caused his life to implode? But perhaps she didn't know that.

"I applaud you," Asivah said.

"Do you?" Haiden met her look for look. "Here I thought you'd resent that I overcame your prophecy."

"Overcame it?" Asivah looked politely bewildered. "On the contrary. You fulfilled it." She obviously saw that they were all lost, because she elaborated. "I confess I didn't realize that my prophecy didn't relate to the human kingdom. We have never considered our leader a monarch before. But it is all clear to me now. Lonik was the main force behind all the subtle changes that have made us view the Imperator as a king, and our home here as a royal capital. He wished to establish a monarchy in Ilgal, in his own way. And he didn't intend to wait until his turn at leadership in order to do it. If not stopped, he would have killed or deposed my grandfather and named himself as monarch. His was the rising kingdom you brought down."

The humans just blinked at her as they all tried to make sense of her words.

"So by choosing *not* to act to bring down my grandfather's dominion, you led to the bringing down of my cousin's rising kingdom. In working against the prophecy as you understood it, you fulfilled it as it was truly meant."

"I'm not sure I like that," said Haiden wryly. "I thought I'd taken control of my own destiny."

"I have no particular interest in whether you like it or not," Asivah said, her pleasant and unemotional tone robbing the words of offense. She turned to Otto. "Our bargain should present no difficulties now, should it?"

"None whatsoever," said Otto. He smiled down at Gisela, sliding his arm around her back. "And although your information turned out not to be especially helpful in finding Gisela, it's all worked out. She's here, she's safe, and she's agreed to marry me."

A shard of regret went through Gisela's heart, and against all her desires, she pulled away from Otto's arm.

"Otto…" She swallowed. "Actually, I haven't agreed to that."

His face fell, confusion marring his usually cheerful features. "I suppose you didn't, did you? Gisela, did I misunderstand? Did I—"

"You didn't misunderstand," she said quickly. "I'm at fault, not you. I wish I could marry you, Otto, truly I do." Her voice was becoming choked, and she paused to collect herself.

"Then why can't you?" Otto asked, his voice unbearably gentle and kind. "I didn't mean to push you too quickly."

She shook her head violently. "It's not that. I spoke literally when I told you that Haiden and I can't leave Ilgal. Our mother is a singer, and she used her magic to curse us to be unable to leave. Trust me, we've tested it. The magic prevents us."

Otto's eyes widened in horror as she spoke. "Gisela, that's terrible. I'm so sorry for all you've been through. But surely there's something we can do. Some way to break the magic."

She shrugged helplessly. "If there is, we don't know it. The magic is strong. She's always rejected her songcraft. Part of her truly refused to believe she had it. I think it grew stronger from being repressed for so long. When it burst out, it wasn't in her control, and it was especially potent."

"It would be," Asivah said, her head tilted with clinical interest. "Repressed magic is often potent. And always hard to control. There would be a way to lift it, though."

"What's the way?" Gisela asked, hardly daring to hope.

"Hard to tell without examining your mother," Asivah said.

"I'm here." The faint voice surprised Gisela. She'd expected her mother to flee after Haiden's admonition.

"Are you willing to lift the curse, Mother?" Gisela asked.

"I don't think I can," said her mother, looking defeated. "I don't know how to wield magic. I didn't even mean to use magic when I said those words. And even if I knew how, I don't have the strength. I'm weaker now than I was then."

She certainly looked it. She seemed to have aged twenty years in the five since Gisela and Haiden had lived with her.

"I suspect there's a good reason for that," Asivah said. With a curt order, she sent another elf running back to the tree palace for supplies. They all waited in tense silence until the elf returned.

Asivah took a long golden ribbon from him, running it first across their mother's forehead, then chest, then stomach. Next she did the same to both Gisela and Haiden.

"As I thought," she said, satisfied. "The curse she placed on you is a kind of core magic. The most dangerous and unpredictable type of heart magic. Not something they'd teach in your academy. It seems inexpertly done, and, as we've already said, it's potent. It's constantly connected to her heart, which makes it dangerous."

"What do you mean?" Gisela asked nervously.

"It creates a link between the singer who formed it and the subject. The magic is tied to the singer's heart. In short, she cursed you not to leave Ilgal while her heart continues. She's still fueling it. That's why she's so weakened. It's required constant effort from her core since the moment the magic was crafted."

"What are you saying?" Haiden asked slowly. "That we're stuck here until our mother dies?"

Asivah considered him. "That's one way to phrase it. Another would be that if your mother dies, you're free of the magic."

Gisela recoiled. She and Haiden looked at each other, then,

unwillingly, both pairs of eyes flicked to their mother. She looked small, Gisela realized. In her memories, Gisela was so small and her mother was so big. But now...

"Perhaps it would be for the best." The whispered words came from their mother, and Gisela could tell they rattled Haiden as much as they did her. "I haven't known a moment's peace since you left."

"No." Gisela's voice was strong. "Absolutely not. Regardless of what you've done, we'd never consider that." She looked at her brother. "Would we, Haiden?"

He regarded his mother in silence for the longest three seconds of Gisela's life. Then he turned to look at his sister, something in him relaxing.

"No. We wouldn't."

"Why would you care if I live or die?" asked their mother miserably.

"Because you're our mother," said Gisela. "We loved each other once." Otto's grip was firm and comforting on her hand, and her voice softened as she let down her barriers and let the memories flood in. "When something is precious, it's better to be sad remembering it than happy forgetting it," she said aloud.

Her mother looked up at her in amazement, clearly recognizing her own words from long ago.

"I'm so sorry," she said, her voice a hoarse whisper. Her eyes passed to Haiden. "I was so terribly wrong, and I'm so sorry."

Gisela couldn't bring herself to answer, and Haiden also remained silent. It was too much too soon. But she was confident in her determination not to let her mother die over the curse she'd inadvertently cast on her children. She turned to Asivah.

"Isn't there some way to stop the flow of the magic without killing her?"

"There is," said Asivah. "We have talismans in my grandfather's armory that can break the hold of any magic. But they are very powerful, and very valuable. I would require an exchange."

"I have nothing to give," said Gisela.

"Not from you." Asivah's eyes were on Otto. "From him."

"I have access to plenty of gold," said Otto.

The elf shook her head, the tips of her ears wiggling. "I don't want gold."

"You can't have our firstborn child," Otto said flatly.

Heat rushed over Gisela at this casual mention of their future children, but Asivah seemed more inclined to be amused.

"Changelings don't interest me," she informed the prince. "I want a guarantee that we'll be allowed to keep our city where it is."

Otto frowned. "I thought there must be more to the tale of the elf city moving. So humans were displaced after all, were they?"

"They were," Gisela confirmed sadly. "Lorraine is one of them. She's the one who led this attack. Their original grievance was legitimate, I think. But their actions in response..." She shook her head. "They abducted singers and caged them like animals, and they murdered the families of some who wouldn't cooperate."

"They've gone far beyond the point where Father could give them what they seek," Otto agreed gravely. "Any who've survived today will be taken to Terenford to face justice, not restored to their lands within Ilgal." He considered Asivah. "I won't pretend to agree with what your people did several years ago. But I also can't pretend much would be gained from trying to undo it now."

"Does that mean you're willing to make the bargain proposed?" Asivah asked.

Otto looked down at Gisela, certainty in his eyes. "I am," he said, squeezing her hand again.

She responded to the pressure, not sure whether to be touched or terrified at the risks he was willing to take in order to win a future with her.

Both, realistically.

"Witnessed." Many elven voices murmured the words from around them.

Asivah didn't waste any time, striding off toward her grandfather. She had a brief conversation with the Imperator, who was overseeing the six elves now lifting up Lonik's body on a stretcher. The Imperator's eyes fell on the group of humans, his gaze penetrating. Gisela could tell nothing from his demeanor.

But apparently he was positively disposed toward the bargain. After a moment, Asivah stepped away from her grandfather, and another elf went scurrying toward the palace. When she returned, she bore a talisman unlike any Gisela had ever seen. It was a thick, golden rope. As Asivah lifted it from its velvet cushion and uncoiled it, Gisela realized it was literally made from gold, the metal glinting in the fading light of the afternoon.

"The three of you must stand close together," said Asivah imperiously.

Gisela, Haiden, and their mother obeyed, discomfort clear on all sides as their shoulders touched. The elf wound the rope around them, weaving it between their arms and bodies until they were linked.

"Assistance," Asivah said, and three elves stepped forward.

Passing a jar of some kind of salve between them, they coated the chain, smearing the salve onto the trio where the metal connected with their skin as well.

"It draws the magic out of you and into the talisman," said Asivah. "It's potent magic, and it's deeply woven into you. It will take some time."

The process was repeated several times, until Asivah

declared herself satisfied. Gisela expected the elf to unwind the chain, but instead, she gave the order and several elves set to work destroying it.

"Careful," said Otto anxiously, as Gisela felt the cool metal of the flat of one of the elves' blades against her skin.

None of the elves deigned to reply, and in a few minutes, the chain was gone. Looking down at the broken links on the grass, Gisela was surprised to see that it no longer looked like gold. Rusted, tarnished sections of chain littered the area around them.

"Did it work?" Otto asked anxiously.

Gisela rolled her shoulders back, trying to sense whether anything was different. "I don't know."

"You can't tell?" Haiden sounded incredulous. "The pressure is gone. I didn't even realize it was there, but I can feel its absence." He closed his eyes and drew in a deep breath. "It feels amazing."

"I feel it, too." Their mother's soft voice caused him to open his eyes. "I feel...energy in me again."

"Of course it worked," said Asivah, sounding offended that they'd questioned it. She looked at Otto. "Our bargain is in force."

"I won't forget it," he assured her.

He held out his hands, and Gisela took them without hesitation. Drawing her close, he searched her eyes.

"You're free now, Gisela. To start whatever life you choose. Will you start a new one with me?"

"Yes," she said simply. Her heart was aglow, but her mind had no fancy words to mark the moment.

"Are you truly willing to leave Ilgal to be with me?" Otto asked gravely.

"I am," Gisela assured him. "I love this forest, but it holds complicated memories, many of them memories of being trapped. I'm eager for a new chapter."

"You'll have it," Otto assured her. He bit his lip. "In spite of what people think, it's not the easiest life, being royal. A lot of it will feel ridiculous." His voice turned wry. "A lot of it *is* ridiculous."

Gisela smiled up at him. She didn't doubt the truth of his words, and she was wise enough to realize there would be many great challenges ahead, most of which she couldn't foresee yet. But she also felt completely and utterly at peace with her decision, for the first time in a long time. She didn't second guess it.

"I have full confidence that we can face it together," she said.

His eyes lighting up, Otto drew her against him, resting his cheek on the top of her head as he held her. After a moment, Gisela pulled back, realizing her large oversight. Honestly, the fact that she'd even forgotten felt significant in itself.

"Haiden, what about you? Will you come to Terenford with us?"

Her brother looked surprised. "You're not going to tell me I have to?"

"Of course not," said Gisela, pained by this evidence of her overbearing habits. "You're free now to choose your own trail, just like I am."

Haiden looked pleased, and still a little surprised. "I think I will come. At least for a while. I'd like to see what the capital is like."

"We'll show you all the very best parts of city life," said Otto enthusiastically.

"Of course we will," Valerie agreed brightly. "I'll take you to the Academy of Song, Haiden. You'll love it."

Haiden lit up at once, turning toward her. "Do you think there are classes I could take? Do they accept students at any time, or only once a year?"

Leaving the singers to their discussion, Gisela turned smiling eyes back up to Otto. "I'm sure they'll accept such a well-connected student at any time, won't they, Otto?"

"Of course they will," said Otto promptly, recognizing his cue. "I'll arrange it the moment we arrive. Well," he amended. "After I show you your new home, that is." He gave her a squeeze. "I really think you'll love the castle." He drew in a quick breath. "And Rosa! You'll love her, and she'll adore you. I'll write to her as soon as we reach the city, and ask her to bring that husband of hers for another visit."

"That sounds perfect," said Gisela contentedly. She leaned her head against his chest, murmuring the words for no one's benefit but her own. "My new home." It was a long time since she'd had a true home. It was about time to build another.

"So we're to return to Terenford, Your Highness?" Lady Louisa's practical voice broke into the conversation.

"Yes, of course," said Otto. "Without delay. My father needs to be apprised of all that's passed."

"Yes, that's true enough," said the countess. She sighed. "I suppose a new plan will need to be made, since our mission failed so spectacularly." She eyed Haiden. "Only one singer recruited in all this time."

Gisela felt Otto's arms deflate. He'd clearly forgotten temporarily about his original purpose in coming to Ilgal.

"Actually," she said, drawing back and looking eagerly up at him. "A lot more than one. Lorraine had three dozen trapped in that pit." She glanced around, taking in the various singers who'd entered the clearing and were now standing about, seeming dazed and unsure what to do. "All of whom you just freed from terrible magic. I wouldn't be surprised if they all agree to help you."

"Help him what?" The shrewd voice made her jump. She

hadn't realized any of the liberated singers were close enough to hear.

"We have a plan to form an organized team of singers to move throughout Ilgal and help dissipate the over-concentration of magic," Otto explained calmly. "It's a model being attempted in Selvana as we speak, and we believe it could be effective here."

The singer eyed him warily. "And what if we don't agree to help?"

"Then you are, of course, free to return to your homes," Otto assured him. "No one will be required to help. It's a voluntary assignment."

"But if we succeed, it will mean that your loved ones who aren't singers will be able to stay in Ilgal without being crushed from the inside out by the magic," Haiden commented.

"Even those willing to assist should return to their families first," Otto added. "The crown will provide any assistance needed in helping you reach your destination safely. This trip was only intended to gather names of those willing to take part. Any who wish to help should provide their details to me, and we will arrange a meeting in a few months' time."

Gisela could see many of the singers exchanging looks, clearly interested in the opportunity to help rescue their home from the growing magic. It wasn't impossible that they would all sign up.

"It seems everything has come together," Otto said, his voice a murmur for her ears alone.

She smiled mischievously back at him. "The trails seem to have wound their circuitous way to the right destination, don't they?"

"I don't mind where they lead from here," said Otto comfortably, his arms fitting so naturally around her. "As long as we're walking those trails together."

# Gisela

"Gisela, they're here!"

Gisela looked up from her contemplation of the library shelf, her heart lifting as it always did when she heard that voice. She poked her head around the shelving to see her betrothed hurrying toward her.

"Their carriage has just pulled up," Otto said eagerly.

"Oh. Right. They're here."

Nerves rushed over Gisela as she caught up with what he was saying. She'd been at the castle in Terenford for four weeks, and so far it had been smoother than she'd dared hope it would be. Some of the servants looked at her askance, and she still found herself often overwhelmed—hiding in the library pretending to read up on the kingdom's history was a favorite pastime, for example. But King Ryker and Queen Ada had been incredibly welcoming. She'd braced for disappointment, perhaps even anger when they learned that the king's only son and heir had betrothed himself to a peasant girl from the forest. But if they felt those things, they'd kept them private. Perhaps it helped that Queen Ada had herself been both a commoner and an inhabitant of Ilgal before marrying the king.

But relieved as she was to have overcome the hurdle of meeting the king and queen with surprising success, Gisela had the sense that gaining Rosa's approval was more meaningful in Otto's eyes. His fondness for his stepsister was one of the things that had drawn her to him. Now she could only hope she wouldn't have cause to regret the pair's closeness.

"Don't worry," Otto told her, the smile that was pulling up one corner of his mouth telling her that he knew what she was thinking. "She'll love you."

"How do you know?" asked Gisela despairingly.

"Because I love you." He spoke the words so simply, as if they were nothing. But to Gisela, they were everything. "Come on."

Seizing her hand, Otto pulled her out of the library and toward the castle's entrance. They left the building in time to see a black carriage pull up, drawn by four handsome and well-matched horses.

Still tugging Gisela with him, Otto sprang down the castle steps, barely reaching the carriage when it was flung open and a dark-haired girl with a straight nose and high cheekbones tumbled out. She was dressed magnificently, but she wore the gown with a casual cheerfulness Gisela had yet to observe in any other courtier.

"Otto! You survived the deeps of Ilgal." Princess Rosa threw her arms around her stepbrother and squeezed. "And you brought home a wife!"

"Not yet, but won't be long now, we hope," said Otto brightly. "Rosa, Emmett," he nodded to a dark-haired man now stepping out of the carriage behind his wife. "This is Gisela."

Gisela smiled, trying not to look as nervous as she felt. Struggling to remember the training she'd already begun, she started to lower herself into a curtsy.

"Don't worry about all that nonsense," said Rosa cheerfully, taking both of her hands and nipping her curtsy attempt in the bud. "I'm so pleased to meet you, Gisela. We have so much to talk about." She shot her stepbrother a cheeky look. "Me, endless stories that will embarrass Otto past the point of redemption. And you, tales of Ilgal. It feels an age since I've been in the forest!"

"We passed through it on the journey from Lernvale," Prince Emmett said mildly.

"Oh, you know what I mean, that doesn't count." Princess Rosa waved off her husband's words with a shapely hand.

"It's wonderful to make your acquaintance, Gisela," said Prince Emmett, the picture of calm courtesy next to his wife's exuberance. "I look forward to getting to know you better in the future."

"Emmett is very good at the stiff royal decorum," Rosa confided in Gisela, linking arms with her and leading her up the steps to where her mother and stepfather waited. "But he's actually great fun underneath it all."

"I'm glad," said Gisela, her lips twitching. It was difficult to remain nervous in Princess Rosa's presence.

"Is that your brother?" the princess asked, nodding to Haiden, who'd appeared in the castle doorway behind the king and queen. "The singer who apparently brought down an elf rebellion?"

"That's not quite what happened," said Gisela, pained. "But yes, that's Haiden."

"Ah, rumor is never entirely accurate," said Princess Rosa wisely. "I know all about sensational stories." She threw a grin back over her shoulder to where Otto and Emmett were climbing the steps together. "I did marry a wild wolf-man, after all."

She broke off from Gisela to greet King Ryker and Queen Ada, and soon they were all ushered into a comfortable parlor where refreshments were waiting.

"I'm dying to hear all about your adventures in the forest, Otto," said Rosa, settling onto a cushioned seat alongside her husband. She shot Gisela a smile. "And the story of your romance, of course."

"They're one and the same, really," said Otto. He gave a brief version of his various experiences in Ilgal. Even keeping details to a minimum, it took some time, and Rosa listened avidly throughout.

"So what's happened with the singers? Did they sign up?"

"Most of them," said Otto. "And others are coming out of hiding now Lorraine's ring has been broken up." He sent a proud glance toward his father. "At this rate, we expect to be ready to start work as soon as we receive a report regarding the Selvanan experience."

"Yes, Otto performed his task excellently," said King Ryker. "And in addition, communication has never been more open with the elves. The Imperator even came to Terenford to meet with me. We spoke at length, and have agreed to share information regarding our findings on the recent attacks perpetrated among both our kinds."

"The information we've gleaned from Lorraine's lackeys hasn't brought any great surprises," Otto commented. "She was honest with Gisela about her motivations and intentions, and inquiries have confirmed that they spent a long time both gathering singers and acquiring talismans in preparation for their strike. We're confident the threat is neutralized now."

"It sounds like the interrogation of the elves who were working with the Imperator's heir have been less successful," King Ryker commented, taking a sip from his tankard.

Otto nodded, explaining for Princess Rosa and Prince Emmett's benefit. "It's been confirmed that the immediate goal was to see Lonik installed as Imperator, with the secondary goal of driving humans from Ilgal. And a number have admitted that they were sending gold and information to a group outside the forest. But even with Lonik gone, they're very reluctant to reveal who that group is."

"The interrogations are ongoing," said King Ryker. "I imagine the Imperator will get the information he seeks." He gave his head a slow shake. "He's not an individual I would relish crossing."

"Yes, elves' ways are incomprehensible to humans, I think," said Gisela softly, thinking of the way the Imperator had effectively executed his own grandson. "I wouldn't wish to live among them."

Prince Emmett shifted in his seat, and his wife looked at him inquiringly, apparently reading something in his body language that Gisela didn't know him well enough to see.

"What's on your mind, Emmett?"

"Just thinking of Farrin and Bianca," answered the Medullan prince. "My brother and my sister-in-law, who is Selvana's queen," he added.

It was unnecessary. Even as isolated forest-dwellers, Gisela and Haiden had heard of Selvana's young singer queen with the snow-white hair, and knew that she'd married Medulle's younger prince.

"They both lived among elves. Farrin for two years. He claims that elves can be nothing like us in some ways, but in others they're almost human." He gave his head a little shake. "But that's not what struck me." His eyes sought King Ryker's. "You said that the elves were working with someone outside their forest, and won't reveal who, even after their activities have been permanently stopped. Well, they had the same experience in Selvana. Some renegade elves tried to kill Bianca, and they definitely weren't working for any of her known enemies. They wouldn't say who they worked for, but when they were captured, they were overheard talking about employers.

Employers who wanted to keep the magic in Selvana wild, and opposed any attempt to tame it. They apparently said the employers would have to mine magic elsewhere when their current source runs out. Farrin speculates that they'd agreed to set Selvana up as a near endless supply of magic for whoever this *employer* was."

"Do you think the current source they spoke of was Ilgal?" Otto demanded, sitting up straighter.

"I don't know," said Prince Emmett, frowning. "But I don't think so. I'm...intimately familiar with the strength of the magic in Ilgal, and it doesn't seem to me as though anyone's been drawing excessively from it."

"Definitely not," Otto agreed. "That's the whole issue we're trying to resolve." He smiled humorlessly. "Maybe it would help us if this mysterious party was drawing magic from Ilgal."

"I don't like the sound of that," said Gisela uneasily. "It depends how much magic they were drawing."

"Agreed," said Haiden. "We know nothing about this group. What if they were mining enough magic to turn Ilgal into a wasteland?"

"We can't allow that," said Princess Rosa briskly. "We'll leave the wasteland to northern Frossenland."

As she said the words, the princess got an arrested look on her face, and the whole room fell silent for a moment. Gisela could sense in everyone else the same feeling she had, of trying to pull threads together that almost met but didn't quite. There was something they were all missing.

"Speaking of Frossenland," said Princess Rosa, breaking the spell, "I assume you've all heard the sensational news about Prince Herleif? King Herleif, I should say?"

"We certainly have!" Otto assured her, turning in his seat to better engage in some light-hearted royal gossip. "The castle talked of nothing else for a week when the news came through. I can hardly believe he's still alive!"

"And that he reappeared from the oblivion of assumed death with a wife!" Rosa said. She grinned at Otto. "He got the job done though, unlike you. They were already married when they emerged, none of this juvenile getting approval from the proper authorities nonsense."

Otto threw a cushion at his stepsister, surprising Gisela with the display of informality. She exchanged a smile with Haiden, feeling herself relax a little more. It was nice having Princess Rosa around.

"I'll have you know our wedding date is set," said Otto with dignity. "You're to attend, thank you very much."

"We've been summoned, Emmett," said Princess Rosa to her husband. "And not at all politely. Medulle's honor has been insulted. Shall we declare war on Teren?"

"Rosa, will you stop speaking nonsense?" Queen Ada said in a long-suffering voice.

"Probably not anytime soon," said Princess Rosa cheerfully.

King Ryker asked Emmett a question, and the conversation flowed on. Princess Rosa turned to Gisela, speaking in an undertone she clearly intended to be conspiratorial.

"Mothers—I can't decide whether we're a greater trial to them, or them to us."

Gisela froze at the casual words, and Princess Rosa's expression immediately changed.

"Gisela, I'm so sorry!" There was no trace of her impudent banter now, true penitence in her voice instead. "I forgot, like an utter fool."

"It's all right," said Gisela quickly. "Truly. I know you didn't mean any offense." She gave the princess a wan smile. "It's not a forbidden topic. I can talk about my mother without falling apart."

"Of course," said Princess Rosa, nodding awkwardly. She studied Gisela's face. "Where are your parents?"

"They're still in Ilgal," said Gisela, her eyes on Haiden. The conversation was thankfully too quiet for him to hear. He was still touchier about their parents than she was, and she didn't blame him. "In the home we grew up in, I imagine."

"You...you didn't seek any kind of punishment?" Princess Rosa asked delicately.

Gisela shook her head. "And we don't intend to. Haiden and I are agreed on that. And Otto," she added as an afterthought. "What my mother did was wrong, and terrible. But in her own twisted way, she thought she was serving her kingdom. She knows now that she was wrong about Haiden's prophecy, and both she and our father have shown some signs they wish to make amends. I don't know how possible that will be, but we're all confident that they don't pose any danger to anyone else."

"Only to their own children," murmured Princess Rosa darkly.

Gisela sighed. "We've invited them to the wedding," she said. "It will be a start."

She looked up as a shadow darkened the settee. Haiden was approaching, and with a smile, she made room for him to join them.

"What are you two talking about?" he asked, with the confidence of a fifteen-year-old.

"You now, hopefully," said Princess Rosa. "Tell me about your plans, Haiden. I hear you're studying at the academy?"

He nodded. "I am, and it's fantastic. I'll definitely finish out my allotted years there. It's good that there are rooms at the academy, so those of us not from the capital can live on site. I can't imagine losing time to travel when there's so much to learn and not nearly enough hours in the day in which to learn it."

Princess Rosa smiled. "It sounds like you've found where you're supposed to be."

"Yes, for now, most definitely," Haiden said.

Gisela frowned, but Princess Rosa beat her to the question.

"For now? What do you mean by that? What plans do you have after the academy?"

Haiden shrugged, seeming reluctant to elaborate. "I'm not sure exactly. But I don't think I'll hang around Terenford forever."

"Where then?" Gisela pressed. "You want to go back to Ilgal?"

He shook his head. "Not anytime soon. I think..." He looked at his sister, a hint of defiance in his eyes. "Well, I think I might head east once I'm trained."

"East?" she repeated blankly. "You mean to Frossenland?"

"Further," said Haiden.

"To Vadolis?" Gisela just felt bewildered as she named the eastern-most kingdom in Providore. "What's there?"

"Information, maybe," shrugged Haiden. He hesitated, then plunged on. "I want to learn more about the Reviled Lands. I think it might help me to reconnect with the history that made our mother what she is."

"What made her what she is was being raised to value a distant generational memory over her own flesh and blood in the present," said Gisela flatly.

"Yes, I know," said Haiden. "But that doesn't mean I don't have questions."

Gisela bit her lip, not convinced he was telling her the full story. She had a niggling fear that he was still trying to outrun the prophecy that had defined his life. But that was over, completed, fully explained. She wished he could be free of it, in his heart as well as in his circumstances.

But she supposed that was his battle to fight, not hers. That's what Otto would say. It wasn't easy, but she was trying to let her brother live his own life and make his own mistakes. And if nothing else, her relationship with Haiden was drastically improved because of it. He'd actually come to her for advice once or twice in the last few weeks, rather than spurning the guidance she offered unasked. He would figure his future out, and he'd do it without her leading him there.

Gisela's eyes passed to Otto, in conversation with his father. Her own future would be full of enough excitement, challenges, and surprises to keep her occupied.

Otto looked up suddenly, perhaps feeling her gaze on him. The warm smile he only wore for her lit up his face, softening his already pleasant features and making him the most handsome man in the world.

Yes, her own future would be full of plenty of adventure. And she couldn't wait to run into it with barriers down and heart open. Or at least, that was what she would try to do. She knew it would take time and patience for her to learn to open herself. But Otto had been all the support she could dream of in that process so far, not pushing, not rushing, always believing in her, always ready to really listen and to forgive.

It would be a process, but she wasn't afraid of what was ahead. Not when she would walk into it hand in hand with someone she could trust with every part of her being.

# NOTE FROM THE AUTHOR

Thank you for reading *Song of Trails*. I hope you enjoyed returning to the world of Providore. I would be so grateful if you would consider leaving a review on Amazon—it would really make a difference!

If you want to finally get to the bottom of what exactly is going on with the elves and the giants, and get lost in a childhood sweethearts love story, check out *Song of Vines*, the sixth and final installment of *The Singer Tales*. You'll find more adventure, fantasy, mystery, and hard-won happily ever afters!

Join up to my mailing list at deborah gracewhite.com to be kept up to date on new releases, specials, and giveaways, such as bonus chapters. You'll receive some great freebies, too, including *An Expectation of Magic*, a novella which is a prequel to my completed YA fantasy series *The Vazula Chronicles*.

Plus, you'll receive *Dragon's Sight*, an 8,000 word prequel to my completed YA fantasy trilogy *The Kyona Chronicles.*

Again, thanks for entering the world of Providore! I hope to see you back again.

*Also by Deborah Grace White*

## The Vazula Chronicles: YA Fantasy

## The Kingdom Tales: Fairy Tale Retellings

## The Singer Tales: Fairy Tale Retellings

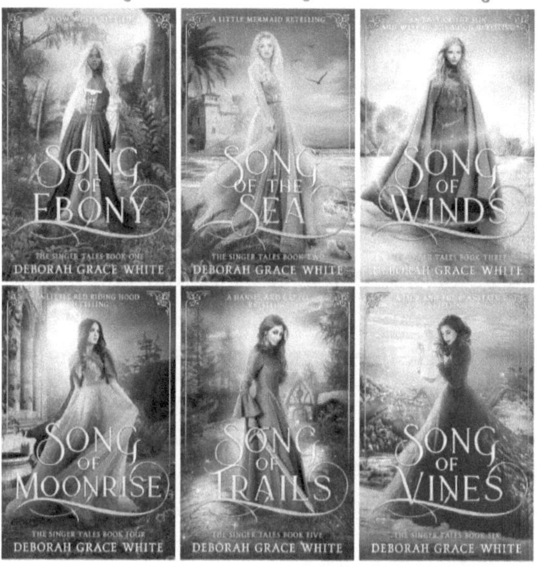

## The Unlucky Prince: Fairy Tale Retelling
### (Once Upon a Prince Multi-Author Series)

# ACKNOWLEDGMENTS

As always, I want to hugely thank my wonderful team for helping me get *Song of Trails* ready for publication.

Ray, my incredible husband and cheer squad, for your encouragement and feedback. My betas for going above and beyond with this one: Dad, Tamara, Mel W, and Adrian. Shae for a thorough and fantastic proofread. Any remaining errors are of course my own.

Thanks also to Karri for the cover that so beautifully captures the mystery of Ilgal and the indomitable spirit of Gisela, and to Becca for the gorgeous map that continues to bring Providore to life.

To you, the reader, thank you for giving me the privilege of being an author.

And most importantly, to God, the only one we can truly trust without reservation, in all situations.

# ABOUT THE AUTHOR

I've been a reader since I can remember, growing up on a wide range of books, from classic literature to light-hearted romps. The love of reading has traveled with me unchanged across multiple continents, and carried me from my own childhood all the way to having children of my own.

But if reading is like looking through a window into a magical and beautiful world, beginning to write my own stories was like discovering that I could open that window and climb right out into fantasyland.

I cannot believe how privileged I am to actually be living that childhood dream and publishing my own novels. I do so from my hometown of Adelaide, Australia, where I live with my husband and our three little ones.

I've never outgrown my love of young adult stories, so the genre of young adult fantasy was always going to be my niche. Feel free to email me at deborah@deborahgracewhite.com and introduce yourself! Or subscribe to my mailing list at deborah gracewhite.com for free giveaways, sales, and updates.